I0717479
False
Start
usa today bestselling author
echo grayce

For my husband, Jim, who is just as offended as I am when family and friends see our house for the first time and ask why I'm the one with the big office.
The patriarchy is strong y'all.
Burn that bullshit to the ground!

For the man-child who keeps stumbling across my ads for this book and drops bullshit comments each time about how my heroine looks like she should be in jail...
Go suck a jenkity dick.
May the putrid stench of sweaty man-berries with the haunting aroma of fermented fromunda cheese fill your nasal cavities with every smack of those short and curly bristled balls against your chin.

Finally, there are plenty of sports romances worshipping at the altar of men.
Fuck 'em, this one's for us!

Peace out...
xoxo, Echo.

a special thank you...

This series wouldn't have been possible without the help of a few amazing roller derby players who answered all of my questions... even the weird ones!

Catye (Catastrophe) Jones
Evan (Evanity) Stewart
Danielle (Cookie) Mahoney
Jenn (Jenn-I-Fear) Cooper

A special thank you to Jenn Cooper for proofreading and editing for accuracy of the sport! I'll keep you supplied with all the hardcover books after you helped me make this the best book possible!

a word of warning

Before you dive into Cain and Maisy's story, I just want to
warn you about a couple triggers. Cain's sister is pregnant
and she has complications in the book that would fall
under the umbrella of birth trauma. Please proceed with
caution.

Also, Cain and Lilith have a complicated childhood after
being raised by an abusive father. The abuse
doesn't happen on the page, but there is mention of
drugs, violence, and death.

Thank you from the bottom of my heart for choosing my
book out of the sea of amazing books out there to read.
That's all any of us want as authors... for our readers to
have a kick ass experience, find books that give them all the
feels, and leave them happy from the inside out.

I hope you love Cain and Maisy just as much as I do!
I wish you happy reading and lifetime full of
mind-blowing orgasms, LOL.

Echo Grayce

If you're reading this, Mom, I guess that means you too,
but gross!
To my girls, if you're reading this… you're grounded.

xoxo,
echo

meet the team...

CORE TEAM MEMBERS: THE ORIGINALS

#5 - MAYHEM (Maisy Flynn)
Jammer
#M60 - ANARCH-EVE (Eve McAllister)
Blocker
#88 - HAZY EIGHTS (Marty Hayes)
Pivot
#13 - RORY HIGHNESS (Rory Turner)
Blocker
#99 - LOWE BAR (Sean Lowe)
Blocker
#90210 - HOT WEST (Zara West)
Pivot

COACH : Cain "PRIEST" Bishop

REST OF THE TEAM:

#867-5309 - DIXIE DOM (Dixie North)

Blocker
#13 - LICK-OR-TREAT (Lexi Alexander)
Pivot
#11 - SLEEPING BOOTY (Sierra Ashmore)
Blocker
#555 - GET HUSSY (Carmen Brooks)
Jammer
#666 - HATE PUCK (Harley Owens)
Blocker
#69 - SPREAD 'EM (Kendall Mercer)
Jammer
#911 - WALL OF DUTY (Wrenlie Fulton)
Blocker
#24/7 - COME QUEEN (Emerson Walsh)
Blocker

a crash course on roller derby... pun intended!

This is not required reading, but… if you're curious, this is your crash course on the single coolest fucking sport in the world!

POSITIONS:

REVERSE COWGIRL:

I caught you, you schmexxy lush… there's no reverse cowgirl in derby. But no one can hold it against a player if she can't help but, climb and ride, Coach Hung-Like-A-Horse. He's a goddamn vagina whisperer, all broody glares and veiny forearms. And he doesn't realize it which makes him twice as dangerous to hearts and ovaries.

Okay, for real now…

The JAMMER:

The only skater who can score points for the team. She's the badass with the star on her helmet. She starts each jam behind the pack and has to get through the pack and lap them once (called a non-scoring pass) before she can begin racking up points.

The BLOCKER:

The skater whose job is to block the other team's jammer while also helping her own team's jammer to score. Multitasking at it's finest!

The PIVOT:

The blocker at the front of the pack who regulates pack speed. Hopefully she's got a little dom in her, LOL, because she runs this shit. And get this, she also has the ability to change places with the jammer, *hello inner switch*, (via a panty swap-sounds cool, right?). She's the powerhouse
with the stripe on her helmet.

TERMINOLOGY EXPLAINED:

You'll see some of these in this book and throughout the rest of the series. I use them sparingly so you can still love the book and know jack shit about roller derby. Come back to these any time or feel free to skip them all together!

BOUT: A 60 minute roller derby match broken into two-30 minute periods. Banked track roller derby is broken into four-15 minute quarters.

JAM: A period of play up to two minutes. Banked track jams are only sixty seconds long.

FRESH MEAT: Newbies on the team.

LEAD JAMMER: The first of the two jammers who legally bust through the pack.

NSO: A non-skating official. They help with tracking penalties, timing the penalty box, and score keeping. They usually have cool derby names too. More on that later!

PACK: The mass of blockers from both teams skating around the track.

PANTY: A stretchy helmet cover that is used to designate the jammer (with a star) or a pivot (with a stripe).

PASSING THE STAR: A strategic play where the jammer removes her helmet cover and gives it to the pivot, enabling the pivot to become the new jammer and score points.

QUADS: Skates with four wheels positioned two in front and two in back, contrasted with inline skates. Quads only in derby!

RINK RASH: A burn injury caused by skin skidding along the rink floor. Ouch!

DERBY KISSES: Cute name for the brutal bruises you collect from the game. Cute name, hurts just the same. Some of this shit is brutal. Like, healing for months brutal. But they get up and do it all again because women are badasses!

FLAT TRACK: The oval-shaped track where all the action happens. Both flat tracks and banked tracks surround an infield with benches for the team, coaches, and officials.

BANKED TRACK: This is a track on a banked slant, think NASCAR Racing… Bristol in particular for any racing fans out there. Look, I like cars, okay? Don't judge me, LOL. This is what most people think of when they think of old school roller derby.

BASTARD BOARDS: Banked tracks are constructed with sections of masonite. The pieces are often referred to as bastard boards. You will see this in the book. One mention. Hot and sweaty coach inspecting every bolt in his veiny forearm glory. You're welcome!

COPING: The piping running along the bottom of a banked track. Think PVC piping.

NINE MONTH INJURY: Nine months guys… the uterus is occupied, and the skater is off the track while she brews a human.

ASSIST: An action by one player to help another player gain advantage. An assist can include pushing, pulling, redirecting, or whipping another skater. More on whipping later. No BDSM involved!

BLOCKING ZONES: Parts of the body which are legal to hit on another skater. Legal blocking zones: the arms from the shoulder to above the elbow, torso, hips, butt, and the mid and upper thigh. Illegal blocking zones: elbows, forearms, hands, head, and any part of the leg below the mid-thigh.

FALLING SMALL: Trying to keep your body as small as possible when hitting the ground to prevent other skaters from tripping over you and causing injury.

FALSE START: A minor penalty when a player crosses the designated starting line before the appropriate whistle is blown–no jumping the gun-no blowing your load early in this sport, LMAO.

HIP WHIP (Title for Book 2): An assist where a player (usually the jammer) grabs her teammate's hips, gives them a hard pull, thrusting herself forward with the momentum.

LOW BLOCK (Title for Book 3): Derby term for contact with an opposing team member that targets the other skaters feet or legs causing them to fall or stumble.

JAM LINE (Title for Book 4): A starting line on the track, behind the pivot line. Jammers may touch, but not cross, the line. If the jammer crosses the line before the second whistle, it's a false start.

GRAND SLAM (Title for Book 5): When a jammer succeeds in lapping the opposing team's jammer.

TURN STOP (Title or Book 6): A stopping technique in which a skater reverses direction from forward to backwards before stopping, usually by going up on her toe stops. Also, cool AF to watch. There are so many vids on TikTok with skaters doing this. Their skills are absolutely mesmerizing.

derby in action...

Careful, this shit is addicting!
Don't take my word for it… see for yourself.
Visit my website to see my roller derby inspiration in
action.

https://geni.us/RollerDerbyGoodness

Maisy

Psssst!

Yeah, you.

Look, I'm hijacking the prologue to set some-thing straight. Coach Hung-Like-A-Horse had his say on the back cover, but now it's my turn. I cannot let that cocky shit have the last word.

Look, it goes a little something like this…

Yes, he's the scandalous coach everyone warned me to stay away from… and I had every intention of taking their advice despite my curiosity. Even when my inner moth saw the flame and whispered, "Why hello, old friend."

Still, I managed to squash my baser instincts. Go me.

After all, why would I want to talk to the older, brooding grump, with the body of a god and the graying hairline that's far sexier than it should be? Especially after we locked eyes during the single most humiliating moment of my life from where I lay stuck to the track after being annihilated by my nemesis?

All I wanted when I stepped up to the bar was a strong drink and a fat bag of ice. But noooooo… he just had to open his mouth, coming at me with the unsolicited play by play of my most recent humiliation which he blamed all on me. On me!

He's as rude as he is cocky.

And I had every intention of staying the hell away from the judgmental fucker. Well, until it all went to shit…

The youth center we adore is in trouble and without an infusion of cash, it won't make it another year. We need money. Big money. All of a sudden the banked track exhibition we dismissed months ago isn't so easy to dismiss and the answer is clear.

Drag the disgraced Anaconda-In-His-Shorts-Smuggling coach out of retirement to train us.

Half the town will hate us and teaming up with the controversial coach will almost certainly cost us our shot at joining the Women's Roller Derby Federation—something we've been working toward for years, but these kids and their happiness is all that matters.

Misfits stick together.

Only, when I approached him, he couldn't get away fast enough. When I chased him down the sidewalk, he just walked faster.

It's too bad he doesn't want to help, but I'm not taking no for an answer. Even if his arched brow, stormy eyes, and square jaw have me ready to submit to him, not the other way around.

But *his* submission has a price.

Now that I'm pinned against the wall, his hand cupping my jaw, forcing my face up to his… it's becoming crystal clear what this arrangement might really cost me.

Fuck.

Maisy

S harp, jagged pain speared through my side, making me suck in a hard, deep breath. My teeth dug into my mouthguard as I growled low in my throat. Glancing up at the pack as they skated into position, I met Tilly the Hun's mean eyes. They crinkled at the corners when they narrowed, not with age, but with spite. The sneer spread over her face, a glimpse of the cold black heart that chugged inside her chest.

Of course, the last bout of the season had to be against her team. Why wouldn't it? We'd go head-to-head, our personal bitter rivalry a living, breathing heartbeat on the track. Each smackdown she delivered trying to gouge the armor of my confidence.

She refused to stop swinging at me.

And no matter how many times she came at me, no matter how hard, I refused to stay down.

Tilly's calculating smile promised more retribution to be delivered the minute the ref blew the whistle to start the jam.

Retaliation for landing on her turf.

Punishment for being an outsider in her town.

Reckoning for refusing to leave.

Every bout, every blow of the whistle when our skates

met the track in the same jam, she played out her need for revenge.

And I showed up front and center for the battle between us that would never be over.

Because in life, and especially in roller derby, when they knock you down, you get back up.

You always get back up.

Pathetic and emotionally bankrupt Tilly had no clue she'd been preparing me for this sport for a decade. She'd been hardening me with brutality to take hit after hit, building my endurance.

Fueling my tenacity, all to her own detriment.

She thought she could scare me away?

Fuck no.

As long as derby existed, she'd have to keep facing me. She'd never have this sport on her terms.

Free from me.

With one last glance over her shoulder, our eyes connected, and I grinned.

The gauntlet dropped with the shrill peel of the referee's whistle cutting through the air. Pushing off my toe stops, I tapped into the adrenaline, the anger burning low in my belly whenever I saw Tilly's face—heard her poisonous voice—and lunged forward, looking for a way around or through the pack.

Pockets opened but closed a fraction of a second later as bodies collided, muscles flexed, and determination-laced grunts filled the air.

Tuned into the calls from my blockers, I pushed at barriers, waiting for something to give.

Moving to the outside, I kept my eyes on the inside, looking for space to get through. Throwing my shoulder as though I planned to cut around the outside, pushing the boundaries, I lurched forward and the two blockers in front of me crowded right, keeping their bodies tight together, closing the gap, giving me the opportunity to dart around them in the middle.

The shouts melded together. The cheers of the crowd bled into the calls from my teammates. Sweat trickled into my eyes, the warm sting forcing me to blink.

Bite "N" Switch, their biggest blocker, with her head half turned, always watching and readjusting to thwart my every attempt to break through the pack while trying to propel her own jammer through the chaos, stumbled back after a solid hit from my teammate, Anarch-Eve.

Their showdown left Tilly trapped in the middle.

Away from me.

Despite the gap in front of me, another pocket opened on the inside. With Tilly pinned, I had a shot this time. Adrenaline surged through my veins, my instincts screaming for me to go for it.

I could never resist going for the inside.

Something about that boundary line called me every single time.

My shoulder brushed past their pivot, MissAdventure. Just two more strides and I could surge forward. I had it this time. I totally had it. With Eve on Tilly, nothing could stop me.

Our tangled skates threatened to topple me over, but I yanked my foot free while keeping my balance on my left. My edges flexed from the force of my weight. With a swing of my arms to propel my upper body, and a hop... I slipped ahead.

Fuck yes!

A sickening thud obliterated the cheer of the crowd. The air whooshed from my lungs as the sharp pain exploded in my ribs once again. My wheels ripped away from the floor, gravity and my trajectory turning them into lead weights on my feet.

Time slowed, our rivalry playing out like a scene in an action movie where victory was all but certain.

But whose victory?

She was the bad guy.

But maybe I was a bad guy too.

Maybe we weren't the lead characters at all. Maybe our names were both lost in the second half of the credits. The font smaller. The roles forgettable. Secondary characters adding to the body count.

Names on the tip of viewers' tongues, but never quite remembered.

Soaring off the track, I kept my arms tucked in, fighting the urge to catch myself. I caught Tilly's determined gaze one last time, standing where I had been, gloved hands clutched on her knee pads, her lungs heaving, victory in her glare.

Closing my eyes, I waited for it.

The one thing this sport guaranteed.

Pain.

I envisioned the next few seconds. The ones that came after the landing. My mind already determined to get back on the track. My brain calculating the next steps to get up.

My side and hip crashed against the concrete, a slice of pain slashing through my pelvis from the unyielding cold surface.

The blow ricocheted through me, rattling me all the way to my bones, sucking the breath from my heaving lungs until my stomach hollowed out with the loss of air.

The whistle cut through the ringing in my ears, saving me from having to pretend I didn't just get pummeled by a freight train. Saving me from exposing my weakness… that maybe this time, no matter how much I prepared, no matter how much I wanted to win, I might not have been able to bounce right back up and on the track.

Dragging a gulp of air into my lungs, I blinked furiously trying to clear my vision. The blurry crowd finally coming into focus.

And him.

His cool, hooded gaze radiated boredom. Detached and so still in the restless crowd, he leaned back in his seat in the front row, his leg casually stretched out, his bent arm hooked over the back of his metal folding chair, leaving his fingers dangling carelessly.

"Hey, you good?" Eve asked, panting over me, cutting off my view and reaching out to help me up.

"Yeah." I clasped her offered hand. My hip buckled when I straightened, the stab of pain slicing through me, making my eyes burn. Tightening my muscles, I locked my knees until I had my balance.

On my feet once again, I cocked my head until my neck cracked as Eve skated away. Glancing back at the crowd, my focus homed in on the now-empty metal chair. From the corner of my eye, I caught sight of the door clicking shut.

Not impressed, dude?

Yeah, me either.

Maisy

Cars, pickups, and a few company vans filled the parking lot next to Banked Track, the single hottest bar—well, only bar in Galloway Bay.

Okay, so maybe not the only bar. There were a few watering holes on the outskirts of our coastal Maine town. The kind that looked like abandoned outbuildings during the day with sagging rooflines, missing shingles, cracked windowpanes, and neon signs which probably hadn't worked since the seventies.

I know I sure as hell never recalled seeing them lit.

The sort of places where warm beer was always on tap for weathered fisherman, relic sea riders ranging somewhere between fifty and corpse, all with the same deep carved wrinkles in their sea-worn faces.

Generations of locals who struggled to survive their love affair with a romanticized profession flocked to the forgettable dives, wanting the quiet anonymity of drinking away their mountain of sorrows and all-too-limited successes with little fanfare and the drone of a muffled television keeping them company.

But for the rest of us, the outcasts, the townies, occasional tourists, and definitely derby girls, Banked Track was the sole nightlife of Galloway Bay. Tinged with the scent of salt air that crashed along our rocky coast and wrapped in the charm of rough brick walls, the atmosphere lulled even the most sullen into a good time.

And the saving grace—the sconces glowing with warm light and muted just enough you could get away with not recognizing a one-night stand you snagged from the scarred bar stools there.

Not that there were many one-night stands. Small-town bed-hopping had a way of making the rounds; next thing you knew, you were in the express lane of the local grocery store, minding your own, just a girl trying to snag a bit of salted caramel liquor to keep her company on a cold, lonely night and bam!

Not so subtle whispers of your escapades from the over-forty gossips who only gave a shit because they weren't getting any at home.

Not that it happened to me often, but when it did, I shrugged it off. Sleeping with your high school sweetheart for the past two decades, realizing that you may actually die with having only fucked one guy throughout your ho-hum life had to sting.

I couldn't imagine any sex being good enough that I'd want to be married to it for the rest of my life.

And I'd had some damn good sex.

A blast of heat washed over my frozen cheeks the minute I yanked open the door, driving away the vibration of my chattering teeth reverberating through my battered body from the minute I got out of my car.

Okay, in my car. Because the heater sucked. But the car ran and that was good enough. I was never behind the wheel for more than a few minutes anyway. Anything longer than around town, like our bouts in Augusta, Port-land, and Rockland, I hitched a ride with a teammate.

They appreciated the gas money and I appreciated not sitting broken down on the turnpike.

If I even made it to the turnpike.

"Toast, toast, toast," my team chanted, raising their shot glasses as I uncoiled my scarf and limped over to join them.

Eve handed me a shot glass and narrowed her eyes. "You're limping."

"So what else is new."

"Maybe you should get that hip checked."

"I'm walking, right?"

"Yeah, and snarling which means you're hurting."

"Alcohol and ice. That's all I need." I raised my glass and took in the skeptical glances from my core team. The originals: Eve, Marty, Rory, Sean, and Zara. "To stiff dicks, perky tits, bitches getting every last bit of karma they deserve… oh, and that straight piece in Tetris." I knocked back the shot, slapped the glass on the table, lifted the pile of hair off my neck, and fanned my face for the flush I knew would rush my Irish skin in a matter of seconds.

"Girl, you are fired up tonight," Marty said on a laugh.

"Enjoy it." My voice hissed on the burn in my throat. "I won't be this full of fuckery until I have to face off with Tilly the wench again."

"Don't you mean Hun? Tilly the Hun?" Zara said, ever the serious one of the group.

"No."

"Ooooooookay then," Zara said, glancing away.

I almost felt bad. Almost.

While I seriously wanted to stab Tilly in the fucking eye, I was madder at myself and the fact that I continued to play right into her juvenile games. Every time I did, I only emboldened her to continue with her shit, committing myself to the miserable cycle of giving Tilly endless satis-faction.

Frankly, I just wanted to stop talking about it.

And that ice. I needed that fucking ice.

Flipping my head down, I wrapped the bandana around my hair and tied it in a knot to hold my sweaty and now-cold hair off my face.

"Did you guys order the next round yet?" This bitch was getting her drink on tonight.

A little Three Dog Night pumped through the speakers low in the background, almost impossible to discern, but the familiar beat crawled in my chest and took hold of my body, wrapping me in a familiar memory like a warm pair of arms. Each note transporting me to another time, another place, to the last time I had a family.

"Oh no. She's got that look in her eye," Sean said with a snicker.

Eve glowered at me. "Yeah, we ordered the next round. Now put that face away."

Slinging my arm around Eve, I bobbed my head, a slow grin curving my lips.

Eve flicked me a glance and rolled her eyes. "You and your classic rock folky shit."

Pressing my cheek to hers, I closed my eyes. "You love it and you know it."

Eve snorted. "I love you, so I put up with it."

The liquor swept through my veins, carrying away the first few seeds of discontent. The song was a sign and I planned to roll with the message it delivered.

Hips swaying, a smile spreading over my lips, I gave Eve no choice but to sway along with me.

Her hip bumped mine, my muscles seized, and I bit my lip. "Ouch, shit. Ice."

"I'll get it," Eve said, pulling away.

"Hey," I said, stopping her. "I've got it." Dropping a quick, hard kiss on her lips, I made my way to the bar where I knew the song would be louder.

Patti Perkins, owner of Banked Track and the original derby queen from Galloway Bay, slung her towel over her shoulder and slapped her palms on the polished cherry bar. "Heard you had a rough night."

I glanced away with a shrug. "Word travels fast. Can I beg you for a bag of ice? Super cold."

She threw her head back and laughed, her frizzy, frosted hair paying homage to the eighties brushing her shoulders. "Super cold ice, you got it, Maze."

I rolled my eyes at the way she shortened my name. Something that used to drive me nuts, but sort of caught on and hell if anything I said was going to stop it. I could forgive her for that one… after all she had a special place in my heart, giving me my first job when I knew damn well she wasn't looking for help.

"You let her get in your head." His voice rumbled from his throat, cocky and rich, the kind of timbre a woman craved dancing over the skin of her inner thigh.

The beat forgotten, I flicked a glance in the direction of the deep, unfamiliar voice.

Him.

Casual fucker from the front row.

He tipped back a longneck bottle, his gaze never leaving mine even when they closed to slits.

"Really? And how the hell would you know that?" I would entertain him. Why not? He'd toss out his observations, this guy I'd never once seen at a single bout; he'd make it embarrassingly clear he didn't know shit about derby, and I'd go back to my drinks, ice in hand, and the rockin' fucking tunes in my head keeping me happy.

"She manipulated you to the inside every single time

and you never failed to fall for it. The minute you got there, the refs were too busy concentrating on your feet to see her throwing you elbows." His lip curled with distaste. "Six times."

Okay, he knew a little bit more than nothing.

"Here you go, Maze. Let me know when you need a refresh," Patti said with a couple pats to my cheek, something I normally liked, except on the heels of the dude's assessment of my game play, the endearing gesture only making me feel immature and stupid.

Kind of appropriate all things considered, but a kick in the tits just the same.

"Thanks. His next beer is on me," I said with a nod toward the judgmental bastard at the end of the bar.

Patti raised an eyebrow and glanced between the two of us.

"For the unsolicited play-by-play."

Heading back to the corner booth we always settled into after bouts, a coveted spot in the bar that Patti reserved for us so no matter if it was just the six of us or the whole team, we'd have room, I dropped into a chair, my back firmly to the bar.

More importantly, my back to the asshole hell-bent on taking my inventory.

My teeth clenched the minute the ice hit my hip, both from the shocking cold soaking through my thin shorts and the deep-seated throb playing a tempo of its own through my fucking pelvis.

Thank fuck our drinks had been delivered while I was gone. The Banked Track, a mixed drink Patti invented, the kind of concoction strong enough to put hair on your chest, or maybe even stop your heart.

I didn't care… because it started out with a heavy root beer flavor.

Too bad it ended with a swift punch of paint thinner.

I'd just stay away from open flame. No biggie.

Think I'm kidding? Right there in the drink menu, in parenthesis next to The Banked Track—a stern warning about the consumer's new flame rating after consumption.

Three gulps in, the root beer flavor so strong it filled my sinuses, I set the glass down and blinked up at my team —well, some of my team.

All eyes on me, silently studying me, I started to squirm in my seat, until my hip screamed in protest. "What?"

"You have no idea who you were talking to, do you?" Rory said, sneaking a glance past me, presumably to the dude.

"Sure, some bar rat who thinks he can mansplain derby to me. Call me fucking shocked."

Rory shook her head, her ordinarily confident voice dropping to a breathy whisper. "That's not a bar rat... that's Priest."

"He's a priest? What the fuck are you talking about?"

"No, just Priest," Rory said with a shake of her head.

"I wouldn't mind praying at that altar," Zara said, casting a quick side-glance at the bar.

"He was a roller derby coach here about ten years ago," Marty went on. "*The* roller derby coach. He was fucking brilliant... and gorgeous to boot. Like seriously, next level looks here. The women flocked to him."

Okay, so not mansplaining. But still, I didn't ask for his opinion and he just couldn't help but give it.

A few of my teammates salivated with breathy delight from the glances they stole of him across the bar.

Yeah, he was good looking. The way he filled out a sweater and his jeans should have been declared borderline obscene. His wide jaw and seductive mouth didn't hurt anything either... but ultimately, it was his deep, rough voice that set off a damn ache tried to seep into my you-can-just-fuck-off-with-your-assessment attitude.

In thirty seconds of conversation, he went from the kind of guy with the power to tickle my lady bits with just a smug glance, to the words coming out of his mouth making me want to roll my skates right over that face of his, to the low rumble finish of his voice destroying my underwear.

"I can't believe he came back after what happened," Sean whispered. "I hope you're ready, because Galloway Bay is about to explode."

"Well, maybe not all of Galloway Bay, but the squeakiest wheels in our town are definitely not team Priest." Rory said, lifting her glass to her lips. "But then that's what happens when you stack your team with underage talent only to have one of Galloway Bay's most promising teens end up in a wheelchair on your watch. I don't have to wonder why so many people in this town would love to go all Game of Thrones up in this bitch and mount his head on a pike."

"In town for all of five minutes and making friends already I see," Patti said with a bit of side-eye and a whole lot of signature smirk on her mauve-painted mouth.

Taking the last swallow of my beer and reaching for the "fuck you" round Mayhem bought me, I nodded. "Something like that."

Maisy Mayhem… well, not tonight she wasn't. She was playing with feelings. I couldn't even call it vengeance. At least if it had been, she might have had a chance. She was all reaction.

A goddamned jammer on the defensive would always lose.

Six elbows to her ribs. Same side every time.

Tilly needed a good hard knock on her ass, but Mayhem wouldn't be delivering it anytime soon unless she figured out how to get out of her own head… and let go of whatever was fucking with her heart.

Emotional investment wielded great power, but not when it was built on a foundation of bitterness and pain.

She was icing her hip now, but tomorrow she'd be struggling to take a deep breath. Their refs made shit rookie mistakes out there. They only needed one of them focused on the floor. But no, they all stared down at the concrete while Tilly took complete advantage of their inattention.

They needed more training.

Maisy needed to run her emotions, not let them run her.

And Tilly? Tilly had always been a problem. Her reputation in amateur leagues was common knowledge in New England… and maybe farther. She needed a coach strong enough to bend her to their will, someone hard and swift—and no bullshit—who could get her to comply.

Because the woman had demons and they were running the show. They'd kicked into overdrive tonight on that track.

Question was… what did those demons have to do with Mayhem?

I glanced over at the woman in question and found her rubbing near her spine where it met her ribs.

Not my problem. Not my circus.

Not anymore.

"Maisy's a good girl. I expect you to go easy on that one," Patti warned me.

I had no damn intentions of going easy or hard on her. Again, not my circus. "Good girl, huh? Well, she did buy me a beer."

"No, she didn't. I'm putting it on your tab."

"Bummer," I said with a grunt, tipping the bottle to my lips.

"You can damn well afford it. She, however… cannot." Patti rested her hand on her cocked hip and looked over at the corner booth where the team leaned in, their attention on each other as their pivot, Hazy Eights, filled them in on something noteworthy, keeping them enthralled, their drinks forgotten. Patti's face softened and a smile reminiscent of her Pinup Patti days on the track spread over her face. "Maisy's my favorite. I know a mother's not supposed to have them, but I can't help it. Underneath that makeup, those tattoos, and borderline foul mouth is a tender heart."

Patti never had kids, but when she took someone under her wing, she may as well have birthed them herself for how protective she became. The look on her face left zero doubt. She'd claimed all six of them here tonight as her own.

And she would slice off the balls of any man who dared do one of them dirty, all with a smile on her face. When she was done, she'd fry them up in the back and serve them with blue cheese dressing and celery sticks for garnish.

My balls weren't looking for an adventure—thanks.

Besides, they were young. The ladies, not my balls. Probably ten years younger than me. Just babies.

Plus, they were derby… and I wasn't.

I never would be again.

"It's fine. I don't plan to find out."

"Uh-huh. Sure," she said, turning that shrewd gaze on me. "So, when did you get into town?"

"This afternoon." My gaze snapped to the corner and found Mayhem blatantly watching me while her team darted guilty glances my way.

Subtle, ladies.

Problem solved… her buddies were filling her in and that's all it would take for her to steer clear of me anyway.

"Not even one night home and you've already been to a bout. Like I said, go easy on that one."

Not my style—but then, I'm not her coach so there's that.

I shrugged. "It was the last bout of the season. I'll be long gone before the next season kicks into gear."

"Now that's unfortunate," Patti said as she reached out and cupped my cheek, showing me I was also one of the lucky few under her wing.

Instinct told me to lean into that affection as much as I itched to run from it.

When I let people get close, they got hurt. Time and again. The adventure always changed, but the outcome… the same every single time.

"It's damn good to see you again. You look tired. You should sleep more." She patted my cheek once—hard—and turned to the pass between the bar and crammed kitchen that churned out a small menu of American favorites.

Okay, she smacked me—kind of—as though she could sense my unease, so she made it playful, giving me a way to retreat.

I'd tip the shit out of her when I settled up.

She dropped a basket next to my beer. "For you." Leaning on her elbows, she settled in and snagged a mozzarella stick. "So, have you seen her yet?"

Lulling me with fried food… so freaking Patti of her. "No," I said, my clipped voice harder than I intended.

"You plan to?"

"Yes."

"Her parents aren't going to be happy about that."

I met her gaze but said nothing. It didn't matter what her parents thought. I was in town; I would see her. They had no say. Not anymore.

"Oooooh, bound up tighter than a colon seized up by a five-day cheese binge."

I dropped the cheese stick I'd picked up. "That's disgusting."

"And all too common around these parts. You ever see a seventy-year-old man grunting out a cheddar log?"

"And with that, I'm never eating cheese again. Tell me you didn't meet this seventy-year-old cheese addict online."

"Sorry to break it to you, but there's more cheese in your future. You're going to eat it and you're going to like it," Patti said, plunking down a double cheeseburger and cheese fries in front of me. "And don't worry, I didn't meet him online… he's local."

"I didn't order this."

She pointed her index finger at me and huffed out an exasperated breath. "I'm taking care of you for a few minutes. Now stop interfering. Hey, at least it's not cheddar."

"Fair point."

"Enough small talk, Cain. Spill… what brought you home?"

"Lilith is having complications and Jordan can't get back just yet from his deployment. So here I am."

She straightened, her mouth pressing into a thin line. "She's going to be okay though, right? And the baby?"

"They're going to be fine, but if she goes into labor early, we don't want her to be alone."

"Already a good uncle. Look at you."

"Yeah, well, jury's still out on that."

"The only jury is the one you've got locked in that head of yours. Being sequestered has an end date. You should give them a break," she said, rapping her knuckles against the bar and turning toward the crew at the end of the bar calling her name. "Duty calls. Don't leave without checking in with me. Got it?"

"You're the boss."

"See, now if everyone could just get that through their head as a given, life would be so much easier." She tossed the words over her shoulder with a laugh and a twinkle in her eye that had me smiling back.

The flex of those facial muscles felt foreign, and I had to wonder how long it had actually been since I had something to grin about.

My skin tingled and the hair stood up on my neck. Turning to the likely source, I found Mayhem now seated in the booth, her hostile stare roaming over me.

I had to wonder if my assessment of her shit play put that pinched look on her face or if it was the result of the gossip fed to her by her teammates.

Whatever.

Turning back to my burger, I did as I was told and ate. I wasn't stupid. Patti wouldn't give me a lecture if I turned down her food. She wouldn't cuff me. She'd hit me with another nightmare inducing anecdote, maybe not about cheese, but it seems likely geriatric colons might be involved.

The woman in question glanced over at me, her eyes narrowed.

Yeah, I'd do as I was told.

Pick your battles, Bishop… this one wasn't worth it.

Frustration pulsed through me with renewed energy since I rolled into Galloway Bay. This town had been my salvation and eventually my home until karma found me and took a devastating swipe, turning every part of my haven into a festering reminder that I didn't deserve the sanctuary it offered.

I carried the broken parts of me from a shitty life, into this idyllic place. Relieved to have broken free from my nightmare, I failed to notice the broken pieces in me planting seeds that later flared to life in the fertile earth here. Standing ready to shatter any illusions I might have of peace.

Peace didn't exist. Turmoil… and ironically, mayhem, I had those in spades.

The last of my burger down, I wiped my mouth and tossed my napkin on my plate. What flicker of good mood I'd found soured to shit.

This frame of mind called for hard liquor, a willing woman, or better… both.

But nope, I get to go home and deal with my sister.

My pregnant, moody, perceptive sister.

Life really knew how to deliver a merciless double nipple twist.

Tossing a hundred-dollar bill on the bar, I slid off the stool, but stopped when I spotted Patti waving her hands at me, rushing over with a takeout bag.

"Take this to your sister for me. On the house. Pregnancy is the one time you can eat your feelings with no judgment."

"Pregnancy or not, it's no one's business what we choose to put in our mouths."

"From your lips to God's ears."

"What is it?"

"Prosciutto and Brussels sprout panini with her favorite pepper jack. Five minutes in that air fryer of hers and it will be just like it came fresh from the pass."

"Brussels sprouts? She doesn't like the vile little bastards."

"Well, she does now… apparently that baby loves him some Brussels sprouts too."

"Must get it from his dad. Thanks." I wrapped my arms around her and gave her a squeeze. The lingering scent of her familiar floral perfume eased something bound tight in my chest and I closed my eyes.

"Welcome home," she murmured before kissing me on the cheek, only to swipe at my skin a second later to wipe the lipstick print she no doubt left there.

"It's temporary," I said over my shoulder as I turned for the door.

"We'll see," she called to my retreating back.

Galloway Bay would never be what it once was for me. Too many mistakes and long memories would make sure of that.

It could never be home again, no matter how much I wished it could be.

CAIN

Gravel crunched under my tires as I turned off Old Mill Road onto the winding driveway to the farm. Between the sound and the winking of stars peeking through the pine trees lining the drive, the night ignited dozens of memories, each taking aim at my most vulnerable places.

Gnashing my teeth, I forced them out of my head, knowing even if I planted the seeds of my warmest memories here, those seeds would only grow so far before the broken pieces of me, already flourishing in their maturity, choked them out, leaving them withered piles of lifeless hope.

I'd dared to hope for more once. I'd even reached for what I didn't deserve only to be knocked on my ass for my audacity.

Damaged goods.

It never failed. Being home played games with my head and assaulted the fragments left of my bitter heart.

Rolling to a stop, I turned off the engine and clutched the wheel. Lamplight burned in the picture window in the living room as it had for decades from sundown until sun up every single night. A gift from my grandmother to my grandfather when they first bought the farm, she insisted it would always be on no matter how late he had to stay up, no matter what went wrong in the middle of the night, lighting the way back to her.

Lilith insisted it would do the same for me, for as long as it took.

She was pushy like that.

Colors flickered from the TV bathing the room in a colorful glow. The fluorescents over the kitchen sink illuminated my sister's profile as she rubbed her round belly, a peaceful smile on her lips as she talked to her unborn son.

Okay, so maybe it didn't all turn to shit. Lilith would get her happy ending. She'd always have peace.

She'd been through so much. She saw too damn much, but here in this town, in this farmhouse full of warm memories and familiar scents, she could raise her family with the love and nurturing we'd lost the day our mother died.

The minute I walked in, she would ask where I was. If I told her the truth, it'd start a fight.

Just like that, I was grateful for the panini bag sitting next to me… even if it did have Brussels sprouts lurking in it.

Shedding my impulse to avoid her, I headed inside. Clicking the door shut behind me, I turned the deadbolt before facing her.

"Hey, where have you been?" Lilith asked, cocking a hip against the counter and crossing her arms.

See, called it.

"Stopped in at Banked Track for a bit. Patti sent you this nightmare. Says you like it." I handed over the bag and tossed my keys on the drop-leaf table before heading to the fridge for one last beer, wishing it was something a hell of a lot stronger.

Lilith's senses only got stronger now that she hovered

on the brink of motherhood. Now, if she just wouldn't aim her keen talents on me, I might survive the next couple of months.

She peeled open the bag and her lips twitched. "For three hours?"

"You watching the clock now?" With a flick of my thumb and middle finger, I shot the cap at the key rack by the cellar door and watched it sink in the trash can, just like our grandpa taught me when I was a kid.

"You know he's up there cheering right now. Probably nudging Gram and saying, 'Now that's my boy.'"

My lips twitched. "Yeah, that sounds about right."

She turned her back on me and worked on getting her sandwich into the air fryer Patti knew she had, but I didn't.

There was a lot to unpack with how out of touch I was with my own baby sister, but today had already been a bitch between the drive up here and the bout. Especially if knowledge of a small appliance could push my buttons.

"So, before you ended up at Banked Track… where'd you go?"

"I drove around for a while."

She glared at me over her shoulder, wordlessly calling me on my bullshit.

"You went to the bout up at Sid's, didn't you?"

Sid's Aviation, a relic of an airport even before I was born, sat mostly unused, but Sid's grandchildren so far had refused to sell despite some seriously lucrative offers. Selling meant the recreation derby league would likely lose the hangar they practiced and played in, and with derby being a big deal in Sid's family for several generations, they would likely hang on as long as they possibly could.

"And if I did?" I asked, stretching my neck, tugging at the knots lodging in my tight muscles as she gave me the third degree.

"You haven't even slept in your bed once and already you're at it with the damn derby again."

She sounded just like Patti—well, Patti with less tact.

"It was the last bout on the schedule… I think I'd have to go to more than one to classify it as being at it."

She slapped her palms on the counter. "It's not a joke, Cain."

"No, it's not," I snapped. "But drilling me like I'm some addict that just fell off the wagon is pretty damn insulting, so if you want me to listen to what you have to say, how about you remember who's older and have a little respect."

She hung her head, her voice turning sad, slicing away at me with every syllable. "Roller derby cost me my only living brother. They took ever—"

"No," I said, my voice hard and low.

Pushing away from the wall, I stepped up to her and took her rigid shoulders in my hands. I dropped a kiss on the top of her head and the tension radiating from her into my palms eased a fraction. "They didn't take anything. I screwed up. There's no one to blame here but me."

"You and I both know that's not entirely true."

"I was the coach—the adult, Lilith. It's on me."

"God, that damn cop integrity of yours," she said with a heavy sigh. "You're here for such a short amount of time. Why would you risk dredging it up all over again? People are going to talk now."

"People were going to talk anyway. There was no avoiding that. You need help and I want to give it. When Jordan gets back, I'm gone. It's two months, tops." I wrapped my arms around her shoulders and dropped my chin on her head. For a second, just a second, it was like she was that little girl again. "Besides, what kind of trouble can I cause between now and then?"

"You forget I know you better than anyone."

"I'll be good. Scouts honor. It's the off-season so while there might be talk for a few days, it will die down. I promise."

"I wish I understood why you can't stay away from the sport. I love it too… and I love our family ties to it. But for you, it's just—I don't know, it's beating with a life of its own inside you."

"Women took it over and made it their own. Our grandmother being one of them. There's something rather poetic about that after how it all started."

She patted my hand where it rested on her shoulder and sighed. "Very true and not many men would recognize it. So, was the bout any good?"

"Not very. A waste of time."

"I don't know, a couple of the teams in the area are applying for the Women's Roller Derby Federation so they're getting better. Maybe it was just a bad night."

"Where'd you hear about the WRDF?"

"Patti mentioned it."

"Huh, she didn't say anything to me about it."

"Why would she… you're not staying and even if you were…" Her words trailed off, leaving a heavy silence wedged between us full of harsh allegations and scandal.

Two months loomed before me, the time stretching out until it felt more like two years. Too tired to finish my beer, I let Lilith go. "If you don't need anything, I'm going to head on up to bed," I said, pouring the rest of my drink down the sink.

"Wait, you've got to try just one bite."

"It's Brussels sprouts. I think the fuck not."

"Oh, come on. You'll love it. I swear. I hated the little bastards too, until this panini. It's power to convert Brussels sprout haters everywhere is downright diabolical."

"This is my punishment for tonight, isn't it?"

"If that's how you want to look at it, fine. Just try it, would you?" she said with her hand out, half of the sandwich clutched between her fingertips.

"Fine." I grabbed her hand, brought it to my mouth, and took a good-sized bite. Because if I didn't, she'd make me take another.

I waited for the bitterness to explode in my mouth, preparing to choke it down with a smile on my face, but to my surprise, I detected none, only a mild sweetness complimented with the rich smoked meat and the kick of pepper jack. "Well damn, give me half," I said, snagging the piece from her fingers before heading for the stairs.

"Hey!"

"What?"

"I thought you didn't like Brussels sprouts?" she said with the same mocking tone she'd hammered me with when we were kids.

"What can I say, you converted me."

"Thief," she called out right before I reached the stairs.

"Nag."

"I love you, butthead."

I leaned over the bannister and winked. "Love you too, squirt."

Maisy

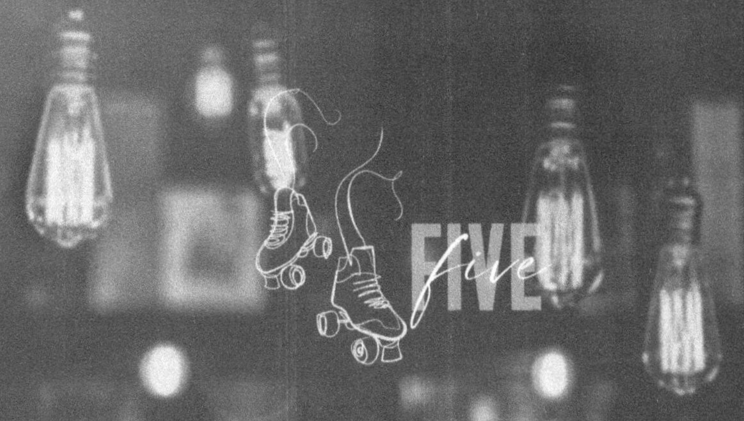

"Heard you had a hell of a night last night, Maisy Jane."

"Up late gossiping, were you?" I said, grabbing the coffee filters to start a fresh pot of decaf, because I was down to one refill left for good ol' Milton. Not that he wanted decaf, but what he didn't know would likely keep his crusty ass alive.

At least on my watch.

From the day his wife Mary stopped by, worried about his heart palpitations, I'd begun switching out his brew. I didn't do it all in one shot, mind you. Some things required finesse—in other words, ten percent increments.

My boy finally joined the world of full decaf just last week and I couldn't be prouder. This must be what it's like for a mother whose baby walks for the first time.

Mary tried to keep him home, cooking him breakfast so she could control his diet better, but he missed being on his boat and he craved the sea. So he spent his mornings here, the only diner for fifty miles that sat next to a rocky cliff overlooking the Atlantic.

That's where I took over, giving Mary a little peace of mind while Milton gave me some real live entertainment… and most days the sailor didn't disappoint.

Every morning he bellied on up to the counter and settled in, his back turned toward his true love, giving it the cold shoulder.

Stubborn shit. Maybe that's why I liked him so much.

"Aw hell, Maisy, I overheard them talking about it over at the general store. You know I don't do that gossiping nonsense."

Sure, he didn't. "What would you call this?"

"Going to the source."

"Fair enough. It was a shitty night. Not one I want to repeat." Grabbing the carafe, I hopped over to where he sat on a cracked black vinyl stool. Or at least I tried to hop over, only to have my momentum reduced to a hobble as a fresh wave of slicing pain sucked the next words right out of my throat. My muscles locked tight and I squeezed my eyes shut while the ache rocked through me, a stark reminder why hopping, gliding, dancing, grinding against my mattress with forbidden coach fantasies—basically why existing was a god-awful idea at the moment.

Bushy gray eyebrows bunched over his cloudy blue eyes. "You okay, kid?"

"I will be. Just my body reminding me I'm not super-human after all." I loved derby. I even appreciated the aches and pains, within reason. But the ice pick wedged in my lungs threatened to steal the simple pleasures I get from the crack of dawn squad who kept me company every morning at The Shipwreck.

It's bad enough I couldn't take a deep breath which meant I missed my morning inhale of smoked meat tinged with strong coffee and pastries brought fresh each morning by Audrey from Crum Cakes.

Every day for five years, exactly twenty minutes into my shift, the tables and counter still empty, the coffee brewed, and the first of the local bacon and sausage sizzling on the griddle, I'd unpack those sugar bombs and let the quiet settle over me while I breathed in the scent of the closest thing I had to home.

Each time I soaked it in and committed it to memory, I pretended I belonged to these people and they belonged to me.

I missed that this morning and it left me out of sorts and almost as grumbly as Milton over there.

Plus, the pain killed my dancing time. How the hell was I supposed to not dance a little when the oldies station pumped out Dion and the Belmonts at the top of the hour? I'd rather give up Crum Cakes for the day than lose my groove.

"What's this I hear about not being superhuman, darlin'?" Gerald said, shuffling up to the counter, all set to take the seat next to Milton.

"Oh no, you don't," I said, snapping my fingers at Gerald. He matched Milton in the stubbornness department, but they didn't play nice together. "Move over. You know the rule, one stool between the two of you at all times."

"She's in a mood," Gerald muttered.

"No leaning either, Gerald," I called out as I grabbed Milton's food out of the window.

"Damn woman's got eyes in the back of her head."

Setting Milton's piping hot eggs over easy, home fries, and the bacon I wasn't supposed to let him have in front of him, I shot Gerald a look. "And don't you forget it. Now, you look at the menu while I take Sheriff Chase's order." I glanced between both of them, making sure they were looking at me so there'd be no misunderstanding. "Be good. Don't make me punish you."

"How exactly you gonna do that?" Milton said with a scowl.

I crossed my arms and arched my brow, adopting Patti's best "why don't you try me" expression. "I'll take away your salt."

Gerald smirked. "I'd listen to her. She's stronger than you."

"Shut it, Gerald," Milton said with a glower at his… nemesis? Friend? Some days it was hard to tell.

Rolling my eyes, I bit back a grin as I walked away. A smile would only encourage them, and I'd lose all control on a morning when I didn't have the energy or stamina for more.

I loved the old farts, but they'd better behave. With the relentless pain keeping me company, they might just be able to overpower me at the moment. Not that they'd put their hands on me, but they'd put their hands on each other a time or two and I'd had to get between them.

They were spry little turds at six in the morning. That's what happens when you go to bed at eight.

As for me, I think my eyes finally closed at about one. Which was stupid on my part when I had to clock in at five in the morning, but after the information dump on a certain sexy, shunned coach at Banked Track the night before, and the pain from the shittiest bout of the season, there was no amount of alcohol powerful enough to silence the shitstorm in my head and the throbbing vibrating through my body with every breath.

Pulling out my pad, I tapped my pen against the paper and smiled at the robust, hulking man dwarfing the corner table. "Good morning, Sheriff. What can I get for you this morning?"

"Morning, Maisy. I'm actually waiting for someone, so if I could just get a cup of coffee while—oh, never mind, he's here."

"Sorry, I'm late."

I froze at the familiar voice behind me and sunk my teeth into my lip to stifle the yelp from the spasm it set off in my back.

Moving aside, I gave him room while he peeled off his jacket and wrapped it around the back of his chair. Worn blue jeans stretched tight over muscular thighs as he slid into his seat. The cable knit sweater he favored the night before had been replaced by a white t-shirt covered with unbuttoned blue-and-black flannel, the sleeves rolled up to just past his elbows.

Light-brown hair sprinkled over corded muscles. A spattering of freckles dotted his skin. Thick veins peeked out from the underside of his forearms as he interlaced his long fingers and propped his joined hands on the table.

There should be a law against a flaming asshole having so much hand and arm porn at his disposal.

Fucking forearms.

"Mayhem," he said quietly with a brief nod. His deep molten voice dragging out the word longer than normal.

"Priest," I deadpanned despite the dust storm that had just surged up my esophagus, turning the inside of my mouth into the Sahara.

The sheriff's tired eyes widened, and he glanced between the two of us. "You two know each other?"

His lips twitched. "You might say that."

His smug tone made my fingers itch to reach out and touch him—hard—but I fought the urge to smack him in the back of the head with a menu. Awfully adult of me all things considered. "Only if you're a liar. No, we don't know each other."

"I know that tone," the sheriff said with a husky laugh. "You're in trouble, Bishop."

"There's a shocker," Priest muttered with a dismissive snort.

The sheriff leaned back in his seat and crossed his meaty arms. "Don't let his surly disposition fool you, Maisy. He's got more integrity than anyone I know."

"Hmmm, is that right?" I flicked a glance at the stubborn man in question. Mired in scandal, whispered about around town, but beloved by Patti and now the sheriff.

The pieces didn't fit, but I wouldn't ask around, it wasn't my style. I sure as hell didn't like the whispering around town about me over the years before I formed a few bonds here, so I wouldn't be a party to doing the same to someone else.

I'd always been a transplant to this town where familial roots run deep, with no real ties but for derby, and it took me five years of living here before I even found that. Our team had plans. That meant not blowing it and losing the semi-comfortable little pocket in the world I'd struggled to make here. And getting close to Priest could only mean casting doubt on our team and ruining every bit of hard work we'd been putting in for so long.

He'd turned his attention on me for a brief moment in time, but the time passed. The season was over. I'd stay out of his way and if he was as wonderful as the sheriff thought he was, he'd stay out of mine. "I'll be back in a minute with coffee and to take your order."

By the time I made it back to the counter, Gerald had moved over next to Milton. "What did I say?" I snapped, filling two mugs with one hand while reaching for the salt shaker in front of Milton with the other.

Every day they trained me more and more for motherhood I wasn't even sure I wanted.

"Hey, hey, hey," he said, trying to beat me to the goods. "He came my way, Maisy Jane. I'm the victim here."

I pulled my hand back and left the salt in front of him,

then pierced Gerald with a hard glare. "You remember, I touch your food before you do. Understood?"

"Damn, yes," Gerald said, flicking off his cap and scratching his head before dropping the hat back on. "My drill sergeants were nicer than you."

"Yeah, well, they had weapons to keep you in line. All I have is fear."

"Back in my day a woman used her feminine wiles to get what she wanted."

"Back in your day, women couldn't have credit cards without their husband's signatures." I rounded the counter, two coffees perched on my tray, and stopped between the two men, pressing a kiss to each of their cheeks. "Now, be good while mama's away."

CAIN

Mayhem made damn good coffee. Strong, but not bitter. Nope. She saved the bitterness for the hostile glare she shot me when she set my plate of food in front of me.

Glancing over my shoulder as she left, I caught sight of Gerald creeping his hand toward Milton's second helping of bacon. "God, some shit never changes. You got your cuffs ready?"

Sheriff Chase grinned. "Won't need 'em."

"If Milton catches him, Gerald's going to be sporting a fork in his hand as a new accessory."

"They'll mind. Just watch," the sheriff said, jutting his chin in their direction.

She had her back to them now, leaning against the counter, remote in hand, bringing up the local news. Without taking her eyes off the screen, she darted out her hand and caught Gerald's as he crept in on Milton's bacon.

"I know five-year-olds who have better manners than you," she snapped.

Gerald shook his head with disgust. "Nasty little buggers. Pick their noses and eat it."

"Yes," she hummed in a sweet tone, "and what does that tell you?"

The sheriff chuckled as she slapped down the morning paper in front of Gerald. "I've got a juicy story for you on the front cover. Defense spending cut again. It'll give you something to bitch about until your food's done."

A smile crept over my face again as I turned to face my mentor.

"I told you. She's good with those two, not that she'd ever admit it. Tried to compliment her once and she got this pained look on her face. I swear she'd rather eat mud than have someone give her any sort of praise."

"I don't remember her. I guess she's not local," I said, feeling him out for information while I dug into my omelet.

"Not local. You were still in town when they arrived though," he said, pointing at me with his fork, the sausage link bobbing on the end of it. "You might remember. Her mama was Daisy Flynn."

"She had some sort of medical emergency, right? They didn't get to her in time."

"Something like that," he said, lowering his voice, his eyes on the counter. "They found her slumped by the doors of the health center. Figured she must have been waiting for them to open, but it was too late. Diabetic coma. She died three days later."

It happened on my first day back in town after my team won their first semi-final in Portland. But I still had two days off before I went back to work. By the time I'd clocked back in, the situation had been handled.

"Where's her father?"

"Never could find him. Maisy doesn't even know his name, so that didn't help."

"Other family?" I took a bite of the thick toast slathered with butter. Shit, I missed the food here. Not that Boston didn't have good food, but this... this tasted like home.

"None that we could find. They only landed here because this is where Daisy's car broke down. She got a job over at the Beacon Motel and they gave her and Maisy a room to live in as part of her pay."

Just a kid sleeping in a hole in the wall motel while her mom slipped away. Her mother probably hadn't woken her up to tell her she was running out.

The toast lost its appeal and I tossed it on my plate. "Where did she go after?"

"Where they all go at that age. Bay Wilderness."

My jaw clenched so hard my temples throbbed with it. "But that's for troubled youth."

"She was fourteen and all of our foster homes were full. At least the ones in town, and she didn't want to leave."

"So, she chose it?" I told myself I was only seeking information, but with every new detail, my blood pumped harder and faster. I couldn't afford to care, but I couldn't stop myself from wanting—needing—to know more.

"In a way, yes. I would say it worked out. Who knows, might just be where she got her talents for herding stubborn old fisherman. Thanks to her keeping them in line, for the first time in ten years, Milton let that restraining order on Gerald lapse."

"Her doing, huh?"

"Maisy's blunt with them, but affectionate. They know if they don't let the old shit go, they'll lose her and she's the bright spot in their day."

"I haven't seen that side of her yet." But I saw something. Something I didn't want to examine too closely.

She'd definitely decided where I belonged, and she was right.

Even as my mind knew keeping my distance was best,

something in me just wanted to poke at her. Activate that temper.

Go head-to-head and see who came out on top.

"I don't suppose you'll be in town long enough to see it. She doesn't trust easily, and we can't seem to get you to stick around," the sheriff said, his hard eyes settling on me.

I walked right into that one. I leaned back in my chair and turned my focus to the sunlight bathing the ripples of saltwater jumping on the surface of the ocean in a golden glow. "It's better for everyone if I'm gone."

The sheriff heaved a heavy sigh. "It wasn't your fault."

"That's what everyone keeps saying."

"When are you going to believe it?" the sheriff demanded with a hard rap of his knuckles rattling the table between them. The utensils on the sheriff's now mostly empty plate rattled with the force.

Undaunted by the heat in his words, I looked him dead in the eye. "I'm not."

"That sense of responsibility you've got is going to be the death of you."

"Better than a lack of responsibility being the death of others."

Heat crept up my neck and my skin burned under the sheriff's stare. The one man who knew all of it. The past and the present. The bad, and the downright disastrous.

Because there sure as hell wasn't any good.

Sheriff Chase whistled low and leaned back in his chair. "You, son, are dancing with some old ghosts. You've gone back in time, clean past the accident and straight on back to your brother, haven't you?"

Ah, there was the sore spot, always festering. Always making me wonder what the outcome would have been if I'd done something different.

If I'd been different.

"Wouldn't you?"

"You were a kid, and your dad was a coward."

"So was I, but I moved on. Made a life here just like you all said I should. Just like you all told me I deserved," I hurled the words at him, resentment wrapped around my heart for the way I let them all convince me I deserved more. Could be more.

I wouldn't fall for it today.

Not ever again.

The sheriff shot daggers at me with his narrowed eyes, but he couldn't scare me. I'd seen far worse than him.

"I had the start of a solid career I could be proud of on a small-town police force. I got involved with my community, with my heritage, and you know how that all turned out."

The sheriff scraped his hand along his chin. "We have an opening coming up this spring. I was kind of hoping with Lilith having a baby I could convince you to take it, but you're too far gone, aren't you?"

"It's better for the town, better for my family and my nephew if I go."

"Nothing heals if you keep running from it, son. You've got to face the ugly shit. Have hard conversations. When Sanders called me, told me he was sending a boy and his baby sister our way, sending them home where they belonged, he made me promise to look out for you."

"I know."

"Just because he's gone doesn't mean I've forgotten. I have every intention of seeing that promise through."

"In Boston—"

"You work shit hours and have no friends. You're not living in Boston, you're existing," the sheriff said, glancing over at the counter where Maisy favored her good hip and flinched when she laughed at something Gerald said.

The rib.

"She took six elbows to the ribs last night."

Sheriff Chase cocked his head and smiled. "Did she? You were there to see it?"

"I walked right into that trap."

"You did, but it's not like I wouldn't have heard about it anyway. Word around town travels faster than the empanadas from that food truck over on Route One tearing through a colon."

"What in the fresh hell is the fascination this town has with digestion all of a sudden?"

"On that note, I need to get to the station," the sheriff said with a gruff laugh. "I'm leaving that position open for a while. You're my first choice."

"Not going to hap—"

"Don't even bother, son. I'm more stubborn than you and I'll win."

I stood and reached for the sheriff's hand. "I'm paying for breakfast then."

"Joke's on you, I'm going to let you." The sheriff's hand fell away, and he glanced up at Maisy and tipped his hat. "You get some rest now, Maisy Jane. Tell Scooter he outdid himself with the omelets."

"Will do. Stay safe out there," she said, giving him a quick smile.

"Always."

Mayhem crossed her arms and tapped her foot, her temperature cooling a good forty degrees with the sheriff's retreating back. "Anything else I can get for you?"

"The check."

"Done." She reached for the order pad tucked into her jeans pocket, wobbled, sucked in a jagged breath, caught her balance, and slapped the receipt on the table.

Fucking hell. "Tell me about the rib."

She flicked me an irritated glance, all but telling me to fuck off with her wary eyes. "There's nothing wrong with my rib. Now, if you ask me about my back, that's a whole different story."

"Show me."

"Yeah, I don't think so," she said with a snort.

I reached for her arm before she could storm off. "You have a chiropractor?"

She glanced down at my fingers wrapped around her elbow. "Of course. I also have a money tree growing out my ass. Wanna see?"

"Cute."

"That's unfortunate, I wasn't trying to be."

"I'll dismiss it as the pain talking and not your glowing personality."

"Or you could just call it what it is. I don't like you," she spat back.

"Most people don't."

"Now that I believe."

With two fingers tucked between my lips, I blew, letting out a whistle that had every patron turning our way. Not really my intention, but that was the only way to get Scooter's attention.

The retired fisherman popped his head up in the pass and glowered. "What?"

"Maisy's taking five."

"She's the only one out there."

"Ahh, let her go. We can get along for a few minutes," Milton said with a wave of his hand as he sipped away at his coffee.

"Five minutes. That's it," Scooter said, pointing his greasy spatula at us through the pass.

"Come on."

"You're nuts."

"And you're maddening. Now move it."

"Yes, Coach," she said with a roll of her eyes. But I noticed the way her steps faltered with the snide comment.

Because… the rib.

I was going to take care of that sucker and say farewell to Mayhem once and for all.

I led her through the side exit the employees used. The same one I used for a year washing dishes as a teenager here at night, when the menu switched from gut-busting breakfasts to fried fish and seafood fresh from the ocean.

The spring-loaded door slammed shut behind us, reminding me of all the times I used to cut out here to kiss my girlfriend, Shelby.

Okay, putting that memory away now.

I gave the railing a hard shake to make sure it was solid. Falling fifteen feet to the lower parking lot, probably not the help she was looking for.

Not that she wanted any help, but she sure as hell was going to get it, whether she liked it or not.

She hugged herself against the cold. "I've seen this part in the movies. This is where you toss my ass over. Let me tell you something, if I go, you go."

Maisy

"Are you ever not a smart-ass?" Priest said, cutting me with a hard glare from warm brown eyes that crinkled at the corners.

Brown fucking eyes like melted chocolate, with threads of caramel swirled in. Eyes of a languid lover smoldering with heat and promise.

God, I hate that I noticed. And maybe that was my problem with him all along.

His presence.

Commanding attention with a heavy silence, he held it in his grasp with the storm raging in his eyes, making me want to get closer and run all at the same time.

Making me want to hear his secrets, but only from him so he could consume me with the way they rolled off his scathing tongue.

All starting from the very first moment our eyes met from where he sat on a metal folding chair outside the track.

If only he'd keep his mouth shut because every observation, every question, every biting reply washed over me like the frigid, unforgiving Atlantic in early February.

And that was the only reason my nipples had perked up.

The cold water.

Not the eyes.

Or the forearms. Yeah, I hadn't forgotten those. If anything, I may have imagined sinking my teeth into them.

I flashed him a grin, my smile dialed to eat-me-fucker. "Smart-ass is the only mood I've got."

Shoving his hand through his short-cropped hair, he shook his head. "One thing I didn't miss? The attitudes."

"I can't begin to imagine why you even care about a pinched nerve." I fought the urge to spin away from the gust of air sweeping through the parking lot. My Henley tee had nothing on frigid late fall air. Early December temperatures sat firmly in the mid-thirties, but with the breeze rolling in off the ocean, the chill bit into my skin leaving a bone-deep cold even the sun burning in the cloudless sky couldn't penetrate.

"It's not a pinched nerve," he muttered as he snatched his jacket from his elbow. His confidence, the arrogance, it poked at me and sizzled like a brand sparking my own flash of temper.

I gnashed my teeth and swallowed the snarl that bubbled in my throat. "So, this is about being right? Aren't you a fucking charmer? It's my body. I think I'm the first one to know when something goes wrong in there *and* I'd know if it was a rib."

Arms hanging casually at his sides, but his shoulders rigid and ready to fight, he took a step toward me, the jacket swaying from where it dangled from his fingertips. "I think you don't know shit about your own body. If you did, you'd know it's your rib."

"Fine, Doc. How is it possible for it to be my rib?" I asked, hoping to give him enough rope to hang himself. There's no way he had a hundred percent accuracy rate in the confidence department. Especially considering his history.

He snorted as if the answer was obvious. The sound, a verbal pat on the head dismissing me like I was daft. "Because you took six elbows last night playing like shit. That's all it takes. Lucky for you, I can fix it."

He poked at the festering wound that never really healed. I knew I let Tilly get to me. I sure as hell didn't need him to swoop into town and point out the obvious. Every time I let her get in my head, I told myself it was the last time. But the minute our skates met the concrete in the same jam, I was right back there—seething—stuck in a constant loop of taking hits from her, some of her worst barbs whispered with poison until I was that kid again.

Alone.

Terrified.

And defenseless.

Fortunately, I had no such history with the six-foot-tall mountain of conceit smirking before me. I took a step back, glanced over the railing to the ground below, then eyed him from head to toe. "You know, forget me taking you over the railing with me. How about I just shove your ass over and be done with you?"

"You wish. More like you're going to lean against that railing, cross your arms over your chest like a good girl, and I'm going to bend you over backward and see how flexible you really are."

We both froze, the suggestive words hanging between us for a beat, two beats, and three.

"That's a whole lot of your front against my front and I'm not cool with that." The conviction in my voice just seconds before fled entirely, abandoning me when I needed the armor the most.

"I'm not thrilled about it either." His eyes fell away

from mine and his gaze traveled over me, touching every point from my chin to my fucking feet. He might as well have reached out a finger and danced it over every single sensitive place on the points in between.

I wanted to cross my arms, but I wouldn't. Fuck him. I wouldn't let him put me even more on the defensive. He was the one with the tattered reputation in this town. I just needed to make sure he didn't taint mine while he was back here doing whatever the hell he was doing.

"Why do you even care?"

"Hell if I know. Come on." He took my arm, the heat from his palm reaching through the thin cotton to my skin.

The rough way his fingers curled around me should have pissed me off. I should have yanked my arm away, but no. After the way he eye-fucked me before, my inner lusty bitch betrayed me and leaned into the pressure while wondering what it would be like to feel the same grip on my hips, my breasts, the inside of my thigh—he was too close. Too much.

Too fucking much.

Letting me go, he tossed his jacket over the cold metal and wrapped it around the railing three times before taking both of my arms. One step at a time, eyes on mine, he backed me right up to the worn leather. The clean scent of his morning shower teased my nose and despite the heap of reasons it was the worst possible thing to do, I caught myself leaning in for more.

"What are you doing?" he asked, giving me a hard look, a whole lot like the one he shot me the night before while I was stuck to the concrete.

"Just waiting for you to show off your skills so I can get back to work. You think you can hurry it up? I don't want to clean up bloodshed in there. Scooter doesn't pay me enough for that."

"I'd love to. Now, lean back," he said, lining me up with his jacket. "Does that feel like it's hitting the spot?"

I rocked back and forth. "Ummm, maybe?"

He cocked his head and blew out a breath. "You don't know?"

"Well, it's hard to te—hey!"

Stepping into me, invading every last inch of my space, he reached around, his palm landing on my lower back. "I'll work my way up, you tell me when I find it," he said, his voice full of impatience, his breath brushing over my temple as he stepped into me, impossibly close.

Thank fuck he wasn't looking me in the eye right now because my body had decided to take complete leave of all sense and zero in on the heat radiating from him, the pressure making tracks along the edge of my spine, and the sound of his breath way too close to my ear.

All I had to do was remember the way he owned that chair last night, sitting like a cocky man giving zero fucks, spoiling for a fight. Abrasiveness rolling off him like the rumble of a Harley roaring to life.

Flaming asshole, flaming asshole, flaming asshole.

"Ow!" I hopped away from the pain, my back arching, but with Priest wrapped around me, it meant practically climbing into him.

Chest to chest, hip to hip, the force making him wobble back enough he darted his hand out and curled it around my waist.

"Easy," he said, his voice low and gravelly. "Now move with me." His feet and thighs bracketed mine and God help me, the position left his hips nestled into mine. My skin grew hot and tight. My cheeks burned. And my breathing had shallowed while my body took over my sense of reason, every warning system I had, and nestled against him in all of his yummy places.

"I'm going to line you up. Good. That's good. Right there."

Everything he said, the rumble of his deep words, his grip on me—washed over me. Directions in a voice coated with sex, igniting dirty fantasies, making me want to suck the lingering scent of black coffee on his breath straight from his mouth.

I'd lost all ability to say anything. The deep breaths necessary to form words meant my breasts pressing harder into his chest. With the way my body betrayed my simmering rage at the fucker, my nipples would be carving our initials over his heart in three seconds flat if I let them.

With his feet turned slightly out so the tips of my toes rested against his instep, his hands dropped to my palms, his fingers curling around mine and bringing them to my chest.

"Cross your arms," he rasped, his dark gaze locked on mine, "and keep your fingertips on your shoulders."

"Is this going to hurt?" You know, besides the painful throb of my clit screaming at me to grind against him. My mother had a thing for assholes, and it looked like I might have inherited that quirk of the DNA.

"Not at all."

"You're fucking lying to me, aren't you?"

"Language," he warned, the corner of his mouth tipping into a grin.

Don't fall for it. Flaming asshole, flaming asshole, flaming asshole.

My new mantra on repeat, it echoed a reminder to my lusty areas to sit the fuck down already. I had a date with my vibrator tonight. I hope he had a safe word. He was so going to need it.

"You really think you have anything to say about my lang—"

"Maisy?" My words stopped dead at the sound of my name humming from his lips. Lips that now swiped aside the few strands of hair framing my face only to settle along my temple with just the slightest pressure so I couldn't tell if it was his position that had his mouth brushing over my skin like a caress or if it was intentional.

"Yeah?" It came out as a squeak with the meager breath I'd managed to take.

"Take a deep breath," he said, his voice low and sure while leaning into me.

My little rebel heart surrendered and fell over with its legs in the air at the command, obliterating any comeback.

He settled his forearm across my folded arms while his other arm wrapped around my upper back.

I closed my eyes, the image of us naked with his forearm over my throat while he fucked me mercilessly making me squeak in horny misery.

Take a deep breath, my ass.

Two vibrators tonight. Yeah, I said it. Use your imagination. The goal… to be walking funny when I started my shift in the morning. Not from the "rib" Mr. Fucking Manners was so convinced it was, but because I'd fucked myself ruthlessly with the best man-made dude parts my income at The Shipwreck could buy.

Before I could exhale, he snapped me back, probably not more than a few inches, but the click and searing pain tearing through me told me he either fixed it or he just broke me for good.

I couldn't stop the grunt slipping from my lips. Fighting my urge to sink to the wood, I dropped my head forward, not even caring that it meant resting my forehead on his forearm. Would he notice if I just sunk my teeth into his flesh right now?

My eyes watered as his fingers probed my back again.

"Got it," he said, finding the tender spot, only this time it didn't make me jump when he pressed against it.

"Yeah, you think?"

"That's going to be better. You'll be sore for a while, but no more sharp pains."

"This better not have ruined my orgasm plans."

He choked out a laugh. Lowering his arm, he took a step back before cupping my elbows and guiding my hands off my shoulders. "Depends on your tolerance for pain and how ambitious you get. Your girlfriend doesn't look particularly gentle."

"My girlfriend?"

"Anarch-Eve," he said as he unraveled his jacket.

"She's not my girlfriend."

"You kissed her the other night," he said, the arched brow of his silently calling bullshit. "Twice."

"Observant of you to notice, but she's not my girlfriend. She was, but that was a long time ago."

He cocked his head and pierced me with his stare. "Not so sure about that if you're still kissing her."

I balled my fists at my sides but stopped short of stomping while sheer frustration rocketed through me, leaving a hot flush over my skin. "You're not sure if I'm single after I just told you I was? Wow, you really are a pompous asshole, aren't you?" And why did I care so much? Really? Did I need this guy to know I was single? No. I don't.

Horny lies. All horny lies.

He shrugged off my assessment of his assholery. "I only meant maybe your business isn't finish—"

I held up my hand to shut him up, but I did good and resisted the urge to smack him silly. "She's my family. God, for a second I thought I saw signs of an actual human being in there. I almost thanked you, but now I'm back to wanting to knee you in the balls."

And angry fuck you, but yeah, that will be my little secret.

"Good, our relationship is restored."

"We don't *have* a relationship."

"No, but I'm also not your enemy," he said quietly.

"Maybe not, but you sure as hell aren't my friend."

"Noted." His mouth pressed into a thin, hard line and the muscle in his cheek jumped. He had so many things he wanted to say judging from his expression, but with the restraint of a saint, he didn't let anything more slip past his lips. Turning away, he jogged down the first few steps to the lower parking lot.

I stared at his retreating back one question racing through my mind knowing this might be the only chance I'd get to ask the man himself. "Is it true what they say about you?"

His hand locked on the railing, he stopped mid-step and glanced back at me over his shoulder. "Doesn't matter. People decided what they believe a long time ago."

I stepped to the edge of the stairs. "It matters to me."

"Why?"

"I don't know."

He glanced away, his eyes shuttered, erecting a solid wall between the two of us. "Looks like it's about to get busy in there," he said, jutting his chin in the direction of two cars that had just rolled into the parking lot. "See you around, Mayhem."

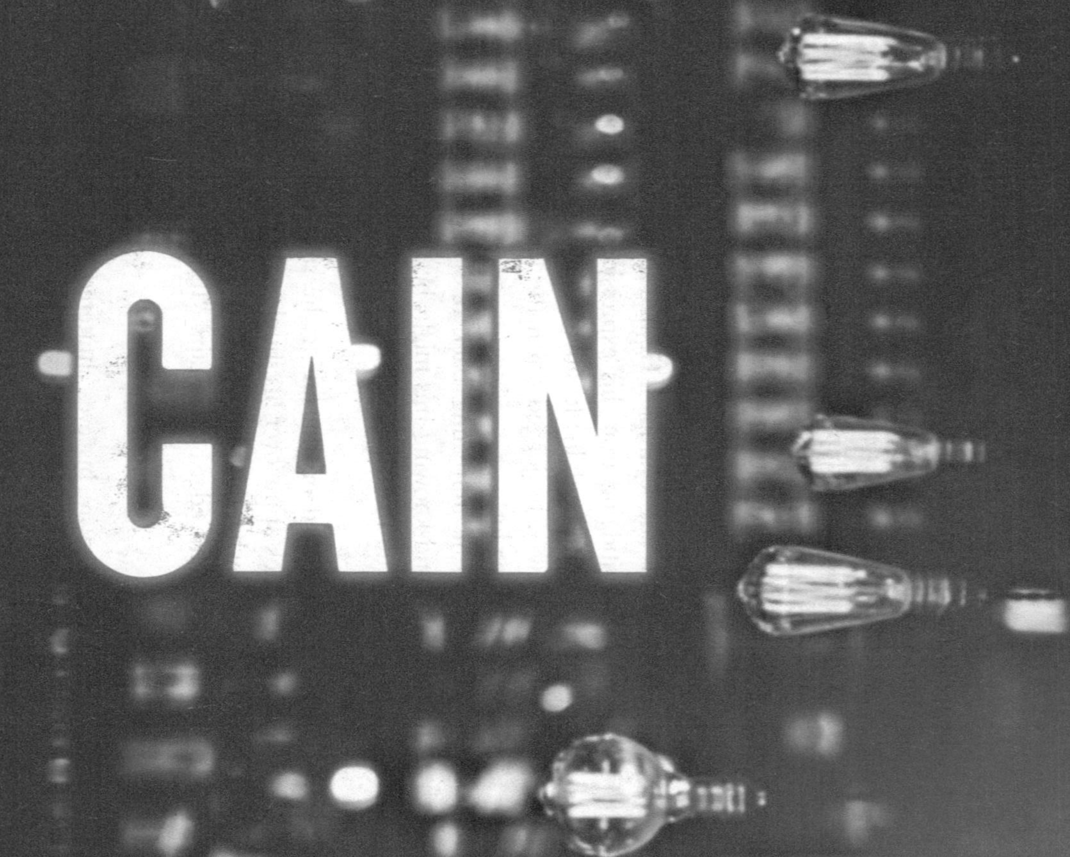

CAIN

Lana's two-bedroom cottage sat tucked on the corner of Main Street and Alden Avenue alongside Bay Park, close to the Galloway Bay library, and on the direct route for Coastal Transport Services.

I made sure of all three before I bought it.

Her parents wanted her to live with them. Hell, if I were a parent, I'd probably feel the same. If it had been Lilith even, I'd raise all sorts of hell to get my way when it came to her wellbeing. But they overplayed their hand and railed against Lana's every effort to move out, going so far as to take her to court.

Undeterred, Lana set her own course, she always had, even when she was a dumb kid. How the hell they didn't realize after raising her that she'd never let them get away with controlling her in the long term, I'd never know. There was no way someone as tenacious and determined as Lana would ever be happy living with her parents. She knew her mind, even if she was impulsive as hell.

It was the same fiercely independent spark in her that made her such a force on the track.

For a while anyway.

The same kind of spark I saw in Mayhem when she

didn't have to go head to head with Tilly in a jam, under the influence of whatever demons held her in their grip.

What the fuck am I doing?

Not here parked in Lana's driveway. I always come here when I'm in town. But getting involved with Mayhem? Totally new territory for me.

Or trying to get involved.

Okay, that didn't sound right. There was no getting or trying to get involved. Two months and I'd be out of here.

Caring maybe?

Nope, that was worse. Way worse.

Shit.

Flexing my hands on the wheel, I snapped the back of my head against the headrest and closed my eyes.

Big mistake.

She was there. In the darkness behind my closed eyelids. In the constant replay of the other morning at The Shipwreck.

Fucking with my head.

Fucking with my promises.

This was what? The hundredth, two hundredth replay by now?

Vivid, as though she stood before me again, the wisps of red hair slipped from her bandana and fluttered over her cheeks. The glimpses of pain etched in her eyes I caught when she thought no one was paying attention. The steely determination in their cool blue depths as she shot daggers at me.

For the first time in years, I didn't feel like I was going through the motions. Wake up, shower, put on my uniform, punch the clock, go home, eat a flavorless dinner, watch a game, fall into bed, rinse and repeat.

I'd be lying if I didn't admit that dabbling in the land of the living lit a craving in me for my family, my home.

And for some reason, for the mouthy derby girl who wore her mysteriously-wounded heart on her sleeve.

That stubborn lift of her chin, the almost permanent narrowing of her suspicious eyes, and that pierced eyebrow raised in defiance of every word out of my mouth pushed at something deep in me I wanted to ignite and let burn out of control. With only a handful of minutes, a whole bunch of attitude, and the intimate confessions in the form of orgasm plans she let slip from her lips while she leaned on my arm, she'd tapped into a part of me that had been dormant for a lot longer than ten years.

She made me feel out of control in a way I hadn't felt since I was a teenager. An angry kid who'd reeled in the haze of ruin when he lost his mom. Who under the influence of the absolute devastation left behind, made the worst mistake of his life fracturing his already wounded family to the point of crippling heartbreak.

It was only the beginning of catastrophic mistakes I would make, could make, when I let people in. Mayhem thought the gossip around Galloway Bay about me was bad?

If only she knew the truth.

Twin brothers. One alive. One dead.

One very much to blame, who didn't deserve forgiveness. One who fooled himself into thinking he could move on only to have karma crash around him until he retreated into his misery again.

If I let her get too close, if I let her tap into the long-buried part of me, it wouldn't eek out in a trickle. Oh no. I'd been holding that shit back for so long, it rivaled the force of any turbulent, storm-ravaged sea crashing relentlessly against a rocky coast.

Cracking open that well of pain, anger, and resentment would flood everything and everyone in its path.

Resurrecting the past wouldn't change it. It would only bring agony, but fuck if I could separate the two and make sense of any of it. Even when I knew every encounter with her, with derby, with my mistakes would eventually destroy everyone left in the world I cared about, here I was, itching to challenge her.

I wanted her in my face, full of attitude and insults. Every time I came at her, I wanted her to come back harder. I wanted to push every button she had until I figured out her reactions, her every impulse, and then, only then, I'd bend her to my will. I wanted to teach her how to hammer every one of her weaknesses, pummeling them over and over until all that remained was steely strength.

I wanted to coach.

Needed to coach.

And I couldn't.

Perhaps the most dangerous of all, I wanted to answer her question the other morning, and any that came after. That's how I knew I was in real trouble. So much so I put off coming into town for two days just so I wouldn't run into her or anything derby.

Old me stirred deep inside and for the first time in ten years, I wondered if I'd be able to hold him back. To keep him from falling into this sport, this town, this legacy once again.

If that wasn't bad enough, I'd have to be dead inside to miss the way her body reacted to mine.

News flash, I'm not dead inside.

If anything, I'm a lot less dead inside than I was hoping I would be.

Or need to be, to make it through another fifty-eight days in Galloway Bay.

Thwap. Thwap. Thwap. "Yo!"

I jerked and glanced toward the familiar voice outside my window.

"Stalking doesn't suit you, Coach. It's pretty gross, actually. Can't they take your badge for that?" Lana laughed as she rolled back a few inches, giving me room to open my door.

"Still a smart-ass. Aren't you getting too old for *that*?" The tightness in my chest eased with the playful back and forth. Until my gaze fell to Lana's atrophied, lifeless legs.

Once-thick thighs, heavy with powerful muscles, now laid narrow and almost flat. The jeans that fit snug to her hips laid baggy over legs that would never work again.

"I'm taking notes from Patti's playbook so… never. Besides, you love it and you know it. All the ladies around you saying whatever pops into their heads while you get to be all superior and above that shit." She rolled back until her wheels lined up to the ramp leading into the cottage and waited for me to follow along.

I forced the lump of guilt back with a hard swallow. "That shit? You mean emotional outbursts?"

Her lips quirked with amusement, her rosy cheeks mocking me as her mouth slid into a full grin. "I mean being human."

"Hey, I'm human." The acid churning in my gut was a sure sign.

She rolled her eyes. "You're repressed."

"So you're a therapist now?"

Lifting her chin and her eyes wide, she pierced me with a determined look I recognized. "Almost."

I cocked my head and waited for her to burst out laughing, but nope. "Wait, seriously?"

"Seriously. Come on, Coach. I've got fresh coffee, and you and I have some catching up to do."

I followed her up the ramp, making sure the wood had been completely cleared of snow like I'd hired Powell Landscaping to do over the winter. I paid them well to make sure Lana could move freely around the property and all along the pathways around and through Bay Park, all the way to the library, and the bus stop. Sure, the town cleaned up the roads and sidewalks, but they did under the assumption that people would be navigating them by car or on foot.

Lana wouldn't be doing either.

Never again.

And maneuvering with an electric wheelchair through the unpredictable coastal snow and ice was precarious at best.

Normally Lilith drove through and scoped this out for me, but a bit of the crushing guilt filling my chest relaxed seeing it with my own eyes.

Lana rolled through the door with ease, no slowing down to make sure she didn't scuff the edges.

"You got a new chair. Slides right through. Nice."

Lana snorted and stopped short, tossed me a look over her shoulder, and rolled her eyes again like she used to all time from her position on the track a decade ago. "Please, like you didn't know I got a new chair."

"How would I know?"

"Because you bought it, Moneybags."

"Wasn't me." I followed her into the customized kitchen with low granite countertops and modified appliances, everything designed with her independent living in mind. The builders had made every single surface reachable and usable for her, and judging by the onions, fresh garlic, and root veggies in wire racks along the wall, she didn't leave it just for show.

She was making the best of her life now which should

make me happy, if only it didn't come with a swift punch of how unfair it was that she even had to.

She rolled to the fridge and pulled out heavy cream while I jammed my hands in my pockets and fought the urge to jump in and help. A totally unfamiliar sensation for me, because if this was derby and I were coaching, I wouldn't be trying to take over anything. I'd be putting each player through their paces, making them do it on their own, over and over, pain and frustration layered over more pain and frustration until they figured it out.

They called me Coach Hard-Ass behind my back and they were right. I wasn't their friend. I didn't want to hear about their bruises, exhaustion, or aches and pains. If it didn't affect their ability to play, who cared? Anyone who took the track with skates on their feet had them.

As for the social shit and comradery? Shitty friends and turbulent love lives… they'd better fucking not go there.

She handed me a steaming cup just the way I like it. A splash of cream, no sugar. "You're full of shit."

"How the hell did you know it was me?" Not that it qualified me for the moneybags status she tossed my way. If anything, it left my savings a whole lot lighter, to a point I wasn't exactly comfortable. But then, I didn't deserve to be.

"You told me when you brought it up. You're a bad actor, Coach. You're not one for small talk. Grunts, judgment, and a wide-berth requirement are more your style. Just the fact that you mentioned it told me you felt awkward about it. So you figured if you bring it up, you can deflect the attention and credit. Not exactly complex."

"So what I'm getting is that I'm an unapproachable, predictable prick headed for permanent hermit status. I don't think I like this new degree you're earning."

"I'm sure you don't. Now come here." She crooked her

finger at me, one of the very few people in this world who could without earning permanent disdain.

I leaned down, the fact that she had to ask me to a painful reminder of the damage I could do.

Pinching my sweatshirt, she tugged me in close, and pressed a kiss on my cheek. "Thank you, you crusty asshole. I love it."

"You're welcome."

With a firm shove of her fingertips on my forehead, she pushed me away. "Now stop buying me shit."

"Never."

"I googled the price and almost pooped."

Sinking into the couch next to her, I rested my elbows on my knees and breathed in the coffee before taking my first sip. "Patti has everyone talking about shit in this town."

"Patti is the best damn influence on us all. Leave her alone. Too bad I can't get my parents in Banked Track to soak up some of her wisdom."

"They have a right to how they feel."

"It's been ten years since the accident. They're letting it eat up precious time that should be spent living." She paused, the silence hanging in the air between us. "Kind of like you are."

Ahhh, and there was the right hook. "So tell me, what happened to computer programming?"

She shook her head and laughed. "Wow, I've practically got whiplash from the subject change."

When I said nothing and just held her unwavering stare, she sighed. "It's mind-numbing. I need something with more. More spark. More… I don't know. Autopilot just wasn't working for me. It was either change careers or dabble in hacking."

I laughed thinking of the troublemaker she'd been who'd been so full of talent and potential. Actually, she still was, it was just different now.

Everything was different.

"I'm kind of surprised you hadn't dabbled in it already."

"Who said I haven't? Not that I'm going to confirm or deny said hacking to a cop."

"My badge means nothing in Galloway Bay."

"I'm never putting you in a compromising position again, Coach. So, on that front, no more about the hacking. I'm still working for the county, but by this time next year, I'll be counseling patients. If you stick around, I'll give you a discount." She took a delicate sip of coffee like she was at some high tea complete with a pinky in the air while she called me out.

I snorted into my cup. "I'm not spilling my secrets to you."

"But you have them?"

"Doesn't everybody?" The hot coffee burned a trail down my throat. Normally I'd appreciate the burn and settle on the couch, only Lana decided to start probing me like a crew of extra-terrestrials shoving their technology in my every orifice.

Lana probably wouldn't use lube either.

"Evasive."

"I could use some lessons in combat before I visit you again."

She snapped her fingers and pointed at me with a smug smile on her face. "See, I'm going to kill it at the whole therapy thing."

"You look happy," I said, my voice thick, the sound catching in my throat.

Honey hair framed her face, the long layers brushing her shoulders. Caramel eyes gleamed, the fire inside her lit once again, just fueled by different desires. They softened on me and I fidgeted in my seat.

"I am happy. But you don't look so happy, Coach. What's up?"

"Not a whole lot. Concerned about my sister," I lied.

"You sure this doesn't have something to do with the fact that you were up at Sid's the other night watching Beautifully Brutal take on Girls of Fury? Or that you were seen talking with Beautifully Brutal's best jammer at Banked Track later that night and then again the next day at The Shipwreck."

The coffee betrayed me by skidding to a stop in my throat instead of sliding down. My body went with instinct and tried to force it, just to have it crawl into my sinuses, making my eyes water. I reached for a napkin just to slosh the hot brew over the lip of my mug and down my hand. "Christ."

"Now don't bring him into this," she said with a cluck of her tongue. "So it's true?"

"Yeah, but—"

"You've set your sights on Maisy," she practically sang. "I'm kind of proud of you to be honest. She's fucking hot too. I'm not into chicks, but hell, I'd slide a hand under that skirt. Well done, Coach."

"I didn't set my sights on her," I said low and hard, hoping to convince her. Or me. Okay, more me, because that hot factor was a damn problem.

But worse, she possessed this eerie patience. Like when she waited me out at Banked Track. I took her inventory and she let me. She didn't dissolve into hysterics or accuse me of mansplaining. She took my words, without surrendering to them or admitting I was right, and squirreled them away like pieces to a puzzle.

I had a feeling she did the same at The Shipwreck too. Just filing away clues until she could pull them all out and build a picture of me that might even take me by surprise.

The idea of her figuring me out before I figured out myself had my gut bottoming out in a free fall.

"Then why were you kissing her?"

"I just—wait, what? I wasn't kissing her." My ears burned and I knew they'd flamed red at the tips like a green teenage boy, for God's sake.

Lana shrugged. "That's not the word around town. Apparently, you had her in one hell of a kiss outside of her work. Had her bent over the railing on the side deck and everything. Ovaries around town are exploding with every retelling of the story."

I jammed my hand through my hair, forgetting that I cut most of it off, and set my coffee on the table in front of me. "There was no kissing. Who the hell is telling everyone I was kissing her? She had a rib out of place. I fixed it. End of story."

"Well, you know how these things are. Stories get embellished."

"You think?"

"But you want to kiss her."

"This is a trap. I feel it." And fuck yeah, I wanted to kiss her. I was pretty sure the feeling was mutual, only it looked like the both of us were smart enough to not act on it.

I still didn't know if I was happy about our mutual sense of caution and responsibility.

"You don't have to answer that. The fact that you didn't immediately say no was answer enough."

"I'm going to need a nap after this visit."

"That's not my fault. Must be because you're getting old."

"I'm not getting old."

"You're in your mid-thirties with no girlfriend, no wife, hell, you don't even have a pet. You're stuck. No shame in admitting it."

"I've only got five years on you and you're in exactly the same boat." On firmer ground and relatively sure I wouldn't drown myself in Lana's living room, I picked up my cup again and took a gulp of coffee.

"Ahhh, but I'm not. I have a boyfriend."

Fuuuuccccckkkkkkk! I coughed, sputtered, and pounded a fist against my chest, trying to clear my esophagus.

"When did this happen?" I choked out, my eyes watering again, and a tickle in my sinuses trying to strong-arm me into a sneezing fit.

"A few months ago."

"I'm surprised Patti didn't say anything. She loves spreading news like this."

"She doesn't know. Unlike you, I'm good at keeping my business private. Plus, I'm saving this news for when I really need it."

I spun on the couch until I faced her head-on. "Who is this guy? What does he do? He better not be taking advantage of you."

She patted my hand and laughed. "He's a physical therapist and no, he's not taking advantage of me. I put him in his place right away."

"Your physical therapist?"

"Not anymore. That would be unethical."

"Says the woman dabbling in hacking. Okay, spill."

"I told him I was worried that I couldn't have an orgasm."

"Whoa! Hold up," I said, throwing my hands in the air between us. "I've changed my mind; I don't want to hear."

"Shut up," she said, smacking away my hands. "You're a big boy. There's no way a guy as hot as you hasn't taken a tour or a thousand around a vag, so buck up."

"Hot maybe, but then there's that glowing personality of mine that you reminded me of." I closed my eyes and sighed. When I opened them, she was very much waiting for me to get on board with what was to come. "And here I thought my biggest worry was that I might get stuck delivering my own sister's baby. This is worse. Way worse."

"So, I asked him how that works out for people like me. You know what that shit said? He told me to try to ring my bell and let him know how it worked out. I bet that wasn't in the employee handbook. Like I hadn't tried that already," she said with another roll of her eyes while I simultaneously died inside. "Yeesh. What is it with you guys anyway? I got so mad I rang his bells instead. Punched him right in the sac."

"Jesus, Lana. You assaulted him?"

"Sure, but it worked out. He apologized for making it seem like he didn't take me seriously, and I told him he could make it up to me by being a willing participant in my orgasm experiment. Good news," she said with a lift of her cup like she was toasting her good fortune, "I can definitely have orgasms."

"God, you just had to tell me that when you know damn well I can't get good and drunk to mind scrub that right out of my head."

"Maybe. I might enjoy watching you squirm a little. The point is, Coach. I'm good. He's good. He's very good. Most importantly, I wouldn't change a thing." She laid her hand over mine and squeezed. "I'm right where I'm supposed to be."

I turned my palm over and laced my fingers with hers and cleared my thick throat. "Glad to hear it."

"But what about you, Coach? Are you right where you're supposed to be?"

Maisy

Marty, Sean, Rory, and Zara stumbled through my door, their arms laden with grocery bags.

"You didn't answer your phone," Marty said, blowing her long bangs out of her face. "I sent you a flyer on Insta for a banked track charity exhibition in Philly. I thought maybe we could take a road trip, check it out. Full-blown slumber party time in a suite complete with greasy Philly cheesesteaks."

"I turned my ringer off," I said as I reached out to snag a few bags and drop them in the kitchen. "I keep getting calls from this same number over and over in New York. They never leave a message so it's total bullshit. So much for no call registries."

"Every other call on my phone either pops up spam risk or it's an automated bullshit message to tell me my auto warranty is about to expire. Not sure how, since I've never owned a car with a warranty," Sean said with a snort.

Snow fell from their hair and jackets as they kicked off their boots in my modest entryway. Really it was a five by seven rug in front of my door. Just inches beyond it, my living room with barely enough space for the six of us to dance.

For that reason alone, when the whole team met up, we crashed Rory's place—really her aunt's place—just outside of town. Her aunt hated the idea of leaving it empty fifty weeks out of the year, so she asked Rory to stay there year-around rent-free, and Rory worked double shifts for the two weeks her aunt was in town so she didn't murder her with a corkscrew.

Rory insisted orange wasn't her color.

I pointed out Maine inmates wore blue for the most part and even then, the colors changed depending on security level.

Rory didn't appreciate the distinction.

Tonight was the core six. The originals. The misfits of the team who'd been consistently at every scrimmage and in every bout, without fail, for four years now.

Basically, the ones who had no life outside of derby.

Or made derby their life.

Distinguishing between the two really depended if you're a glass half empty or half full sort.

Most days, I'm glass half full.

Especially days like today, when my favorite people filled my tiny home. I never really told them, but I loved having them here. So much so, I steered them toward staying overnight every single time. It finally became routine and now they just automatically tossed a change of clothes in their bags when they came over, ready to crash on the couch, three in a bed, in the oversized bean bag chair in the corner, wherever they could find a soft spot to land.

A vagabond at heart, my mother drifted around the country with me in tow for the better part of my life. A young, single mother with no real history and no family didn't inspire a lot of confidence in other parents so sleepovers were nonexistent in the tiny studio apartments and rented rooms my mother could afford.

My apartment might have been a total of seven hundred square feet tops tucked over Banked Track. Not much more than my mother could manage for me, but then, I'm not a kid anymore and at the mercy of judgmental asshole parents of childhood friends. Hell, even if I were, I'd be hard-pressed to leave. I love it here. The brick building dominated the edge of Main Street since the early 1800s. Two stories, but tall enough to have been three, it had history, character, and a clear view of the comings and goings in town.

Despite my meager square footage, I had old cast-iron radiator heaters that chugged away, warming me to the bone. I got to pad along scuffed wood floors gouged with decades worth of scars, each with their own story I would never know, but sealed and clean with a subtle shine that made me smile.

The clawfoot bathtub didn't hurt my feelings either. Especially after rough bouts or long days on my feet at The Shipwreck.

Cozy, warm, and something no one could take away from me.

A home.

Sure, it wasn't much, but I'd earned every dollar that paid for each piece of secondhand furniture that filled it. It wouldn't make the front page of magazines or be featured on any savvy home shows, but then perfection was overrated.

Perfection didn't have secret stories to tell. You didn't sink into perfection and make warm memories.

Most nights like these, with the snow coming down in sheets, I'd sit on the low-slung ledge of my tall windows and watch townspeople strolling along the sidewalk between the white twinkling lights that burned every night from just after Halloween all the way into early spring, casting a gentle glow along the way.

Other nights I popped downstairs to chat with Patti and steal glances of the old black and white framed photos from her derby days hanging over the bar. I imagined the sights, sounds, smells that must have filled the last of the banked track derby bouts of the seventies. What those moments in the spotlight meant to women in the midst of some of the most significant moments of the women's rights movement. Women clawing their way free from the control of powerful men and coming to realize sometimes breaking free wasn't done with bold moves, but with subterfuge using a corrupt system against itself to come out on top.

Those echoes of the past called to me, making this place the absolute right place for me.

I snatched up a few bags and hauled them to the kitchen while they struggled out of their jackets, hung up their purses and keys, and lined up their boots out of the way of the door.

"Where's Eve?" I called out to them when after a couple minutes she still hadn't come through the door.

"She's running late. She said Astrid, Kelsie, and Sonya stopped by with some information about the WRDF that we might find useful. She'll be along in a bit to fill us in," Marty said as she sailed into my kitchen, grabbed the stockpot, and began filling it with water.

She had five pounds of shrimp fresh off the boats, her usual contribution to girls' night. Not that we minded. The tasty little fuckers were gone inside of an hour every single time.

"The paperwork is sent so I hope it's not something

that would have given us a leg up for the actual application."

Marty flipped her thick dark hair up in a knot at the back of her neck and pushed up the sleeves of her sweater before turning the water off and settling the pot over the gas burner. With a series of rapid clicks and a whoosh, the burner flared to life. "Honestly, it's probably just talk. Kelsie's grandma is back at the salon and gossiping up a storm. I swear she's trying to make up for the six months out with that broken hip, all in one week."

The mutterings around town had been light since Martha had been sidelined. A damn blessing. The silence. Not the hip. That would make me an asshole.

Especially when I was sporting a hell of a bruise on mine that still needed to be iced three times a day.

At least my pinched—ugh, my rib didn't hurt anymore.

Flaming asshole.

And he was right… not that he needed to know. The last thing I needed was him in my space gloating.

"She had a few things to say about you," Sean said, grabbing a brick of cheddar cheese, knife, and cutting board before settling in at the drop leaf two-seater table also looking out over Main Street.

"What the hell did I do?"

Rory cocked a hip against the doorframe into the tiny kitchen and crossed her arms. "Word around town is you've been fraternizing with the coach."

"If fraternizing is serving him his breakfast, I guess I'm guilty." But it was more than breakfast. It just wasn't what they were implying with their shrewd glances. It was more the haunted look in his eyes from the other morning that was never far away and made me wonder if I hurt him. Or embarrassed him. I still didn't know and I hated that three days later, I still cared.

Could a guy like him even be embarrassed? Or hurt? Probably not. He was so damn sure he was right, that kind of confidence probably came from one hell of a track record being just that.

Right.

Flaming asshole.

Okay, that might be my jealousy talking. I wish I ran around with that kind of certainty.

Zara passed a six-pack over Rory's shoulder. I snagged one as I passed it on to Marty.

"I heard he had you in one hell of a lip-lock on The Shipwreck's smoking deck," Zara said with a wink as she popped open a bag of Doritos.

"Hey! There was no locking of lips." Okay, I didn't need this shit swirling around town. Not with a coach who may or may not have cheated by letting an underage girl play on his team.

I was still on the fence with that part of his story. I had a hard time believing a cop would knowingly allow an underage player on his team, no matter how good she was. It just didn't jibe with the aloof guy who lounged in the front row at our bout.

I would expect someone who wants to win at any cost to be snarlier than that. Mean maybe, borderline cruel in his pursuit of a win.

Mean and cruel were not words that fit with a guy who noticed a rib out of place on a stranger and fixed it.

"But you were on the deck with him," Rory said as she peeked into the pot of water on the stove that had just started to steam.

"For a few minutes," I said, glad I was getting this discussion out of the way before Eve got here. We hadn't been a thing in almost a year, but things were more over for me than they were for her. I didn't want to hurt her anymore. I did everything I could to keep it from spilling over onto the team. Dating hadn't been my brightest idea, but the attraction was there so I ran with it without really considering what would happen if it didn't work out.

Or if one of us got in too deep instead of keeping it light and fun. "It wasn't a big deal. I thought I had a pinched nerve. Turns out I had a rib out of place, and he fixed it."

"He's your doctor now?" Eve said, pushing her way into the kitchen.

Shit.

"He's someone who knew what he was talking about and I'm someone with shitty health insurance. Seemed like a no-brainer if I wanted to stay upright."

"He couldn't be here at a worse time. We're going to be under a microscope applying for the WRDF. If they catch wind he's not only here, but sniffing around one of our players, everything we've worked for will be for nothing," Rory said with a wary glance between Eve and me.

I slapped a smile on my face to reassure her, but she only narrowed her eyes and studied me harder.

Cause I was shit at covering my feelings once they bubbled to the surface.

Total and utter shit.

Which was why Tilly managed to crawl under my skin at every bout and tear me apart from the inside out. The ultimate wound that just wouldn't heal.

"I wouldn't call it sniffing around. He met Sheriff Chase for breakfast and I just happened to be working."

"Which naturally led to kissing on the side deck," Rory replied.

"Again… no kissing."

Rory shrugged. "Just making sure."

"Look. It's not like either of us enjoyed being in close

proximity"—God I was a liar—"but the rib hurt and he did fix it so I'm grateful for that. And now I won't be seeing him again. It's not like he lives here or anything."

"If he's meeting with Sheriff Chase, that could be changing. Wayne Savage is retiring this spring so a position is opening up with the police department," Sean said.

"Mmm, I don't know about that. Priest didn't seem that interested in what he had to say."

"And you paid close enough attention to notice that, huh?" Eve said with a disgusted snort.

Maisy

W e'd been at this for four years. Four years leveling up in bouts, playing against WRDF teams, and white-knuckling our way through getting our asses kicked over and over while getting better, training harder, until finally we'd earned our way into enough sanctioned games in a season to make filling out the application worth it.

Glancing around at the somber expressions on the faces of my friends, I had to wonder if this was really Eve being a jealous twat or if maybe my excuses had less with pointing out how unreasonable they were being, and a whole lot more to do with how I was feeling about a certain flaming asshole.

It turned out leveling up our game play was only the beginning of the hard work. Once there, we had to form a committee and a code of conduct. We all had our talents, but it turned out not a single one of us had a desire to touch paperwork or anything having to do with making rules. Our "committee," as we were still getting used to calling it, had more hands-on talents. Eve worked in construction. Rory slung beers behind a bar and effortlessly made every patron, even the assholes, feel like kings and queens. Sean worked as a self-trained pastry chef. Zara worked for a non-profit for homeless youth.

The closest skill set to write a dry as fuck code of conduct was Marty. A certified personal accountant, and when all eyes turned to her, she grunted and said, "I prefer numbers."

But after three months and several votes to address rules we'd never once imagined we'd have to consider, Marty had done it and because she had, she never had to pay for her drinks at Banked Track again. We all covered her, a permanent arrangement that hadn't quite banished the twitch in her left eye left over from her time in the trenches with headings, subheadings, bullet lists, articles— basically all the technical writing layout aspects that made our eyes glaze over.

Eve had even tossed in some custom carpentry work at Rutledge and Brooks law firm to get them to review everything to make sure our code of conduct was complete.

After all of that, and still stumbling in our mind-numbing haze of paperwork, we had training and skills tests for both our players and officials for our team.

In our little corner of the world where people lived modestly, we had players who had a hard time keeping up with equipment needs. Once we managed to overcome that hurdle, it was all about how the hell we would coordinate the schedules in an area where most of us worked nontraditional jobs with odd hours. Add to that the complications of joining a federation and we'd been sapped of every last bit of resources we could scrounge up.

Everyone in this room had sacrificed time, money, peace of mind, and sometimes relationships to march this team toward its ultimate goal of joining the WRDF, and by dabbling in any talk or otherwise with Priest, I was putting it all on the line.

"Shit," I muttered, gulping down the last of the beer I'd been drinking and grabbing another.

"It's okay. It's going to be okay." Zara paced the narrow patch of floor in my living room. "It's not like Priest was a WRDF coach. So he wasn't suspended or anything. From what I Googled, it doesn't even look like there was an investigation."

"You Googled him?"

Why didn't I think of that?

Oh, yeah, because my tits were still vibrating from the close encounter that very well might have looked like a lip-lock for anyone looking on.

Zara shrugged. "Yeah, but it's Maine; there wasn't a lot."

"There wasn't an investigation because he resigned from the police force, gave up derby, and left town. Unfortunately for him, in a small town, that means he all but laid down and confessed to the crime by doing all three," Rory said as she typed something into her phone.

"Crime seems like an awfully strong word," Zara said with a glance. "The girl was only like three months shy or so of her eighteenth birthday. It's not like she was a teenager getting her drink on or anything."

Rory waved away her comment. "You know what I mean."

"She still had no business on that track no matter how good she was. There are junior leagues for a reason," Eve pointed out, a thin sliver of anger burning in her eyes.

Rory shot up in her seat and hunched over her phone. "The girl's parents sure were vocal about the whole thing. At least the mother according to this. They were at the ribbon cutting ceremony of the new physical therapy wing at the hospital about four years ago now, and she, well, let's just say she's still bitter."

I glanced down at the picture on Rory's phone. "What does it say?"

"We're proud to be here and witness the opening of yada, yada, yada, if only the negligence of one of our own in Galloway Bay hadn't cost our Lana her ability to walk, who knows if we would have even needed a place like this."

Marty cringed. "I don't think that came out how she intended. At least I hope that's not how she meant it."

"I don't know about that. She goes on, each comment more awful than the last," Rory said with a wince.

The beer turned bitter on my tongue. "She literally disregarded anyone else who might have a need for physical therapy. I don't even know what to say to that."

Sean moved through the room, offering each of us cheese. "Poor Lana. Damn."

"Well, I didn't see this before. Lana Bradley made a statement to *The East Coaster* in direct response to her mother's comments." Rory scanned her phone, a gleam in her eye and an eager grin spreading over her face. "Oh shit, this is good."

"Well, read it, girl; don't keep it all to yourself," Marty said from the kitchen as she dumped the shrimp in the water.

"Unfortunately, my mother refuses to accept that I'm responsible for where I am today," Rory began. "I knew how old I was when I skated onto the track, and I knew I didn't belong there. Fact of the matter is, I was selfish, and I didn't care. I paid the price for it. Someone I care a whole lot about also paid the price of my selfishness through no fault of his own. It's time to move on. My mother forgets that the world does not revolve around me. The truth, and what she should have acknowledged, is this new physical therapy wing is going to make a huge difference in the quality of life for our community. For the investors who made this happen, thank you. And may I suggest focusing the next infusion of funds on advanced mental health services, particularly for people in denial."

Someone she cares a whole lot about... Priest. I shouldn't be jealous of that. It made no sense to be jealous that this woman I didn't even know, knew him on a much more personal level than I did.

I needed something stronger than a damn beer.

"Very grown-up and ended with a snarky dismount. I dig it," Sean said.

"Through no fault of his own," Zara said quietly. "She's got to be talking about Priest. But how could he not know?"

Marty sucked the beer off her upper lip. "Backed up her birth year by a year when she signed up probably."

"Why are we even hashing this out? It doesn't matter. If everyone just stays away from him, the problem is solved," Eve said.

All eyes swung in my direction.

"Hey, I don't like that tone."

Rory smirked. "We didn't say anything."

"Your eyes said plenty, and they're mouthy little bastards. Put your faces away."

"Well, none of us were hanging out with him. Twice," Zara said with a shrug.

"Banked Track was not my fault. And The Shipwreck —you know what, that wasn't my fault either."

"Dude, are you blushing?" Marty asked.

"What? No!" I scrambled over to the mirror only to find that I was definitely blushing.

"I've never seen you blush before. Didn't know it was possible. Turn red with rage, sure, but blushing? You?" Marty said with a snort, putting me even more on the spot.

"This is going to be a problem. I can feel it," Eve muttered.

"It's not like he's some kind of God and I'm some feckless female just waiting to fall tits up at his feet. You all act like I can't resist the dick. I dated her," I said, pointing at Eve, "for a full year and never even missed the dick." I tossed the words over my shoulder, willing my rogue cheeks to stop breaking out in a flush that had freshly fucked written all over it. I mean, if this was happening over a trip down memory lane, getting a rib set in place, what the hell would happen if—you know what, no if. They were waiting for me to surrender to the if.

No. If.

"Just doing my job," Eve said, the corner of her mouth twitching with the words.

"Look, I'm not looking to hop on a bone because who needs the hassle of a damn man when I can buy one in any size I want and it doesn't talk back," Rory began, "but even I know that guy is like biting into shortbread, finding out it's a gooey chocolate chunk, and an hour later realizing you ate an edible."

"It's simple then. Just say no," Zara said with a straight face, making the rest of us break out in cackling laughter, easing the tension, but not obliterating it altogether.

Cause like she said, Priest was gooey chocolate chunk and while drugs had never been my thing, I was all of a sudden totally down with popping an edible.

CAIN

With a couple quick knocks on the side door at Rockabilly's, I waited to see if Jackson Stone would answer. I should have called, but I itched to do something, anything at this point that got me out of my head and kept me from finding Mayhem.

Yeah. I was itching to see her again.

Restless to the point Lilith was ready to strangle me with the straps of the baby carrier she'd just gotten in the mail, I hightailed it out of there to give her space and give me—well, hell if I knew.

I avoided town. With so much speculation about my interest in Mayhem, the last thing I wanted to do was hover in her space—basically anywhere within a five-mile radius—and feed the voracious gossips.

I didn't need to be giving the town the wrong idea.

Or her.

Or me for that matter.

Because the closer I got, the harder it became to see the boundaries between reason and a colossal mistake in the making. And that was after only two encounters.

It was going to be a hell of a long two months.

Curling my fist, I pounded the door again.

I tried to imagine the guy I knew so well from school

and endless weekends at the skate park running the decades old roller rink, but I could never see him managing the place like an actual grown-up. Definitely not the same as his father and grandfather before him.

After all, he spent his teen years running with the crew of punk kids often banned from the property for getting high in the woods at the edge of the parking lot. Family or not, Old Man Stone, the original owner of Rockabilly's and third generation hard-ass, didn't put up with bullshit.

A laugh crept into my throat as an old memory of him took hold, cigar clenched between his teeth in the corner of his mouth, smoke wafting into his one eye, making him squint. Thick bushy eyebrows low and pinched as he griped about dumbass teens and their wacky tobacky.

Old Man Stone could be a real son of a bitch, but a weathered New Englander to the core, he always shot straight.

Jackson sitting at the 1950s steel tanker of a desk his grandfather coveted as good ol' American craftsmanship? God no. All I could imagine was Jackson, lounging in the high-back chair, his feet propped on the edge of that scarred monstrosity, headphones blasting The Ramones and Beastie Boys as he suffered through his own personal hell—or in this case, his birthright.

But then, sometimes birthrights were a punch in the balls like that.

At least he had a legacy worth taking over. Some of us had a mountain of rot ingrained in us from one parent that we try relentlessly to keep from infecting the good in us from the other parent, leaving us wondering if we really are an even split of our mom and dad or if the bad managed to wield a majority stake in our soul.

This was exactly why I convinced Lilith and Jordan to raise their kids at the family farm we'd inherited fifty/fifty.

This was the chance for something good to come from my mistakes. For smiles and laughter to overwrite the loss and sadness.

With no sign of life from the other side of the door, I pounded louder with enough force to rattle the sheet metal on either side of the frame. I debated giving up for all of a handful of seconds, but I had to burn off the past week and what town was doing to me each day I stayed.

Come on, Jackson.

The blue box monstrosity with swathes of red and yellow signage drew in families from Bangor and Augusta where roller rinks had all but died under the crushing costs of upkeep and stiff competition from growing cities with more modern entertainment options.

Even with the support of the towns surrounding Galloway Bay, I wondered if this place could survive the onslaught of competition, but I also knew if anyone could pull off saving it, it was Jackson Stone.

He'd saved me from myself a time or two with his quick wit, his free spirit, and loyalty.

Maybe that's why I couldn't make myself go now.

I needed a friend—I hated admitting that even to myself. I still had a few in town, but I needed someone who wouldn't try to pick me apart and just let me be. Most of all, I want to see what he made of this place—how much had changed, how much had stayed the same.

I wanted to see if I could find a bit of my youth here, the guy I was before everything went wrong not once, but twice.

And maybe I needed to see for myself he was fine after the disturbing phone call from him a few months earlier.

The door burst open, and Jackson swung out with it, his tall body stretched between his firm grip on the door handle and his feet firmly planted in the doorway. He scanned the area, his shrewd gaze barely visible through the safety glasses shielding his eyes, a laser tag vest strapped to his chest, and a laser gun locked in his hand.

"You alone?" Jackson asked with a quick flick of his chin and pursed lips while he scanned the parking lot.

The tightness in my chest eased with my laugh. His good dose of humor I so desperately needed taking a swipe at my loaded memories. "Dude, you really are never going to grow up, are you?"

Sliding his glasses up a fraction, his familiar hazel eyes, now with the beginnings of crow's feet, met mine. "Why the fuck would I do that?" His mouth split into a lopsided grin as he took a step back. "Come on in, man. It's been too long."

I tapped the vest with my knuckles on my way past him. "Am I interrupting?"

"God, I hope so," he said, scrubbing a hand through the wavy hair falling into his face. "No one should have to face a full day of paperwork. I'd rather someone drive nails through my balls."

The familiar scent of popcorn and commercial carpet cleaner lingered in the air. Gone was the underlying scent of cigarette smoke that seemed to cling for years after the laws that finally outlawed smoking inside. "What the hell is so miserable it has you considering mutilation?"

"Prepping for tax season. I thought I'd get a jump on it, saving myself a few headaches, but the only thing that will do that is a fucking full-time accountant. That's what I get for trying to be responsible. I always thought this adulting shit was a scam. I was right."

I grinned and gestured at his chest. "And the laser tag gear? How does that come into play?"

"I think better with gear on. Reminds me what's at stake if I don't get this shit done. You see the addition on the back? We've got a wild laser tag setup now." He unclipped the vest and tossed it into the chair he'd likely just vacated, a clear sign he didn't plan to plant his ass there again anytime soon. The gun and glasses followed just seconds later.

"Hard to miss. It's purple."

"The whole building will be purple soon."

"Didn't Old Man Stone hate purple?"

Jackson crossed his ankles and propped his shoulder against the wall with a cocky grin. "Yup. Seemed like the upside to me."

"You're going to give him a stroke."

"Nah, as long as I don't resurrect the purple mohawk, he'll be fine. I'll sneak him a cigar when my grandma's not looking to make it up to him. Anyway, enough about me; what took you so long to get your ass over here? I heard you were back in town almost a week ago."

"People didn't waste time talking about it."

"They never do, especially when it comes to you. The gossip about you takes some heat off me, so I'll take it." He poured a couple cups of coffee and glanced over his shoulder. "Hell, what did you expect when the first thing you did was sniff around the derby team?"

"No sniffing, just observing," I said, trying to sound bored with the mutterings around town, despite the spike in my blood pressure from his question.

"You never *just observe* derby," he said, letting out a snort. "Any chance you'll make your stay permanent?"

"I wouldn't do that to the town." Or my sister, brother-in-law, and nephew. I stepped up and took the cup he offered. I considered grabbing the cream but decided against it.

Today was a black-like-my-soul kind of day. Might as well be festive.

"I don't know, the town could use some shaking up. Besides, the ladies are starting to outnumber us around here. It's getting scary."

"Only if you don't understand them. Maybe you should work on that, man."

"Careful, I'll think my mom sent you."

"How's business?" I glanced around the room, really looked at it, and noticed the modern touches. The six metal filing cabinets along the wall, all gone now. In their place a workbench with skate hardware, plates, nuts and washers, bearings, toe stops, wheels of all colors, sizes, and styles. He even had an array of toe caps in a dozen or so colors and an endless variety of laces in varying lengths, colors, and material. Hanging on a pegboard next to the bench, multiple skate tools to change out parts.

The days of the classic high-top quad skates were over. At least here.

On another wall ran a series of monitors mounted along the edge of the ceiling, no doubt overlooking the rink and now the laser tag area. It sure as hell beat the glitchy black-and-white box that used to sit back here, flickering endlessly with a grainy view of the locker section.

Jackson's touches were everywhere, some obvious, some not so obvious, all of them full of pride and dedication.

I underestimated him.

"It's good. Real good actually. Instead of limping along, breaking even, we're finally putting some solid money into the business. No loan on the addition. All profits. My father isn't sure how he feels about it just yet, but more dollar signs will help that along eventually."

"Pissed off you were right and he was wrong, no doubt." I noticed a calendar on a hook, clearly covering another, and flicked the edge to spy what he was hiding.

His gruff laugh filled the room. "Among other things

he's pissed at me about, yeah." He gestured to the calendar with his cup. "You thought you were going to find a set of titties back there, didn't you?"

Fucking Mandalorian.

"With you, one never knows. Could have just as easily been The Golden Girls." Because he was a seriously weird dude who got off on watching repeats of the eighties sitcom when he wasn't causing trouble on skates.

"That's the desk calendar," Jackson said, nodding toward the one piece of furniture that didn't change over the years and the flat calendar spread over the top.

Probably because no one could lift it.

"As for my father, my being right definitely chafed his ass, but I ignored it. When that didn't piss me off the way he hoped, he jumped up my colon about there being no point if I don't settle down and have kids to take over the business."

"Any chance that's on the radar?"

"You could say I've got something in the works where that's concerned, but she's skittish. And I like kids. But it will be on my timeline—actually her timeline—not my father's. I guess I'd ask you the same on the settling down front, but word is you popped bone for Maisy Flynn."

Of course it was. Fucking wonderful.

"I hope they aren't saying it like that. Pretty sure I haven't 'popped bone' since I was fifteen." I took a sip of coffee, the biting flavor punishment on my tongue.

"Well, yeah, you are kind of getting old. Takes more work for the pop, huh?"

"You're a month older than me, Stone."

"Yeah, but poppin' all the damn time."

"I'm not sure I'd be bragging about that. Somehow the town stoner, mid-thirties, running a roller rink, sporting unpredictable wood has child molester vibes written all over it."

He snorted. "I've got stains on my soul, but that will never be one of them. And that's former stoner. I gave that shit up."

"Really? Now that's news in a town where nothing ever changes."

"Yeah, it's not as fun when your dad decides he wants to get high with you. I'm pretty sure I only did it to piss him off, and the day he asked to light one up with me, he sucked every last shred of joy from it."

"You still skate?"

"Fuck yeah, I do," he said, tilting his head. "You?"

"That's why I'm here."

"So that's the tension rolling off you."

Glancing out at the empty rink, I avoided his comment. "You want to talk about that phone call last summer?"

His gaze slid away and he shook his head. "Nope."

"Still processing?"

"I think that's a lifetime sentence where that's concerned. But it's not that." He looked me dead in the eye then. "I respect you and your career. Because I do, the conversation we had last summer will be the only conversation we ever have about that particular situation."

"Understood." He broke the law. And not something little either. But I knew Jackson, in his heart I knew him, and whatever he did, he only did because there was no other choice.

That's a position I understood all too well.

I sucked in a deep breath, memories when I first started skating here with my grandparents, mom, sister, and brother colliding with what came after.

Just after.

When I broke away from my siblings, anger took over as the Devil sitting on my shoulder while I raced around the rink. No matter what I did, how fast I went, my gaze always going to my mother's favorite corner table.

One now used by another family, another smiling mother.

Every pass, that spot a cutting reminder that she'd never sit there again. I'd never see her smile, hear her laugh, or breathe her in when I hugged her.

She'd never again reassure me everything was going to be okay.

Each glance at the corner carving out the good in my heart, leaving gaping holes for the rot to seep in and fill me up from the inside out.

I let that anguish rule my decisions. I let grief push me to run away.

From my grandparents, from the pain, from feeling adrift in a world I'd always thought would hold me to it with unwavering gravity.

Heartbreak and desperation fucked with my head, leading me to manipulate my brother and sister into leaving the security with our grandparents on the farm to go live with our dad.

The price of my disastrous decision was never paid in full.

The balance destined to hang over my head for a lifetime.

What the hell was I doing here?

What business did I have getting involved with anyone, carrying my stains into their lives, making them bear the cost of my mistakes?

This was why I avoided this town. Why I limited myself to brief visits lasting only a handful of days. I could get in and out before my past could be picked apart, before self-torment could take hold. I never had to worry about running into Lana's parents, my presence drawing slivers of resentment to the surface only to spill over, becoming one more thing for Lana to handle.

The weeks to come loomed before me, and if I didn't find something to sink my energy into, some sort of purpose, everything I'd done, the wrongs I couldn't right, would swallow me whole.

I glanced down at my hands, the way my fists clenched tight, the edge of my fingernails digging into my skin, the only outward sign of the storm brewing in me. Muscles rigid, gut churning, the pressure built, the desire to rage terrifying after the years I'd spent learning control.

Words I might have said turned to ash in my mouth. I didn't want to talk anymore. I wanted to burn up every last bit of energy I had, leaving behind exhaustion so heavy I couldn't muster the strength to agonize over the gossip, the town, my mistakes, or the way I could still feel Mayhem's heat which had somehow burrowed in a dangerously vulnerable place inside me that had been cold for more than half of my life.

And I didn't want to skate alone.

God, that sucked to acknowledge because needing someone meant I'd get close. Getting close meant someone would get hurt. But damn, I wanted a friend alongside me.

"Want to tear up the floor with me for a while?" I asked, my throat thick, my voice almost rusty with disuse despite the conversation between us—the timbre exposing just how shredded my spirit was inside me.

"With you, Bishop? Anytime," Jackson said, clapping my shoulder with a reassuring smile. "Let's do this shit."

I jogged out to my truck and grabbed my skates, the relief beginning to push against the anger brewing in my heart.

We laced up and Jackson flicked on the lights suspended over the rink, sending rainbow beams of light—another new addition instead of the standard white—dancing over the gleaming wood. Plugging in his phone to a state-of-the-art sound system way better than the muffled shit from our teen years, he resurrected our youth with a playlist full of angst and grit from the very first beat.

The song vibrated in my chest, rattling me from the inside out. I pushed off, the easy glide of my wheels sweet relief in a fucking abrasive world. My muscles warmed with every glide. The old moves came back as natural as walking.

Moves that had always been a core part of who I was.

The ones my mother taught me.

Jackson kept pace, matching his motions to mine. The tempo commanded our feet. With every move we reawakened the familiar kinship from endless afternoons jam skating as teenagers.

Song after song we skated in tandem. Sweat broke out over my skin and my heart pumped blood so hard and heavy through my veins it echoed in my ears.

On what had to be the twentieth pass, I shed my flannel shirt, balled it up, and ditched it over the wall.

Spins, slides, crazy legs, snake walks, splits, jumps, nothing was off-limits as I pushed physical boundaries, my body occasionally pushing back, reminding me I wasn't sixteen anymore.

I'd feel it by tonight. I might not be able to walk by morning.

And still I pushed faster.

I didn't look at the corner. Couldn't look at the corner. My demons lurked there, waiting for me to falter. Waiting for me to succumb.

I kicked harder, my slides longer and on my heels now,

as jam skating mixed with skate park moves. My momentum careened me dangerously close to the wall, but I didn't care.

I stopped or I didn't.

I'd break or I wouldn't.

And if my recklessness brought me pain, I welcomed it.

The laser lights blurred, the music grew muffled, and the shouts from Mayhem's bout crept into my head. The hungry look in her eyes. The quick shift of her gaze finding tiny gaps. Her body low, tight, and powerful as she exploded through barriers with unrelenting force beyond the physical propelling her.

The air tore from my lungs. I lunged harder, faster, memories taunting me.

Tempting me.

A memory—fuzzy at the edges—but the central scene unfolding with devastating clarity scrubbed Mayhem away, and now Lana burst around a corner, heading to the outside to zip past the pack as lead jammer. One point, two points, then a third. A shoulder from out of nowhere lifting her clean off the floor, suspending her in air, before sending her sliding into the wall.

The impossible angle of her head as she took the brunt of the collision at the base of her neck.

Her still body in a heap. Gasps of onlookers filling the air.

My own whispered prayer when I didn't even realize I knew how to pray anymore.

When I was sure, because of my past sins, God had stopped listening.

Another slide, the drag of my wheels and the force of my body putting impossible pressure on my ankles. Sweat running down my forehead into my eyes.

My brother's angry voice, the word traitor on the tip of

his tongue before he slammed the door and went with our father.

Barreling across the floor again, my vision blurring, my gut squeezing bile into my throat, the screams of my sister when the police showed up at our apartment and told us our father and brother were gone. What's left of my brother in an urn I've spent way too much time sitting in silence with.

You're the oldest. It's your job to protect them when you go.

He's our father, and you're a traitor.

Our daughter will never walk again and it's all your fault.

Voices filled with venom and despair reverberating through my skull snatching the thread of peace I'd struggled so hard to hold on to.

I can't protect anyone.

"Hey, watch out!"

The crack of wood echoed through the air. My thighs burned with the force stopping my lower body dead. My upper body kept going, the benches on the other side of the wall a flash of color as I flipped over the side and landed flat on my back on an unforgiving commercial carpet, the only thing between me and the concrete underneath. My teeth rattled in my skull. A pulsating throb took root inside me as I struggled to suck air into my lungs.

"Fuckin' A, dude. Are you okay?"

I grabbed my chest, still working on moving air. "Shit, that hurt a lot less when we were sixteen," I gasped out.

Jackson barked out a laugh as he yanked the frame of the wall back and forth. "Everything hurt less when we were sixteen."

I craned my neck to look up at him, grateful that I could still move it. "I'll cover the damage. Is it bad?"

"Nah, you're probably lucky it was already loose after some troublemakers rammed one of their buddies into it last week. Already have it scheduled to get fixed after Christmas."

"So you're saying the leeway softened the blow?" Because it sure as hell felt like I hit a brick wall before I definitely landed on concrete.

"Something like that."

I pushed up onto my elbows and took a deep breath of commercial carpet that no longer smelled like shampoo now that I'd decided to bump and grind against it. "Doesn't feel like it."

"Dude, whatever you were outrunning, did you win?" Jackson reached out a hand and helped hoist me up.

"I never do."

Maisy

"**I** don't wanna roller-skate," Leo said as he dragged his feet from the van all the way to the door of Rockabilly's. I had to give it to the little dude, his defiance game was strong.

"You know the deal. You and Noah picked last week, now the girls get to pick this week. And they picked skating."

I'd only said this about five times so far on the six-mile drive here. Each time I managed to keep my voice upbeat while I explained it again, Wes winked at me in the rearview. The father of three's version of, "Stay strong, kid" thus indoctrinating me into an honorary responsible adult club where it was us against them, we were outnumbered, and the power could shift at any minute.

Two against five and if the boys had their way, they'd revolt and get all *Lord of the Flies* up in this shit.

Over roller skates.

Roller skates, for fuck's sake.

But if I handed them skateboards, they'd be all over that shit. I couldn't roll my eyes hard enough at the irony.

I probably owed Milton and Gerald thank-yous for all the involuntary training. They'd been preparing me for this day for six years.

Tonight, I'd reward myself with peppermint schnapps, a deep, warm bath, and a dark and dirty romance. The kind of book you needed to be in the mood to read if you know what I mean.

"So they picked, doesn't mean we have to get on skates though," Noah chimed in, his voice starting out strong and full of conviction, until he saw the look in my eye. Like a week-old balloon finally being shown mercy with a needle, his attitude deflated, his words sliding from defiance to a dull whine.

"And how fun would it have been to play laser tag if the girls sat out last week?" I asked, hoping that maybe I could spark some empathy in the boy.

But he was eight. His empathy bank was like an under-developed, featherless bird.

He only cared how his teenage cousin told him roller-skating was for girls.

I wish I'd known that nugget of bullshit before our season was over so I could have made arrangements to squash that notion right out of Noah's head. He'd be surprised what girls did on roller skates.

So would his butthead of a cousin.

Boys could be such little pricks.

The cousin I mean—technically the jury was still out on Leo and Noah—plus, I sort of adored them even though they weren't living their finest moment.

Well, I had no intentions of going anywhere. Between me and the rest of my team who all volunteered with the Crossroads Youth Center, we'd make sure they didn't become delinquent burdens on society.

No way would I let his cousin win. Not even today when he'd gone and pissed on what was supposed to be a pretty damn awesome day.

Finally, an activity where I could share more of myself.

Not derby me, but the fun memories I had before my mom died. My mother loved skating, and I couldn't remember a time when she didn't have me on skates right alongside her.

This was one of those moments I had to remind myself I was an adult because I was not feeling very adult when it came to Noah's cousin.

Nope, I felt my full-on inner thug coming out. And it wouldn't be a fair fight. Not when I'm derby and he's a sixteen-year-old twerp. A twerp who kept hovering near the youth center with stolen cigarettes he'd offer to little kids when he thought no one was looking.

If it weren't an assault charge, I'd have him on his ass before he could suck in a breath.

Thanks to his shitty influence, I had a decision to make. Battle with Leo and Noah and possibly eat into Ellie, Addison, and Rylee's time on the rink, or let it go and let Wes sit with them while they sulked.

One thing was for sure, Noah and Leo had two choices, skate or sit. Laser tag in every way, shape, or form was off the table.

I didn't even want to hear the words slip from their lips.

Oh, and those video games along the wall? Also off the table.

I really hated that they made me have to be a hard-ass here. This wasn't just their playtime; in a way it was mine too. My time with them not only filled their well, but it filled mine.

And maybe, just maybe I filled up a few of the lonely places from my childhood.

I held the door while five sets of booted feet stomped over the threshold.

Ellie and Addison practically bounced with excitement. Leo and Noah moped, and Rylee, well, her previous excitement seemed to have fled, leaving her with big round eyes and pale cheeks. The girl looked scared enough to poop.

I had my work cut out for me.

Maybe next time they could all agree on a shared mood. Too much to ask?

Probably.

Jackson came around the corner and skidded to a stop, his hand stilling on the towel he rubbed along the edges of his sweaty hair. "Hey Maze, I didn't expect you again this week."

"Last-minute decision. Marty had an appointment. Who needs a day off anyway?"

I did, but there was no way I was going to admit that and take the risk of the kids feeling bad.

Even if I was disappointed in two of them at the moment.

Plus, those childhood nuggets I pilfered vicariously through my little borrowed brood called my name. I'm pretty sure I needed them as much as they needed me.

I didn't know all the details of their lives, but kids didn't spend time at the youth center without damn good reason. Some had parents working two jobs to make ends meet and no one at home after school; some were foster kids, and some of them were like me. They lived in a group home devoid of hugs, love, and individual attention.

At least I'd had years of hugs before I ended up there. The queen of a good snuggle, my mom never let a day go by without letting me know how loved and wanted I was.

When I ended up at Bay Wilderness group home, I was older and a few years wiser than my little crew. I was lucky.

Well, other than having to deal with Tilly.

Or what Tilly had become after she doused our bond with lighter fluid and tossed a match on it.

Someone has to feel bad for her. After all, what does it say when your own mother has to go and die to get away from you?

I'd never know if she knew I stood behind her when she said those words. It didn't matter. The fact that she could say it made her a merciless bitch. One I didn't see clearly until that moment.

Crossroads eventually gave me an escape from her torment.

Tilly went too, but the dynamics changed inside the walls of the youth center. The adults paid close attention. All it took was one of them overhearing the poison dripping from Tilly's tongue one time. From that moment on they kept us separated.

For those few hours a week, they protected me.

Pretty much the only peace I knew until I moved out of Bay Wilderness and left Tilly's misery behind.

What if I were the one standing between these little humans and torment and I just didn't know it?

I looked down at Rylee's pale, worried face dusted with freckles. Cupping her soft, pointed chin, I smiled until my silent reassurance wiped away some of the fear lingering in her eyes.

These guys were too damn young to be feeling all of that uncertainty and hurt. The thought of them lying in their beds at night, sad, maybe hungry, or worse… scared —I knew that gnawing feeling in the gut. I knew it intimately. The uncertainty of tomorrow, and the next day, and the next after that.

What it was like to hear the muffled sobs of the girl in the next bed.

It never really went away. Not for me.

So, while they were with me, they had my undivided attention and much to Leo and Noah's disappointment, consequences for their decisions.

"Well, you know the drill, the floor is yours. How about we get these little guys and girls fitted for skates?"

"Just the girls," Noah muttered.

Jackson yanked his head back and glanced between Leo and Noah. "You guys don't want to skate?"

Neither Leo nor Noah said a word.

"Skating is for girls according to these little dudes. So they're choosing to sit this out."

Jackson crouched down eye level with the boys. "Who told you guys that boys don't skate? I skate."

Noah glanced at Leo, a flicker of doubt moving over his face. "Yeah, but you own the place. You have to skate."

"My grandfather didn't skate. Neither did my dad, and they both owned Rockabilly's before me." Jackson clicked his tongue. "Too bad," Jackson said, ruffling Noah's hair as he stood. "You guys are missing out."

"Could you do me a favor and take the girls to pick some skates while I get these guys settled in with the perfect view of the floor?"

"Anything for you, Maze," he said with a wink. "Come on, ladies. Tell me, do you have a favorite color? I've got skates in a rainbow of colors. I might even have rainbow skates. Let's go see," Jackson said, leading them behind the front counter.

"I can't believe you're going to pass up the VIP attention. Jackson doesn't let just anybody behind that counter, you know." I guided each of them toward the tables with a little nudge when they tried to veer toward the pinball machine.

They stayed silent, didn't make eye contact, and Noah crossed his arms.

Suit yourselves, little dudes.

I led them to the corner and handed cash to Wes.

"Would you do me a favor and hook them up with a couple drinks and snacks while I get the girls on the floor?"

"Sure, but keep your money," he said as he pulled out two chairs for the boys. "I've got it this time around."

I kissed his cheek, his salt-and-pepper whiskers long enough now they no longer doubled as weapons. "You're a sweetheart. Thank you."

By the time I made it over to the girls, they'd all picked their skates and Jackson crouched before them, helping them get laced up.

Dropping onto the floor, I grabbed my skates out of my bag and laced up right alongside them.

"You look like you were out there before we got here. Either that or you were attacked with a fire hose," I said with a laugh.

Jackson's lips twitched and for just a second a look flashed in his eyes that I couldn't quite figure out. "Yup, I was out there."

"Not much fun skating alone."

"It's definitely better with a friend," he agreed before glancing at the girls next to me. "Luckily, you've got three to help you stay upright out there."

"Maisy won't fall. She never falls," Addison said with a grin that bordered on hero worship.

"Hey, I can still fall with the best of them. I definitely fall when I play derby." I pushed up on my feet and held out a hand to Ellie and Addison while Jackson reached out to help Rylee. "You guys will fall, but that's okay. I'll be right there with you. I can even teach you some tricks so you don't hurt yourselves. Sound good?"

Rylee looked up, her eyes wide with fear. "Not falling sounds better."

"Yes, it does, honey," I said with a laugh. "But don't

worry. We're going to go slow, and we won't do anything you're not comfortable with. It's all about having fun."

"What kind of tunes would you ladies like out there?" Jackson asked, scrolling through his phone.

"Jojo Siwa," Ellie said, her eyes lighting up, the only part of her she dared move judging by how rigid she held herself.

"And the Haschak Sisters," Addison added.

Jackson scratched the back of his head and flinched down at his phone. "Good luck with this playlist, Maze."

I rolled a skate buddy in front of each of them. Made of PVC with wheels on the bottom, the prop would keep them upright at first. "Okay, girls, we're heading out there." I glanced back over my shoulder. "Have mercy on my soul and switch that out after a few songs, okay? I'll shoot you a playlist from my Spotify."

"Consider it done."

"Thanks."

I led them onto the floor with a quick glance to the sullen boys in the corner. Wes looked at the girls, grinned, and gave me a thumbs-up. He had three of his own. All girls. Leo and Noah had nothing on that chaos.

The music came on, and I cringed. I reminded myself that I would have been into the same saccharine sweet, high-pitched pop at their age, and laughed at the expressions on the faces of the boys as the speaker right over their ear made sure they experienced that wonderful beat full force.

Hell, maybe that would be enough to chase them onto the floor.

But I wouldn't hold my breath.

"Okay—you guys ready?"

All three girls nodded as they stared down at their feet.

"I have one rule. Just one. When you fall, you get back up. Can you do that for me?"

They nodded in unison, Ellie and Addison with beaming smiles while Rylee bit her lip.

Hopefully she stopped doing that before she fell. It was an emergency room visit waiting to happen.

"The first thing I want you to do… bring your heels together and aim your toes out like a penguin." I shifted into the position on my skates and waited as they settled into the same placement.

Ellie and Addison giggled as they wobbled into place.

But Rylee locked up, her body rigid with every shift. I wanted to hug her and tell her it was going to be okay, but I knew that was about making me feel better and not what Rylee needed. Confidence came from achievement and Rylee showed a lot of vulnerability in the confidence department.

If I had my way, we would blow up those insecurities one at a time until she's all shiny and shit. Until her go-to look is not one of nervousness and fear, but of excitement and discovery.

"Good job. Now, grab your skate buddy and stomp like me. Just follow the beat. You ladies know it, you picked it." I lifted my skates, my moves exaggerated to click against the floor, straight up and down, in time with the music. The girls followed along, each stomp harder as they became braver, their smiles growing wider.

"That's it, just like that."

None of them seemed to notice that they'd started moving forward a couple inches at a time and I sure as shit wasn't saying a word. Let them be surprised.

I rolled backward, keeping an eye on our pace out of the corner of my eye with every intention of steering them around the bend, keeping them going as long as I possibly could.

"Now, bend your knees just a little bit more. Like this. It'll help you balance. That's it, just like that."

They immediately followed my lead and in minutes, their torsos more upright now, the confidence began to show in their bright eyes and big smiles. They even started letting go of their skate buddies with one hand while their heads bopped to the tempo.

"Look at you already. You're doing it, girls; you're really doing it!"

I kept their attention on me, exaggerating my movements, raising my knees almost to the point I practically marched in place. I'm sure I looked absolutely ridiculous, but I didn't care because every minute brought more laughter. Little did they know, with their eyes on mine, they'd begun turning the corner.

Stomp, stomp, stomp.

For ten minutes we kept marching. When Addison started pushing her skate buddy ahead of her a few feet before catching up to it, I knew the time had come to ditch them altogether.

This was where they would fall.

Why the hell did it make my heart ache just thinking about it?

"Okay, how about it, girls? You ready to try without your skate buddies?"

Ellie and Addison squealed in unison while Rylee just smiled up at me, her flushed cheeks chasing away the pale fear.

I crouched down in front of her while the other two distracted themselves rolling their skates back and forth. "Remember what I said. You're going to fall. What's important is you get back up, okay?"

"Okay," she said quietly, lacing her fingers with mine.

"Good." I kissed her knuckles and stood. "Alright, here's what we're going to do. Knees bent, march it out to the beat, arms like mine."

I kept them tucked into my sides to the elbow and then arched them out with my palms facing down.

"We're going to look like we're waddling like penguins, but we don't care, do we?"

"Nooooo!" they called out.

"And when you feel like you're going to fall, get low, your hands out like you're driving a tiny car. Like this," I said, getting into the position. "Now you show me."

They mimicked my moves and made it a whole ten feet when Addison dropped onto her knee, but she popped right back up with a smile just like I said. Not that it was surprising she was the first; she was the most adventurous of the three with Ellie right behind her.

Ellie fell next, landing right on her butt. She winced, then scrambled to her hands and knees, crawling as she scurried back up.

We turned the corner, then the second and the third. The girls never even noticed they'd stopped stomping and had begun gliding.

I crouched low to stay eye level with them while I rolled along backward. This was it, their real first time. They'd never be this again and I was the one here teaching them. I wanted to take pictures. I wanted to record them. I wanted to brag to everyone at The Shipwreck and then do it all over again at Banked Track over drinks. I wanted to fly around the rink in a victory lap; I wanted—Priest.

I spotted him over Addison's shoulder where he leaned against the lockers in faded blue jeans, one leg bent, his thumbs hooked in the edge of his pockets. His black tank top showed off thick ridged muscles running up his arms, arriving at wide shoulders, and proving his orgasm-inspiring forearms were only the beginning.

His face unreadable, his gaze never wavered from mine.

The man didn't even blink.

"Oh… oh… oh no… Maaiiissssyyyyy!"

At the sound of Rylee's frantic cry, my attention snapped back to the girl. She'd picked up speed, the frantic windmilling of her arms doing nothing to help her regain her balance. Terrified eyes locked on mine as I reached for her to slow her momentum, but it was too late. Before I could so much as stand upright, she crashed into me and we both went down.

Rylee's elbow landed right in my stomach as she pushed herself up over me. My grunt turned into a laugh as I smoothed the wisps of hair out of Rylee's worried face. I glanced at Ellie and Addison who stood bent over us, and smiled while I struggled for my next breath.

Maybe I was breathless from going ass over tea kettle while trying to keep myself from crushing Rylee… or maybe the brooding man whose dark hooded eyes still searing through me from where he stood in the shadows sucked all the air from my lungs.

Either way, if this kept up, there'd be an oxygen tank in my future.

"See, girls. I can still fall."

CAIN

Mayhem lay under the heap, her head thrown back in laughter, her cheeks flushed, an open, sweet smile spread across her face.

I let go of the breath I'd been holding in a rush of air. Goosebumps prickled over my neck and my heart rate kicked up a notch.

No longer casually observing her for my own amusement, I voraciously studied her. Every last bit of her.

Her affectionate grin alone delivered a crippling blow to my gut. But that was just the warm-up for the uppercut coming right after when she slipped the errant strands of hair from the scared little girl's forehead, tucked them behind her ears, and cupped her cheek.

The nurturing there punched right through my ribs into my chest and mercilessly rooted around for my heart.

Even drawn to her determination and drive—hell, even the slice of attitude—I'd managed to fortify my barriers. My armor hadn't even taken a hit when I caught a glimpse of humor and vulnerability. I'd clutched on to my willpower and maintained distance, leaving her question hanging in the air between us at The Shipwreck, and walked away for what I thought would be the last time.

I held on to strength and common sense and reminded

myself every time my mind had even flirted with the idea of wavering.

But the love written on her face was the kind of genuine caring I could never resist. Intimate gestures like those weren't scripted; they were as much a part of who a person was as the veins threading through them. The instinctual comfort she offered came from a good heart. Seeing this side of her, when there was no one watching, no one to impress—fucking hell—it did shit to me on the inside I didn't want to admit.

She compelled me to waver for the first real time since I made a silent promise to this town and the people I loved here to protect them from everything… even me.

The smallest of the three girls who'd taken Mayhem out, struggled to get up while the others yanked on her hands and arms to help. Once they made it onto their skates again, Mayhem bounded to her feet effortlessly, no pinch of pain flitting over her face.

Guess that rib felt a hell of a lot better.

So much better she guided them straight into another lap around the floor.

Anyone else would have had the kids take five after a spill like that, but not Mayhem.

Of course, not Mayhem.

If she didn't sweep those little girls right into another lap, the one who fell may never go back out there again. Mayhem gave her the gift of faith. It would leave a mark.

Mayhem left her mark.

Apparently, she left indelible touches everywhere. Banked Track. The Shipwreck. Here.

Inside me.

She met my eyes, the startled confusion on her face just moments before now shrouded in curiosity.

I was pretty sure if I looked in a mirror, I'd find curiosity on my face too.

We stumbled into this tentative dance with one another, both of us shit at hiding our mutual dangerous interest.

One of us better learn how to put on the brakes. Mayhem didn't look like she braked for anything—and despite years of discipline where I'd mastered caution, I didn't want to either.

Shit.

When she turned her attention on the girls again, I let myself watch her despite the Guinness World Record list of reasons why I shouldn't. Off the clock and off the track, she had a softness in her and fuck if I could tear my eyes away.

Acid-washed jeans hugged round hips that moved along with the music pumping through the room. A new song because Jackson had mercy on our souls and dialed back that teenybopper pop playlist. This one, soft and catchy, had Mayhem's brood of beginners mimicking her movements, swaying more with their arms than hips, but their attention off their skates, the hero worship evident with their toothy grins.

The rips in the material stretched across her thighs gave a tantalizing glimpse of the tattoos running up her skin. Covered from the side of her neck, down her arms, over her fingers, and along her thigh made me wonder how many tattoos lay hidden in between.

What was she trying to hide with so much ink?

Or—what was she trying to tell?

I wanted to search over her body and study them all. Graze over them with my fingertips, trace them with my tongue. Memorize their taste with my mouth.

I wanted to know what each permanent piece of ink

etched into her porcelain skin meant to her. What it said about the woman inside. The girl she was before her mother died. The girl she became after. The woman who battled demons on the track and wrangled unruly old men with comfortable affection and humor.

Turning the corner, her back to me now, I swallowed hard.

Worse than the rips on the front of her jeans was the one across the back of her thigh, just a couple inches under the curve of her round ass.

My blood stirred, surging hot and heavy through my veins, burning me up from the inside out as my body reacted to the baggy sweater determined to hang off her shoulder.

With her hair up in a ponytail and bandana, the tattoo stretching over her back and climbing to the base of her neck lay exposed.

Bastard that I was, I took full advantage.

Her flesh just begged for a series of sensual bites.

All of a sudden joking around with Jackson about popping bone didn't seem so funny.

Blinking away the connection, I searched for a polar vortex to sweep through and knock me down a few degrees. I glanced over and caught sight of Wes Myers, a fixture in this town who knew everybody after spending two decades as an ER nurse at the local hospital. He sat at the table with a couple of boys sporting shitty moods etched over their defiant little baby faces.

My mother's corner table.

And there it was, the blast of cold to spank my ass before seeping into my bones.

The boys kept stealing glances at the floor, their skeptical faces morphing into rapt interest the longer they stared.

They didn't look like they were in trouble with the way Wes reclined back in his seat, an unbothered look on his face. If anything, they looked like they wanted to be out there, but something held them back.

"Hey, man, you're still here, huh?" Jackson nudged my arm with his elbow. "I guess I shouldn't be too surprised since you spotted Maze," Jackson said, earning a warning glare from me.

"Don't read anything into it, Jackson." The guy looked all too happy to be gloating in the gossip seeping from every corner of Galloway Bay. Just whose side was he on anyway?

"Wouldn't dream of it," he said, rocking on his heels and just one step away from a jaunty whistle that might make me throat punch him.

"Does she come in here a lot?" I'm a fucking idiot. Hands down, the dumbest shit on the planet. The guy who couldn't resist a temptation, or in this case, a stupid challenge.

The guy who'd stuck his tongue on the 9V battery. The dude who'd stick his tongue to the metal flagpole during recess when it was twenty degrees out. The idiot who took the dare to grab on to an electric fence because how bad could it be? Oh, and that puddle I stood in while doing it? That just made me more of a badass when I pulled it off.

I'm a drowning man, and this asshole sidles on up next to me to help hold my head under water.

"Yeah, but usually the team rotates, and she was here just last week. They all volunteer over at the youth center. Actually, they do time at the food pantry and created a mobile library too with the help of Marty's cousin London who came up for a visit from New York and helped with the logistics."

"What's the deal with the boys sitting with Wes?"

"They said skating is for girls."

Not my problem.

Don't do it, Bishop. Don't you fucking do it.

I pushed away from the locker and turned to him. "And you didn't set them straight?"

"They didn't seem to care what I had to say. Too bad they weren't here fifteen minutes earlier." Jackson glanced at the orange cones he'd put around the edge of the wall I'd crushed. "Maybe half an hour earlier," he said, barking out a laugh. "You were a bad example fifteen minutes ago."

"Yeah, well, maybe I'm a bad influence all the time," I muttered.

"That's Lana's parents talking. What do you say? You up to setting the boys straight after the hit you took, old man?"

"Old man? I could kick your ass right now."

"You could, but unfortunately I know for a fact your sense of honor won't let you."

"Half the people in this town want to skin me alive; the other half of you want to pin some sort of saint medal to my chest." I glanced over at the boys one more time and knew I was screwed. Absolutely fucking screwed.

"That's a small town for ya."

"You up for one more round out there? Maybe we can reprogram the little guys." My legs and lower back ached like a son of a bitch, my body even trying to tell me this was a shitty idea, but my listening skills were hibernating for the winter apparently.

"Sure, let's do it."

CAIN

The song that had Mayhem's hips swaying faded away and for the life of me I couldn't decide if I was relieved about that or not. Didn't matter; I was going to see her body every time I closed my eyes now.

The beat kicked up, and I grasped for the freedom and oblivion on the rink. The lights flashed in time with the remix, a decent blend of hip-hop and funk, and Jackson and I fell into a casual shuffle. Nothing too fancy, just a good dose of speed and a few slick moves of our feet that looked more complicated than they actually were, but would entice kids to strap on some wheels.

The best part, all moves these kids could be doing in short order if Mayhem managed to get them all out there at one time.

I took the lead and added a few turns and dance moves, knowing Jackson would follow along and then take the lead himself as we switched off.

Mayhem ushered her crew to the side wall and lifted each of them onto the edge, while the boys scrambled over from their seats, smiles on their faces. Hell, even Wes had some pepper in his ass and joined them.

Three laps in, all the kids had smiles and one of the

boys had started tugging on Mayhem's sweater to snag her attention.

And in another hit to my pride, just like that I was jealous of a kid who hadn't even reached the double digits.

She nodded down at him and pointed to Jackson and me on the floor before turning back to us, that smile on her face once again, but this time, aimed at me.

I wanted her on the floor with us.

I wanted my hands on her.

Skating had a way of liberating something inside of me. The freedom in the speed, in the movements, the way my heart and soul aligned, acting as a balm on my turbulent past. A temporary fix, a sliver of relief for old wounds, and a euphoric moment of absolution prompting me to do something incredibly stupid.

I crooked my finger in her direction from the straightaway across from her.

She turned to Wes, said something that had him nodding, and the minute we turned the corner and headed for her she was ready.

Dangerous territory and still I couldn't muster up a bit of common sense.

She slid between Jackson and me, gliding seamlessly into our rhythm, leaving me in the best and worst position.

Behind her.

Perfect for my hands that itched to touch, absolute nightmare for my voracious eyes and the part of me wanting to satisfy a recent hunger I couldn't shake.

Backward, to frontward, toe jams into snake walks, she followed along, never missing a switch, her arms swinging, her fingers snapping along with the beat, and a goddamned laugh bubbling from her that branded itself inside me.

With an extra push, I launched myself closer and curled my fingers around her hips.

Her fucking hips.

Remembering her fall from the week before, I made sure not to dig my fingertips in and hurt her, but damn the effort it took to resist.

My hands, the treacherous little bastards, memorized her on contact. My fingertips flexed until they brushed over her waistband and found warm skin.

I wanted her by her hips. Back arched, ass in the air, my fingers tanged in her hair, dragging her head back until her defiant eyes met mine.

Or pinned to the wall all panting breaths as I devoured her from her fresh mouth, straight down to her wet cunt. My name an oath from her lips with every swipe of my tongue over her swollen clit.

Not Priest.

Cain.

Just Cain.

I pulled her back and took her hand. Raising my arm, she ducked under and slid right into the spin.

This.

If we didn't have to leave this moment, I could stay in this town and just do this for the rest of my days.

Dangerous fucking territory.

I needed to remember what I was. What I'd done. What I cost the people I love.

What I could cost her.

Taking her hand, I propelled us ahead of Jackson and handed her off. I needed the distance. To make sure she didn't get the wrong idea.

Okay, to make sure I didn't get the wrong idea.

Jackson touching her grated on my nerves and in the span of a dozen beats, I was snatching her back from my friend, glaring at the fucking knowing grin on his smug face when I did.

Bastard.

We skated off the floor when the song ended. I avoided the table and made my way to the other side where I dropped into a chair and started tugging at my laces. The boys shot over, their avid gazes on my feet.

"That was awesome. I wanna skate like that." The dark-haired boy peered down at me with fire in his eyes.

The minute he got on skates, he'd never get off them. "Have Jackson get you fitted with some skates and get out there then."

"I want skates with flames like yours."

I glanced at the kid full of enthusiasm now, but a stubborn little shit not ten minutes earlier. "You have to earn the flames, my man."

"Sounds like you little dudes had a change of heart. Why don't we go take care of that. Ladies, you want to help me show them the ropes back there?" Jackson ushered the boys and girls to the counter, leaving Mayhem and me alone.

Subtle.

I hope Jackson took a skate in the taint.

Mayhem sat down next to me, her arm brushing mine. "Thank you for that."

"For what?" I muttered, trying to ignore her heat as it seeped into me just from our proximity alone.

"You know for what. When someone says thank you, you then say, 'you're welcome.'"

"Is that right?" I didn't look at her. Couldn't look at her. So I focused on her skates. I expected her to be out here in her derby skates, maybe a set of Moxies, not the classic high-top white skates with a low heel.

I yanked off my first skate and wondered about her

choice to wear those when there were so many better options out there.

None of my business.

"What's the deal with the lace?" Tie-dye laces ran up the leather and through the eyelets, but on the right, a faded, frayed green lace that looked like it had snapped a decade or two ago ran alongside the new one.

Her startled gaze met mine before her eyes darted down to her skates. Fidgeting on the seat, she tucked them under her.

Like she was hiding.

"It, uh—" Her normally confident voice stumbled. "They were my mother's."

"The laces?"

"The skates. The last time she took me skating the lace snapped. I didn't—couldn't… I couldn't bring myself to throw it away."

I tugged on my boots, her words squeezing in my chest impossibly tight. Plagued with this feeling that some other force was writing this story between us, and we would be helpless to change the plot, I crammed my toes in so hard, my foot stomped on the floor.

Propping my elbows on my knees, hunched over, her invisible pain so fucking palpable it washed over me and tried to mix with mine. "Your mother's skates?"

"Yes." Her voice turned soft, laced with an unexpected sound of longing.

I couldn't leave her hanging like that alone as much as I wanted to. As much as I needed to get away from her, from whatever this was, or wanted to become. "I get that."

"You do?"

"Yeah. I used to spend a lot of time here as a kid with my mother. At that same table over there." I glanced over to the corner table, closed my eyes against the slice of pain, and turned back to her again.

"Where is she?" Mayhem swallowed. "Your mother."

"She died." I had to get out of here. I didn't want this heart-to-heart. I didn't want to give a shit. And I definitely didn't want to bond over two dead mothers.

I stood, grabbed my skates, and turned away from her without a glance.

"You don't have to leave." Her words came out in a rush to my retreating back. Like she was desperate to hold on to something.

Only I was a bad bet and the worst possible anchor in any damn storm.

I stopped but didn't turn around. "I think I do. This… whatever this is, it's not a good idea."

"I thought you said you weren't the enemy?" she said quietly, my words coming back to haunt me, like every-thing else in my past. Just one more reminder why this had to stop now, before it went too far. Before I lost the iron fist on my willpower and gave in to the attraction, immersed myself in her, until it soothed my loneliness or worse.

Until she became someone I couldn't walk away from.

I turned to look at her one more time over my shoulder then. "And you said we aren't friends."

Maisy

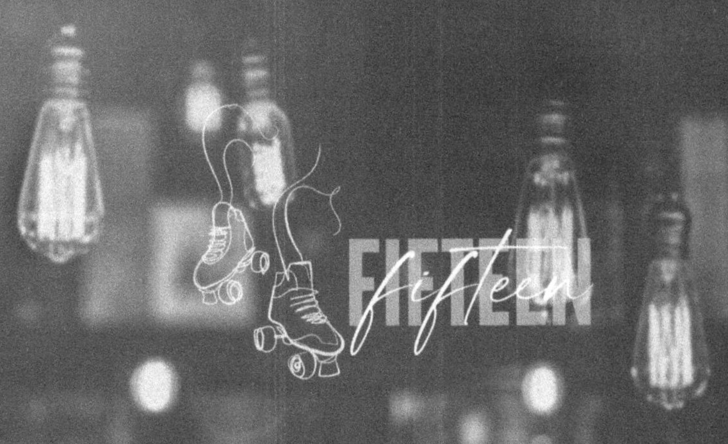

ddison, Ellie, Leo, and Noah fell asleep on their way back to Crossroads. Rylee stayed tucked against my side, her eyes wide open as I threaded my fingers through her soft brown hair, enjoying the quiet where I could replay the best moments from our afternoon at Rockabilly's.

Yeah, that meant the heart-stopping ones too.

Like Priest on that floor.

God, the sight of him on skates, as if he spent more time on wheels than in shoes, sent a bolt of fire lancing through me that had every part of me capable of spine-tingling arousal standing to rapt attention.

And I had questions… so many questions.

Too bad we weren't friends.

I could kick myself for tossing those words out there.

Actually, I could kick him for remembering them so well and tossing them between us like he'd just framed out a wall… with two-by-sixes instead of two-by-fours.

The boy wasn't just building any wall. He was building one to withstand a hurricane.

Derby coach didn't mean skater. It never had. But Priest was a skater through and through. He moved with sleek confidence but fueled with a deep-seated disquiet.

Skates with red leather flames streaking along the sides that inspired so much adoration in Noah, told a secret story.

Only pieces remained out of reach… so many pieces.

He didn't look like a cop.

He didn't look like a disgraced coach.

He didn't look like the bad idea he was… at least according to my team.

If being friends with him could ruin our chances with the WRDF, did I really want to be in the WRDF to begin with? Not that this was solely my decision to make. And if I stood my ground, and my team didn't feel the same—nope, not going there. Even in my head… Not. Going. There.

Hot memories lingered on torturous replay of him skating ahead of Jackson, lean muscular legs in faded blue jeans, his tank top caught on the edge of his thick black belt so whenever he raised his arms higher or swung them faster, he gave me a glimpse of hard abs. And that smile on his face with the way he bit his lip?

He was way more than a gooey cookie, more than an edible, way more than a snack—he was a whole damn meal.

A captain's seafood platter piled high with fried haddock, whole-bellied clams, scallops, and shrimp with none of that pesky slaw on the side to take up space on the plate.

No lemon wedge either.

And fries? Fuck fries. He was a straight-out-of-the-sea-that-day, drool-worthy bag of yum fried in fresh oil.

And this bitch was hungry.

Joining him sent shivers through me, even now. His hand holding mine, the pads of his rough fingertips barely digging into my skin, making me want them on me harder and more insistent. The confidence in the way he guided me, spun me, trusting me to keep up, but confident just the same that if I couldn't, he had this.

Was I really that woman? The one who wanted a guy who could take control and did so without asking first.

Yes, yes, apparently, I am.

The brooding man had all but disappeared except for a few glimpses here and there. Like when I caught him watching us from the shadows near the lockers, and later, when his eyes landed on that table in the corner.

His mother's table.

Every revelation only made me all too aware of how much more there was to learn. A dangerous proposition with my team's application to the WRDF, with Eve ready to snarl at anyone getting close to me, and with the kind of potential this had to annihilate my heart.

Cozying up to the controversial coach wouldn't endear me to a good part of the town and these people were all I had. Sure, the sheriff liked him. So did Patti. But my team?

Lukewarm didn't even loom on the radar.

Rylee wiggled next to me, her eyes wide open as she chewed her lip.

"What's the matter?" I whispered down to her, giving her a snuggle.

"Nothing," Rylee said quietly.

I nudged her little chin. "Hmmm, I don't know about that. When a girl says nothing, it's almost always something."

"How would I get to spend time with you if I can't go to the center anymore?" she asked, her voice small and broken.

I tipped her face up to mine, surprised to see the glistening of tears welling there. "Why wouldn't you get to go to the center anymore?"

"Well, if it closed down or something."

"Honey, the center is not going to close down," I said, squeezing her close.

She glanced away, her voice barely a whisper. "Okay."

"You don't believe me?"

"It's just… well, I heard…"

The tentative beginnings of a confession made me breathless. I swallowed against my suddenly dry throat in an effort to keep my voice strong and reassuring. "What? What did you hear?"

"I was listening in when I shouldn't have been."

A lump of dread lodged in my throat as I told myself to stay calm and keep the conversation light. "You're not going to get in trouble, honey. Just tell me what you heard."

"Mrs. Rutledge said she didn't know where the kids would go after March. Do you know where we're going?"

I glanced around at the kids sleeping peacefully in the van, my stomach pitching. "Maybe she wasn't talking about you. It's hard to know what she was talking about when we don't know what the other person said, right? That's the danger of eavesdropping."

"I didn't mean to. It's just, she sounded worried. Really worried. Like my mom used to sound right before my dad came home."

Rylee's father spent years beating his wife and kids with little to no consequences. Over and over her mother took him back, accepting his apologies, lying to herself, thinking that maybe this time if he did fly into a rage, he'd keep his hands off the kids and only hurt her.

And so what if he did commit to only hurting her. Every yell, curse, slap, punch, and kick, even if only directed toward their mother, was a yell, curse, slap, punch, and kick for them.

Sheriff Chase and his officers repeatedly hauled him

off to jail only to let him out hours later because Rylee's mother made excuses for him or worse, refused to press charges.

Rylee's dad was a pro at making sure to be careful of the visible marks he left on their mother, making it hard to press any sort of lasting charges stick. It wasn't until Rylee borrowed a friend's cell phone overnight and caught one of his worst beatings on video that the kids finally broke free.

Their mother had a long way to go to prove she could handle having her kids back. First, she had to start with getting well herself.

As for Rylee's dad, he'd be behind bars until well after Rylee became an adult.

"Mrs. Rutledge's words gave you that funny feeling in the pit of your tummy?"

Rylee nodded and snuggled in closer.

The sign for Crossroads appeared around the corner, letting me know I only had a couple minutes to make her feel better.

"How about I speak to Mrs. Rutledge and make sure everything's okay? How does that sound?"

She nodded against my chest and sighed. "I'd like that."

"Okay. For now, I don't want you to worry about what you heard okay? March is a long way away and next week we'll talk about it. It's all going to be okay; you'll see."

We bumped over the side street alongside Crossroads and pulled right up to the door. I shuffled the sleepy crew off the van and helped them shed their boots and jackets, reminding them along the way not to just toss them in a heap, but hang them on the hooks where they belonged.

"Can we go skating again next week, Miss Maisy?" Noah asked, rubbing the sleep from his eyes with his fists.

I laughed, his sour mood from earlier today all but forgotten. I bet Noah was going to set his cousin straight the minute he saw him again. "Let me talk to Eve, but I don't see why not."

"Can Mr. Jackson and the man with the flames skate with us again?"

"I'm sure Jackson can, I'm not so sure about Priest though. If I see him, I'll ask. Okay?"

Noah grinned. "Okay," he said right before he took off at a run, chasing after Leo.

Maisy

Once the kids settled into activities with a few of the other staff members, I went in search of Mrs. Rutledge for a few answers.

I just hope she had the ones I wanted to hear. Not that I would tell Rylee because when it came down to it, I couldn't imagine any conversation where the words Rylee overheard were innocent.

I found Mrs. Rutledge standing by the tall windows of her office facing out onto the snow-covered gardens we used each year to teach the kids about responsibility and good nutrition. Turns out kids had a whole lot more interest in eating veggies and fruits if they had a hand in planting, growing, and harvesting them.

Now I had to wonder if the raised beds we'd put in three years ago, all funded through our derby team, had seen their last harvest and we just didn't know it at the time.

I knocked on her open door. "Mrs. Rutledge, do you have a minute?"

She told me to call her Rita a million times, but it seemed weird when she'd been the director at Crossroads from my days here. Looking at her now, with the forlorn expression on her tired face, her eyes heavy with worry, I wanted to call her by her first name. I wanted the kinship she offered when she tore down that barrier.

Especially when her face told me everything I needed to know, and the news wasn't good.

We were in this together... and our ship was sinking.

"Come on in, Maisy. I expected to see you," she said as she turned and leaned on the windowsill, her hands curling over the wood.

"Then it's true?"

"I spotted Rylee outside my door at an unfortunate moment. The minute Rylee overheard me, I knew I'd screwed up, and if she was going to say anything, it would be to you." She slumped even more at the admission. "That little girl adores you. You're the first person who's managed to earn her trust again."

I waited her out and didn't say anything. Couldn't say anything past the ache throbbing in my chest.

"I'm sorry," she said, scrubbing a hand down her weary face.

"What happened?"

"Budget cuts. Assholes who only see dollars, not hearts. If we don't have a waiting list to get into the program, we're not worth funding. All of the above maybe. I don't know. The official word is budget cuts and without an infusion of cash, the program isn't worth saving."

My skin grew hot as anger streaked through me with how callously faceless suits could discard children. The same people who'd used the success of this program as a feather in their conceited little caps for years at church, brunches, and during their golf game, as though they had a hand in what we built here when we're the ones who did the real work. "Fuck that shit."

Rita's lips twitched and she shook her head, but tears welled in her eyes. "Fuck that shit is right."

My past, my present, the memories made, the ones I thought would come to be, they tried to slip away with the news, destined to become fond recollections and lost connections if I didn't do something, but fuck if I knew how to fix this.

I walked over and wrapped my arms around the woman who'd been one of the constants in my life since my mom died. "What can I do?"

She clung to me, her sniffles just making the situation more real. "Unless we find the money to fund the program to the tune of fifty thousand a year, I just don't see a way to turn this around."

I let her go, snatched a tissue from her desk, and handed it to her. "Will you lose your job?"

"No. There are other community programs they'll have me focus on. Basically, they'll shuffle me off to the same place they shuffle the money. Bastards. They'll make me handle budgets using the same cash they're taking from my program without one worry for the kids they'll hurt by shutting us down."

"How long do we have?"

"The end of March. I may be able to get them to stretch it a month, but after that… we're done. They want to use the rest of this year's funds to change over to whatever the hell they intend to do. The kids will go into a few after-school programs, but during the summer—I just don't even want to think about it. They rely so heavily on us then, between the meals, summer school needs for those who are behind, escaping troubled homes. We know there are more than a few of those."

A throb started in the front of my skull as I struggled to hold back tears of frustration. I hated crying, and I knew I had one little girl out there who'd be watching my face when I left, searching for clues to her fate.

At least they weren't angry tears. I hated letting anyone have enough power to drive me to rage crying.

But these tears hurt. They lodged in my throat and made my chest ache. I grabbed a tissue, dabbed my eyes, and fanned my face.

"You didn't see me cry, Mrs. Ru—Rita."

"Well, look at you, you finally did it. You finally called me by my name."

"Yeah, well, I needed you smiling. So smile. Because if you keep crying, I'm going to keep crying, and Rylee is going to be onto both of us."

"We're equals now," she whispered as she took my hands.

"Yes, and we don't have much time." I blew out a rough breath and squeezed her fingers reassuringly before letting them go. "Okay. I'm calling a team meeting, and we're going to figure something out."

"I love you girls so damn much, but don't get your heart set on saving this. Really. It's a lot of money, and the people in this town don't have a lot to spare."

For a split second a weird shift rippled through me, like any last part of me who spent time with these kids only to play, faded into the background and thrust me into true adulthood where worries loomed.

I'd take the responsibility, but hell if I'd let the shift snatch away the fun parts. I wouldn't let it. I'd be the bridge between responsibility and fun. I just needed a crash course on tightropes. Hopefully my good balance would give me a leg up. "No, but I'm willing to squeeze every last person who does," I promised as I headed for the door while my eyes were dry again.

"Yes, well, squeezing people means unexpected piles of shit too, so wear boots."

I laughed, the tightness easing in my chest when I did. "Good advice."

"Maisy?"

Holding the edge of the door, I turned back to her. "Yeah."

"I just want you to know, the time you've spent here with us giving back, working with you after seeing you go through this program yourself—it's been the highlight of my career."

I crossed the room and hugged her hard one last time. "Thank you… but wipe your eyes and prepare to be here for a good long time. We're not going down without one hell of a fight."

"Patti said the drinks are on her tonight, but we've got work to do so don't let it go straight to your head," I told my team as I settled in and straddled my chair.

Almost every player managed to break away and meet me at Banked Track to brainstorm how to save Crossroads. Of course, with everyone here, this left them squeezed into the corner booth made for ten.

They had a couple choices—keep their arms pinned next to them or arms resting straight out on the table.

One choice was a waste of perfectly good free alcohol. We couldn't have that.

I made sure to pick a chair.

After sex-on-skates Priest whipped me into a tizzy with the way he commanded a roller rink, only to be plummeted off a cliff with a devastating blow an hour later at Crossroads, I needed to find my mellow or I wouldn't sleep tonight.

The tears had broken free again when I left the youth center, so I called Patti from the road. I know, I know, hands-free laws, but I made sure to pull over before I dialed and put her on speaker. I had to pull over anyway because trying to see through tears was like trying to find the road in a downpour with no wipers.

Patti had mercy on my pathetic, sobbing, snotting soul and saved the corner booth and the surrounding tables so we could have an emergency meeting. She even helped me get ahold of the entire team, strong-arming them to be here at seven.

Free booze worked wonders. Her idea of strong-arming. The idea was brilliant, really.

"Look at her just handing out alcohol like lollipops," Carmen said, raising a glass toward the bar. "She's the first person to hit up for a donation."

"Wait!" Rory screeched, shooting out of her chair and throwing up a hand between Carmen's puckered lips and her first sip. "I know a bunch of you aren't familiar with the tradition, but let's not jinx this. Maisy… toast!"

"That's just for games," I said, waving off her suggestion. How I ever got into these toasts, I'd never know, but after five or so years, I was rapidly running out of material.

"And you don't think this situation has epic battle written all over it?" Marty said with a snort. "You better toast us. Why risk the bad juju?"

"Fine…" I caught a glimpse of Priest hanging his jacket under the counter before taking a seat at the edge of the bar closest to the exit.

Another sweater.

Another pair of blue jeans.

Another pair of boots.

Another insistent throb of my c-bone.

Flaming asshole.

I really wanted to hold on to that.

But he wasn't. Or he was, but just not in the certified 100% USDA beef kind of way.

I stood and held out my drink. "To fast skates, hard

abs, great hands, powerful jaws… oh, and you know what, another shout-out to that straight piece in Tetris." I gulped down a generous amount of my drink, hissed at the burn, and opened my eyes to find my whole team staring at me, their drinks untouched.

I froze. "What?"

"What the hell kind of toast was that?" Eve sneered.

"Hey! People still play Tetris." I dropped into my seat again and glanced away from her. Not because she put me on the spot, but because the bulldog possessive energy coming from her had me dreading the confrontation looming on our horizon.

I had no intention of burdening the team with our shit. Hell, I didn't think we had shit, but apparently if the first person I was interested in dat—nope.

If the first person I found hot—wow… really not better —set her off this way, we had a problem.

A big fucking problem.

Mutual parting of ways, my ass.

"She's not talking about Tetris, you hussy," Rory said with a smirk.

"She's talking about that quick eye fuck you aimed at Priest and then all but toasted to his attributes," Marty pointed out.

I itched to turn around and glance at him again because my hormones had stellar fucking timing. "Noticing someone walking through the door is eye fucking them now?"

"The way you just did it? Yeah," Zara squeaked, her eyes wide. "I mean, that was evidence for a restraining order right there."

"Whatever."

"What's up with you two?" Rory asked.

"Nothing."

"This is the second time we've been sitting in this spot with your vag vibrating in his proximity," Eve said, slamming her glass on the table. "That's not nothing."

Carmen's gaze darted back and forth between our core crew. "Shit, I need to make time for these meetups because I'm missing way too much of the good stuff."

"Yup, same here. The minute my college classes are done, I'm never missing a Banked Track night again. I don't care if I'm so sick I have the shits. I'll wear diapers," Dixie said, raising her glass before finally taking her first sip.

The conversation about Priest died on that particular picture so I took the opportunity to steer the direction back to the point of our emergency meeting.

"Okay, guys… let's focus. Money. We need to squeeze money out of the people in this town."

Marty nodded toward the bar. "Patti's in for 10K."

I choked on my drink and wiped my mouth as it dribbled down my chin, my gaze shooting to the woman in question as I stood up. The minute I opened my mouth, she slammed the cash register shut and aimed a determined finger in my direction.

"Shut it, child. You'll take my money, and I won't hear another word. You know what, you'll take it again next year too. Just consider it a standing donation for the next, say, five years. We'll reevaluate after that."

Priest's eyebrows furrowed, turning to slashes over cool, dark eyes with what seemed like permanent irritation—well, other than when he had skates on his feet—but his lips quirked with amusement at Patti's words.

He should see a doctor about the two moods of his face.

"She told you," Marty said.

"Focus. What kind of cash do we have to come up with?" Sean asked.

"Fifty grand and that's just for a year. After that we have a revolving funding issue," I sighed. My phone vibrated on the table and started to slide toward the edge. I flipped it over, noticed the same bullshit number, and turned the ringer off.

"Guess we should cancel that girls' trip to the exhibition. We can pool the money we were going to use into this," Marty said.

Rory shrugged, her gaze locked on the pattern she'd begun swirling over the table with her fingernail. "I can manage without the vacation, but that's not going to come close to putting a dent in what we need."

"Too bad we didn't do banked track; we could register and go for the prize. That would keep the youth center going for a few years," Marty said.

The conversation died as we all took keen interest in our drinks all of a sudden. A few sips later, a swelling silence took hold with a life of its own, followed by furtive glances, no one really wanting to be the first one to admit to actually considering the idea.

"How hard could it really be?" Zara asked.

"Pretty damn hard when we don't even have a banked track to practice on. Even under the best of circumstances —which these aren't—we're dead in the water," Eve pointed out. She always had to come in like gangbusters and pop a squat on hope.

Okay, maybe that was my irritation talking. Maybe Eve was just the realistic one and I was the dreamer.

"How much are they to buy?" Zara asked.

"You're kidding, right?" Eve said with a snort. "Probably pretty damn expensive, and then you need room to set one up."

"Sid's Aviation would totally let us set it up there if we had one," Sean chimed in.

"If… and according to my search," Marty said, holding up her phone. "They cost almost as much as one year running Crossroads so we can just get that idea right out of our heads."

"It was a pipe dream anyway. We need real ways to capture dollars in a town where bake sales, auctions, and spaghetti suppers rule. That kind of shit is great, but not for the kind of money we're looking for. We aren't trying to fill a piggy bank, for fuck's sake," Rory said.

Zara nodded toward the bar. "Patti used to do banked track… maybe she knows where there might be one."

"Nothing is near here and I would have thought if there was one we would have heard about it by now. Even if there was one in Boston, you're talking a four-hour drive," I said.

"And we have no experience, guys. Seriously, a few weeks on a banked track, even if we could find one to practice on, it's not going to be enough to have a shot. And who would coach us?" Sean asked.

"Maybe Patti would," Zara said.

"Except she's got a business to run. Listen, I love Patti and all, but she's already spending too much time here. She's been stretched thin with the holidays coming and the extra crowds, covering shifts when bartenders don't show. I've tried to be available to help, but sometimes by the time I get here, she's wrung out," Rory said, casting a worried glance at Patti behind the bar.

I spied Patti over my shoulder, taking in everything. She leaned over the counter, attitude in her cocked hip and crooked grin. But if I looked closely, really looked, I spotted the way her smile slipped a little too soon, the way she rubbed at her temples, and the slump of her shoulders as she pulled on tap handles, filling beer orders.

Patti could offer knowledge, but when it came to hours wrangling a derby team, she just wouldn't be up to it. Not that I'd ever dare say the words outright.

If she caught wind that I even noticed a hint of exhaustion on her face, she'd mount my ass over the bar with her derby memorabilia.

"We need to think realistically, guys. Let's start with sponsorships from our employers. Maybe we can get something going there, especially when we tell them that Patti is putting up 10K for the cause. They might just follow suit," I said.

"It's worth a shot, but this is a hard time of year with Christmas coming in a couple of weeks. But maybe we get them excited about some last-minute tax deductions?" Rory said with a glance at Marty.

Marty stopped tapping her fingers on the table and shrugged. "It's worth a shot."

We spent the next hour making a list of employers and agreed to check in with one another tomorrow to determine if we were getting any nibbles.

One by one we said our goodbyes after our first round. No one wanted to reject Patti's offer of free drinks for the night, but none of us felt right about taking advantage either.

For a few minutes, at least... while we made the list, a buzz of excitement hummed over our group.

We could do this. We had a starting point.

By the time the list was made, and we all stared down at it, the buzz had morphed into the worry settling over us. Like we all knew this might be our only decent shot.

None of us mentioned the obstacles with our plan. How some companies had a process for this and getting an answer could take months or longer. Time the kids didn't have.

This was it. We had no plan B.

I took a trembling breath.

When you didn't have a plan B, you ended up at the mercy of others. You ended up packing your meager belongings and piling them high in the trunk and back seat of a rusted-out sedan.

With no plan B, your mother tells you this is another adventure. New places. New people.

She tells you that you'll love a new school.

You'll have a blast making new friends.

But really, your stomach gnaws on itself in the dark while you try to keep yourself from throwing up the generic SpaghettiOs you had three hours before.

You force a smile.

You pretend to be asleep so you don't have to lie about being excited.

When really, you're one mile closer to the unknown and one mile farther from that little girl who thought she might have finally convinced her mom to let you sleep over. The girl you didn't dare tell your mom about until you knew for sure.

The girl who didn't matter now, because you'd never see her again.

My heart raced in my chest. A wave of dizziness cascaded through me.

"Hey, you okay?" Marty asked. She'd been trapped in the middle of the booth, making her the last one left.

I'd never said a bad word about my mother. I'd never confessed to anyone how many times she broke my heart. I loved her so damn much. Even after all these years without her, the thought of saying anything that stained her memory cut me to the core.

So I smiled, and I buried it.

And I focused on what I had the power to change. Right now, that meant saving the program for the kids. For Rylee. "Yeah, I'm good. Just tired."

"You've had a rough day. You should go get some sleep."

"I will. I just want to check in with Patti first."

"Okay." Just a few steps away, Marty turned back to me. "Maisy… you should probably have a talk with Eve. I thought she was fine, but with all of this—with whatever might be happening with you and anyone else—she's not fine."

"I know," I said quietly, trying to ignore Priest in the background watching us.

"If you need to talk, just hit me up." Marty smiled and turned for the door again.

But I didn't see her leave.

I only saw him.

I took a seat at the bar, several stools away from his penetrating stare.

Needing a minute.

Just a damn minute.

"That was fast… how did it go?" Patti asked, stopping in front of me and slapping her bar towel over her shoulder before she started scooping ice into a highball glass.

"Not great, but not horrible. Depends on how good we'll be at talking our bosses out of their money."

"Well, that sounds about as fun as a root canal. Give me just a second, honey, and we'll talk about it."

"Sure." I studied the black and white images over the bar of Patti in her heyday. It was the action shot all the way to the right, with her arms thrown wide, hair billowing out from under the hideous cap helmets they used to wear, when they chose to wear helmets, and her feet midair as she jumped over a pile of fallen skaters that called to me.

My favorite shot.

The look on her face—hungry, determined, and—fulfilled. With old-school classic white roller skates on her feet laced only halfway to give them more flex. Barely any knee pads or elbow pads to be seen, and the ones who did have them? They were nothing more than bulkier material like what you'd see from a thin winter jacket. As for gloves? What the hell were those?

How much skin did they leave on those banked tracks anyway?

The black and whites left me wondering the color of their polyester shorts and shirts. I'd put my meager earnings on orange, olive green, and brown, some of the less fortunate color combos of the seventies.

Only now did I notice how little Patti talked about the details from those days. Sure, she told stories about getting fancied up in rockabilly clothes, their hair up in pompadours with barrel curls and bandanas. She fondly bitched about the painstaking accuracy needed to execute the perfect exaggerated winged eyeliner and red lips for photo shoots and tours.

But when it came to the down and dirty, when the sweat dragged streaks of mascara down their flushed cheeks, their scuffed uniforms hiding the bruises and track kisses, she let her legacy live in a series of eight pictures hanging over fancy liquor bottles.

Frozen moments in time when women balanced on the cruel hand dealt to them of being paraded around in all the trappings of pageantry. Those stolen moments their only opportunity to command attention long enough to show their power, hunger, and resilience on the track.

They made so much out of a sport with so damn little and virtually no control.

Drawn back to the one picture, my eyes caught on something, something I'd never noticed before.

I narrowed my eyes and leaned in struggling to make out the details.

Black metal piping climbing up exposed brick in the background.

I blinked and blinked again. The pieces in my head sliding together.

Glancing in the direction of the door of Banked Track just past Priest's shoulder, the same kind of piping running up the same kind of exposed brick.

The same kind or the same?

The voices in the bar became a dull hum in the background as I leaned in for a better glimpse.

And found a familiar face.

My ears burned and my stomach fluttered.

A familiar wool cap.

Adrenaline surged through me as my focus narrowed down to one single point.

It couldn't be.

Pushing my drink aside, I scrambled onto the bar and leaned in closer.

Holy shit.

He was decades younger, but I'd know that crooked grin in the front row of the crowd along the edge of the picture anywhere.

Milton.

"Hey, young lady, no shenanigans in my bar!" Patti said as she hurried over.

I looked down to find an irate Patti glaring up at me. "Where was the banked track you played on?"

She glanced at the wall and back at me. "Right here, girlie. Now scoot off my bar, thank you very much. You're a health hazard up there. I won't have you messing with my A rating," she muttered with a huff.

But I didn't move. "You played here? In this very room?"

"Sure did. You can still see the scuffs in the wood floor from the support beams," Patti said, glancing down at her feet, stomping her purple Doc Martens against a deep groove cut into the wood. "Now are you going to get off my damn bar and tell me what in the hell is wrong with you? You sure as hell aren't drunk, you only had one drink."

"I know how we can get the money for Crossroads. Where was your practice track?" Goosebumps raced over my skin as excitement, hope, the makings of a damn miracle bloomed in my chest.

Patti leaned in and propped her hands on the bar. "We practiced here."

My breath stuttered in my throat. "There's no other track?"

"I didn't say that," Patti said, her lips twitching, her gaze sliding over to Priest. "Seems like I remember there being one more around these parts."

Priest glowered at the two of us, slapped his beer on the bar, and dragged his thumb along his bottom lip, his eyes narrowed in a one hundred percent I-think-the-fuck-not-glare. "No."

I slammed down a stack of cash, snatched my jacket, and stomped out of Banked Track, leaving Mayhem on her hands and knees on the bar.

I figured I had about ten seconds tops before she scrambled off and chased me down.

Ten seconds to get to the parking lot, get in my truck, and get the fuck out of here.

And never come to town again.

My breath billowed before me, illuminated by the dull glow of streetlamps in the inky darkness of the frigid night. I pounded down the sidewalk, the image of her voracious eyes combing over Patti's pictures playing through my head.

My amusement at her climbing clean up on the counter swept away by an avalanche of bitterness for what they asked of me even without saying the words.

The bitterness of what I couldn't give them.

But damn, I wanted to.

Too much.

I'd stay at the farm. I'd pay whoever I had to pay for grocery delivery. We'd survive, we could just call it quality time… so much quality, Lilith would be ready to murder me, but then my nephew would be born, Jordan would get home, and I'd be on my way out of town.

"Hey!"

Six damn seconds.

I kept my pace as I whipped around, only to find her chasing me down in that sweater.

That. Fucking. Sweater.

My pulse pounded in my ears. My nostrils flared with the ragged breath I sucked into my lungs.

It didn't even cover her shoulders and the temperature had mercilessly dropped into the low twenties the minute the sun disappeared over the horizon. By now, we'd plummeted to the teens.

I jabbed a finger in the direction of the bar. "Get your ass inside."

She skidded to a stop, propped her hands on her hips, and arched an eyebrow.

I knew that look. Every man on the planet knew that look and all the variations whether it be aimed with stunning precision at them from a girlfriend, a sister, a mother, or a grandmother. "Excuse me?"

"You don't have a jacket," I said, marching back to her, my hands curled into fists because fuck if I didn't want to haul her ass off somewhere warm and private.

Only I couldn't trust myself alone with her. Warm and private meant giving in and tearing off every last shred of clothing so I could fuck her until neither of us could stand.

Glowering down at her, I put every bit of anger and frustration into the force of my words, not caring if they hurt her, because they were the only way to save us from absolute disaster. "Get. Your. Ass. Inside."

Better to hurt her now before the stakes got higher.

Before feelings got involved.

Look at me pretending like they hadn't already.

We'd been nothing but feelings since our eyes met during her bout. We'd been adding good old-fashioned dry logs to that flame ever since, building the kind of heat that didn't flash and die, but simmered, building a base of coals so damn hot it reached into the shadowed recesses of our lives.

"Not until you agree to help us." Her chin wobbled as she shivered before me. She clamped down her teeth, but the telltale tremble of them trying to chatter in the blistering cold remained.

"Goddammit." I yanked my jacket off, wrapped it around her, and held it together so she couldn't shrug it off. "I'll walk you home. Which way?"

She tried to yank away from me. "I don't need you to walk me home; I need you to train us on your track."

I curled my fists tighter into the soft leather, shaking her with every bit of resentment coursing through me, making her rock on her heels before holding her steady. "No."

"Why not?"

"You damn well know why not." I growled. There's no way she didn't know.

And the fact that she did made it damn near impossible to look her in the eye at times.

"You didn't do it," she said quietly. "What they say about you. You didn't do it."

The calm confidence of her words only fueled a dormant rage, now burgeoning inside me again since waking up the minute I rolled into Galloway Bay. I wouldn't stand here while she looked at me with softness, caring, the hushed tone of her voice reverent, like I was some kind of hero.

Not when all I had was a legacy of mistakes that brought others pain.

I tugged her against me. "You don't know a damn

thing about what I did or didn't do," I said, seething with the fine edge of anguish cutting through me. "What I've cost the people I love."

My gaze dropped to her full pink lips and I closed my eyes. Her mouth wasn't mine to taste, should never be mine to taste, and if I took, it would only prove what a selfish bastard I really was. "You'd do good to trust your instincts about me, Mayhem."

She turned her face up to mine. Unflinching, she stared me straight in the eye without so much as a blink. Full of stubbornness and ready for confrontation, she took me head-on. "The funny thing is, I do," she said with quiet finality. "I know who I saw on that rink today. That wasn't a man who'd put an underage girl at risk just to win."

Her eyes dropped to my mouth and I fought the urge to waver. I hung my head and turned away from her, away from temptation.

How many more times would I scour my soul and find scraps of shredded honor before I ran out completely?

"You didn't do it. I don't know why you don't shout it from the damn rooftops. I don't know why you didn't defend yourself; maybe it's time to—"

I pierced her with a scowl. "Leave it alone." I bit out the words in harsh warning. Fury pounded in time with the ripple of my beating heart.

"If that's really what you want, I won't speak of it again… if you train us."

I dragged a hand down my face. She shivered even with my jacket around her; meanwhile, I was all but positive steam billowed off my shoulders.

"You're freezing."

"I'm fine."

"Which way?" I asked, the first stirrings that I might waver trying to take hold.

She yanked away from me and hopped onto the threshold of the door leading to the small second-floor apartment over Banked Track. "There. You walked me home. Happy?"

"Hardly. Now go inside."

She leaned her shoulder against the doorframe like she planned to settle in for a while. "Train us."

"No."

"I won't leave you alone until you agree."

I rubbed the back of my neck, doing anything I could to keep myself from reaching for her. I still didn't know if I put my hands on her if I'd throttle her or kiss her. I was equally worried about both. "You haven't left me alone for a single second since I saw you on that track a week ago."

"I need you to train us. Please," she said, the plea in her voice softer, more desperate.

"I can't."

"Why not?"

"For her whole life, my sister has had one dream. Living here. Raising her family at the farm. If this goes bad, they pay the price."

"What if it doesn't go bad? Did you ever think about that?"

"It always goes bad. If you knew me, you'd know that. But you don't know me, Mayhem. One afternoon at a roller rink doesn't change that."

Fire snapped in her eyes. "So, what about that? What about the kids you met today? My family," she said, jabbing a thumb into her chest. "What happens to them when they lose the one safe place they have? How are you going to feel when that happens and you had the power to help them, but you were too damn scared to do anything about it?" Every word grew more and more raw until her voice broke.

"I'm not scared."

"The fuck you're not," she snapped.

The last of my control fractured and I stepped into her, my hand cupping her jaw, forcing her to look up at me. "You and that foul mouth. Someone should have done something about that a long time ago."

How the hell was I supposed to say no to her? To this woman who loved those kids.

A woman who couldn't bear to throw away a frayed green shoelace because it was the last connection she had to her mother.

She raised her chin even more, despite my hold. Slim fingers wrapped around my wrist, drew my hand down, until my hand settled at her throat.

Her warm, soft, tempting throat.

"Show me someone strong enough to."

My fingers flexed, squeezing the column of her slim, inked neck. Defiance flamed in her eyes and I wondered how far she'd let me go.

She fucked with my head.

She fucked with my heart.

She fucked with everything I believed about myself.

Everything I needed to believe about myself.

She turned the new normal I found upside down and threatened everyone and everything I worked so hard to protect.

I turned the knob to the door and backed her into the dark landing at the foot of the stairs. I pictured her apartment up there, a tiny space I'd helped Patti clean up almost twenty years ago now.

This girl, the one who clung to nostalgia so fiercely she kept a broken lace in an old skate would have turned it into her own utopia. She'd cherish the quirks of register heat and rough plank floors gouged with the scars from the past.

And she'd leave every last inch of the space every bit as touched as it had been before she made it hers.

"No witnesses. See? I called it, you're scared," she panted out. Fire glittered in her eyes, the breathless words sliding from her lips taunting me, despite the power I wielded with the hold I had on her.

"Shut up." I backed her up to the wall, with my hand locked on the vulnerable spot where her neck met her jaw. Her blood pumped heavy under her delicate skin, her rapid pulse fluttering under my pinky.

"Make me."

Oh how she gleefully taunt me judging by the smirk on those bare, pink lips. She instinctively knew which buttons to push and she did so without hesitation. Without an ounce of self-preservation.

The brazen little shit.

I crushed my mouth to hers, the kiss every bit as raw and punishing as it was seductive. I plundered the warm places behind those sharp teeth I wanted her to sink into me.

My hands spread over each side of her head, my fingertips spearing into her hair, holding her under me, giving her no escape.I took and took, stealing her breath for my own, exploiting her willing mouth.

I needed her to steal it back. To be selfish. To push me away. Anything.

As long as she didn't give.

Don't give one damn part of yourself to me.

She reached for me then, a low groan rumbled in her throat. The vibration trembled along my palm and my cock jerked in response. My jacket slid from her shoulders as her palms crawled up my chest, burning a trail along the way as though she had her hands on my bare skin.

Her fingers plunged into my hair, breaking the hold I had on her, her nails scraping my scalp, pulling me in until I didn't know if I was the one wielding the power anymore.

"You want a confession, Mayhem?" I said as I tore my mouth from hers, my lungs heaving as I dragged my lips along the curve of her jaw, to the soft spot just behind her ear.

"Yeah, I'm scared," I admitted, biting the soft flesh of her neck, making her hiss.

"Of this." I licked her skin, memorizing her taste, making her gasp.

"Of you." I dragged my teeth over the rise of her collarbone, the sound of her jagged breath echoing in my head.

"Of me." Dragging her sweater lower, I pressed a series of hot kisses over the curve of her shoulder, her fingernails carving into my skin as she sank her fingertips deeper into my flesh.

"Of what this thing between us will unleash," I said as I returned to her wet mouth. Her eyes fluttered closed and I swallowed the moan that slipped from her lips.

I seduced us both with hot, deep glides of my tongue along hers. Pinning her to the wall with every grind of my hips against her belly, my cock desperately tried to soothe an impossible ache. My hands traced over the skin underneath her sweater, my thumbs finding the curved undersides of her breasts.

I glided my thumbs back and forth, afraid to go further, mustering a shred of willpower so I didn't haul her up the stairs and plunder inside her the way my body demanded.

The soft sound of her sigh whispered through me as the fight shifted and changed.

As I handed her the power to my surrender, praying she wouldn't use it against me.

"I need you," she confessed in a broken whisper against my mouth. "Please. These kids won't have anywhere to go. I won't have anywhere left to go."

She tore her mouth away and dropped her forehead to my chest, her words muffled, but no less desolate. "Don't you get it? Crossroads saved me when my mom died. It still saves me in a town where I have no roots. No family. Nothing of my own. And nowhere in this world to go."

Her words twisted into my heart and echoed there. There was no way out. No right choice.

Don't do it. Don't do it. Don't do it.

"Dammit," I said quietly as I wrapped my arms around her to keep her warm.

To keep me warm.

To hold on as our lives collided and everything spiraled out of control.

Pressing my lips to the top of her head, my heart slammed against my ribs—not with the lust building between us that finally bubbled over, but with dread.

Cold, sharp barbs hooking into tender flesh dread.

"Does that mean yes?" she asked, her arms tightening around me and her fingers curling into the back of my sweater.

"Yeah." I sighed and nodded against the top of her head. "Yeah."

She let out a shuttering breath, relaxing in my arms.

Time to let go.

But I didn't. I couldn't. Instead, my hand defied the logic in my head and curled under her hair, cradling her in my palm while I kissed her temple and breathed in her sweet scent.

She turned her face into me, her lips right there,

hovering just a breath away from mine. "One more thing," she murmured.

"What?" I whispered as I traced her bottom lip with my thumb.

She sighed over my skin and I forgot to breathe. "If you're not the enemy and we're not friends... what is this?"

I laughed, the sound completely devoid of any humor as a lump of fear lodged in my chest right by the part of my heart she'd managed to grip in her tight little fist without knowing it. I brushed her lips with mine, lingering there, not knowing when I'd have her in my arms again.

If I'd have her in my arms again.

I found her lust-filled eyes and held her unfocused stare. "Post-apocalyptic Galloway Bay in the making. Without a doubt."

CAIN

Two days passed since that night at Banked Track. Since the kiss I could still taste even now. Since I caved.

I caved so fucking hard.

While Mayhem convinced her team to put their trust in me, I'd been gathering every last bit of information I'd need, starting with thick stacks of session plans both for flat track and banked track derby I hadn't laid eyes on in ten years.

I hardly used them at the time. I didn't need to. I'd been so immersed in the sport, the components of the game moved like fluid pieces in my head, shifting and changing with new circumstances.

Between playing banked track on my own and coaching flat track, I could easily shift from one to the other.

But a decade had passed since then. Rules changed. Requirements changed. As I stared out at the sea of notes scattered across my grandmother's dining room table, I wondered if I'd be able to pull this off.

If they'd be able to pull this off.

This was the one and only time I got to linger in doubt. The minute the team showed up, I was all coach mode. I knew just how I'd get when I got into the infield again, the echo of skates reverberating from under the bank, the grunts, and shouts.

I'd become the bastard they hated to need.

They'd resist. They'd challenge me.

I would break down their defiance until they complied.

Then I'd build them back up.

That was the only choice with the little time we had.

They'd be going against some of the best. Skaters that practically live on a banked track. They know every bump, every angle, the shift in their center of gravity no longer even a blip on the radar for them.

And they'd look at Beautifully Brutal and laugh.

Flat track derby trying to make a mark on banked track? My team would be the interlopers. The team swooping in thinking they could invade banked track territory and take the prize.

Their competitors would be downright merciless.

But they would also dismiss them.

I was counting on it.

Their mistake would be the key to a shot at victory.

They'd never expect a flat track team to skate into a banked track exhibition and have a chance.

They wouldn't have information on Beautifully Brutal going in. As an amateur league, there'd be little to find. Not yet being members of the WRDF would work in our favor.

Their competitors would have no history to go on. No video footage. No way of knowing my team's bad habits, weaknesses, or strengths. No hints of the dynamic between the players.

And those were the shadows my team had to operate in.

I had attitudes to curb.

I had personal weaknesses to hammer out.

And a love triangle.

A first for me.

Only I would end up dealing with a love triangle as one of the three.

I shouldn't have kissed her. I knew I shouldn't have kissed her even as I continued attacking her mouth like a damn starving man, every slide of our tongues tasting, taking, plunging deeper while tucked away in that hallway chasing away the shivers racking her body until we both burned.

No doubt Eve would see the change. The minute we all shared the same space, she'd home right in on the tension now a raging bonfire.

Mayhem might have thought whatever she had with Eve was over, but for Eve... not so much. She had a tight grip.

Time would tell if she was going to march that possessiveness onto the track, forcing me to face it head-on, or if she'd find the maturity to set it aside.

We had a month to get ready and Christmas coming in a little more than a week. Big plans? Too bad. Canceled. They could open a few presents and eat Christmas dinner. Other than that, if they weren't at work, their asses needed to be on the track, starting with scrimmages to get them adapted to the bank.

They'd have to learn everything all over again. All of their footwork, slides, stops, jumps, control, crossovers, and dozens of other skills—everything had to be practiced hundreds, maybe thousands of times until their bodies forgot the flat track and only reacted to the bank.

I reached out to a few people I knew from my early days and got the details of the exhibition. The rule set they'd follow, the condensed bouts used for elimination rounds on day one, and the format for the final rounds on day two.

Two days.

That was it.

We had one month to train for an exhibition so aggressive it was capable of breaking down even the most seasoned banked track player.

Mayhem texted me—because apparently we did that now—to let me know that the team was on board and they'd be ready to start tomorrow.

That gave me today to make sure the track was ready. I'd inspected it before closing it, just like my grandfather taught me, but that had been a decade ago.

Ten years in an old dairy barn with the fluctuation in temperature and humidity meant I had work to do.

I brushed away the cobwebs along the switch and flicked on the lights hanging in rows along the support beams crisscrossing the ceiling. Almost as cold inside as it was outside, the track lay there barren and silent, covered with a couple dozen silver tarps.

It'd take the whole day to get it ready, but at least I'd flop into bed exhausted to the core tonight.

Maybe then I'd stop playing our kiss through my head.

I'd settle for my cock to stop twitching. Fucking Jackson cursing me with that poppin' bone shit.

I walked the perimeter of the barn, starting each of the four jet force kerosene heaters and making note of their fuel levels. I'd need them for at least six hours a day, a pace I expected the team to protest.

Too bad. They needed my help, not the other way around.

They'd get it my way or no way.

I'd also need an additional hour of fuel before practice to get the temperature to a tolerable level, especially while competing against the cold blasting through the open windows in each corner for ventilation.

I stopped in the front office, if you could call it an office, and left what I salvaged from old scrimmages. The room wasn't much, but with tables along two walls and a lone chair, I'd make it work. I didn't plan to park my ass in there for long anyway.

If my team was going to be uncomfortable, so was I.

I'd be in the infield… and on the track.

Dragging along my grandfather's cart from where he left it tucked in the corner, the familiar squeak of protest from the back left wheel had a smile tugging at my mouth. Piled high with nuts, bolts, tools, and a checklist, I got to work.

You've got to check everything, son, all the panels from the bastards, to the turns, and straightaways, and when you've done that, you get right down to the nuts and bolts. Nothing but the best for your grandmother. You hear?

I'd swear, even though he'd been in the ground for almost seventeen years, he'd stood here with me through every single moment.

In person and in spirit.

Through the good and bad.

One at a time I peeled off the tarps, dust billowing into the air before settling back down again on the concrete floor. After I folded them, I stacked them on shelves along the back wall.

Hours upon hours of memories with my family echoed in this place. The first time I ever put on skates and got on a banked track had been right here with my grandmother. Small but strong and unbelievably fast, she continued to skate well into her seventies. She spent time every day out on this track for at least an hour, claiming the exercise kept her young.

From the onset, she'd started me out racing her. After a few months I finally got fast enough to blast past her out of the first turn.

Then our mother died.

When she did, I took my sorrow out on the Masonite track. No more races. Instead, she stood on the infield, her keen eye never leaving me. Like she sensed the bitterness in me bubbling to a dangerous flash point.

They're orphans now.

I overheard the words, hushed and muffled so I never figured out who'd said them.

We weren't orphans. We had a father.

Somewhere.

With every lap, I skated harder and faster. I shouted out every last bit of anger and misery filling me. I punished this very track for what I'd lost.

For what I'd never get back.

This track had the power to lift me up so fucking high I'd swear I could touch the angels—and the power to cut me so deep my life leeched out with every bit of sweat and streak of furious tears pouring down my cheeks.

My emotions had always gone to war in these four walls.

What emotions would I face off with this time?

With the tarps off, I started at the first of two bastard boards, directly across from one another, the center pieces of the turns on each end of the track. I studied every center bolt, every brush of my fingers over the cold metal bringing a fresh memory of my grandfather's smile and the awe in his voice when he talked about my grandmother.

She knocked me right on my keister from day one, son. Day one. I never even knew what hit me; I just knew I wanted it to hit me again.

Yeah. That sounded about right.

Mayhem.

She'd done the same to me. And here I was, working on a track for her. Just like my grandfather.

Only we wouldn't have the happy ending. She wanted to be in the WRDF and any long-term attention on her team because of me would risk their chances.

She had a goal and all I brought to the table was endless scrutiny.

And I wouldn't throw Lana under the bus to save myself. She'd paid plenty already.

My silence was the final nail in my own coffin.

Happy endings were for everyone else.

So bitter and angry, the lessons I learned in this barn—care and respect from my grandfather, fire and hunger from my grandmother—withered under the suffocating blanket of grief for my mother until it turned to poison.

I let the battle fuck with my head until tunnel vision took over, tempting me into giving my father another chance.

I told my grandmother what I wanted. What I thought was right. My words turning sour in my gut like my soul's warning. She gave me the choice, the adult choice as the older brother, the older twin. The one who'd always looked out for his siblings. She squared her proud shoulders and gave me a firm nod. "If you think it's the right thing to do, then maybe it is the right thing to do," she'd said.

Six months later, my twin dead, my father in jail, my sister screaming every night in her sleep and barely eating, we ended up back at the farm.

I never even went into the house when we arrived. I marched straight to this barn and strapped on my skates.

My grandmother didn't say a word, just followed me and waited for me to skate it out.

We had a shared demon to fight now.

Regret.

I saw it every time I looked into her eyes, and in the mirror each morning.

Eventually she put up obstacles: orange cones, buckets, stools, whatever she could find. Pushing me until the tears dried and all that was left was sweat.

Drowning in my own torment, I didn't recognize what she was doing; I just kept trying to outrun ghosts.

And when I didn't believe in myself anymore, she believed enough for both of us and cracked open the door to a family legacy which until then had only belonged to women.

She trusted me to honor the generations before me.

And she taught me banked track derby.

Every day we worked.

Covered in bruises from head to toe from laying my every emotion on the track, and still she pushed harder, faster, stronger.

Over and over she challenged me, bet me I couldn't get through. Hungry for absolution and hell-bent on proving her wrong, I'd swerve, jump, spin, and navigate my way through until I slayed every single challenge stationary objects could bring.

Leave it to my grandmother to up the ante.

Obstacles flew in from the left, from the right, foam padding in a variety of shapes and weights. Forcing me to learn how to be good on my toes, literally, and mastering speed recovery after getting through the pack or past a pileup.

My grandmother taught me how to coach.

Lilith started to wander in after a while. She never got on the track herself. She wasn't into roller-skating, the way we were, but she loved to watch, to play music, and God could the girl cheer.

Even when I didn't deserve it.

CAIN

"You want some company?" Lilith called from the open doorway.

I dropped a rusted bolt into the bucket at my feet and turned to her. For just a second, I saw that young girl. The one who'd been hurt over and over by my mistakes.

The one who learned to laugh and cheer again despite them.

I wonder what she saw when she looked at me.

I wiped the sweat from my forehead with my sleeve. "Sure."

She dragged her hands along the snaps for the skirting we'd never once put on the track. "How's it going?"

I slid a new bolt into the hole and worked on finger-tightening the nut. "It would have been better if I hadn't left it sitting here for ten years. I'll be replacing bolts for a few hours. Might need to take a run to Dawson's and grab some more."

She yanked on one of the braces going into the corner, her lips twitching. "You're really going to do this, huh?"

"Looks that way." My ratchet clicked with every rota-tion, a sound I'd always loved for some reason.

"And there's nothing I can do to change your mind?"

she asked, crossing her arms and propping her shoulder against the track.

I glanced down at her stomach, spotted the twitch of cotton under her shirt, and grinned. "He's active today."

She laughed. "He's active every day. Now answer the question."

Ahhh, so this was the part where she picked me apart. Might as well get it over with. "There are kids involved."

"And a woman from what I hear."

"Fourteen of them," I said without looking at her as I dropped another bolt in the bucket.

"Galloway Bay is only talking about one of them, though."

"Galloway Bay needs to mind its own business."

"They are."

"Yeah? How's that?" I crouched under the track to slide in another bolt. I squinted up at her as sweat trickled in my eye. "By gossiping about her or by running their mouths about me?"

"Ouch," she said with an exaggerated wince that told me my blunt assessment would do nothing to shut down her little inquiry. "I suppose both. But they're right, though? You and Maisy?"

Or Mayhem... since we weren't on a first name basis yet. I reached under and started loosening another nut on the shittiest section of the track I'd found so far.

"Is there not supposed to be a woman for me, Lilith? Ever?" My gaze snapped up to her. I swiped the sweat trickling toward my eye and grabbed another bolt.

I knew this thing between Mayhem and me was a dead end, but I sure as hell didn't need my sister who had the husband, the baby coming, and the one place that felt like home to the two of us telling me what I did and didn't have the right to.

"I'm not saying that. You know I'm not saying that," she said, her voice softening as she laid her hand on my shoulder.

Anger burned in my throat at the scathing words I swallowed. I cut her a glance that had her sliding her hand away. "So, what are you saying?"

"You forget who you're talking to. I know you won't stay."

"Well," I said, huffing out a breath, "I guess it's good she didn't ask me to."

"She's going to fall for you, you know?"

"Because I'm so irresistible?" A humorless laugh broke free. "I don't see you talking about me falling for her."

"Because I'm starting to figure out it might be a bit late for me to be worrying about that."

"I'm not in love with her," I said quietly, choking the words past the sudden lump in my throat.

I'd known her for all of five minutes. We'd been fighting four minutes and fifty-nine seconds of them.

"Maybe not all in, but you wouldn't have agreed to this if you weren't well on your way," she said with quiet confidence I normally admired, but in this moment loathed. "Is it really worth the pain?"

"Pain's kept me company for how long now? I'll be fine."

She crouched down next to me, wincing as she settled in.

Just like that, I felt like an asshole for climbing under here. "Not your pain… hers."

I thought about my first night home and the personal rivalry she battled on that track going head-to-head with Tilly.

About the mother who never returned to their room at the Beacon Motel.

The frayed green lace of her skate she didn't dare throw away.

Her desperation to save Crossroads.

"She's in pain too." I wanted to snatch the gruff declaration back. Four words that confirmed my sister's every worry.

"Oh," she said on a quiet sigh. She sucked in a breath and slapped her palms on her thighs. "Well—damn. I've run out of all judgment and sisterly warnings."

I dropped my hands to my knees and laughed. My rigid shoulders relaxed and I nudged Lilith's chin. When the hell had she become a woman? A full-blown adult woman who didn't need her big brother anymore. "Don't worry, it'll only take a few hours with me for them to realize what a bastard I am. That'll solve everything."

"They'll eventually respect you for it." She grabbed ahold of one of the supports, pushed to her feet, and started to turn.

"Lilith?"

She stopped, her gaze fixing on mine. "Hmm?"

"I won't screw up this time."

Those eyes that saw everything softened, turning sad. "You didn't screw up last time. And when it comes to our brother—"

Her words sliced into my chest, the only place I could keep my twin safe now. With him gone, the only thing I could protect was his memory. "Don't go there."

"Abel made his own choices."

Son of a bitch. "I'm the oldest."

Her hands went to her lower back where she dug her fingertips into her muscles. "By six minutes, Cain. You're the oldest by six damn minutes. You're putting how many years' worth of responsibility on six minutes?"

"Six minutes is still older. And you need off this

concrete." I nodded to the door, hoping she'd take the hint. "You should go inside."

"Yeah, well... just so you know, you're not the smartest."

"Ouch."

She cocked her head with a smug grin on her face. "Someone had to tell you."

I grinned up at her. "Point taken, Mouth."

She bent down and wiped my cheek before pressing a kiss to it. "And you're a damn good coach."

She'd never said those words. My history coaching had only inspired attitude and frustration from her—with me, with the way this town turned against me after Lana's accident, and with how I refused to help her understand.

Relief slid through me, my skin tingling with the rush, knowing that even now, after all that I'd done, the mistakes I'd made, my sister believed in me. "Thank you."

"Okay," she said, clapping her hands and rubbing them together. "Since I can't talk you out of the heartbreak you're headed for, what can I do to help?"

"Just keep my nephew in for another month while we train."

"You'll need to go to Philly with them—"

"I'm not leaving you."

"Cain, they're going to need you there."

"I said I'm not leaving." I shot her the same look I gave suspects when they took advantage of my demeanor and got mouthy. Hell, I had to keep up my skills for when I went back to Boston. Just the thought had an ache flaring to life in my chest.

"Okay, we'll talk about that part at another time—"

"Looking forward to it," I muttered.

"Hey, don't make me practice my mom voice on you."

"You don't have a—"

A knock echoed through the room, cutting off what I was about to say. I climbed to my feet, grabbed a rag, and walked around to the straightaway, my feet rooting to the spot when I saw the familiar face standing there.

"Word around town is Beautifully Brutal is training to save Crossroads," Tilly said from the door. "I want in."

Maisy

After two soul-sucking days of double shifts at The Shipwreck wrangling the families rolling into town for the impending Christmas holiday, followed by two nights spent trying to talk my team into this plan, I just wanted to lay here after my shift and bask in the Christmas lights from the two-foot tree on my end table.

I wanted to shove my face so deep in their glow I'd need sunglasses and SPF50.

Was that too damn much to ask?

I'd done so much taming of tantrums, assuaging of egos, and kissing of disgruntled ass in the past two days, I needed a therapist, a chiropractor, and an asshole bleaching kit for my mouth after all the assholes I'd had to lick to bend people to my will.

Ass licking in porn—intriguing.

Ass licking in real life thus far—unpredictable, with a bit of crunch, salty as fuck, and plagued with pesky rogue hairs.

Shut up, we've all been there.

All it took was a man too macho to consider a bit of manscaping.

An overeager thrust of his hips jamming his man wand so deep down your throat his balls try to crawl in too.

And a ball hair or three with no manners.

Next thing you know you've placed a Prime order on the Zon for mega tweezers long enough to untangle short and curlies from your uvula next time because chugging drinks didn't wash them down this time.

And really, no cocktail existed strong enough to forget they lay back there tickling your throat until they decided to have mercy on your soul and slide down.

The last short and curly I'd been forced to deal with in the past twenty-four hours came in the form of Patti's— um, well, that didn't sound right.

You know what I mean.

The woman spent two nights giving me side-eye for climbing on her bar despite sending her a slammin' edible arrangement from Crum Cakes. And I sprung for the cinnamon bun as big as her seventies hair.

But it wasn't until Mike from Dawson's Hardware tried to be funny by suggesting Patti start paying me to perform up on the bar that she turned that side-eye on him and silently declared me in the clear.

Well, I should be in the clear. This was partly her fault. I wouldn't have known there was another banked track around here had it not been for her.

Because Priest sure as hell wasn't offering up that shit.

Pulling secrets—or hell, just straight-up information out of him was like trying to drag a cat into a bathtub of water and pit bulls.

Same could be said for convincing my team to agree to work with him. The exhibition had definite appeal for them. His track did too.

As for his involvement… more than half the team gave a swift no.

But my determination had grown sharp, barbed claws hooking into the idea of his training us like a horny bitch coming out of a year-long self-imposed dry spell. She was all ravenous and shit clutching onto the idea with the enthusiasm of a horny nun given a hall pass and a ticket to Magic Mike tour.

Sister Mary Maisy didn't waste opportunities. She dug her nails into the scrumptious ass cheeks of a sweaty rock-hard dancer while she wrapped her thighs around him and squeezed him so fucking tight she tried to crack his hips like walnuts.

Basically, I'd refused to take no for an answer.

At the same time, I got it. I completely understood their trepidation.

We'd put in hundreds of hours into our compliance and application to the WRDF. Time away from our families, our friends, hours of sleep lost when we were already stretched so thin.

Plus, we had money into this.

Real money.

Money we would not get back.

With this being a mostly quiet small town, scandal had a hell of a long shelf life. There were more than a few mouths around here willing to spread the word. And it had already begun.

You'd think they had better things to do with Christmas around the corner, but nope. Fueled with festive cocktails, more family around than ever to regale with tales, and embellishments these people had injected the salacious chatter with a hulking round of steroids until it flowed as smooth as rum-spiked eggnog.

But at what point did it stop? Ten years? Clearly not.

What about twenty?

Never?

Did we really need to be worried that somehow word would get to the WRDF?

And so what if word did get to them? Were they going to deny our application based on gossip? If they were, why would we even want to become a WRDF team anyway?

Sure, we wanted to grow derby in our area and up our game play, but did we really need them to do it? If left with no other choice, why couldn't we just start our own junior leagues, recruit members, build more teams on our own?

I didn't point that part out just yet. I decided to vent my doses of reality to my team in manageable nuggets. They were already on edge. Even the people who'd readily agreed to Priest's involvement were fidgeting like they were fifteen again, storing contraband in the form of a half-naked varsity football player in their closet sporting 100% activated boy peen.

No sense in applying pressure on that constant worry because it was bad enough word had already gotten around about Crossroads coming to an end and at some point someone had overheard us talking about the charity exhibition so hope started to take root.

Now Galloway Bay had its very own raging wildfire sweeping through town.

We'd just asked a bunch of our employers for donations, but the minute word got around—the very next day—how we were going for the charity prize, those requests fell by the wayside and became the secondary focus to the glory of the underdog. Storytellers all over town had started elevating us to some weird hero status, counting on us to save all.

Guys… this was the long shot of long shots.

I hated to break it to them, but we needed our plan A *and* plan B.

We needed prayer chains, rabbit's feet, crystals, horseshoes, fuzzy dice, ladybugs, shamrocks… hell, we could use leprechauns shooting out of our butts right now, sputtering, "I'm after me lucky charms."

But fuck if I'd let doubt fall from my lips. I'd lay everything I had on that track for those kids leading up to the exhibition and all the way through it. Rylee's worried face, as real as if she were right in front of me, popped into my head and a band tightened around my chest. I shuddered out a breath.

And the image sliding into place right after… Priest's angry mouth and flashing eyes a split second before he mercilessly ate me alive.

So fucking gruff and grumpy, and when pushed, the control he clung too snapped.

My heart rolled a series of slow, hard thumps in my chest before taking off at a sprint. Heat slid through me. My skin grew hot and tight.

I pierced his complacency and when the grump surrendered all that remained was the blaze engulfing his every emotion, the bewitching flames making me want to burn too.

And that's when the stubborn man slid his hands from the vice grip he had on my jaw, flexed his fingers around my throat, and set me on fire right along with him.

Devouring me.

And I wanted to do it again. I wanted to do it naked.

There should probably be some sort of break between the images flashing through my scattered imagination. A Parental Advisory: Explicit Warning.

My flaming girl bits mobilized… good thing they came with their very own sprinkler system.

God, I was getting punchy.

I shot off the couch and glanced at the clock. Nine

minutes. I rested for nine damn minutes. If you could call the mental acrobatics I'd just gone through rest.

Jamming my feet into my boots, I grabbed my duffel and I headed out the door. If I was going to be this restless, I'd put that energy into something useful.

I took a deep breath of crisp, cold air. A few familiar locals waved, nodded, and smiled as they hurried to and from their cars into the shops on Main Street. Janice Chase, the sheriff's sister who ran the Galloway Bay library, called out just as I reached the parking lot.

"Make sure you bring in those little ones to see us. We've got brand-new books they're going to love. Oh! And we have that camp series Addison has been waiting for," she said with a wave.

"I'll try to get them in next week," I called back.

"If you can tear them away from Rockabilly's. Am I right?" Janice called back with a wink.

"Yeah." I forced out a laugh as my stomach pitched to my toes. Our issues went so much further than steering the kids away from the roller rink.

We needed to figure out how we were going to manage this training and continue our time with the kids at Crossroads.

We couldn't give up a solid month's worth of visits with them to train. It was too much for their little hearts and feelings, and with the battle ahead, we needed a constant reminder of what we were fighting for.

We needed more of the kids, not less.

Well, shit.

I fired up my car, aimed the vents away from me until my little sedan heated up, with what little heat it chugged out, and rolled out of town. Despite the sun and cloudless sky, the cool temperatures helped the snow cling to the towering pines. Blankets of white shimmered in the sun where it draped over heavy limbs.

I didn't need directions. Everyone, even a transplant like me, knew where to find Bishop Farm. Priest's family had been a fixture in this town for generations. The once-dairy farm hadn't seen cattle in decades, but now had expansive gardens that supplied local restaurants, adding to their locally grown pride. And the transformation throughout the generations hung in aged, grainy photos in various local diners, shops, and even in Banked Track.

Those gardens languished for a short time after Stella Bishop died, but before long, Lilith moved to the farm, hired help, and in three years managed to get them flourishing once again.

I knew *that* story of the Bishops.

Hell, if I knew much else. Again, that whole difficulty pulling information from the tight-ass coach. The timing of the scandal didn't help.

I'd just lost my mom.

I didn't care about anything happening in Galloway Bay; I was too busy fighting to stay.

My skin prickled as I pulled into the drive at Bishop Farm a half hour before the rest of the team.

What was it like to have this connection to a place? To people? To a town? To have generations of family, traditions, and memories to cherish when life kicked you in the tits?

And once you had it, how the hell did you ever walk away?

The two-story white house came into view. Flanked by two chimneys trickling with tufts of smoke, it stretched toward a massive red barn with the added length of additions over the years, eventually ending at the newest section —a two-story two-car garage.

Heavy green snow-covered window boxes lay empty, but spilled colorful blooms from early spring until after Halloween.

The kind of house you only saw in idyllic Christmas cards.

The kind of place you wanted to get cozy, wrap up in a quilt, and watch the snowfall outside the quiet picture window for hours.

The kind of house I'd never had.

I gulped back an embarrassing wave of longing and tightened my hands on the wheel.

I'd planned to arrive with my team to bridge the gap between their hostile wariness and his reluctance. But after a kiss that was better than all the good sex I've ever had combined—including the sex with myself—I needed to see him alone.

We had some ground rules to establish.

My tires crunched and squeaked over the snow as I pulled up next to his truck. I caught a glimpse of his Massachusetts plates, a shiny, white reminder this was temporary.

This would all be over eventually, and I'd go back to my biggest worry of keeping Milton and Gerald from killing one another, the next derby season, and building Rylee's confidence.

I should probably add building a few boundaries with Eve to that list too.

Slinging my bag over my shoulder, I eyed the open door to the barn on the hill.

"He's up there already."

I whipped around and found Lilith leaning out the screen door, the frame propped on her round belly. Her smile had been dialed to the required politeness, but the way she narrowed her eyes, her brows wrinkled as her gaze swept over me and suspicion stamped all over it.

"You're Maisy," she said. No question and not quite accusation. But salty.

"And you're Lilith."

"Cain's sister, yes."

Ahhhh, gotcha. You're something to him, I'm nothing to him, and this is you letting me know where we stand when it comes to YOUR brother. Got it.

Chilly, but then, being an outsider wasn't exactly new to me. "Well, Lilith… it was nice to meet you. I'm going to head up and get to work." I didn't wait for a reply, just tore up the ground between my car and the hill, stomping over the packed path that had been heavily sanded for traction, the roiling in my gut a familiar feeling.

Outsider.

Always an outsider.

Well, I may be an outsider, but then… so was he.

Maisy

I stopped at the door and spotted his familiar shoulders as he raced around the corner.

An outsider to his own heritage. Mistakes keeping him away from something he ached for. Keeping him away from people he'd die for.

I'd never seen a banked track in person.

Hell, I wasn't really seeing it now.

Because the man there commanded every last bit of my attention.

The track howled drowning out The Clash playing in the background with the echo of Priest's skates as he shot down the straightaways. Tucking in his shoulder, he snapped around the inside corner only to speed up down the other side.

Crouched low, his mouth hard, his eyes haunted, he leaned into his power and tore up the surface with every crossover of his feet and swing of his arms. The skates with the flames keeping up with every brutal demand to go faster from whatever he tried to outrun up there.

Because he was definitely running.

The same energy that radiated from him from where he sat in that metal folding chair, from the bar at Banked Track, from the tortured sound of his voice when he told me to get my ass back inside Banked Track the other night —the hint of desperation—it lay unveiled here.

He hadn't cared that I stood there on the sidewalk with no jacket.

He cared that I'd found a crack to burrow into. A weak spot in that aloof armor he'd clutched for a decade.

And he hated that he couldn't run.

This was what he wouldn't let others see. But it lingered behind the shimmering threadbare parts of his defense. If you turned to him fast enough, caught him off guard for just a split second—you could spot the turmoil simmering below the surface.

Here lay his safe place.

He raced around the banked track, his mask gone, a mountain of complications revealed.

I should have turned away and given him his privacy in this moment. Or at the very least, announced my presence.

But I couldn't tear my eyes away from the mysteries swirling around him. Taunting and unfinished, as though they ached to murmur truths he refused to let slip past his lips.

They wanted to be set free.

This track was his confidant, the outlet for his pain, and—his lover.

He may have abandoned it over time, but he always came back. They had secrets, the two of them. Secrets they whispered between one another with every glide of his skates over the Masonite, and I was the outsider here too.

This was more than agreeing to help a youth center survive. This was so much more than acting on mutual attraction.

These were living, breathing wounds he struggled against. There was safety in the familiar, even if it brought you excruciating pain.

When he held my face in his hands, his soul desperate to protect itself from me—from whatever was happening between us—I didn't just ask him to help us win an exhibition. I asked him to face whatever haunted him and break it wide open.

My excitement over his agreement crumbled to dust in a pile of apprehension. The weight of his yes crushed my heart where it stumbled in my chest.

And it was too fucking late to run. Whatever unmarked road we'd turned on, that fucker was one lane with grass growing up in the center, and all we could do was see where it ended up.

With rules in place.

He spotted me then. Straightening, his hands went to his hips as he coasted along the straightaway toward where I stood.

His chest heaving, sweat powering down his face, he glided to a clean stop.

"Your sister loves me."

His lips twitched and I had to remind myself that it didn't matter that I knew how his mouth tasted now. Too much was at stake.

For both of us.

"I'm sure," he said with a snort.

"We're going to be best friends." I shrugged like I didn't care what she thought of me, but I did. More than I wanted to. But only because of him. "I'm thinking we need matching bracelets."

"She'll warm up. She's—cautious."

"Seems to run in the family."

"You're early." He chugged back half a bottle of water I hadn't noticed perched on the rail ignoring my comment.

"We need to go over the rules."

He crouched down and eyed me from the bank. "We will, when everyone gets here."

"Not those rules—our rules."

"Our rules, huh?" he said with an amused chuckle. A deceptively light indicator of his mood, if it weren't for those telling eyes of his and the muscle ticking when he clenched his jaw. "And what rules would those be?"

"About kissing—"

His eyes flashed.

I forgot to breathe.

"And stuff like that." Confidence—the fickle fucker, abandoned me and the words came out as little more than a croak.

With a shake of his head, Priest wrapped his fingers round the handrails and swung out onto the concrete barn floor, all lithe and agile like he spent all day everyday just like this. His skates landed with an ominous echoing click.

"I'm all ears, Mayhem." He rolled toward me as he said it—seductively—inches at a time. All deliberate movements with that deep sexy rumble and distinct lilt telling me he was only appeasing me.

I started backing up. "We shouldn't do that anymore."

He lifted his t-shirt and ran it over the beads of sweat running down his face and temples.

Holy fucking abs. Not bare abs either. He had grown-ass man abs. Sprinkled with hair, and in this case a damp trail shooting straight into the shorts hanging low on his hips.

My internal sprinkler system heard the call. I tried not to squirm and failed miserably as I squeezed my thighs together.

"You sure?" His shoulders bunched and flexed as he continued to stalk me like prey. "You don't sound so sure." Quiet words, a question and threat all at the same time, fell

from his lips. His shoulders bunched and flexed as he continued to stalk me like prey.

"Yes—" My back hit the wall, giving me nowhere else to go, but he kept on coming, that deep dimple in his cheek I wanted to run my thumb over flirting with me the whole time. "It was great and all—

His eyebrows slashed down over narrowed eyes. "Just great?"

"You know what I mean. But since you'll be training us… "

"Mayhem, the Red Sox making it to the world series is great. Grilling ribeye to medium rare every single time, also great. But that kiss—," He stared at my mouth while he bit his bottom lip. It snapped black slowly, glistening now from where he brushed it with his tongue, "Was enough to make me forget my past while daring me to rewrite the future fate carved out for me a long damn time ago."

A tremor lanced my heart and left it hammering to a foolish beat. "That—I—But… "

"No kissing once training starts. Got it." But he moved in even closer, his hands pressing flat against the wall on either side of my head.

"What are you doing?" I asked, my voice husky and tight. His heat rolled over me, and I fought the urge to rub up against him. Damp hair in spikes, skin glazed with sweat, and I didn't care. I wanted to lick him from head to toe like a fucking ice cream cone dripping in the ninety-degree heat.

Lick, lick, lick, lick—and then bite into that creamy mass of deliciousness.

"Training hasn't started yet," he hummed, his voice low and hot.

My head thunked against the wood as I ran out of room to retreat. "But—"

He slanted his hungry mouth over mine. And just in case any part of me came to my senses, his palm slid over my hip, across my back, and straight up my spine, until his hand locked on the back of my neck. His long fingers threaded through my hair, gripping my bandana, tugging my head back.

My duffel slipped from my fingertips and my hand curled into his damp T-shirt, twisting the cotton, pulling him in for more.

I had no fucking clue how I was going to stick to my own agreement. A blend of anger, surrender, and desperation—our kiss the other night wrung me inside out, leaving me vulnerable.

Today—this kindred craving we found in the last quiet breaths before our lips met would prove impossible to ignore.

And even harder to let go of when this was all over.

Thick and hard he pushed against me, settling there, his teeth sinking into my bottom lip, delivering a distinct flash of sharp pain before following it with a purposeful swipe of his hot tongue. He let out a rough growl that had my clit throbbing in agony.

"I bet you kiss all the girls in this barn," I murmured into his hot mouth—to reel him in, to reel me in, who knew… maybe both of us.

His fingers flexed on the back of my neck while his free hand slid to the front of my throat, his thumb nudging my chin up giving me no choice but to look at him and only him.

Those fucking eyes. Always haunted. Pleading with me to run even as they begged me to stay. I would swear they were an irresistible gateway to another time, another place.

Another version of himself he kept hidden away.

"I've never kissed anyone in this barn."

Because this barn is your sanctuary and the track—your lover.

I never had a chance to breathe life into the words. He stole them when he took my mouth again, his tongue swiping at mine before retreating—until I drew it back by sucking it between my teeth.

He groaned then, his hips flexing, driving some seriously lengthy dick against me.

My eyes drifted shut and rolled back.

I bet he knew how to use every last inch of it.

"Mayhem?" he murmured against my mouth.

"Hmmm," I said before sinking my teeth into his bottom lip the way he did just moments ago.

He hissed and pressed his forehead to mine when I released the tender flesh. "I want you to remember something."

"Mmmhmmm," I hummed as I scored my nails over his chest, eliciting a hungry sound from low in his throat.

"You said you trust your instincts about me. Just remember that." He took my hand and settled my palm against his thundering heart. His ragged breath brushed my cheek as his dark eyes raked over me. "When we get started today. Remember... there's a reason for everything."

CAIN

Fourteen pairs of eyes stared back at me from my very own infield. Their temperatures ranging from thoroughly kissed slow burn to ice age deep freeze.

Eve's chilly mood came complete with ice balls lined with razor blades.

It's almost as if she knew not twenty minutes ago I had her ex-girlfriend pinned to the barn wall, her lips under mine, every inch of her front pressed against every inch of mine something neither of us were too thrilled at the idea of when I fixed her rib.

Jesus, what was I doing?

All of it. Really, what the hell was I doing?

I told myself I wouldn't touch her today. I'd convinced myself that our kiss the other night had been a mistake. Nothing more than two frustrated and desperate people taking it out on one another—and scratching an itch while we were at it.

There was no point in going down this road with Mayhem because I had a job waiting in Boston.

And she had the world to save.

I wouldn't stay.

And I wouldn't ask her to leave.

The minute I tasted her in the shadows of her dark

hallway, I wanted to taste her everywhere. I hadn't gotten every hot breath, every moan, and every dig of her fingertips out of my head since.

Now I got to face the temptation for the next month, day in, day out, hour after hour, minute after agonizing minute.

As for Mayhem's rule, it was a hell of a lot easier to follow with her team here. Really, I only had to stick to Mayhem's rules for another hour, because then she'd be sticking it to me.

They had on their gear: knee pads, elbow pads, wrist-guards—everything other than their helmets and mouth-guards—they stood ready to do this. At least physically.

But one thing I knew about this team from the one time I'd seen them in a bout. They push back when pushed.

They were going to need that.

And sometimes to their detriment. But we'd work on that.

Time to see if they had what it took to ride it out.

"Before we get started…" I glanced down at my notes. "I've got the information and format of the exhibition. They're using the RCDL rulebook. Lucky you it's about half as thick as the WRDF rule book you're used to. I've printed them out for you. Grab a copy on your way out tonight. Make sure you've read it before you walk back through that door tomorrow."

Someone scoffed and I snapped my head up to look at the team. "Problem?"

"Yeah," Eve said. "We have the same twenty-four hours in a day that you do. Not all of us are here on vacation. Between our jobs and practice and sleep, you expect us to read it all in twenty-four hours. It's not enough time."

"Make the time or don't walk back through that door."

"What the fuck?" she bit back.

"You need my help, not the other way around. If you want it, you're going to do it my way."

"Bullsh—"

I pinned her to the spot with a hard look that cut off her words. "You're all here to save Crossroads, right?"

Mayhem stepped out and turned to them. She didn't say a word, but her eyes sure as hell had plenty to say judging by the way they looked around at one another, their chins dipped low, before giving me reluctant nods.

"You have twenty-eight days," I said after Mayhem stepped back into the line. "That's it. Twenty-eight days to learn the same skills as teams who have been doing this for a decade. You'll either do it my way, or you can walk out that door. Anyone can be replaced."

A few of them shifted on their skates and glanced at one another; a couple others started to roll their eyes, but seemed to think better of it, and Eve looked like she was ready to set me on fire.

Bastard status reached.

But a few emerged as quiet forces, their energy cooling the attitudes on the team.

Not surprising, Mayhem was one of them. Hazy Eights for sure since she'd never once let what she was thinking cross her face and the jury was still out, but probably Hot West. With her serious, wide-eyed expression, she was either dedicated or terrified.

I could work with either. So, I had three out of fourteen with me.

Swell.

"Okay—first, the main differences between flat track and banked track that you'll learn in the RCDL—jams are only sixty seconds. Penalties are served during the following jam. And lead jammer status changes." I met

Mayhem's eyes. "Being the first jammer out of the pack guarantees you nothing."

I waited for it, for some hint of attitude, but her lips—lips I'd been kissing not so long ago—only twitched with amusement.

Good.

My girl was up for the challenge.

I froze.

Not mine. Christ.

"Day one will follow the abbreviated game format you'll find in section 2.2 of the RCDL. Two quarters. Quick elimination rounds. Think sprints, not marathons. You either have it, or you don't. Let's make sure you have it." I tossed the notes on the bench. "Get on the bank. I want fifty laps."

They strapped on their helmets, slid their mouthguards over their teeth, and headed for the jam line on the track. Just watching them get on the bank told me a hell of a lot I needed to know from the onset, just by how comfortable they were climbing on, getting into position, and taking off.

Almost all of them hesitated at the coping where the track dropped off an inch and a half or so along the bottom edge.

Well, they could avoid it now, but they'd be getting to know it really well in about fifteen minutes.

Watching them settle in and take off, I'd bet half or more of them had been skaters for years, a hefty portion of them probably having spent a bunch of time at skate parks.

If I was right, it would be a hell of a start. Better than I expected, but still so far to go.

By ten laps in, I spotted a few smiles out there.

The first time flying around those corners, there was nothing like it.

Enjoy it, ladies… once banked track gets inside you, you never get it out.

Their strides lengthened and with each lap, they naturally started to curl their shoulders in and lean into the inside of the track.

Their feet synced next until about halfway through their laps they skated tight and fast, their legs and feet moving together like an orchestrated performance.

I studied each of them and made notes on the roster of players Mayhem brought with her. Made sure I had their names straight since the one time I'd watched them, I'd been focused on one of them in particular.

The one I wanted to be focused on now.

That hungry look came into her eyes again, but this time clean and uninhibited by hurt and anger. Her gaze turned into laser sharp focus on the track before her. Everything narrowing down to the bodies surrounding her and the goal ahead.

I just had to harness it. Make that determination impenetrable.

I had to stack her against her biggest weakness.

And she might just hate me for it.

By the time they reached fifty laps, I rolled over and skated the infield along with them while they slowed to a coast. They crept closer to the coping, but none of them crossed just yet.

I skated backward and kept their pace. "Don't let it get in your head. Just stagger your feet and roll right off the coping. You're all going to get really familiar with that part of the track, especially you, Mayhem, since you can't resist the inside. You're not out of play until you touch the infield so you can use it to your advantage."

One by one they rolled off the track. A wobble here,

arms thrown out there, a little squeak, but everyone stayed upright.

Upright was good.

"Good, now get back on, climb to the top, and skate down and over the coping. Give me a hundred."

"Hey, Mayhem," Rory said as she climbed up the bank for the eighty-third time. "Your coach is a real asshole, you know that? Fuck."

"It's for the kids. Just remember it's for the kids," I said, my thighs burning from climbing the bank, sweat dripping from my face landing with a fat splatter against the track.

"Yeah, tell that to my fucking quads. They're already trash," Marty chimed in.

"Just think, if a guy pisses you off while you're riding him, you can crush his pelvis with your new muscles," I said, trying to keep it positive while my thigh muscles burned and quivered under my skin.

"If a guy pisses her off? You mean when. *When* a guy pisses her off," Marty said with a snort.

Where did she manage to find the air to snort?

If I sucked in a quick burst of air right now, I'd die. I could barely wheeze at this point.

Maybe that's what Priest wanted. If we run, he gets his track back and his life gets a whole lot less complicated.

We'd barely started, but all it took was adding a little incline and it was like hitting the gym for the first time in months after the round of food holidays and fifteen extra pounds.

I'd imagined all the ways Priest could make me lose my breath, bruising kisses laced with angry surrender, hot fore-play—a total assault of his big hands, hard thrusts with that bat in his shorts, but this… there was nothing sexy about this. Because ladies got jock sweat too and right now, I was pretty sure I was sweating myself what looked like the outline of crotchless underwear with a case of swamp ass not far behind.

That had kissing repellent written all over it.

I'd go take a roll in the snow if that didn't mean putting on a steam show fit for a sauna with my roasting hoo-ha.

I was smuggling a damn swamp cooler in my pants at this point.

"Ah, but I'm talking about said pissing off when she's riding him only," I finally managed to scrape out past my heavy breaths.

"Me too," Marty said.

"You know, she's not wrong—God, this hurts—but I swear dudes always forget about literally everything when we get on top," Rory began between gasps, her words on pause while we skated off the track and coping, only to turn and begin our climb to do it all over again. "They fucking lie back with their hands folded behind their heads, happy to let us do everything. I mean, dude, I'll do the hip work. At least then I know I'm going to come, but if you don't at least give me some nipple action and touch them like you mean it, I might just tear this dick off with my rocking' Kegels."

"Pelvic muscles might end up being the only muscles that don't hurt by the time we're done," Marty said before blowing out a hard breath and swiping the sweat off her forehead with her bare forearm.

"Ours maybe, but Mayhem's on the other hand," Rory

said with a side glance at me. "Priest has her all hot and bothered. I'm willing to bet all this time together has her flexing those fuckers like a new mother who pees herself every time the wind blows."

Eve glared at us then, the fact that she heard us written all over her face.

"If I flex anything else right now, I'll die." I attempted humor to brush off their comments, hoping to appease Eve. But Rory wasn't wrong. And she needed to shut up.

And tonight… after my shit day, after what was proving to be the shittiest practice of shittiest practices, I'd talk to Eve. I needed to just be honest, not only about Priest, but about her and me.

No more riding this whole *life is just too full right now and I'm not looking for anything serious, but it's been fun* excuse. I needed to make it abundantly clear that while I love her, I just didn't think in the end either of us would be happy.

Truth was, she was too eager to protect me. I thought I wanted that in a partner after losing my mom and spending years at the mercy of a system designed to send kids on their way the minute they aged out with no real support. But when her idea of protecting me turned to stifling me and not giving me room to make decisions without barreling over me—or worse—thinking she could make decisions for me, I knew it had to end.

I rolled down the bank one last time, rested my hands on my hips, and took a deep breath as I continued across the infield.

"Holy shit," Sean said, her eyes focused on something past us.

"Oh, hell no," Eve spat. "No. No. And in case you didn't hear me… fuck no!"

"What the hell is she doing here?" Marty said.

Their voices collided and I spun in the direction they

faced… to find Tilly standing in the doorway, uniform on, her duffel slung over her shoulder.

"She," Priest said, his unyielding gaze on mine, "is your fifteenth player."

My teammates all started in at once, their voices rising with anger, but the sound disappeared with the buzz of white-hot rage filling my head.

Remember… there's a reason for everything.

There were no evasive glances this time around. None of my teammates hung their heads being confronted with their less than grateful reception to Priest's help. Nope, they were all hands on hips, chin jutting indignation, circling Priest and ripping into him.

Not that I could hear them.

Because my blood surged through my veins like I'd sucked down a handful of speed before practice started.

My stomach ached; a band squeezed my chest like a vise—everything hurt.

Body… and heart.

He'd found the one part of me that just wouldn't heal no matter what and he'd poured acid into it. I blinked back tears, grateful for the sweat burning my eyes to hide the way he cut me deep.

I wouldn't let him have that power over me.

It was bad enough I let Tilly.

Here I was, paralyzed with betrayal, and my team defending me. I never realized we'd arrived at this place where they saw me as weak, too weak to speak up for myself. I thought this was between me and Eve.

Maybe not.

Maybe what was going on between Eve and me had bled onto the team as a whole.

We had work to do to change the dynamic—and very little time to do it.

To start, I needed to defend myself.

Just not like this. Not in some dressing down in front of everyone.

"Guys... stop." When their chatter died down, but didn't stop completely, I raise my voice. "Just stop!" My voice almost broke—almost.

And the way Priest cut a glance at me made me think he heard it.

I didn't know why he did this. At the moment I didn't care. I hurt too much to care. The only thing keeping me from bursting apart in a million little pieces—the big picture—the kids hanging in the balance.

My team's rumblings faded away and an awkward silence filled the room.

Priest looked at me, but those feelings, his thoughts, he kept them close. He didn't show me one damn thing to reassure me that he hadn't done this to be cruel.

All I had was the echo of his words in my head.

And the memory of raw kisses that weren't polished or by design. If anything, they were pieces of our hearts— bursting from the cages we'd tried to keep them locked in —finding their way around old wounds, clawing their way through the scar tissue we'd both built up to protect us from others.

From ourselves.

"We need all the help we can get," he said, his voice low and final. "A fifteenth player means three fresh sets of five. It's one more powerful player to use to your advantage. She's in it for Crossroads too. She knows what hangs in the balance."

The bit of camaraderie that had bloomed in reluctant smiles and winces of pain on my team's faces retreated to wary distrust. Maybe not back to the beginning, but he practically demolished the fragile bridge he'd built in the past hour with this addition.

I didn't feel one bit of sympathy for him. Not at all.

"You," he said, pointing at Tilly who'd made her way onto the track and into the infield. "No dirty play. You throw even one elbow here and you're out. Got it?"

Tilly nodded like she was in boot camp. "Got it."

Ass kisser.

But then, she'd always been. It wasn't how she behaved when everyone was looking. It was the words she'd sharpened, delivered on her cruel tongue when no one else was listening that had been the problem.

"No warnings. You know the rules, you know what I expect. No second chances." His mouth had thinned into a hard, angry line. His eyes narrowed, irritability in the set of his rigid shoulders. A complete one eighty from how he dealt with us even in the beginning when Eve pushed his boundaries.

Maybe he wasn't as comfortable with this addition as he let us all believe.

Or maybe he was one hell of an actor.

"Understood," Tilly said.

"Good. Get your gear on and get your ass on the track." He turned to us then and I thought I saw it, a flash of apology in his eyes. "Laps!" he snapped. "One skating forward. One skating backward. Don't roll off that bank until you've done another fifty."

Guess I imagined it.

Maybe I didn't go back far enough in the instinct department because it looked like I should have been trusting my flaming asshole instincts all along.

Maisy

TWENTY-SIX

I eyed my door at the sound of the knock on the other side and immediately regretted coming straight home. A ball of restless agitation settled in my gut and fuck if anyone thought I was hiding and licking my wounds.

I wanted to drop-kick a certain coach right in the grapes for the stunt he pulled.

And I needed someone to talk it over with, but after the stunning realization that my team had turned into this hardened shell on the outside, treating me like some shiny, dainty pearl on the inside, I sure as hell couldn't talk to any of them.

Because we still needed him.

Especially now that we not only had money into applying to the WRDE, but we'd paid to register for the exhibition and had travel expenses coming for that too.

I couldn't say he didn't warn me of impending doom —he did, kinda.

The fucker.

But I deserved a hell of a lot more than some vague warning while he busied himself collecting another hot kiss on a technicality.

If he tried to kiss me now, I'd bite his tongue off.

And that better not be him on the other side of the door.

I'd literally take anyone else. Maybe even Tilly and that was saying something. At least with her I knew what to expect. I hadn't managed to let her shitty comments roll off just yet, but she didn't have any new material.

If anything, her willingness to stand there while Priest hammered into her the expectations as we all looked on was new. Authority had never really been her thing, landing her in Bay Wilderness to begin with when her family decided she was too much of a behavioral issue and signed her over to the state.

Something I always pitied when we were teenagers. Not that I told her that.

For her to take Priest's rules without a flicker of nastiness in her eyes or a sneer twitching at the corner of her lips was new territory entirely.

I opened the door, ready to give whoever was on the other side hell, when Eve sailed right past me and let herself in.

"We need to talk," she said, her voice bone-white with fury.

I threw the door shut behind her. "Yes, we do—"

"We can't trust him," she said, cutting me off.

I sighed. I'd put a whole lot more value in her words if they were really about him, but this had our personal relationship written all over it.

This newfound clarity could kiss my ass. "And why is that?"

She whirled on me then, her jaw slack, and huffed out a livid breath. "He brought Tilly onto the team without saying a fucking word. That's not reason enough?"

He did say a word... just not the right ones, but that was between him and me.

"No, it's not. We have a youth center hanging in the balance. So no, it's not enough." And because it didn't make sense. He knew how important this was to me. He knew, dammit. He saw me with my kids. He skated with my kids. The guy who ran from me three nights ago—the guy who said no over and over—the guy who relented… he didn't do it to lay some sort of trap so he could be cruel.

"So you're just going to let him run all over you and get away with it?"

"Don't piss me off, Eve. I'm exhausted and I have just enough anger to unleash on him. I'm not interested in wasting it with you."

"Good," she said, beginning to pace. "You do that. While you're at it—"

"No more. Just knock this shit off. You're not going to run all over me in the name of what he did. Do you really think I'm that weak that you can just plow right through me and what I want?"

She stopped and whipped around. "And you want him?"

"That's what this is really about, isn't it?"

Hurt crept into her eyes and for a second, instincts told me to waver—to back off and leave this alone, but that's what got me here. Avoiding the hard shit. Keeping the peace. Fearing the loss of the few connections I had in Galloway Bay.

And I'd had her for longer than almost anyone else.

I wanted a lot of things. Yeah, I wanted him. But right now, in this moment, I wanted some damn respect—and I didn't want to lose Eve. I had to risk losing her by putting my foot down to have any hope of keeping her. Because I couldn't unsee the dynamic and its power to destroy everything if I didn't grow up and speak out.

"What you're doing right now is no different than

what he just did. Actually, it's worse. Instead of just being indignant about what he did—which sucked by the way—you bulldozed in here, not trusting me to take care of me."

At least Priest had given me that. In a way, by not telling me first, he showed me he trusted me to handle it. To be an adult. He did it with the information at hand. Oh, he was still wrong. So fucking wrong. And he'd pay for it. But from a coach's standpoint, I could see the appeal. Tilly was a strong, agile force on the track when she wasn't targeting me over childhood slights. Take those out of the equation and our chances only grew.

"I'm thinking about you," she pleaded as she took a step toward me.

I took a step back. "No, you're not. You're thinking about us being together again—and we're over, Eve. We talked about this."

"Don't you think I know that?"

"No, I don't."

"The rest of the team spoke up at the practice. It's not like I'm the only one who feels this way."

"Yes, and are they here right now? I told everyone to stop and what did they do? They respected it."

Eve pulled her shoulders back, a showing of stubborn pride for her. "I don't know how to not protect you."

"I know. And that's my fault. You came into my life at a really scary time and it felt good to have someone take over a little bit. To have a best friend I could count on to have my back. But at some point, it felt a little too good—too easy. It's bled into our team, Eve. I didn't see it until tonight. And we can't afford that."

"So, what are you saying, that you don't want me as a best friend now?"

"No, I'm saying I want you as my best friend again.

We're not there right now. I can't talk to you about—it's just not the same."

"I still love you." She said the words—her voice so low and full of pain it made it hard for me to breathe.

"And I still love you. But it's different for me than it is for you and I don't know how to help you get over that. I don't know if I'm even the right person. But I know I need you to let me go. I need you to respect my decisions. You can't say you love me and that you want to protect me, while taking away my choices. It's the same thing he did to me tonight."

"And you choose him?"

"To coach us, yes."

"But you want more?"

"It doesn't matter what I want, because I can't have it."

She stepped into me, backed me right against the wall, and kissed me, tugging my bottom lip between her teeth like I used to love.

And I felt nothing. No spark. No want. No need.

Just regret. So much regret that I might have ruined my single most important friendship by crossing the line into more.

She stilled then, her eyelids slowly opening, her ice-blue eyes on mine. "It really is over, isn't it?"

I cupped her cheek, the wounded look in her eyes squeezing my heart as we lost something in that moment. A piece we had before we turned into lovers—something that attached itself to the attraction that flickered between us, only to die when that mutual attraction faltered.

She still wanted me—which might very well be her pride talking—but that look in her eyes told me she felt it too.

"It's really over," I whispered, wishing I could hug her, but knowing I'd be sending her the wrong message if I did.

If I ever wanted to be able to hug her again, I couldn't wrap my arms around her now.

She leaned her forehead on mine, her fingers curled around the back of my neck. "God, I love you so fucking much. I don't want to let you go."

"Or are you afraid of finding the one who's really right for you, Eve? They're out there somewhere and when you find them, nothing in your world will ever be the same again and that's the way it's supposed to be. They're going to be the last person you expect." My throat turned thick and burned with unshed tears as I let her go, praying this was the way to finding our friendship again. "Don't miss out on it because you're holding on too tight to me."

She swallowed hard and took a step back. Her eyes turning glassy with tears, I knew she'd sooner gouge her own eyes out than shed them in front of me as she headed for the door.

Turning the handle, she gave the door a hard tug, the familiar squeak cutting into the heavy silence of our final goodbye. "So, practice tomorrow, then?" she said without looking me in the eye.

"Practice tomorrow," I said quietly.

"I hate to admit this and if you remind me tomorrow, I'll deny I said it, but—he sees something in you on that track." She turned to me then as the first tear tracked down her cheek. "Despite it, he's still a bastard for what he pulled today."

"Wow, that was a chilly goodbye," Lilith said the minute I stepped through the doorway.

"They're just tired." And pissed at me, but then, there will be more where that came from.

Coaching had changed in ten years.

Or maybe I'd changed in ten years.

I used to step out there so damn sure of myself, but this time, I silently wore my old mistakes like a pair of wet jeans. I was all jerky movements, barked orders, and I suspected—fucking it up.

My life for the last decade had been ruled by regulation, policy, and law. I held on to the absolute in that. I drew comfort from it.

I sought absolution in it.

But now I wondered if it had numbed me to some of the nuances of human interaction.

The nuances of women.

Because with one move, my team wanted to skin me alive.

My team.

They were mine, dammit. I don't care if we'd only been out there for a day. Somewhere along the way, after giving in and agreeing to this, I'd started wanting it, too.

This was a shot to get it right when I'd gotten so many things wrong.

I could leave this town on a high this time instead of weighed down by regrets and a trail of destruction in my wake.

"Oh, they're tired too," she agreed. "Turn around."

"Why?" I said but turned to hang up my jacket.

She skimmed her fingers over my shoulders, smoothing my shirt. "Just figured I'd count the knives in your back."

With nothing better to do with her time than cook that little nephew of mine, she was definitely working on that skill of seeing everything.

Every. Damn. Thing.

"It's fine. They'll get over it." But a bit of spark in Mayhem's eyes died tonight—the exact opposite of what I expected to see when Tilly showed up, making me all but sure I'd misjudged the situation or I was missing something. Something big.

"What did you do?" she said, propping her hip against the counter and popping a piece of chocolate in her mouth.

I glanced over my shoulder as I leaned in to snag a bottle of cold water from the fridge. "What makes you think I did something?"

She gestured with another piece of chocolate. "You're a man."

She'd gotten so sassy. It's a wonder Jordan got her to close her mouth long enough to knock her up. "They're pissed about Tilly being on the team."

"Seems kind of stupid to be pissed at you when they agreed to it."

My skin prickled. I tossed back three long gulps before I turned to her—my throat still dry—with guilt. "I didn't ask them."

"I'm sorry?" Her voice had gone all high-pitched now, telling me I was in for it and whose side she was definitely going to take in this particular hurdle.

I was a man on my own. Cool. Not exactly new territory for me. "I. Didn't. Ask. Them."

"Woooowwwww. Dick move, Cain."

I glanced away and shrugged. "Thanks."

"No, really. I mean, I said you were a good coach and I meant it, but this…"

"Yeah, I get it, Lil." I sucked down the last of the water and crushed the bottle in my hands. "You think I fucked up." Tossing the bottle toward the recyclables, I watched it glance off the corner, spin, and pitch right back out onto the floor.

"No—I know you fucked up," she said, reaching for the bottle.

I grabbed her arm to stop her and snatched up the bottle with my other hand. "Stop, I've got it."

She blew out an exasperated breath. "I'm not breakable."

"I'm not okay with you picking up after me."

"Fine, I'll go back to what I'm good at then, irritating the shit out of you."

"Great." I snorted.

"Maybe you're rusty with this whole coaching thing. It's only day one. I mean, it's a hell of a mistake to make on day one, but you've always been a bit of an overachiever. Go big, am I right?"

"Your confidence in me is astounding. Thanks."

She crossed her arms and settled in. "If it's part of a master plan, enlighten me."

"Tilly and Mayhem have a problem with one another."

"You're supposed to be convincing me why you're not an idiot."

"Working on it." Only I was trying to convince myself now too because all of a sudden, my stellar idea didn't seem so stellar. "The issue isn't so much Mayhem. Her biggest problem is she lets Tilly get in her head. Tilly's the one who likes to play dirty and throw elbows."

"Wait—hold up," Lilith said, holding her hand up to stop me.

"What?"

She shook her head and shifted her weight, the wince on her face telling me she'd gotten uncomfortable on her feet. "That's not having a problem with one another. That's one person bullying another."

I pulled out a chair. "Here, sit."

She shuffled over, sat down, and glanced up at me. "How exactly do you expect Maisy to set aside the way she's been treated?"

"I, uh—" It's not what I intended when I agreed to let Tilly on the team. I hadn't even considered what I was asking Maisy to do—fucking hell—or would have been asking her if I actually, you know, asked her.

"Did Tilly apologize?"

"Shit." I jammed my hand through my hair and glanced at the clock.

"Like I suspected, you're the one who fucked up."

"Son of a bitch." It was late, but practice had only just broken up. Maybe I could do some damage control.

She laughed up at me, her hand roaming over her belly. "You're in the doghouse with the new girlfriend."

"She's not my girlfriend." I snatched my jacket off the hook and jammed my arms through the sleeves.

"I saw you guys kissing in the barn."

My zipper whistled through the air as I yanked it up. "Stop snooping."

She shrugged, but her eyes danced. "Hey, I was just checking to see if you guys needed anything."

So glad I could be a source of entertainment for my restless sister. By falling on my face. A lot. "Yeah, we did. Privacy."

"You needed a hose turned on you. Besides, this property is half mine. It's not snooping when you're part owner."

"That half isn't yours. I have to go into town. Will you be okay if I'm gone for an hour?"

"I'll manage. How long do I wait before I call 9-1-1 so they can start looking for your body?"

"Cute."

"I thought so," she said with a laugh. "Hey, Cain?" she called.

I stopped one foot out the door. "Yeah."

"Start with I'm sorry. Now say it with me… IIIIII'mm-mmmm soooooooorrrrrry."

I slammed the door on the sound of her cackling behind me. So glad I could provide her such quality entertainment.

I went back in my head to the moment the team circled me, giving me shit for Tilly's addition, but it was Mayhem, the look on her face, the way she stood apart that had me hitting the gas, pushing the cushion local cops gave people over the limit.

Stunned.

I told myself she was calm. The anchor for her team, but I'd misread what that meant—how much she could take.

She'd been completely blindsided.

So much so her first instinct wasn't even anger.

I climbed the stairs to her apartment first and knocked for

a good five minutes, talking to the door, convinced she was in there but just ignoring me. I spotted her car in the parking lot, so it's not like she'd gone far, and after what I put them through on the track on top of her day job, she didn't go for a walk.

Which left Banked Track. And maybe Patti on my side.

I found Mayhem perched on a bar stool with Rory behind the counter, their heads together, their faces serious.

Five or six other patrons lingered through the place as they wound down for the night.

Good, less witnesses.

"We need to talk," I said, the words coming out harder than I'd intended.

And completely unwelcome by the two fuck-you glances Rory and Mayhem aimed my way.

Mayhem slowly straightened and held up her glass like a toast. "Well, if it isn't Coach Flaming Asshole," she said right before knocking back a gulp of her drink. "Have a seat. Rory, I'll pay you extra to spit in his beer."

Rory glared and scoffed as she dug her towel into a highball glass she'd just grabbed. "I'd do it for free."

"I'll pass on the beer. Thanks." I might have better luck in a pit of cobras. I propped my foot on the stool next to Mayhem only to have her slice me a cold, hard glance.

"I said have a seat, but I did not say that seat could be next to me."

"Are you serious?"

She turned her heavy-lidded glare back to her drink. "You have no idea."

"Fine." I dragged out the stool one seat down and faced her. "I might have fucked up tonight."

"Nope. Not close enough," she said with a snap of her fingers. "You did fuck up tonight. There's no might have. Might have is what you say when you might have left the toilet seat up or you might have walked through the house with wet boots. There's no might in inviting the biggest flaming twat in existence onto our team without saying a word about it. You did do that, and the least you could do is own it."

"I fucked up," I said, waiting for her to turn to me. When she finally did, the betrayal I saw in her eyes took me to another time, another place, another mistake, and made it hard to speak. "I'm sorry."

She searched my face, silent until her shoulders slumped. "Nope, that's not satisfying either." Turning away, she wrapped her fingers around her glass.

"I'll tell her she's off the team."

She froze with her glass halfway to her lips and cut me a glance. "If you do that, I'm going to beat you with my skate, I swear to God."

"You don't want me to kick her off the team?"

"I didn't want her on the team to begin with, but that ship sailed. It's gone. Now that you put me in this position, you've made me more fuel for her fire." She leaned on the bar and tilted her head. "What do you think happens if Tilly is kicked off because of me? Because you damn well know after watching the shit she pulled in that bout that she will definitely blame it all on me."

"Son of a bitch."

"See it now, hotshot? For a cop, you sure are slow." She slammed her glass down, looked at Rory, and pointed over her shoulder. "Stop worrying about me, I've got this. Pay attention to Gerald. He's serving himself now."

Rory whipped around. "Shit!"

"You can't turn your back on him," Mayhem said, turning away from me again, glancing into the bottom of her glass like the amount of liquid left was an hourglass— the liquor the sand—telling her just how much longer she had to suffer my presence.

"Where's Patti?" It wasn't like her to not be here—to let Rory cover her when the woman knew the team had their first practice tonight. She'd want to be here, with all of them, living vicariously through every detail.

"She wasn't feeling well," she said, saying as few words as possible, making me pull the conversation out of her one stubborn word at a time.

"I took your power away."

She sucked in a sharp breath. "You sure did."

A weight settled in my chest. I swallowed the unexpected knot wedged in my throat and forced the words past my lips. "And I weaponized you for her."

"Yup."

"Are you going to tell me what the deal is between you and Tilly?"

"Nope. Now, if you'd asked me before—" She shrugged and pulled a twenty from her bag and tossed it on the counter. "Doesn't matter now." But her mouth trembled when she said it—just one of a dozen different ways she showed me it mattered.

"You're just going to let me go into this blind?"

"How does it feel?" she snapped as she slid off the stool.

Rory glanced between the two of us and moved in closer. Ready to protect Mayhem—from me.

In the span of one disastrous move, I now stood apart from the team—maybe even more separated than Tilly. God, that was a kick in the balls right there.

Mayhem started past me without even a glance, and I couldn't let her go. My sister was right… I was already well on my way to falling in love with her, and if I let her walk away from me now, she might walk away from me for good.

I curled my fingers around her arm and let them slide down over her wrist to her hand.

"I have to regrets right now and Tilly isn't even the biggest one."

She slowed to a stop next to me and closed her eyes. "What's your biggest?" She whispered.

"Agreeing to that damn no kissing rule."

Afraid to breathe, I waited to see what she would do when my palm slid against hers.

She glanced down at our hands, her index finger twitching against my skin. I felt the shudder move through her a split second before she lightly laced her fingers with mine.

"I won't let her hurt you," I promised her, squeezing her hand gently, afraid to push her any farther.

Damp, bright-blue eyes heavy with unshed tears ripped into me with a glimpse of what I'd done to her.

"You can't protect me," she murmured as she let my fingers go and walked out the door.

I can't protect anyone.

But for the first time since Abel died, my instinct wasn't to run from trying.

Maisy

My hair follicles hurt.

No really… all it took was a breeze wafting through the open doorway to make me whimper.

And I still had two hours of practice left to go.

"Push, Mayhem!"

Push this, fucker.

"Get up, get up, get up!"

What the hell did he think I was doing? I just barely got down here. Like really, guy.

"Find your balance!"

I know he better not just be yelling that at me.

"Stay low!"

Demanding bastard.

"That's it. Take five," he called.

Marty hunched over and braced her hands on her knees as she gasped out a breath. "I don't even want to skate off the bank because I'm going to blink and have to get back on."

"I'm not moving. I'm just going to be here trying not to die," Rory said as she clung to the padded rail, her chest laboring to move air.

"He's got a real boner for being up your ass today," Marty said with a quick glance in my direction.

"He's got a boner to get up her ass every day," Sean said as she snickered.

Where the hell did she find the extra air for that?

"Has he gotten his boner near your ass yet, Maze?" Rory asked.

"Don't fucking call me Maze. I don't want to have to use my last burst of energy to kick your ass."

Rory glared. "Hey, you let Patti call you Maze."

"Because I'm afraid Patti will kick *my* ass. Besides, no one lets Patti do anything. She just does it."

"Maybe he'd lighten up if you just do the deed already. You want it. He wants it. I'm ready to hear about some bone action," Marty said.

Sean squatted low and propelled herself back up with a wince. "I bet he's got a really great bone. Like worth molding for a sex toy. Every once in a while he turns a certain way in those shorts and—"

All of our gazes swung in her direction and froze.

"Like you guys haven't noticed," she said, blowing a strand of hair out of her face. "But he's still paying for letting Tilly on the team."

"She's kept her ass in line. I'll give her that," Rory said, straightening and stretching her arms over her head.

Something cold hit my shoulder, and I glanced up to find Tilly tapping a water bottle against my skin.

"Thirsty?"

I tensed but took the bottle from her. "Uh, yeah, thanks."

No smile. Expressionless eyes. Without another word, she handed the bottle to me and skated away.

I looked around to see if she'd handed out a bunch of them or only brought one for me, but I couldn't tell.

Carmen, Dixie, Lexi, and Cat all had water, but they were already half gone at this point. Besides, they stood in a tight circle with Zara, all lips flapping and hand gestures, talking about something that had them all fired up.

My gaze landed on Tilly only to find her watching me from the edge of the infield as she tipped her bottle back.

What the fuck did this mean?

"Make sure the seal's intact," Marty muttered.

"Funny." I pushed off and started a lap around the track. And yeah, I made sure *I* broke the seal.

We still hadn't done an all-out jam yet. Instead, Priest kept us on the bank relearning every basic skill. Hours upon hours he hammered us with endless stops, starts, blocks, transitions, duck walks, duck runs, push drills, swoop and block drills, everything we needed to learn to stay upright on a bank while getting hit from each side.

He didn't miss a single thing, his shrewd eyes scanning, studying, always watching every move.

If we did it wrong, slacked, or looked tired—he called us out.

He called us out hard.

He also made it hella hard for a girl to have a private couple of seconds to pick a fucking wedgie, that was for damn sure.

When he wasn't penetrating our brains with his superhuman stare, he yelled, waved his hands in frustration, scribbled notes, paced, and skated.

Overall, he was a merciless son of a bitch.

I wanted to hate him, and right when I was almost at that point, he climbed on the bank with us. He didn't demand one thing that he couldn't or wouldn't do himself up there.

The man didn't have to say he had integrity, he showed

it with his every single action, making it really freaking hard to stay mad at him for his misstep.

Until the son of a bitch broke us into the three sets of five he was so bloody fond of.

Guess who was in my set of five.

Tilly the Fucking Cyborg. That was her new name.

A name that matched her blank fucking expression.

He put the jammers on the spot first, examining our footwork as we tried to break through and dash around the blockers in front of us. Testing our ability to hop, spin away from a block to dart around and through the pack, and our skill at gaining speed when we broke free.

When I'd told him he would make me a target if he kicked Tilly off the team, he clearly took it to heart by going the complete other direction in making us work together. Apparently, he wanted to send the message that not only was I cool with Tilly on the team, but we were ready for matching tattoos or some bonding shit.

Super.

Everything changed on the bank; our balance changed depending on where we were on the track. The angle of our hips being on a constant tilt threw every other part of us off. But after a week, we finally had it.

If anything, being on flat ground felt weird as hell, but at least when we transitioned to the infield, we didn't look like calves taking their first steps anymore. Sad visual, but true—although, appropriate being in an old dairy barn and all.

Finally happy with our progress—if you called a grunt and a little less resting asshole face, happy—we moved on to jumps so when the time came and bodies hit the track in a jam, we could avoid running over our teammates and hurting ourselves.

At least that was the theory.

We scoffed at his never-ending need to drive the skills home—earning a dark glare—his new natural state over the past week since he found me at Banked Track pouring out my bruised heart to Rory.

He kept everything absolute derby. Nothing personal. But all the things we weren't saying, built up there between us. I could feel it. The air practically vibrated around us.

After all, even my team noticed. The shits probably formed a betting pool behind my back.

The unease made me itchy.

And bitchy.

They thought I needed to get fucked.

But really, I needed to unclench. I was wound so fucking tight I might snap, a completely new sensation for me.

Okay, they also thought the prescription for that was a good seven inches or so of girthy goodness, and they were probably right.

With every bit of control I gained on this track, I lost control over something else. I'd become so fucking disgruntled and short with everyone, even Milton and Gerald had stopped making jokes and prodding each other. Instead, they stopped in for breakfast like their hour there was obligatory, and grumbled into their coffees over my recent lack of charm.

Apparently, they didn't appreciate my new prison guard energy.

But I didn't know how to let go of it and I had to guard my heart.

Though silent, I'd catch Priest watching me, not the judgmental kind of stare from the first night I saw him, but something else.

Dejected and grim, but with flashes of longing so fucking cutting I'd forget to breathe.

I'd spot it, he'd blink, and it would be gone, or he'd turn away, his focus needed elsewhere. Even though he spent a fair amount of time on that track with us, he held himself apart from us—from me—ever since that night at Banked Track.

I didn't like it.

I didn't know how to change it.

And my every instinct begged me to roll right off the track and wrap my arms around him—only I knew I couldn't.

When I'd finally let myself look away from him and return my attention to the team, I'd find Eve watching me, her face hollow. Her mouth tight.

I found myself searching out Tilly of all people. When I found her, she'd look at me with a blank stare, something I found a whole lot more uncomfortable than her attitude. At least I knew what she was thinking when she was attacking me.

This whole blank look came straight out of horror movies, for fuck's sake.

And now she'd flipped the script and done something nice, which only felt more sinister.

I didn't know when our showdown was coming, but it had to be coming. Right?

Or maybe she was trying and I was the asshole here.

I couldn't tell anymore. All I knew was we were getting better, but nothing was right. Not one damn thing.

The void in her eyes—the one she'd just aimed my way for the hundredth time this week—had my nerves stretched so tight, I had to get out of here before I snapped.

Even if for just a few minutes.

I skated off the track straight to the bench and yanked on my laces.

"What are you doing?" Priest asked, skating right up to me.

I flicked him a glance. "I need a break."

Hands on his hips, he glowered down at me. "You just had a break."

I straightened and kicked off my skate. "Goddammit, Priest… back off."

"What's going on with you?"

"God, you've got to be kidding me," I muttered as my phone started to vibrate again with another bullshit call. I slipped it from my duffel, but didn't recognize the number, and tossed it back into my bag as I kicked off my second skate. "I need one damn minute where I'm not under a fucking microscope. If you've got a problem with that, you're going to have to pin me to this fucking floor and force these skates back on my feet. Unless you're prepared to do so, back off."

I shot up to my feet and he jumped back, his eyes widened and his head jerking back.

"Yeah, I thought you'd see it my way," I said, jamming my arms into the sleeves of my jacket. Here I was, ready to stand up for myself, practically vibrating to take someone on, and all of a sudden, I had all the space in the world and none of these fuckers were giving me any material to work with.

Maisy

twenty-nine

I headed for the house to stop at the bathroom before I committed ten minutes to freezing my tits off in my car and then maybe, just maybe I'd make it through the rest of practice without setting someone on fire.

I knocked on the door even though Priest told us not to worry about it, that Lilith would be expecting us to be in and out using the bathroom, because frankly, I didn't give a shit what he said.

Chilly toward me or not, I was not disrespecting this woman's home.

"Hello," I called as I opened the door. "Just stopping in for a bathroom break."

The door to the half bath we'd been using by the laundry room was closed so I knocked, just in case. One of my teammates likely closed it all the way when they were done, a habit that drove me absolutely bonkers, but one of them always did it at my apartment. I'd rather knock for no reason than walk in and have a getting-to-know-you session mid wipe.

I knocked a second time even as I reached for the doorknob, only to have it not give under the twist of my hand. A second later, a muffled moan came from the other side of the door.

A prickle of dread skittered along the back of my neck and down my spine as I flattened my hand on the wood. "Lilith? Are you okay in there?"

"I'm not su—re," she said, her words breaking on a sob. "I don't think I can move."

My heart knocked against my ribs as all the images of what I might find behind the door started flashing through my head. I gave the knob a hard twist again. "It's locked. Can you reach the lock?"

"I think so," she said with a low moan.

At the sound of the telltale click, I turned the handle and forced myself to stay calm no matter what waited for me on the other side. I didn't know which of the horrific scenes to expect, but Lilith on her knees on the floor clutching her side wasn't even close.

There's something to be said for imagining the worst when reality swoops in and tells you to slow your dramatic roll.

Relief slid through me and my muscles unclenched a fraction to see the baby was still where he was supposed to be. For now.

The toilet paper holder hung crooked where it had been yanked from the wall as though she tried to pull herself up with it. The roll had flopped off and unraveled only to come to a stop somewhere behind the toilet.

If she tried to pull herself up like that and fell back down, with no one here to hear her... shit. "Is it the baby?"

A fat tear rolled down her cheek and her lips trembled as she bit back a sob. "I don't know. It's too early."

I rubbed her back and her shoulders slumped at my touch. "Does it feel like contractions?"

"It's hard to tell. I've never had them," she said, a touch of snark lacing her voice.

Another good sign. I'd take any sort of fight in her, even if she wanted to aim it at me.

"Did your water break or are you bleeding?"

"No," she gasped as she dug her fingertips into her abdomen.

"Okay, listen, I want to get you off your knees. Let's get you up and sitting and I'm going to get your brother."

"Thank you." She sighed. "God, I'm sorry you have to see me like this."

"Don't worry about it. I've seen a woman deglove her finger on the track." I winced, the image flashing in my head whenever I mentioned it. I'd seen bones break and pop out the skin that was better than that damn finger.

"I don't know what that is, but it sounds awful."

"Yeah, I still have nightmares. Don't google it. No one is that bored."

I got her up on her feet and guided her hands around my shoulders. I didn't dare try to lead her from the bathroom to the kitchen table just yet with the tight squeeze through the narrow doorway. "Keep your arms around my neck for just a second okay."

"Yeah," she whispered as she tightened her grip and groaned in my ear. "It hurts."

"I know; we're going to get you help." I wrapped my arm around her, holding her tight. Flicking the toilet seat down, I snatched a couple towels from the shelf over the toilet to cover the lid to make her as comfortable as possible while I ran up to the barn.

"Okay, just hold on to me and ease yourself down. Go slow."

She whimpered as she lowered onto the seat. Settling in, she sighed and rubbed at her knees. "Thank you."

"How long were you stuck in here like this?"

"A half hour maybe." She leaned against the wall, the

blood all but drained from her face leaving her white and ashen with sweat dotting her temples. "I kept trying to get up, but the pain would shoot around to my back," she said, her voice breathless.

Thirty fucking minutes stuck on the cold bathroom floor wondering when help was going to come.

Priest was going to blame himself for this. There was no way he wouldn't. How do you convince a guy like him that sometimes shit just happened?

Nothing came with a guarantee, but you tried anyway.

You *did* anyway.

You talked to people, let them in knowing one day they'd be gone. Little old men who bickered like brothers —little old men you pretended were the grandfathers you never had.

Things went wrong and you lost people you love.

Life would not always bend to your will like a derby team. Life wasn't coaching; it was living. Surrendering to what went wrong so you could fall in love with the moments that went so right.

Lilith was right here. Every minute he stayed away was a moment wasted. A moment I wish I could have back with my mother.

I squeezed Lilith's hand. "Sit tight for just a minute, I'm going to get your brother."

"This is going to mess with your practice."

"Don't worry about our practice. The baby's more important."

She let out a short laugh. "He's running you ragged, huh?"

"That too, but we asked for it. Sit tight." I ran to the barn, every gasp of air burning my throat. Skidding to a stop at the threshold, I stuck two fingers in my mouth and let out a whistle that had everyone turning to the door.

Priest glowered at me and jabbed a finger at the track. "Get your ass on the bank," he snapped before turning his back on me.

"You've gotta come down to the house." I gasped out the words and at the sound of my tone his face snapped up. "It's your sister."

His notes hit the floor. In seconds he went from skates to boots and tore out the door past me.

"Where is she?" he yelled over his shoulder as he ran down the hill.

"Bathroom. I found her in there stuck on her knees. She thinks she was there for about thirty minutes."

"Is she—"

"Her water didn't break and she doesn't think she's having contractions."

"Good. That's good."

The cold air sliced in and out of me as I kept pace next to him, trying not to fall on my ass despite the sand tossed down the path. "She didn't have her phone on her. I didn't have mine on me either, so I didn't call 9-1-1."

"It's okay. I'll take her in. It'll be faster."

"EMTs have medical training. Maybe—"

"I have medical training. I'm a cop," he said, cutting me off. He ran over the threshold, slid around the corner, and stopped in front of the bathroom.

"Sorry," Lilith gasped out when she looked up at her brother. "Bad timing."

He crouched down in front of her and smoothed her hair back from her face. The smile he gave her—I—God, he should smile more often. It changed something in Lilith the minute he did. "Don't apologize. That's why I'm here."

Clenched and tense until that point, Lilith released a breath and took in another deep one behind it, the strain bracketing her mouth softening.

"Something's not right, Cain. The pain—it's too early. If he's born now, his lungs—"

"Shhh, one thing at a time." He cupped her head and kept her focused on him. "Hospital first. We don't worry until there's something to worry about." Taking her hand, he got her to her feet and guided her just outside the bathroom before scooping her up and tucking her against his chest.

Her arms went around his neck and her head landed on his shoulder, the tears falling freely now. "I'm scared."

"I know you are, but I've got you. I've always got you."

But the words weren't really true, were they? Because he'd leave.

I held the door and followed him outside to open the passenger door of the truck.

"Thanks," he said, sliding his sister onto the front seat, buckling her in, and closing the door. "Keep going. I'll let you know what's happening as soon as I know."

"I'm sending them home. You don't need to be worrying about us up here."

"You don't have to—"

"Take care of Lilith. I've got this."

"Thank you," he said, pressing a kiss to my forehead.

I closed my eyes, tried not to read too much into it, and took a step back. "No kissing rule. Now go."

CAIN

She thinks she was there for about thirty minutes.

Mayhem's words haunted me from the minute medics wheeled Lilith into the back.

My sister was stuck on her knees on the goddamned bathroom floor for half an hour and I had no clue. All while I was in the barn training, barking orders, trying to figure out what the fuck has happened to the chemistry on the track because something was off.

No phone on me. No phone on Lilith. Fuck.

Shit needed to change. My sister came first. She had to come first.

I stared out the wall of windows into the darkness, looking for answers as to how to split my time between two commitments. Answers, the pesky little bastards, they just didn't want to come.

She'd been in with the doctors for almost an hour now. An hour and no word.

For the thousandth time I kicked myself for not trying hard enough to convince her to come to Boston and stay with me near some of the best hospitals in the country. Not that Bay Medical Center was bad. Just limited. They didn't even have a twenty-four-hour anesthesiologist on staff, ruling out something as common as an epidural if she decided she wanted one.

I wanted Lilith to have everything. Every damn thing.

The emergency department waiting room hadn't changed a whole hell of a lot since I was kid. The same metal framed chairs with blue vinyl. The same cherry wood end tables and chunky white lamps.

Hell, probably the same magazines.

I'd stood in this room too many times over the years. I waited here for them to tell me my mother was going to be okay. I waited after my grandfather's heart attack for the same. I stood here searching for some sort of hope again when they brought my grandmother in.

And eventually, I waited here to find out Lana's condition.

Almost every single time the staff stepped out those double doors, I waited for good news, and they brought me tragedy.

I didn't know how to expect anything different.

Warm arms slid around me, Mayhem's tattooed hands locking over my stomach.

I blinked down at them for a minute, wondering if I was finally losing what was left of my damn mind after a nearly impossible week of watching her battle back from the way I hurt her.

I really outdid myself this time. I put her at risk and the way I did it tied my hands so I couldn't even help her without putting her more at risk.

Closing my eyes, I laid my hand over hers. Another selfish step where I took what I wanted—what I needed— knowing I could only cause her more pain in the end.

Everyone who got close to me ended up hurt and there wasn't one damn thing I could do to stop it.

"How is she?" she murmured from behind me.

But I wanted her in front of me.

I wanted her skin under my hands and her heat against my chest. I didn't want to be alone one more time in this room, trying to figure out how I'd survive one more heartache I was powerless to stop.

Lacing my fingers with hers, I tugged her around to stand before me and pulled her in. Hanging my head, I buried my face in the curve of her neck for a minute. Just a minute.

"I haven't heard anything yet," I said as I took a deep breath while her arms tightened around me. Those pieces that felt like they might just burst apart held together. By her.

I closed my eyes and took everything she offered, my hands splaying over her back, memorizing the dip of her muscles, the valley of her spine—who we were in this moment so damn different than the first time I was this close to her just weeks ago.

"She's going to be okay," she whispered, her warm breath sliding along my neck making me shiver.

"How do you know?"

"Because you were there, and you did the right thing. You got her here fast."

"Life's never been that easy for me."

"Today it is."

"Cain?"

At the sound of the nurse calling me—the same nurse who'd called my name before in this waiting room—I turned while keeping Mayhem in my arms, a knot in my chest making it hard to take a breath. "How is she?"

"She's going to be fine. The doctor will be out in just a minute to fill you in," she said with a reassuring smile.

"Thank you." I squeezed Mayhem again and scrubbed my hand over my face. "She's going to be fine. Jesus."

"Well, no offense to him, but I was kind of hoping to take credit for this one," Mayhem said with a relieved laugh as she peered up at me with her chin propped on my chest.

"The credit's yours. I'm glad you came." I framed her face with my hands and slid my fingers into her hair. "You're exhausted."

"I'm stressed."

"And exhausted. You should go get some rest." I dug my fingers into her scalp, enjoying the way her mouth fell open. Really enjoying the way she sank her teeth into her bottom lip.

She hummed, the vibration sinking into the pads of my fingers. "You get to boss me around on the track, not off it."

"If that were true you never would have gone down to the house and found my sister."

"*On* the track, Coach," she said as her eyes narrowed to slits before sliding closed. "You tried to boss me around on the infield."

Her pulse fluttered in the soft skin of her throat along the column of her neck and my mouth ran dry. "I'm glad you didn't listen."

"Me too," she whispered.

I dragged my thumb over the edge of her jaw. The blood rushed through me, my heart kicking up a notch. This was what I wanted. To be touching her. Always touching her. "Lilith said you were sweet with her."

She hissed, her head falling back farther. "Yeah, well, don't tell anybody."

"This is cozy," Lana called from across the room.

"Shit."

"What?" Mayhem blinked up at me, her eyes unfocused.

"Lana."

Lana rolled over, a knowing smirk on her face. "So this is the girlfriend everyone's been talking about around town."

"Don't start shit, Lana," I warned her even as I knew it would do no good. The girl—woman had always said exactly what she wanted to, when she wanted to.

"I'm Maisy," she said with a smile, reaching out her hand, not doing one thing to dispute the girlfriend designation.

What the hell did that mean?

And if that was the case, why the hell did we have a kissing rule?

"Lana Bradley. Nice to finally meet you," she said, shaking Mayhem's hand as she turned her all too perceptive gaze on me. "And you... why the hell didn't you tell me you have a banked track?"

"Sure, that would have been a brilliant idea."

"Hey!" Lana said. "Just for that I want in. I've gotta see this."

I sliced a hand through the air between us. "No way in hell."

Mayhem swatted my shoulder.

"What?"

"Don't be a bellend," she muttered.

"A what?"

"Ooooh, I like her. She called you a bellend. You should know what it is, you have one... it's the glans of the pe—"

"What the hell are you doing talking to him?" Lana's mother shrieked from across the room. Her cheeks flamed as she headed right for us.

"Christ," Lana bit out. "She was supposed to wait for me by the gift shop."

"It's fine. Just go." I needed her to go. I didn't need Mayhem to witness this. To see this confrontation in her eyes every time she looked at me from here on out.

"No. I haven't even seen Zach yet, dammit. She's got some stellar fucking timing as always."

Lana's mother elbowed her way between us and jabbed a pointed finger at me. "You! Stay the hell away from my daughter."

I held my hands up and forced my voice to stay calm. "Look—"

"No, you look. You've done enough. Look at her—just look!" she spat, pointing that finger at me again.

A knot of disgust lodged inside me, heavy with dread. My skin grew hot and tight, shame roiling through me until it choked me and kept me from being able to look Mayhem in the eye.

"Mom, stop!"

"After everything you've done, you think you can just come gallivanting into town again and right back into coaching. Not on my watch."

The energy shifted and my arm fell away from Mayhem as she launched herself in front of me.

"Hey!" Mayhem snapped, forcing Lana's mother back. "You stick that finger in his face one more time and you're going to need a doctor yourself. Knock it off."

Everyone froze.

"Holy shit," Lana whispered.

This right here was the problem. My mistakes were never going away. There would always be someone looking to tear into me for what happened.

I could take it. Did take it.

But the people I love didn't have to.

"Mayhem, don't." I wanted her to defend herself like that. Not me.

"No," she said with a sharp glance at me, her eyes shining with barely banked rage. "You know what? No, dammit. I won't have someone attacking you right in front of me after everything you're doing to help us. I won't have it."

"Stay away from my daughter. Do you hear me? And you," she said, this time looking at Mayhem, but thinking better of pointing a finger at her. "You think your team will have success while you're connected to him. Think again." Lana's mother stormed off back the way she came.

Lana sat in her chair, rubbing her forehead. "I'm sorry. She's the last thing you needed tonight."

"She has a right to how she feels, Lana. It's not your fault."

"What?" Mayhem said, turning on me. "She does not have the right to tear into you whenever she wants. How the hell is anyone supposed to move on with her lashing out like that? And why the hell did you just stand there and take it?"

My skin prickled. Trapped between secrets that weren't mine to tell and what I wanted, what I needed, frustration bubbled up inside me. Tired, scared for my sister, and so damn sick of being tempted by what I couldn't have, humiliation took complete control of my mouth. "Me taking it? You're one to talk."

Lana flinched and dug her fingers against her temples. "Oh, Coach... not the right reaction."

"What the hell is that supposed to mean?" Mayhem demanded.

"Six elbows to the ribs. That's what I mean."

"And you invited her on the team despite it. So who's the asshole here?"

I knew who the asshole was and yeah, I was still pissed

at myself for fucking that one up, but pride. Fucking pride. "I'll tell you what, I'll stop taking it as soon as you do."

Her eyes flashed, the look there, I was pretty sure I had pushed her to a new territory. Barely banked fury. "Tell Lilith I hope she feels better."

"Wait." I reached for her, but she shook me off.

"You want to come to our practice, you've got it," she said, resting her hand on Lana's shoulder. "Give me a call at The Shipwreck in the morning and we'll work out the details."

Lana and I watched her head for the door. When it slid shut behind her, Lana looked up at me. "You're great with the ladies."

"My fucking kryptonite."

"Does this mean she's not your girlfriend?"

"Fuck if I know."

I wasn't wrong. If it was something she cared about, she was all over it, but when it came to protecting herself, she backed down.

But the way I said it—where I chose to say it, wrong in every conceivable way.

The team was good. Damn good. Every last one of them workhorses who didn't run their mouths when it was time to get to work. If I could figure out what the hell was going on with Mayhem—what she kept locked up in there—they might even have the chance to be brilliant.

And every clue pointed to Tilly.

Tilly, even on her best behavior, would always have power over Mayhem if she didn't confront whatever history they had. Because right now, Tilly hadn't done one damn thing on that track to step out of line and it was like that might actually be fucking with Mayhem worse than if she did.

"I think it's time for the truth, Coach," Lana said quietly.

"That's not for me to decide."

"You've been protecting me way too long. It's costing you too much," Lana said with a shrug. "Anyway, what can they do with the truth now? Statute of limitations doesn't really apply here, right?"

"No. But it's a small town. People will talk."

"They already do… but not going to lie, Coach… I just don't care." She glanced past me and smiled.

A tall, broad-shouldered guy with an easy smile on his face walked over. "I got hung up. Sorry about that." He squatted down and pulled Lana in for a sound kiss. "Hi," he murmured to her quietly.

I backed up a step, feeling like an interloper. An old interloper.

"Coach, this is Zach. Zach, my old—uh, former derby coach," Lana said with a wink like she could read my mind.

I reached out and shook the man's hand. "Cain Bishop."

"You're the guy who's had my little delinquent's back."

"Guilty."

"Cain Bishop?" the nurse called from the reception desk. "You can go in now."

Lana took my hand. "Coach? If I come clean, it doesn't screw you, right?"

"Nah. As you can see, I'm really good at getting myself in trouble all on my own."

"Spectacular at it," she said, tugging me in to collect the kiss on the cheek I always had for her before I headed in to see Lilith.

Two hours passed before I was finally able to head to my truck. Of course, I would have stayed overnight if that's what Lilith needed. Or even what she wanted. A urinary tract infection—I'd never been so damn relieved to hear those words. They'd keep her overnight, giving her antibiotics through an IV and monitoring my nephew while they did, and if everything went according to plan, she'd be able to go home by lunchtime tomorrow.

She was tired and uncomfortable, but my nephew was safe.

The sound of his strong heart echoing through the monitors gave me a smile after a spectacularly shitty night.

I'd never heard his heartbeat before. He wasn't even mine, but I hoped I'd get to hear it again.

Jordan was missing so much being overseas.

And my sister was missing the experience of having her husband right there for everything.

Having me wasn't the same... she missed her other half and I missed him for her.

Or maybe I missed mine.

Or what could be mine... for now.

Mayhem and I skipped friendship and tipped right over into acting on our feelings. And we'd barely had time to do that before we ventured into coach and player only to have me fuck it all up only an hour into that.

Now I didn't know what we were. Or even what we could be.

Because in the end, I still planned to walk away.

If Lana went through with it, told the truth—the whole truth—I wouldn't necessarily be so welcome on the police force.

I knew what she'd done and said nothing despite my obligation to uphold the law, something that still didn't sit well with me all these years later, but she was a dumb kid who'd done dumb kid shit. Something that cost her huge. Reporting it seemed like acid in the wound.

They couldn't do anything to her any worse than she'd done to herself.

"Hey."

I glanced up to find Mayhem leaning against her car, dragging the toe of her shoe on the damp asphalt, her eyes anywhere but on mine.

"Hey." I stopped before her and slid my hands in my pockets so I wouldn't reach for her.

"I tried to leave. I even made it out of the parking lot, but I couldn't go without seeing if Lilith was okay."

"She's okay. UTI. She's staying overnight."

"The baby?"

"He's good."

"I threatened to put a woman in a hospital bed tonight," she mumbled, her brows knitting together.

I chuckled and kicked the toe of her boot. "You did."

She glanced toward the glass doors to the ER. "I've never done that. I don't—why did I do that?"

"You're angry."

We both were. Angry, stuck, and scared.

"But I didn't even know that woman. I just—I could see Lana jerking in that chair like she wanted to stand up and be seen and I just—her mother didn't even see her." She ground her fingertips into her temples and shook her head. "God, I never want to see that again."

"You're a protector," I said quietly, knowing I was about to make one more assessment she wouldn't appreciate tonight, but also knowing if something didn't give, we'd stay here. Stuck right here, just spinning.

"I guess," she said with a shrug.

"At least when it comes to everyone but yourself."

She stilled, her lips twisting with scorn as she glared up at me. "How are you any different with how you just stood there and let her treat you that way?"

"Lana's mother can't hurt me. She can rage, she can make me uncomfortable, but she can't take anything from me."

She pushed away from the side of her car and shook her head with her keys clenched tight in her fist. "If she's part of the reason you don't stay… she already has."

"Hustle up, you've got hot dates hugging the kick rails today for warm-up!" Priest called out as he tossed pads over the rails into the infield.

He had a spark of energy today I hadn't seen in him since Lilith spent the night at the hospital. I hadn't realized how much I counted on his mood to set the tone for us, until spotting him just ten minutes before with more color in his face and those tension lines bracketing his mouth all but gone.

He'd become a part of us in the few weeks we'd been training. It made me wonder about after. What it would be like to return to the flat track without him.

Maybe as a WRDF team, maybe not. It would be months until we'd hear for sure.

"Sometimes he's just way too excited about torturing us," Tilly muttered.

It's the first thing she'd said to me, really said to me since joining the team. Thirsty didn't count. I mean, you gave someone water when you cared about them and wanted them to be okay, but you also gave them water when you didn't want them to die on your watch lest you be accused of their death.

I spun around to look before I actually believed full on

that she had directed her comment at me, but everyone had spread out on other benches to gear up, Carmen, Rory, Eve, and Sean stretched on the concrete in the corner.

Marty, the showoff, was already on the bank doing warm-up laps. Must be nice to work at a desk so you could be nice and fresh for practice.

Actually, I'd probably lose my mind behind a desk, so maybe cell deep exhaustion wasn't so bad.

"Right," I said quietly, unsure of this treacherous new territory.

Was it fur-lined or wrapped with razor wire?

Were we supposed to become friends now? Again?

How the hell was I supposed to forget all the nasty things she'd said over the years to poke me, prod me, the way she used my mother to torture me?

But how was I supposed to move on if nothing changed?

Here I was, twenty-four and still living in the past. Worse than that, I was trapped in the ninth grade. Who the fuck wanted that bullshit?

"Shit," Tilly whispered as she dug through her bag furiously.

I didn't glance over this time and instead kept my focus on padding up. "What's wrong?"

"One of my wristguards is missing. I have a new puppy and he's constantly stealing my shit. He's got a fetish for anything with my dried sweat."

"Boys are gross." God, that sounded lame. "You've, uh, you've always wanted a dog. I think—well, thought. Anyway," I said with a jerky nod. "Koda, right?"

Christ, this was as stop and go as an old man with a prostate problem trying to take a leak.

"Yeah. And now Koda has one of my wristguards. The furry little freak."

"I've got an extra pair." I tossed them on the bench next to her and finished strapping on my knee pads.

She half turned. "Thanks."

"No problem."

We didn't look at one another, instead, started building some weird tentative bond over water, furry mutts, and sweaty wristguards. We weren't going to win any awards with our stumbling attempts at coexisting, but maybe I'd get to the point where Tilly wasn't the first thing I worried about when I got on that track.

And maybe this is what Priest was trying to say.

This was getting in my way… and he could see it.

Well, fine. But I still wanted to bite him.

Especially when he was just as guilty. Only he'd attached some sort of just-trying-to-be-honorable-paying-for-my-mistakes badge on his lack of defense, leaving mine looking like fear.

God, that sucked.

I'd rather eat one of Tilly's sweaty wristguards than choke down that truth. You know, if she could find them.

The time to really let Tilly have it had passed, and I wasn't even sure I wanted it back. It was like having a knock-down, drag-out fight and thinking of a bunch of points, good one-liners, and quips well after the fact.

When you wanted to recreate the moment so much that you tried to niggle the person into the same fight again so you could give those digs life, even as you knew they'd never land with just the same oomph as if you'd said them from the beginning.

You know, manipulative girl shit.

We all did it.

We were fucking pros at it.

So now I reached that point I had to try not to recreate it, right? I mean, it shouldn't be so hard since I'd never said a single nasty word about her parents and it's not like I couldn't have, but I didn't.

You're welcome, Tilly.

This was really a one-sided thing.

Going back to that place meant taking barbs—again—and with everything ahead of me and the way I lashed out the other night at Lana's mother, I should probably avoid that. I'd just never wanted to hurt her the way she hurt me.

To do so meant turning her back into Tilly the Cyborg again or worse, Tilly the Wench.

So tentative pseudo friendship it was.

Without another word, we skated over to the bank and climbed up to join the rest of the team.

"Today we're starting with boundaries. The kick rail and handrails on the track in Philly will have a bit more flex than the ones here," Priest said as he curled his fingers around the padded rail and yanked, resulting in barely any give. "It's designed to absorb some of the force when you hit. You'll learn to appreciate that."

"Bashing into the railing… looking forward to it," Eve said with a spark in her eye I hadn't seen in what felt like forever. The anger that gave her a barbed edge since our goodbye seemed to be softening.

I hoped it was… not for me, for her.

"Give and take," he said, his lips twitching at the corners. "You'll send others into the railing too."

She smiled. "That's the part I'm looking forward to."

He laughed and started to skate backward with us following him like a cluster of ducklings as he laid out the plan. "You need to get used to bumping into the kick rail," he said, kicking it as he said it, "and not letting it slow you down. You'll feel the drag on the edge of your skate. You're going to get driven into it a lot. I don't want it in your head when you do," he said, his eyes on mine.

Gee, I wonder if he was thinking about me when he said that?

Blink. Blink. Blink.

Subtle, Coach, subtle.

"We're going to do laps. Keep your skate along the edge at all times. The track is going to pull you down. If you stray, steer back."

"Don't make it obvious you're looking, but girl, his shorts are doing that thing again," Rory said behind me, followed by a hum of pure female appreciation.

My eyes went right to the front of his shorts and I rolled my lips inward with what I saw.

"There are two ways to fight the pull…" he started.

Could he maybe use different words? Slide, tug—ummm, never mind.

"Keep your right skate along the rail while you pump with your left. Or you can do reverse crossovers with your left foot to keep you propelled at the top of the track. You'll master both. I want your feet to know exactly what to do by feel. Then we're moving on to transitions and jumps."

I sighed and bit my bottom lip, watching the red material move back and forth, back and forth.

"Mayhem!"

I shot up straight, lost my balance, and righted myself. "What? Damn!"

A wry smile curled over his lips. "You're going to want some of that super cold ice you're so fond of when we're done."

Was he talking about the jumps or the outline of his junk?

"He caught you staring," Rory said, snorting out a giggle from behind me.

"Shut up."

"I wonder if he's a shower *and* a grower?" she said since she clearly didn't know what shut up meant.

My skate dragged along the kick rail and I stumbled. "Oh. My. God. Would you stop?" I hissed over my shoulder.

"I think she already knows," Marty said, squeezing in tight behind Rory.

"We haven't done anything," I mumbled.

I wanted to. I really fucking wanted to.

But he had those flaming asshole tendencies that made me want to choke him.

And that damn no kissing rule.

I wasn't breaking it on principle. He wasn't breaking it on honor.

One of us needed to end the misery.

I had a feeling if I was the one driven to cross the line first, I was going to suck his face clean off his skull.

And Rory would be asking why I'm not sucking the anaconda in his pants.

Well, I wanted that fucker too.

"Yeah, but you don't have to do much more than kiss for him to grind that eager son of a bitch against you," Rory said. "He looks like he'd be a total grinder."

"We have a no kissing rule."

"Girl, why?" Marty asked. "Get frustrated and pissed off out here on the track, then work that shit out on his dick off the track. Seems like a no-brainer."

"Says the woman who has more energy than all of us off this track since she doesn't stand for eight to ten hours a day before she gets here," I said.

"Shit, I'd roll out of a casket to ride that fucking pole,"

Marty said.

"Okay, I know you guys are fucking around, but I'm really going to need you to stop talking about wanting to hop on his dick or we aren't going to be able to be friends anymore. Like, because I'm going to put you in that casket."

Rory held her hands up. "Ouch… okay. Can I just say, I'm gonna be hella happy when we stop this repetitious shit."

"Same," I agreed.

"Just keep watching his dick. It's good for passing the time. Swings like a fucking pendulum in his shorts. You'll be hypnotized."

I stumbled again, lost my balance, and jammed my tit on the handrail. "Rory, dammit!" I bit out.

"*You* watch his dick. I didn't say I was going to watch it," she said.

We both knew she was totally going to watch it.

We spent almost an hour on the kick rail forward and backward when the pendulum decided to call for a water break.

"Did anyone else listen in when he was on his cell. He's up to something," Zara asked, making her way up to us.

"What did he say?" Marty asked.

"Something about getting them here by two o'clock," Zara said.

"Did you hear who he was talking to?" I asked.

"Nope, but it won't be long now," Zara said, pointing at the clock over the barn door.

I stole glances of Priest in the infield, pulling apart pads, cones, and chunks of foam in all different shapes and sizes. A few minutes shy of two, he started glancing at the door every few seconds.

What the hell was he up to?

Maison

I'd just swallowed the last of my water and sucked down half a granola bar when I heard voices at the door.

"Maisy!" Rylee squealed the minute she saw me and ran for the edge of the track.

My chest squeezed painfully tight. Tears burned in my throat and filled my eyes. Adrenaline kicked through my veins until I swayed on my feet with the rush of it.

I'd missed them so damn much.

I'd had to give almost every minute of my time with them to do this… to protect my time with them in the future.

I skated up the track to the edge, yanked off my helmet, and dropped on my knees to reach for her. Pulling her up on the track, I swallowed her with my arms and breathed in the scent of strawberry shampoo that I hadn't even realized I only associated with her.

"We haven't seen you in so long," she murmured against my chest, sending a wave of fresh tears down my face.

I hadn't known I needed this. I needed them.

I needed to remind myself what I was here for, what was at stake if I couldn't pull this off.

"I missed you too, honey," I whispered against her hair with an extra squeeze. "So, so much."

It wasn't about having a favorite. I loved them all just the same.

But Rylee reminded me so much of me after my mom died.

Always hanging back. A little unsure. Not wanting to make waves out of fear.

She's the one who needed the extra hugs, the constant encouragement, and the safety net while she grew braver.

And I needed to give them to her as much as she needed to receive them.

Addison, Ellie, Noah, and Leo all made it onto the track next with Priest's help. One at a time he lifted them up until I squeezed my entire cluster in my arms again. Even Noah and Leo who were usually above hugs swooped onto the pile.

I gulped back tears in my throat and met Priest's eyes.

Thank you.

I mouthed the words and he winked, leaving me blinking through a fresh round of tears before going to lift the other kids onto the track.

Wes walked over and propped a shoulder against the rail next to us. "It's a good thing you're doing here, Maisy. I'm proud of you."

"Thank you," I said, kissing the top of Addison and Ellie's heads. "Someone had to save our afternoons at Rockabilly's."

"It's more than that, and you know it. I see it. But you're right, I'm looking forward to hanging on to those trips too. If you make this happen, I'll even get my very own pair of skates and humiliate myself out there. You think those skate buddies come in jumbo?"

I choked on a laugh and swiped away the tears on my cheeks. "I'll have one made for you myself."

Priest disappeared for a few minutes, but when he came back, he had Lilith on his arm. He settled her in a chair, helped unload the kids off the bank, and ordered us all back on the track and back to work.

He'd turned three sections into obstacle courses of sorts while we were visiting with the kids before he went to the house to get his sister.

He told us to line up for laps, and with each new lap, he'd call out what he wanted us to do.

Spin out transitions where we wouldn't just veer left or right around the obstacle, but we'd spin away from it and skate on by. Then bean dips, pretending each barrier was an opponent ready to deliver a blow with their shoulder, where we dropped low on our way past with a twist to avoid the hit, giving the opponent our backs—an illegal target zone.

The kids watched with excited smiles on their faces, their rapt attention absorbing everything, but it was the jumps that had them on their feet cheering.

Running on our toes, transitioning to duck walks to push on our edges, and then shifting into a glide to gain speed, we'd skate low around the corners and freestyle jump the pads and cones along the straightaway before coming around again.

Over and over in a line, we'd just go with it, whatever we felt like doing, performing for the kids, teaching those boys exactly why skating was cool, and watching their eyes light up at our moves.

Tilly skated ahead of me, smiling at a cluster of kids she worked with, giving them a wink—the move distracting her just enough she miscalculated her speed when she jumped.

Her skate caught, she stumbled, but rolled, rolling to a stop across the track just past the padding in front of me.

Right in front of me. Too damn close.

If I jumped, I was never going to clear the padding and Tilly.

Her eyes widened and she froze.

If I went for it, for the whole leap and didn't clear her, I was going to do damage, real damage. Broken bones kind of damage.

In front of a room full of kids.

Fuck.

I could hear my team yelling, Priest yelling, their hollers muffled and urgent.

Everything slowed, the echo of my breath a jagged tear through my windpipe, our eyes locking, and only the fraction of a second to make a decision and pray it was right.

Don't move, Tilly.

I leaped, giving it everything I had, my thighs and calves flexing, my left foot digging in its edge, straightening my knee to launch me over the pads, and come down on my front wheels and toe stop in the narrow gap on the other side where I'd give one last push up on a double-toed hop and clear her.

If I didn't time it just right, I'd hit her.

I had no idea how much space there was from this angle. Inches, maybe… but no more than a foot between the backside of the pad and Tilly's body.

I focused on that gap. Willed myself to land in that gap.

My skate came down with a hard grind against the track. My wheel started to slip but stopped when my toe stop made solid contact with the Masonite.

At least I hoped it was the Masonite.

I couldn't look. I didn't want to know. If I looked and I

was hurting her, I'd never clear the next jump over, the one right in line with her neck and shoulders.

Pushing one last time, I dragged in a heavy breath, and launched myself over her, swinging my arms, arching my back—anything to give myself more momentum.

Landing on the other side, I skidded and spun until I was aimed back at Tilly, my lungs heaving with the exertion it took to get over her.

She pushed herself up, stumbling to her feet, her face white and coated in sweat. Patting her hands up and down her chest, she grinned. "Fuck yeah."

Her hand went up for a high five.

Relief surged through me, leaving me light-headed.

Sweat poured down my face only to be soaked up by the strap buckled under my chin. A laugh burst free as I rolled toward her and slapped her palm. As naturally as I did the last time I high-fived her, I dropped my hand low to slap hers again on the underside, going in for a fist bump, and a finger lock followed by the hip bump we did as kids.

We both stared down at our hands, the tips of our fingers naturally interlaced the same way they had been so many years ago, a time when we were best friends, when we used to do this handshake a dozen times a day easy.

I couldn't speak past the lump in my throat. Past missing her.

"Thanks, girl," she said quietly. The words relieved and heavy at the same time.

Thanks, girl.

The same way she'd said it when we were kids, and I got her a new pair of pants on the first day we met when she got stuck in the bathroom with a surprise period that obliterated her khakis.

Our fingers slid apart, and Tilly rolled back, her eyes narrowed in confusion. Her skin ashen.

Probably just like mine.

"Yes! That's what I'm talking about," Priest yelled, climbing onto the track. He grabbed my arms and spun me toward him, my team right behind him swallowing every free inch of track until Tilly disappeared in the cluster. "That is what you're capable of. What I've been trying to get you to see."

"Survival instincts," I said, smiling.

"Exactly. That's what you can do when you've got total focus. I'm so damn proud of you," he said breathlessly. He grinned down at me, his eyes narrowed, his gaze on my mouth. "Fuck the rules," he mumbled right before he fisted the material of my tank top and dragged me under his mouth for a quick, hot kiss.

His taste filled me up, his tongue stealing a quick taste, leaving me a panting mess on skates.

He let me go, his lips moving to my ear, making me tremble from head to toe. "Now get your sweet ass back out there and do it again."

"Yes, sir." I said the words with way too much enthusiasm judging by the way he dragged his thumb over his bottom lip and swept a hot glance over me.

"Sir, huh? I think I like that."

"Go away, you're making it hard to concentrate," I said, giving him a shove that he only laughed off.

We worked for another hour, until the kids had to leave. I crouched down outside of the track and collected all the squeezes they'd give me. Only when they were loaded in the van, the last of their waves visible disappearing around the corner, did I head back for the infield.

"You guys did good today. Really damn good. Get out of here early tonight. Go celebrate," Priest said before skating back to the bench with his gear.

I headed over and stopped in front of him. "We'll

probably stop in at Banked Track. Did you want to join us?"

"Mmmmm," he hummed as he wrapped his hands around my hips and pulled me between his knees. "I'm going to stay with Lilith tonight. I'm not ready to leave her just yet."

"You're awfully handsy all of a sudden, you know," I said, even though my hands had already gone to his shoulders.

With the way his shorts flirted with me earlier, I needed to do something with my hands. This seemed pretty innocent considering the fuck-me vibes swinging in his yum-yum zone.

Plus, there was Eve and I didn't want to do anything so in her face that it caused her more pain. I'd take my cues from her where that was concerned... and we were getting there.

His head fell back, the skin over his Adam's apple stretched taut. "Would you rather I break your rule again?"

I wanted to bite him there. Right. Fucking. There. "Not yet."

"But soon?"

"We'll see," I said, skating out of his arms and heading for my duffel.

We packed up in under ten minutes and our cars rolled like a damn caravan right into town and filled the parking lot.

No one died... and we had some fucking celebrating to do.

Milton and Gerald sat at the end of the counter chatting it up with Patti.

"I hope you two are being good for Patti," I called out.

"They're beered up, happy as clams over here, both of

them exposing their tender underbellies like good little dogs."

"Damn, Patti! Way to lay a guy low," Gerald grumbled.

I ducked over, wrapped an arm around each of their shoulders, and kissed both of them on the cheek. "I'm proud of you boys for getting along. Makes me much freer with my kisses."

"Well, hell, Maisy Jane, if you'd told me that's all it would take, I would have started behaving a long time ago," Milton said, kissing my cheek and patting my back. "Keep being good for Patti over here. I've got to join my team. We've got some celebrating to do."

"No climbing my bar, missy," Patti warned as I backed away.

"Wouldn't dream of it," I said with a wink.

I spotted Rita in the opposite corner with her husband, Len. "Did you have a hand in getting those kids cleared to go out to the farm today?" I called to her.

She winked as Len took her hand and kissed her knuckles. "That might have been me."

"I owe you, huge. Thank you."

Rory let out a whistle, snagging Patti's attention. "A round of Banked Tracks—"

Tilly watched all the commotion with a cautious look on her face. I knew she wouldn't like our usual, but I also knew she probably felt just awkward and out of place enough, she'd never say so after taking the first sip and would just suffer through it to fit in.

I had her back.

"Pick something else tonight, guys. Tilly doesn't like root beer. Besides, we could use a special drink for tonight to celebrate."

"That's cool. What do you like?" Zara asked as she passed the drink menu to Tilly.

"I'll be right back. That big ass bottle of water I sucked down on the drive here is knocking."

I ducked into the bathroom, did my business, washed my hands, caught my face in the mirror, and froze.

Clear, bright eyes stared back at me. A healthy pink hue glowed on my happily flushed cheeks. My chin tilted with confidence, my chest out and shoulders back.

I didn't recognize myself.

And it's exactly what I kidded myself into thinking I looked like all along.

This was the look I wanted Rylee to have on her face.

Well, shit. My team would just have to win some money and make sure I got to stick around long enough to help Rylee achieve it.

I headed back to the derby booth and spotted Tilly's empty seat. "Where's Tilly?"

Rory shrugged. "She said she had to go. Guess we can order those Banked Tracks after all."

Maisy

thirty-three

"Jackson left his dad in charge of the cash register so he could be here helping us today. Let's make it worth it," Priest said from the edge of the track as we got ready for a full day.

Fucking weekend practices were the worst. Long hours, packed lunches reminiscent of days with the less discerning palates we needed to actually find them awesome, and sun shining over fresh snow crystals blanketing the ground from the night before whispering to us to come out and play.

I need a play day so freaking bad.

In true Jackson form, he'd managed to snag a pink tank top for his stint reffing from the infield. He'd even gone so far as to scrawl Beautifully Brutal over the chest in thick Sharpie. And on the back, the number 6-6-6 with a scribble of the grim reaper wielding a scythe, his evil laughter spelled out in a word bubble over his head.

Rory watched him skate by, spotted the back of his tank, and choked on her coffee. "We should see if he's willing to be one of our officials."

"You know, it's not a bad idea," Sean said as she clicked the buckle to her helmet. "Then, if anything happened to our deal with Sid's, we'd have a direct line on somewhere else to play… you know, since Jackson would have a vested interest and all. He'd make a great skate mechanic too."

I pulled on my wrist guard and glanced up at Jackson and Priest, their heads together as they scanned their notes. "I'm kind of digging this plan."

"Or we could use Sid's for our very own banked track and use Rockabilly's for flat track," Marty said. "I'd be up for it."

My fingers froze and my heart perked up its tired little head after the wave of adrenaline and pure fucking joy from having the kids here to watch us waned far too fast. Not that I wasn't still driven. I was. I just wanted my kids. Wes could totally drive them here every few days for mandatory hugs, couldn't he?

"What do you mean, start our own league?" I said as I tucked a nonstick gauze pad on the inside of my elbows. Anything to help soak up the buckets of sweat coming my way today. If I could get out of this unchafed, it'd be a damn miracle.

"We could. If we really wanted to," Marty said, her crooked grin telling me she was latching on to the idea.

The money girl, guys. The money girl was latching on to the idea.

She never got all tingly for ideas that cost a bunch of money. Or meant more paperwork for her.

This definitely sounded like a recipe for paperwork.

And attorneys, permits, insurance companies, basically any entity designed to both protect you by making you all legal like and make your eye twitch.

I dropped down to the bench and glanced up. "But what about the WRDF?"

"We can still do that *and* this. And if that doesn't work

out, maybe we could just do this," Marty said with a half shrug.

But there was no reason for it to not work out, unless the WRDF took issues with us working with Priest, even if that working was only temporary. Unless Marty was thinking about him staying which she shouldn't, because he wasn't.

Tilly skated past without a hint of interest in what we were talking about and tossed my wristguards with a barely audible "thanks" before she skated off to the other side of the infield.

My stomach plummeted to my toes, a familiar apprehension creeping in on me. A hesitance that would unfold on the track and have Priest tearing me a new asshole.

"What's up with her?" I asked as I watched her go.

Rory shook her head, her mouth grim. "She's been weird ever since last night."

"Did she get a call or something while I was in the bathroom?"

"Nope. She just got really quiet and said she had to go," Rory said, giving Tilly a dose of side-eye.

I watched Tilly out of the corner of my eye as she pulled on her elbow pads, followed by her wristguards, and gave a firm tug to the strap under her chin to tighten her helmet. She stood alone, avoiding eye contact, her mouth tight, and a crease between her eyebrows.

"Okay, ladies, round up," Priest called. He waited for us to skate in a circle around him and glanced down at his notepad. "On team one: Hate Puck, Spread 'Em, Wall of Duty, Lick-Or-Treat, and... Come Queen." Priest scratched his head. "And they say guys are pigs."

"I don't know, I kind of like them," Jackson said with a grin.

"You would," Priest said, scoffing at him. "Team two:

Anarch-Eve, Hazy Eights, Tilly the Hun, Mayhem, and Hot West. Get on the bank and let's do this." He skated past me, his palm landing on my hip. "Hey," he said quietly, his lips brushing over my temple, sending a shot of pure fucking lust straight into my shorts. "Kick some ass."

I leaned into him, siphoning the feel of hot, hard, towering man pressed up against me for every second I could. "Did you at least wear underwear today?"

"I did," he said with a laugh. "Didn't want any injuries up there."

"What, like poking an eye out?" I said with what I thought would be a snort but came out a hell of lot more like a whimper.

"Sounds like you might be about ready to get rid of that no kissing rule," he murmured as he dragged a lazy finger along the edge of my collarbone over the word "belonging" tattooed in script there.

"Or maybe you destroyed it when you got all manhandley with me out on the track the other day," I said, forcing the words when his touch had sucked all the air out of the room, but enjoying the way he opened up ever since I managed to avoid steamrolling my own player on the track.

The rigid set of his shoulders had eased. He didn't tunnel his hands through his hair in frustrated spurts quite as much, and he smiled showing off that deep dimple along the edge of his cheek I didn't get to see nearly enough of.

Happiness looked damn good on the man.

A hot, promising grin curled his lips. "Don't give me any ideas, Mayhem. We've got a long day ahead of us."

"Hey, I'm not the one all reaching out to touch someone," I said despite doing just that when I swatted his ass as I skated away, giving him a firm squeeze while I was at it.

We started out slow, not because he had us start out that way, but apparently now that we were actually doing this in full force, we'd gone all duh when putting the moves together. We'd turned into a nightmare cheesy montage of 1980's bloopers from *Cocoon* full of agonizingly slow exaggerated movements and unsure glances.

Followed by the surprised look you get when you trust a fart only to have it betray you.

Gerald almost melted the vinyl of a bar stool one day with one of those.

I had to do something about what was unfolding here. I was a jammer. I set the tone with my takeoff in a way. If I just came in hard, fast, and confident, they'd follow.

Clearly the anaconda smuggler on the infield agreed since he started pacing alongside us, shouting the entire time.

"Go harder!"

"You're not one team on the bank now, you're opponents. Act like it!"

"Push, push, push!"

"Mayhem, don't make me come up there!"

That one got everyone's attention.

If he was going to stomp around like that, he should just wear his sneakers, it'd be better for his arches.

Two hours in, we finally managed to blast past the awkwardness and go for it. Bodies crashed into rails, players slid down the track and hopped back on with ease, gaps opened and closed, and I managed to shoot through the pack and zip around the corner to battle Carmen for lead jammer position several times over.

By lunch, the jitters gone, we sat on the infield benches, grabbing more water than food, our feet tapping to the beat of the music Priest pumped into the barn.

He stood by the front office with Jackson, their heads

together, while Jackson scrolled through his phone. In the few quiet minutes, I could actually study him, so I took full advantage.

But studying meant wanting, if it was possible to want more than I already did.

I'd developed a taste for a bit of self-torture.

How did I know? Because my yearning went way beyond the physical. I wanted him here. In Galloway Bay. I wanted him to take his power back and stay.

Finally beyond the monotony of constant repetitive footwork and finally dipping our toes in the fire that came with real derby, my body hummed with energy. It skittered under my skin, making it nearly impossible to sit still.

My brain latched on and turned that energy into fantasy.

What if?

What if Priest had followed me up to my apartment the night we mauled each other in my hallway?

What if he hadn't brought Tilly onto the team without warning me?

That was easy—I would have set fire to the no kissing rule in the first week no doubt.

I'd spent almost three weeks staring at his buffet of broad shoulders, arms corded with hard muscle and thick veins, and a rather spectacular ass, round, solid, and so damn out of reach at the moment.

"You look like you want to bite right into his ass cheek like it's an apple," Marty said next to me.

I sighed, my quiet moment all too brief. "I bet he snaps like a Red Delicious. The clear, crisp pop, and not too sweet."

"You should just do something about that already. When you guys sniff around each other with so many white-hot glances that you have the rest of us taking cold showers, it's time. Past fucking time," Marty said. "I mean, my down below is on permanent vibrate at this point so hop on that and give us all the details."

"Would you think less of me if I admitted I was afraid of falling for him only to watch him go?"

"Oh, girl," Marty said with a wince. "You already fell for him, so you might as well take the time you have. You never know, he may surprise you. Or you'll surprise him."

"Lunch is over! Hustle up; we're switching up teams," Priest called out as he hopped onto the track along the straightaway where it was lowest to the floor. His skates never once slipping from the grip he made by digging in his edges.

There really was something to be said for a guy who had so much control on wheels.

"Okay, team one: Mayhem, Anarch-Eve, Dixie Dom, Lick-Or-Treat, and Sleeping Booty. Team two: Hazy Eights, Lowe Bar, Rory Highness, Tilly the Hun, and Get Hussy. Get out there and push it!"

We skated into position, the blockers stepping in and around each other. One of their blockers moved, one of our blockers followed.

Right now, Eve stayed pressed to Tilly, moving with her every adjustment, never letting her break away.

My stomach rolled, the old instincts, old fears trying to creep back.

No.

Not this time.

We were teammates and I didn't crush her to dust with my skate the other day. We'd evolved.

All the old shit, it was over.

The starting whistle pierced the air and I dug in my edge taking off at a run on my toe stops. Three steps and a stride had me reaching the pack. In a tight cluster of bodies and legs I fought to get through, trying to wedge into small openings to push my body through and break them apart.

I spun out reaching around the high side along the rail, but Rory was right there to close the gap and send me toward the bottom of the track. I found another gap along the bottom, took advantage of the coping, only to have Tilly plant her left skate in front of mine and drive me out of bounds.

Whistle after whistle, play after play, Tilly didn't stop. She never once threw an elbow, she even managed to avoid an illegal hit when I dipped and gave her my back, but she never backed off of me either.

Like there were two different jams going on out there.

She and I.

And everyone else.

Eight jams in, and I just couldn't pass her.

It was me. All me.

She'd gotten in my head again, and I'd let it happen. Here we were, on the same team, no more bullying, no more spite, and she was still fucking with me.

With one final drive of her hips, she sent me into the infield and the whistle blew. I rolled along the inside, mumbling to myself, my fingers steepled over my head while I rested my hands on my helmet.

It's not the same. Let it go. Just let it go.

"Praying to your dead mother?"

Maisy

The whispered sneer slithered over my shoulder. A second later, Tilly skated past me, the smirk right back on her mouth, every bit of progress we'd made obliterated and fuck if I knew why.

I'd never escape this. As long as we coexisted in this town, I'd never escape this or her. She'd find a way to steal every piece of joy I carved for myself.

Every safe place.

My sport.

Even my kids by sabotaging our chances at the exhibition.

My heart hammered behind my ribs, the blood stampeded through my head, and my control snapped.

Memories cascaded through my mind like a stack of pictures slipping from slack fingertips.

My mother tossing the end of her broken and frayed green lace in the trash the last time we skated together.

Waking up alone in our shared room, shivering under a blue flowered quilt the morning she died.

The police at the door telling me I had to go with them.

Every night from then on in a bunkbed, my scratchy standard issue blanket jammed against my ear to drown out the melody of employees' shoes squeaking on the linoleum, screams of kids lashing out in pain and fear, and the sobs of lonely, heartsick girls in the darkness after the lights went out.

The echo of a lifetime collection of her words all came flooding back, cracking open the recently sealed tomb of my pain.

The taunts, the insults, relentless everywhere I turned until she snatched away every bit of comfort I managed to find in a scary world where I was well and truly all alone.

No mother, no father, no family to speak of.

No family friends.

Just me.

Never belonging.

A haze covered my eyes, and all I could see were my hands wrapping around her throat. I cut my edge into the concrete, pushed off, and lunged for her, a scream of fury tearing from my lungs. The minute my forearm slid over her shoulder, I bent my elbow, wrapping around her neck.

She grunted right before I squeezed the sound right from her throat as we crashed into the cold, hard ground.

The roaring in my head only grew when I rolled her over under me and met her wide eyes. I drew my hand back, my fingers clenched into a tight fist and punched her. Pain exploded in my knuckle when it caught the edge of her helmet, but I didn't care. Blood burst across her skin over her eye, and I drew my hand back and hit her again to spill some more.

"Oh shit!"

"Grab her!"

Hands reached out for me, but I threw them off.

I wrapped my fingers around the strap of her helmet and shook her. "Don't you ever talk about her again! *Ever!*" I screamed, my skin tight, my lips peeled back from my teeth. My heart exploded in my chest, my thighs squeezing her waist as I tried to crush her right here on the concrete while I pulled my fist back a third time.

Powerful fingers locked on my forearm. "Stop!" Priest's commanding voice cut through the voices of my team, but not through the haze of violence rioting inside me.

His fault.

I spun around and met his narrowed dark eyes, the flicker of disappointment there—that was his fault too. A storm of animosity burst from somewhere deep in my heart. I wanted to hurt him the way he hurt me.

For how this one mistake continued to hurt me.

Drawing back my other hand, I swung at him.

The gasps of my teammates cut through the haze filling my head.

His eyes widened as he ducked my hand, and when he straightened, he pierced me with a cold, hard glare. "You took a swing at me." His tone dropped impossibly low, his words lethal and deathly calm.

I couldn't speak, I could only lash out again, but this time, before I could even pull my hand all the way back, he lifted me clean off the concrete and threw me over his shoulder.

"Put me down, you son of a bitch! I hate you." I beat on his back as I tried to twist out from under the arm pinning me to his shoulder. I kicked my skates in the air and yanked his shirt. "Put. Me. Down!"

My arms grew heavy, my lungs ached, and angry tears filled my eyes as he slid us both under the rail and off the track, never letting me down while he did it.

Proficient fucker.

His skates pounded the concrete floor, the reverberation shooting through him and into me so hard my teeth rattled with it, and my mouthguard fell out with a wet splatter as he stalked away from my team.

"Practice is over! Go home!" he bellowed as he snapped open the door to his office and slammed it shut behind him, making the glass behind the blinds quake.

Dropping me on my skates, he backed me right up against the wall. "What the fuck was that?"

"You don't know? Maybe I wasn't doing it right then," I spat before bringing my palm up and slapping him with everything I had, the sound of my palm snapping across his cheek a crack of thunder before an ominous silence filled the room.

His nostrils flared, his brows dropped low over his now black eyes. With a flick of his fingers, my chinstrap popped free and my helmet skittered across the floor. Grabbing me by the jaw, his hand trembled against me as he held me there with the pads of his rough fingers sinking into my skin.

I lifted my chin and refused to look away. He fucked up, not me.

He wanted me to stand up for myself?

Fine. I did.

Now what?

"You hit me." He growled the words against my mouth as he sucked in a furious breath, nuzzling his nose against my cheek.

I dug my nails into the skin just above the back of his shorts and yanked him to me. "Let go of me, and I'll do it again."

He ground against me, hard and ready, the promise of him dragging a ragged hiss from between my lips.

"You'd like that, but no—that's not what we're doing now. You had your shot. You won't get another."

I reached for him, my hands wrapping around his balls through his shorts and squeezing.

"Joke's on you, Mayhem. I like it hard."

He curled his hand into the waistband of my shorts at my hip and jerked the fabric down. Panting against me as he teased the corner of my mouth with his lips, his hand shot along the elastic, the back of his hand grazing right over my hot center right before he dragged down the fabric on the other hip.

"We have a rule," I gasped out as his lips slid closer and my body defied me by clenching impossibly tight, leaving me wet with furious lust.

"No kissing. Got it," he said with a jerky nod as he continued to yank back and forth until he had my shorts around my knees.

"I hate you." I bit out the words, my body defying my head with every thrust of my hips against him.

Seeking. Wanting. Needing him inside me.

"We both know that's a fucking lie," he said as he dragged his own shorts down his thighs.

"You're an asshole."

He let out a scathing laugh. "This isn't news."

"What are you doing?"

"I'm going to fuck that attitude right out of you."

I plunged my hands under his shirt and met hot, smooth skin. "What if I want to do the fucking?"

He pressed his forehead against mine. "You already have, Mayhem. I'm here breaking all the rules for you. I've torn open every fucking wound I have... for you," he said, his words full of torment. "You've fucked me from every goddamn direction but one," he said before swooping his arm behind both of my knees, squeezing my thighs together as he scooped me up, leaving my legs draped over his arm and off to his side. Taking another half step into me, he forced my knees to my chest with the cold wall digging harder into my back.

Leaving me exposed.

So fucking wet and exposed.

"Two assaults. Guess if you actually stuck around instead of running away, you'd be on the payroll and obligated to arrest me," I said, delivering the words with a scathing edge while I bucked in his arms, daring him to do his worst as the head of his cock grazed over me.

A shimmer of guilt rippled in his eyes before he blinked it away, gnashed his teeth, and plunged hard and deep.

CAIN

My chest swelled with my labored furious breaths. My muscles seized with my initial shock at her hand cracking against my skin.

Even as I knew I deserved it.

That I'd earned it a long time ago with my first betrayal.

Knowing she should punish me again because there'd be a next time.

But there was no price I wouldn't pay to finally watch her break free.

Because taking control back, taking that freedom it gave, even if it came with a complete break with sanity and reason in the heat of the moment, meant I wouldn't destroy her when I walked away.

And walk away I would, because no matter how hard I tried, I hadn't figured out how to break free of my own prison, and the only way to keep people I loved close was by dragging them in with me.

I'd be leaving her here safe in this town I loved, long before my presence could change the course she'd set for herself. Before I could tarnish the bonds she'd made and the family she'd created here.

Guilt by association would destroy what she'd built.

My atonement couldn't restore the damage done.

The stains of the past always bled through the fabric of the present.

Maybe if I'd known then that she was in my future, I would have made different choices.

I never would have left. My brother would be alive.

And Lana wouldn't be serving a life sentence in that chair.

The pain never really subsided. It spread through me, just waiting for moments like this when it could forge together into a hard, hot blade slicing away at me from the inside out, making me frenzied for something, anything to force it back into the recesses again.

A sweet respite in pleasure, even if it came poisoned with betrayal.

Dark driving need took over as I slammed into her wet heat.

Her body stiffened in my arms even as her pussy clamped on to me, pulsing despite the pinch of pain clouding her eyes at the intrusion. I mercilessly stole every last pocket of space while demanding more, taking more, forcing her to stretch to the brink.

Her head dropped back against the wall with a thud. Her lips broke apart on a sharp inhale just to slide into a jagged groan.

Back arched, her breasts squeezed against my chest, the clothing separating us only adding to the frustration. Her neck stretched out before me, the cords taut, bringing the tattoos to life with the way they slid along her throat with every flex.

Tears shimmered in her eyes, and I hissed between my teeth as I fought the urge to pull back and slam into her again.

There was no relief for my pain if I had to punish her to get it.

"You did this to me," she said, her voice breaking, the adrenaline surging through her only moments before, slowly receding as she struggled past the tears clogging her throat.

The imprint of her hand burned on my cheek. The outline of her fingers carrying the bulk of the sting.

"I know," I said taking a ragged breath.

I hurt everyone I love.

Everyone.

"You let her in where she could hurt me," she said as one hand pushed against my shoulder even as she sunk her nails into my ass with the other and pulled me in deeper, animosity and need warring between us.

"I'm sorry," I rasped. "God, I'm so fucking sorry."

"Fuck your words. Show me," she whispered, her voice rough.

Eyes locked on hers, my heart squeezed as a hot tear rolled over the edge of her eyelid and cascaded down her flushed cheek.

I captured it with my lips at the edge of her jaw, the salty flavor ripe on my tongue as I drew out of her, shivered at the cold air hitting my wet cock, and drove back into her again.

Her fingers locked in my hair as she yanked my mouth under hers, her tongue diving for mine as I rocked into her, each thrust driving her up against the wall as she gasped against my lips.

The kissing rule lay dead at our feet, lifeless and cold.

And now I understood why she'd grasped on and erected that barrier between us to begin with.

Danger lay here.

In the feeling.

In the way her body accommodated mine, her survival instincts all but nonexistent as she let the wolf right through the front door. Pulsed for him even, in every squeeze of her muscles around my throbbing cock begging for more.

Taking everything on the most primal level.

No flirting. No teasing. No foreplay.

Just primitive fucking. One step from vulgarity.

The vulnerable, intimate sounds spilling from her heated mouth fueled me faster and harder as we both spiraled into this attraction between us. As our bruised hearts called to one another despite reason.

Despite the dead end ahead.

Ignoring the frantic warning screams in the distance to turn back.

Eyes wild on mine, she sucked in a breath as she locked on my cock, ruthlessly squeezing, making me fight for every thrust.

A fractured cry tore from her throat as she bathed me with her wet release, her eyes glazing over as she quaked from the inside out.

She wasn't seeing me anymore.

But fuck did I see her.

Her passion and her energy finally breaking free on the track, and in my arms. Lost in pleasure, her chest heaving as she fought for every breath, she milked me. The sensation coiled tight, becoming so intense every thrust into her drew my balls up tighter until she became sweet pain, a live wire I was helpless to resist.

Refusing to dive off the edge alone, she anchored herself to me with the bite of her sharp nails carving into my skin while plunging barbs into my heart with the plea in her bright eyes.

Trapped, succumbing to everything she demanded, I toppled over with her.

Gasping breaths filled the room, each of us trying to gain control over our racing hearts. I cupped her chin and held her there while I took her warm, deliciously sweet mouth one last time before reality came crashing in, fucking up everything we found in this moment.

"Did you just fuck me with your skates on?" she whispered over my lips.

A laugh rumbled deep in my chest. "Hell yeah, I did." I brushed a final kiss over her lips before taking a step back, easing her legs down at a more comfortable angle. "Like being on wheels could stop me."

"God, that went straight to your head, didn't it?" she asked with a loopy grin.

"Probably." I gave her a lazy smile while her own skated feet dangled over my arm.

She reached for my hair, tugged, the satisfied smile curving her mouth falling away in an instant, a painful cry slipping through her lips.

Yanking her hand back, she winced. "Shit."

Lowering her onto her skates, I steadied her until she got her balance, and carefully lifted her swelling hand. "We have to get that looked at."

Maisy

Stupid, stupid, stupid.

That's me.

Stupid.

And walking funny.

That part wasn't stupid.

Priest marched me into the ER with a towel-wrapped icepack around my throbbing hand.

I was tired. Just sick and damn tired of the whole thing. And frankly, a bit worried about this newfound taste for violence I had.

Priest's cheek still carried the mark from my hand even an hour later.

I hit a cop. Like, really hit a cop. Not one in this jurisdiction and it was a damn good thing he liked me and all, but holy fuck, I hit a fucking cop.

"Grab a seat and I'll get you checked in," he murmured, pressing a kiss to my forehead before steering me off to the waiting area.

I sought peace in the gently falling snow and headed for the atrium section of the waiting room. Fat flakes drifting from the sky offered welcome distraction from the incessant beat of my heart pulsing in my swollen hand.

Pretty sure I wasn't supposed to feel it there.

Rounding the corner, I skidded to a stop when I spotted Tilly. She lay slumped in one of the few chairs, her legs spread out, her head tipped back with a bag of ice on her eye.

She looked almost young again. Stripped of all expression, with her eyes closed, her face almost peaceful.

I'd seen her icing her face once before. Only we were fifteen and she'd been laughing at a joke I told her, flipped off the back of the swing she'd been lazily kicking herself on, only to have it nail her in the bridge of her nose when she sat up.

She'd bled down the front of her shirt—well, my shirt—my favorite, that I'd only ever let her borrow.

This had to end. This standoff between us robbing us of time and joy. Every face-off costing us precious things we wanted.

I dropped into the seat and slumped alongside her. "Aren't you tired? I know I'm fucking tired."

She cracked open her good eye and sunk even lower with a heavy sigh. "Yeah, so fucking tired."

"You were my best friend," I said quietly.

"Until you left me." Resigned hurt. That was the only way to describe her tone. Like it was one more letdown on the mountain of letdowns and she couldn't let it go.

"I didn't want to. I did everything I could to stay."

She sighed. "I know. Fuck—I know." She shifted the ice and hissed as she settled the pack against the goose egg that was her eyebrow. "I heard you begging them—asking them to find a foster home that would take us both. You always did dream big."

"What you said about my mother—"

"It was a low blow. I guess… I just panicked. We fell into step on the track—"

"No, the first time. At Bay Wilderness. When you told those girls that my mother had to die to get away from me…"

She shook her head and swallowed hard. "I should have never said it. I never once meant it. You were leaving and I was going to be alone. The thought of that place at night, the crying, the fighting—living through that without my best friend; I latched on to whatever I could, whoever I could. And I was so damn hurt that my parents just signed me away. They were off living it up somewhere, and I was reduced to a problem child on paper with a list of defects —all unlovable."

All these years and she still carried it. Maybe more than the rest of us, but then the damage ran deeper with her, the twist of the knife in her back just the beginning of the betrayal. Total abandonment all because she didn't conform to their idea of what she should be. Instead of accepting her, they slapped labels on her: difficult, stubborn, rebellious, and destructive. Her rich family, with all the money in the world, didn't even pretend they cared by sending her off to boarding school or abroad under the guise of giving her a top-notch education or life experience —nope, they signed over their rights to the state, sold their properties in Galloway Bay and the surrounding areas and left.

They left her here where she'd have to forge a new life in the ruin of her old one. She'd catch glimpses of the places she called hers but would never be hers again. There was an extra dose of torture in that, and I didn't have to wonder why it turned into savagery to survive.

"I loved you," I whispered next to her, not quite ready to admit that I still did. Not sure she had earned the words.

"I know… you were so easy with love it was terrifying. Your mom taught you that."

"She did."

"What my family did to me, it doesn't excuse what I did to you. It will never make it right. Those girls, there was only one way in with them. I had to speak their language," she said, her voice thick with shame. "Cruelty. When I fell into step with them, I proved my parents right, and I've been trying to live with that ever since."

"I remember a time it being us against them. I miss that." I reached for her hand then and curled my fingers around hers. "I miss you."

"I miss you too. So much I freaked. The team—they take their cues from you, you know," she said with a quick squeeze of my fingers. "They were all ready to let me in the minute you did. If I made it into that circle and lost you again, I didn't know what I'd do."

I shrugged. "We aren't those kids anymore. We aren't at the mercy of others. If you want to keep me, keep me." My heart limped toward the signs of hope at putting this to rest. "And I'll keep you."

"Not so sure Priest will let me stay on the team after what happened."

The man in question had appeared from around the corner and leaned against a pillar just seconds before, hanging back watching, but with less than ten feet between us, no doubt hearing our every word.

"Probably not," I said as I met his eyes, smiling at the twitch at the corner of his mouth. "I guess it's a good thing it's not up to him."

His dark eyebrow shot up, and he cocked his head.

"You sure about that?" Tilly asked, sneaking a peek at me from her good eye.

I nodded. "Yup, I slapped him silly too."

"You didn't land that punch."

"Not the first one, no, but look," I said, pointing at the man himself.

Tilly pushed up in her chair and leaned toward Priest. "Ooooh, a direct hit. Wanna borrow my ice pack?"

"I'm good, thanks." He slid his hands in his pockets and crossed one ankle over the other, settling in. Giving us space, but not letting me out of his sight. Tilly had to earn that trust back with good behavior I guess.

Or maybe I was the one he needed to watch out for.

"Let's start over." I gave her a cocky nod of my chin and narrowed my eyes all suspicious-like as though this was our first meetup in the yard at a state prison. "What are you in for?"

Tilly pursed her lips and bobbed her head. "Some crazy bitch lunged at me like I was Thor carrying a pizza in one hand and a six-pack in the other. Apparently, she didn't like my beer choice so she pummeled my face."

"How do you know she didn't like the beer?"

"Cause she took off with the pizza," Tilly said, hitching a thumb at Priest. "A total misunderstanding. She might have had rabies. Animal control is on the lookout on account of the attack being in daylight and all."

We stared at each other for a beat before bursting out in laughter.

"Ouch," Tilly said with a wince. "Laughing hurts. Damn," she hissed. "So what about you?"

"Dumb bitch tried to pass off skunk piss as quality beer. Had to whoop her ass. She won't do that again."

Tilly glanced up at my hair and smirked. "You gonna get that sex hair checked out while you're here? Looks like a medical condition."

"I'll have them check that first, because the hand? Pshawww. Totally doesn't hurt."

A piece I didn't know I'd been missing slid into place. I dropped my head on Tilly's shoulder to have her tilt hers against mine just seconds later. Our physical injuries were the last remnants of our internal wounds rising to the surface.

Where they could finally heal once and for all.

"We didn't need one more thing stacked against us." We finally walked into my apartment four hours later, Priest right behind me carrying bags of food from Banked Track.

I'd kept my ass in his truck where I would most likely stay out of trouble. My hand had finally quieted to the dull ache, tingling instead of the heartbeat dancing under the skin there just a couple hours earlier, and I just wanted to sneak away to somewhere warm, quiet, and question free.

Word would get around soon enough that one of those girls from the derby team finally snapped. By the time the story made the rounds, they'd no doubt have Tilly in the ICU on life support, or at the very least permanently disfigured with stories of a gruesome eye popping out of the socket injury.

Total fiction, but hey, this town had a knack for fiction. It'd be nice if they'd start using that particular talent for good instead of evil.

Question was, how the hell did I think I was going to fare when I was a transplant here at best and Priest still had to face backlash for a situation no one actually knew the real details of and he was one of their own?

"At least it's only a sprain," he said, quelling the worry

that tried to worm its way into the fray. His voice gave me no indication as to whether I had totally fucked our shot out there.

We played with injuries all the time. It came with the territory. Going hard had consequences. We all accepted them.

But this was a new level for me, for all of us really. I'd never intentionally hurt another player.

And because of my outburst, I had a sprained hand and Tilly had six stitches. We got an unceremonious send off with a smart-ass warning about looking into anger management from Sheriff Chase who was lovely enough to stop in when the hospital reported a possible assault to make sure neither of us wanted to press charges.

Totally unnecessary.

Okay, Priest said it *was* necessary, but still, I couldn't trust that guy's opinion, being so by the book and hell-bent on self-punishment and all.

I'd always been the person who cooled off tempers—I mean, look at Milton and Gerald—but then I came all strutting in, full of unresolved feelings with a taste for whoop ass and flirted with the letter of the law.

A few letters of them.

I couldn't remember which ones specifically… not really my area of expertise.

I sent a message to my teammates to let them know we were okay and called a truce. They invited us out for dinner, but between the practice, the sex—can he get a hallelujah, please—and four hours in the ER, all I wanted was food and a shower.

Actually, I'd love the shower first, but the scent of those steak tips whispered pretty nothings in my ear and sighed my name.

And Priest was here.

Since I didn't know where we were in *that* department, I really wasn't sure what to do next. I mean, most guys, you know, right? Hot stranger and someone you barely knew—hey, no judgment—hot, drive-by quickie sex in public, that didn't even equate to a dinner commitment or a ride home necessarily. A movie and laid-back bite to eat, that could go either way. A fancy date that you made a waxing appointment for, yeah, probably a good roll after that once everyone had their fill of drinks. Maybe they'd stay over, maybe not. But no one would be offended in the end either way.

Hard, angry fuck, following two bursts of violence punishable by law against a barn wall almost fully clothed, both in skates?

I'm not even sure subreddits had the answers for that one.

So, shower after food it was. I figured by the time I struggled through peeling off my clothes one-handed and rinsed a full bottle of shampoo through my hair on account of my one bum hand and no other way to get the job done, I'd be ready for ibuprofen and falling into bed for a few hours of sweet oblivion.

Had to fill up my reserves for the ass I needed to kick tomorrow.

The Shipwreck was going to suck balls in the morning. Hairy ones. Sweaty, hairy balls. With ball cheese.

"Level with me, how bad is this going to hurt when we go to the exhibition?"

He made himself at home and headed right for my kitchen where he started sliding takeout boxes out of the bags. "Pretty bad by the end. Jackson will keep it wrapped for you though, and he'll make sure you have everything you need to take care of it throughout."

What started as a hum in my ears the minute he

mentioned Jackson's name had reached a crescendo by the time he finished his sentence. "Jackson?"

He flattened his palms on the table but didn't look at me. "He's going with you guys… as your coach."

"Oh."

His eyes flashed to mine then. "I have to stay with Lilith until Jordan makes it back. I can't leave town, even for a couple nights."

Well, fuck him… when the hell did I ask him to anyway?

New at wielding this temper, I took a breath and bit back the words. Adrenaline was a tricky fucker. Once activated, it hid behind corners just waiting to pop up and see if you needed backup. Enabling little bastard. "I didn't ask you to."

"I know, but—"

"It's fine, Priest. Really. I get it." And I did, I just hated it. But since his devotion to his sister was one of his best qualities, I had to suck it up. "Now give me food, dammit, before I gnaw off an arm or something."

He handed me a box, found the exact right drawer, and handed me a fork. "I'd rather you gnaw the leg."

"I'm sure you would." I rolled my eyes but laughed at his rather predictable attempt at dude humor. I mean, he wasn't at his best right now either so who was I to judge.

And he wasn't exactly wrong; that leg sounded a hell of a lot better than any arm.

Serious bout of temper averted, I stabbed a hunk of medium rare beef and popped the entire thing in my mouth.

We settled in on the floor, our backs against the couch, our legs stretched out over the carpet.

I leaned over and peeked in his container. "What'd you get?"

"Brussels sprout panini," he said as he eyed it like it might just take a bite out of him instead of the other way around.

"Why are you glaring at it?"

He held the first half in his hand and eyed the innards. "I don't like Brussels sprouts."

I bit back a laugh at the horror written all over his face. "Then why did you order it?"

"Because the stealth little bastards are addictive with prosciutto and melted cheese. It's witchcraft."

"It's Patti's invention."

"Like I said, witchcraft. I should have known what she was capable of considering she won this place in a card game," he said, taking a healthy bite.

I turned, propped my shoulders against the couch, and offered him a chunk of steak. "What?"

"She never told you?" he asked, taking my hand to guide the bite to his mouth.

"Hell no, she never told me." He was totally not doing it to be sexy, but my nipples perked up anyway.

Food made me horny. What can I say?

"She won it playing strip poker."

He offered me a bite of his sandwich; his hot, dark eyes locked on me as a piece of the prosciutto brushed against my chin before I captured it with my upper lip.

His gaze dropped to my mouth, his thumb brushing over the spot, and I forgot to breathe. I gulped the bite down as my eyes slid shut, and I swayed toward him.

"This mouth," he murmured, his lips brushing over mine. "So sweet sometimes, but others... I never know what's coming next."

Me. I was coming next. Again.

Whatever.

I so wanted to go where he was going, but something

kept poking at me. Not him. Unfortunately, but about Patti. "But I thought the ultimate prize in strip poker is the getting to the naked part?"

"It is," he said before sinking his teeth into my bottom lip. "Mmmm, so much better than food."

I laughed against his mouth. "Says the guy feeling all sorts of lukewarm about the Brussels sprouts."

His hot eyes met mine for a brief second before a sexy grin tipped the corners of his mouth and in one smooth, slow move, he found my neck, his thumb nudging my jaw up higher, giving him better access as he licked and sucked the skin there.

"So, uh—" Damn what he did with his mouth. I squeezed my thighs together and cleared my throat. "How, umm—" I blew out a breath as tingling heat shot up my spine. "How did she end up with this if naked is the end game?"

"I didn't ask," he mumbled against my skin, nipping his way to my ear. "And don't plan to. If I ever want to have wood again, I need to keep all thoughts of Patti and naked and anything beyond way the hell out of my head."

I laid my palm against his cheek, the one I slapped, and he stilled. "I don't think wood is a problem of yours."

"Doesn't seem so, no," he said, facing me now, his hooded gaze dark and unreadable.

My heart squeezed, humiliation bubbling inside me, remembering the look of utter disappointment on his face after what I did to Tilly only to be replaced by the absolute shock after I smacked him.

"I'm sorry I hit you," I whispered. "I—I've never done that before."

"It's forgotten."

"Forgiven, not forgotten. Please," I said, brushing my lips softly over his cheek. "Because I never want to do it again. The way you looked at me after…" I swallowed hard and my eyes burned.

We stared at one another for several beats, my fingers tracing over his cheekbone, neither one of us saying what we both knew—he wouldn't stick around long enough for that to be a problem.

He took my hand and pressed his lips to the center of my palm—a kiss that went straight to all my vulnerable places.

"I hurt you. It was such an easy miscalculation on my part and it changed you."

His choice of words, a clue to what he was thinking, feeling—to the future and what he'd do. Why he always chose to go. "You did, but that's no excuse for what I did. You're human. You fucked up. I've now fucked up. I will again in a different way. It's what we do. And it's why we don't forget."

"Forgiven then," he said, tucking a strand of hair behind my ear.

Maisy

"**Y**ou look tired. Why don't we get you cleaned up?" Priest moved our boxes and stood, reached out a hand to pull me to my feet, and nudged me down the hall in front of him.

"Well, it's the least you can do since you might have knocked me up."

He skidded to a stop and froze behind me for a beat—or ten. His hands tightened on my biceps, his forehead bumping against the back of my head.

"Fuck," he bit out, his hot breath landing on my neck, flirting with the wisps of hair there. Because of course I'd be getting aroused while he was in the middle of a heart attack.

"Yes, we did…" I hummed the words, a smile twitching at the corners of my mouth, but not quite ready to stop fucking with him.

"Condoms."

"Those are important."

"I'm sorry, I—how many cows over the years were inseminated in that barn and now—"

I spun on him then because my newfound control was not going to hold up this curve in the road. "Okay, I'm going to need you to stop right there because Jesus. Relax, big boy. I was fucking with you. I never met my father. I don't even know his name. Do you really think I don't handle my business where unwanted pregnancy is concerned?"

"No. But you were with Eve before this so I—"

"I have an IUD. You don't have to worry about fatherhood in nine months."

The blood drained from his face even more when I put him and fatherhood in the same sentence and I sputtered out a laugh.

"Now, do I have anything to worry about? Been dickie dunking in polluted holes?"

"No, there hasn't been anyone, in—quite a while actually."

"Let's leave it at that then, because the thought of anyone else touching you gives me feelings. I don't like it."

His lips twitched and I rolled my eyes. By the time I refocused on him he stood there grinning like an idiot.

"Shut up."

He held up his hands and shrugged. "I didn't say anything."

"No, but that smile of yours is really fucking loud. Now, about this getting me cleaned up thing… do you have a list of the services you provide in that regard?"

"For you, anything," he said, walking me back into my room.

"My hair. I don't know how the hell I'm going to wash my hair."

"You aren't. I am." He pressed a kiss to my forehead and my heart tripped.

I freed my braids as he got the shower going. He waited for the water to steam and added cold before having me check to make sure it wasn't too hot.

Surprisingly, I slid my tank over my busted stump and

worked it over my head, all on my own. But there was no way I'd be able to get the sports bra off. Not for lack of trying. Because I was totally bringing sexy back with the yank and tug until I had one boob out and the band twisted up my back like some backwoods, homemade bondage nightmare.

Kneeling down on one knee, he slid my shorts and underwear off in one swift glide, waiting for me to step out of them before tossing them in the hamper.

Did I mention I was still one tit out here?

Not that he noticed, because he'd taken keen interest in my hip all of a sudden, the look on his face making my mouth go dry.

He ran his fingers over the yellowing bruise from the last bout of the season.

The first time we saw one another.

"It never bothered me before," he said quietly.

"What?" I tunneled my fingers into his thick, dark hair.

Maybe this was why we waited for so long to get to this point. Why we skirted the attraction. Once we got here, it all came so naturally to us. The closeness and intimacy.

Two broken halves of an imperfect whole.

There was nothing quite as heartbreaking as finding out you might have a home out there in another person, only old ghosts held him in their clutches making anything lasting all but impossible.

"The bruises. I know you've got to be covered with them. It's never bothered me before. My own players, I didn't want to hear about it. Didn't care. But seeing them on you... it's different."

He said so little yet revealed everything with his admission and I wondered if maybe, just maybe he'd come around to the idea that he could stay.

He could have his family.

He could have me.

Pressing a firm kiss against my skin, he pushed onto his feet, hooked his fingertips under my bra and took it with him, careful of my hand along the way.

Heart racing, the ground turned to quicksand underneath me and I reached for something, anything to get me on solid footing again.

Because I'd completely fallen for him. Not a single piece left of me to lose, I was silently giving him everything I had, even knowing the odds were stacked against us.

I needed funny.

Or I'd cry.

Shit.

"The first time you're seeing me naked is to groom me. I don't know how to feel about that." Oooh, yes. That was good. Totally believable that I hadn't just realized how utterly fucked I was—or would be when he left.

He didn't look down. He could have. Most guys would, but he kept his eyes on mine before dropping a kiss on my lips. Curling both hands around the hem of his shirt, he tugged it over his head. "I have a solution for that."

Him naked. Another nail in my coffin.

One brief moment became my undoing—the one where he still held his arms over his head, the black cotton having yet to drag over his face—where his muscles flexed, his abs stretching and contracting with his movements. The skin over his ribs shifting. Hard ridges and lickable valleys with a dusting of hair spread across his chest to funnel down his sternum, stomach, before finally disappearing behind the waistband of his shorts.

No ink.

Just pure, healthy, athletic man.

Watching him undress should come with a surgeon general warning.

The shorts dropped next, and I'm pretty sure I swallowed my tongue at the sight of him, heavy and hard.

I couldn't speak past the lump in my throat.

He was in me.

That was in me.

On roller skates.

I kind of felt bad for my teammates to be honest… they were totally missing out.

"You get a good look?"

"Yes, and how uncool of you to mention it. Thank you."

He laughed, took my hand, and helped me balance as I climbed under the hot spray. I tipped my head back, let the water soak into my hair before leaning back farther to let it wash over my face.

When I swayed, disoriented between holding my hand up over my head to keep it out of the spray, tilting my head back, and just plain being wiped out, he was there. His large hands sliding over the wet skin at the curve of my waist, long fingers flexing and curling against me, holding me steady.

I opened my eyes, water dripping from my lashes and running down my cheeks to find him studying me, his expression unreadable, yet unwavering.

Haunted.

Outrunning his past.

Standing right before me, but like he could vanish at any minute.

Spinning me away from him, he smoothed his hand up my one arm while resting my forearm of my injured hand against the wall, keeping it elevated, but giving me support.

His hands worked through my hair first, the scent of cocoa butter filling the steamy air. The pads of his fingers digging into my scalp sent shivers of pure bliss down my spine.

My senses reeled, everything heightened. The brush of his thighs against mine, his forearms sweeping over my shoulders as he reached for the shelf, his sudsy fingertips grazing over my collarbone… a place that already stood out as one of his favorite ways to touch me.

And quickly becoming my favorite way to be touched.

The ache he set off inside me took over leaving my hand all but forgotten as I waited with bated breath for every glide of his fingers over my skin.

He didn't grab a washcloth; he completely ignored the loofa hanging from the hook, and instead ran the soap over me, skimming the slippery bar over curves and dipping and swirling it in the valleys.

"Jesus, this body, Mayhem. Strong, endless curves, and all of these stories carved in ink under your skin. I can't get enough."

My head fell back the minute his lips made contact with the back of my neck. His ragged breath filled my ear as his mouth opened and closed over my skin following along the curve of my shoulder.

Rough, delicious hands grazed over my breasts, circled my nipples, his fingertips making impressions in my fevered skin along the way.

He pinched the tight peak, dragging a hiss from between my lips. Flexing his hips, his cock strained against me.

A rough groan rumbled from his chest. "If you keep teasing me with that round ass of yours, I'm going to take it." With his arm still wrapped around me, his hand went straight to my throat.

I bit my lip and ground against him again. "Maybe that's what I'm looking for."

Every time his fingers flexed along the column of my neck and squeezed, my inner feminist toppled over with her legs in the air, breathless with anticipation.

"Not until your hand is better." His thumb jutted under my jaw, pushing my chin higher, exposing more skin for him to savor.

"Because when I bury my cock in your ass, I want you on your hands and knees."

My body flushed, my nipples tightened, begging to be touched.

"I want you fisting the sheets, while I make you cry and beg as I eat every last inch of that pretty pink cunt. I want you good and relaxed before I move to that tight little asshole and eat that too."

Oh. My. God.

Arousal—hot and tight, lanced through me.

He pinched my nipple then, hard, earning a squeak that quickly turned into a snarl when he abandoned them leaving a throbbing ache behind.

How could one man make me want to throttle him and tie him up and fuck him into oblivion all at the same time.

Keeping me locked there upright against him he glided his cock back and forth along the crease of my ass, dirty words spilling from his wicked mouth.

Imprisoned in his grip, trapped between his tall, hard body and the shower wall, I couldn't seek any sort of relief. Just suffering.

Horny. Hot. Suffering.

And the son of a bitch knew it every time I gulped, gasped, growled, and whimpered because my every reaction to him vibrated against the palm locked on my throat.

"Who knew the coach would be a dirty fucker with a thing for hand necklaces." My body succumbed to instinct and tried to suck in a lung full of air when his fingers squeezed.

He hummed against my temple and my knees buckled.

"There's just something about this pretty little inked neck that makes me insane with want, Mayhem," he said dragging his nose along my cheek and over the curve of my jaw.

"From day one I've either wanted to strangle you or fuck you. You're absolutely maddening." He bit along the tendon flexing there. "I never wanted my hands around a woman's throat… until you. Now I never want to stop."

The tip of his nose cruised back up and brushed over my ear before he settled his lips there. "And you know what? I think you like it."

Shuddering as his breath caressed the shell of my ear, I tipped my head back until I could see him from the corner of my eye. He had total control over me and god fucking help me, as much as I loved it, I needed to knock him off balance.

I arched my back and my greedy ass rubbed even harder against him burying his thick ridge between my cheeks. My breath caught when the head stopped abruptly, nestling right against the hole he wanted to take so bad.

His low growl made me grin and sent a quiver shooting straight to my aching clit.

"Mmmm, I love hand necklaces," the words slipped from my lips in a breathless quiver. God, was that really my voice? "But coach—just so you know, I have a thing for pearls too."

Maisy

Hungry lust flared in his dark eyes as Priest pierced me with a smoldering stare. His hand locked on my wrist keeping my injured hand against the shower wall while he squeezed my neck and dragged my mouth up to his.

Deep and hard he drugged me with a possessive devouring kiss. The kind of claiming that marked me from the inside out. With every swipe of his voracious tongue, he branded himself inside me. My toes ached, but I didn't care because my fucking heart grew wings and soared.

"Hmmmm, this inked skin painted with my cum." A satisfied hum rumbled through his chest as he murmured the dirty words against my wet mouth. "I think this neck might have been made just for my pearls, Mayhem."

A hot ache grew in my throat. My skin prickled. Feelings, so many dangerous feelings bubbled to the surface where I tried to choke them back down.

Because if I were made for him, what would happen when he chose to walk away?

My heart pinched as I took a step toward a dangerous edge, but in my next breath, as though he could hear my thoughts, he dragged me back into the moment by locking his gaze on mine and sinking his teeth into my bottom lip.

Wet, slippery hands skated along my belly until he settled right between my thighs, cupping me. His long, rough fingers tracing over me, dipping into my swollen, aching pussy.

Over and over, he devoured my mewling cries with deep sweeps of his tongue, nips of his teeth, while those fingers swept over me in long languid strokes.

It started as a delicious tingle he stoked with persistence until it bloomed into a throb bordering pain.

He tore his mouth from mine, his breathing raged and raw. "I swear this tight little cunt of yours is just pulsating."

I groaned as his finger ignited an aching between my lips with every swipe toward my throbbing clit. But never touching it.

The fucker.

"Stop fucking with me and give me what I need."

Dense steam swallowed us, creating this tiny cocoon of torture where he whipped me into a seething frenzy. I jerked my hips in frustration, chasing his wicked fingers, with his deep, amused laugh echoing in my ear.

"Not yet, my little hellion. I'm making up for not giving this dripping wet cunt the attention it deserved the first time around. You think you need release… I think you need to be worshipped."

He continued to torture me, swirling, playing—never relenting until my throat strained against the hand he kept locked there, the whimper shimmying up my throat against his palm only making him squeeze tighter as my body spasmed with hot need under his unyielding exploration.

And when he finally pinched my clit, rubbing this thumb and finger back and forth while he held the tight bundle of nerves in his grip, I broke.

Searing heat exploded from the inside out, the burn coursing under the surface of my skin. I gasped at the flash of fire. A sob tore from my lips at the rush sweeping through me obliterating everything worry, every bit of pain.

"That's it baby. Come for me."

Gruff and seductive, his voice washed over me, my body surrendering to his command. Wave after wave ripped through me, with his erotic whispers of encouragement in my ear, I rode out every last ripple of my orgasm until my knees finally buckled.

I'd never need another drink.

No drug could match this.

No other man, or woman, had the power to coil me so tight and give me exquisite relief in the same moment.

Just this man, his touch, his kiss, his unshakeable dedication.

And every minute only made me more desperate for him to stay.

To be in my circle and be in his.

To live in my heart.

The more I wanted him—all of him—the more I needed to know why I couldn't have him. Why he would be the second loss capable of devastating me.

With the water finally giving out, he lifted me out of the tub and dried us both from head to toe, squeezing every last bit of water he could from the strands of hair along my back.

"I don't want to be alone." I traced my finger over a swirl of hair on his chest. "I don't think you do either," I said quietly. "Stay… just for a little while."

Muscles jumped under the pads of my fingers and my gaze lingered, fascinated to have so much power over his reactions with just a simple touch.

"If I stay, you won't get rest."

"Fuck rest."

"You and that f-word have one hell of a tight bond. Did you take vows or something? Till death do you part."

"Or until I get a better offer."

Shadows crept into his molten chocolate eyes. He didn't say a word, just led me to my bed, laid me down, stacking pillows in front of me to prop up my hand, and climbed in behind me.

Lying there peacefully—his chest against my back, his hand skimming over my hip—I finally asked the question I'd been avoiding all this time, "Your father... where is he?"

His hand stilled at first, his chest swelling with his deep breath. "Jail." One word jagged and raw.

Four letters and whatever I asked after them became like a cap on a soda bottle. If you twisted carefully, success. If you weren't careful... explosion.

"Is he the reason you're a cop?"

"One of them," he said quietly.

"What did he do?" I whispered, my heart beating thick and heavy in my chest.

"He turned his kids into drug mules in a low-level drug operation."

I bit my lip, my sharp intake of breath turning into a hiss. His answer, the way he said it, holding himself apart as though his father was just another case—nothing more, nothing less.

As though Priest wasn't one of those kids.

My heart pinched. "And he's paying for it now?"

"If you want to call it that," he said, his voice taut with bitterness.

"What would you call it?"

"Getting off easy."

"Why?" I whispered.

"Because he left in a patrol car. My twin brother left in

a body bag." The slicing bitter edge in his voice revealed a well of pain still holding so many secrets.

But I wouldn't go there. Not tonight. When he'd have to go to the farm soon and be alone in his bed with tortured memories and no one to hold him.

I reached back, forgetting about my sprained hand, but he caught it and stopped me.

"No, keep it on the pillow."

"But—"

"No. No more talking about my brother," he said, his voice ending in a low growl as he took a ragged breath against my skin as his palm locked over my thigh.

He was going to bury his pain in me, with sex. I could feel it, and I was going to let him.

"Why?" I gasped out as the head of his cock slid against me.

"Because all I have left is his memory." He shuddered against me then, his breathing labored. "It's the only part of him I can keep safe now."

One brother survived, one didn't.

And he'd protect his brother from everyone, including me.

I had more questions than answers.

"You've only ever had your mother." He whispered the words along the shell of my ear as he lifted my leg and draped it over his own, exposing me.

"Yes," I said past my thick throat as we resurrected the people we lost, in just this sliver in time.

The absence of the people in our pasts we still longed for, becoming sharp knives of our present carving safer paths we mindlessly followed to avoid being hurt again.

"How did you move on?" he asked quietly, his fingers flexing on my thigh as if I had the secret to ending his pain if only he held on tight enough.

"I live for both of us now."

His arm curled around my waist, his fingers going straight to my breast, as he buried his face in my hair. Dragging in a deep inhale laden with personal agony, he thrusted inside me.

My body bucked at the invasion, a sharp cry tearing from my lips.

He stilled and I bit back a frustrated growl. "Don't. Don't you dare stop." I reached behind me and speared my fingers through his hair, pulling his mouth down to mine. "Stop protecting me." My forehead pressed to his, my mouth hovering so close my lips brushed over his with my words. "Let me handle the pain. I want it. I want you and I don't care how much it'll hurt."

I wasn't just talking about this moment and the tortured look in his eyes confirmed he knew it too. My gaze never wavered. I never blinked. I held his stare until his eyelids sank shut, his jaw clenched, and his hand locked around my ribcage.

Until he gave in and gave me everything he had the power to give me.

And when he trust into me for a second time, he did it with every bit of heartache I'd reawakened. He fucked me hard and deep. Running from demons. Branding me. Desperately holding onto me with enough force I'd be carrying the bruises from his fingertips on my skin for weeks to come.

Tears streaked down my cheeks as the peak closed in. Everything hurt. My body, my heart, and my soul in tattered ruins as he poured his pain into me, filling me up until I overflowed with it. Until I drowned in his despair where the only thing that could offer a hint of relief would be the oblivion of giving into the pleasure every ruthless thrust promised.

"I'm so close. Just… more. I need more." I turned to him over my shoulder, our position shifting just enough he slid even deeper. "Give me everything."

Teeth clenched, he bore down on me, sweat blooming over his skin and trailing down his temple.

Anger filled him now, the energy pulsated from him in heavy waves and a feral smile spread over my face because the controlled coach was finally letting himself feel everything.

Me.

Us.

The possibilities.

And he hated it as much as he yearned for it.

"Come on. Break damn you," he growled, his lips peeled back from his teeth as he gave me a hard shake.

In that moment, I couldn't tell if he meant me or him, but my body responded. My breath stalled in my lungs as I shattered. He took my mouth, swallowing my guttural scream as the burn started in my fucking toes and scorched it's way to the top of my scalp. Every bit of arousal he'd stoked in me with each brutal thrust flooded us both.

He toppled with me then, his harsh broken grunts spilling into my mouth as he rocked through the pleasure. As bone-deep relief tipped with pain washed away every bit of misery we'd carried into this bed with us, leaving us unburdened, even if only for a little while.

Maisy

"I've got a surprise for you ladies today," Priest said as he faced us on the track, skates on, fully padded, a helmet dangling from his fingers.

So the man planned to pull out all the stops to distract me and knock me off my game with all of his man goods on the track now too?

Low blow, *sir*.

Bring it.

Today was our last practice before we fly to Philly for the exhibition, I thought that meant we'd go hard, with him hammering us with every skill we learned, both old and new, from start to finish. Only the sly smile on his face and the familiar audience he'd gathered outside the track told a different story.

We were in for fun today.

He'd lined one side of the track with chairs. Lana and Zach kept their heads together as she pointed at different parts of the setup from infield to the bank, likely explaining the game. Milton and Gerald fawned over Lilith as she rubbed her growing belly. She had more color in her cheeks now, her face a bit rounder, her hair a glossy sheet over her shoulder. She radiated motherhood from the inside out, a huge change from how I'd found her the week before, which helped explain Priest's newfound playful mood. The more he worried about Lilith, the more we all suffered.

But in a good way. Every bit of tension born of his fear, or frustration, made him work harder and the more he gave, the more we rose to meet his every challenge.

Patti whispered to a woman I'd never seen before, and if I had to take a guess from the wistful look on Patti's face followed by her spirited laugh, she'd started pulling out some of her favorite stories from her days as Pinup Patti.

Even Scooter came out which meant he'd closed The Shipwreck for this.

No pressure or anything.

If the man was going to close his restaurant for a special occasion, we better be on our A-game and ready to deliver.

"Today it's the guys versus the ladies," Priest said, sticking his fingers in his mouth to let out a sharp whistle.

Music thumped out of the sound system Priest set up along the far wall. The beat filled the air, not loud enough to make it hard for us to hear, but hella loud enough to kick up our heart rate and give us a thirst for some good ol' ass kicking.

The door to the office—yeah, that office—flew open and Jackson came skating out first in full gear followed by three big-ass dudes I didn't recognize.

All in padding.

All strapping on helmets.

All adept at skating.

Oozing smooth moves and confidence, they glided up and hopped onto the track.

This was gonna be good.

"I know we're supposed to play against them and all, but damn—I kind of just want to eat them," Rory said with an appreciative gleam in her eye. "You think any of them are single?"

"Focus. We're not dating here," I warned as I totally appreciated the guys towering over us as they skated past.

"Says the one of us riding the coach like a hobby horse," Sean added.

I glanced around, looking for Eve, gauging her reaction, and even *she* smiled.

Thank fuck.

"You bet your sweet ass I am. And, guys, he's a shower and a grower. In case you were wondering."

"Leave it to a coach as hot as Priest to have a hidden collection of man candy on skates," Marty said.

We let out a collective sigh when they skated up behind Priest and flanked him—hands folded behind their backs, feet shoulder width apart.

That kind of male showing, smooth skin, corded muscles, and tattoos should be fucking illegal in this concentration in a small town like Galloway Bay.

"Anyone else want to take bets on whether or not they're brothers?" Eve asked. "I always thought I was a little more gay than bi, but this wall of muscle is making me rethink my position."

"Ladies, meet Mason, Garrett, and Talon. They're experienced, so don't think they're just going to roll over and take it today. They're going to give you a fight. I expect you to give it right back."

Zach carried Lana across the track and set her up in a manual wheelchair in the infield. The look on her face, the way her eyes lit up with passion and longing, made me wish I'd had a chance to see her in action before the accident.

Her mischievousness and determination would have been a potent combo.

No wonder Priest was drawn to her. He's a man who likes to harness strengths, and being a cop channels them to the good, not evil.

I would have loved to have her as a teammate. We could have really fucked with him. Who knows, maybe we can still find a way.

A shrill whistle sliced through the air, and we all snapped around to where Lana sat.

"Sorry, just making sure it works." She shrugged but grinned with that sly smile of hers, the same one she got when she was in the ER and thought she'd managed to sneak away from her mother.

Older than me, but in a lot of ways so much younger and a prankster at heart, she and Priest were so different yet so much alike—both hesitating to break free.

Her from her mother, him from the past.

I wondered if he realized it.

But her time was coming. More precocious, and in love, she'd have to break free soon.

And who knows, maybe a taste of the bank would give her the final push.

"Hustle up and pick your first five. Best out of ten jams. And don't be afraid of Talon. He may be big, but just the mere mention of his grandma wielding her cane turns him into a total pussy cat."

"You're a real asshole, Priest," Talon said, shooting him a dark look.

"Never tried to sell myself as anything else. Now get your helmet on or I'll have my girlfriend kick your ass."

"Not man enough to do it yourself," Talon tossed back.

"Sure, but why when she's so much sexier doing it?"

His girlfriend, huh. Maybe all he needed was a few rules. Like about wandering off and shit.

If only it were that easy to keep him.

We skated off the track, each team heading for their benches, until Priest reached out and took my elbow, spinning me around to face him. "Hey, you better kick our asses out there today."

"Count on it," I said, smiling up at him.

He traced his fingertips along my eyebrow, over my temple, and down my cheek before sliding those long fingers around the back of my neck.

I swayed on my skates, blood rushing straight to my head. Seeing the wristguards on him as he did it, knowing we'd go head-to-head on the track—yes, fucking please.

He gave me all sorts of lusty thoughts like this.

Like laying him out like a damn buffet and biting into him.

Thanks, Rory, for the total food horn dog influence.

"Watch out for the hand," he murmured as he hovered over my lips.

"Yes, Coach," I said on a rush of breath.

"Hey! Stop trying to sex up our best jammer," Rory said with a snap of her fingers and a slap of her thigh. "Mayhem. Come."

Marty threw her head back and laughed. "I think she just did."

Eve skated up to Marty and knocked into her shoulder while making a show of studying me. "Mmmm, not yet, but she's close. I've seen that face."

"Oh. My. God. Guys… stop!"

Priest leaned in, that fiery gaze of his on my mouth, but I pushed at his chest and watched him roll back on his skates. "No kissing."

"That rule is retired. Permanently," he said, coming to a stop. "Get your ass over here, Mayhem."

"Fine," I said as I pushed off and rolled right to him.

"But keep it PG. You have a way of short-circuiting my systems, and I'm pretty sure that's cheating."

He slanted that registered weapon of a mouth—the first go-to in his arsenal—and settled over mine, slow, soft, with a quick shot of pressure before he lifted his lips—just a glimpse at sexual energy rippling inside him.

"I knew it. Cheater," I murmured giving him one last shove.

CAIN

I had to force myself to concentrate because the look in Mayhem's eyes right now—fierce, calculating, so fucking in tune with the players on the track—nailed me in every vulnerable spot I didn't even know I had.

She'd been nailing me since the moment I rolled into town.

At the bout.

At The Shipwreck.

Definitely at Rockabilly's.

Obliterating me when she climbed on that bar at Banked Track.

And she did it without even trying.

Lana blew the whistle with the lungs of a damn opera singer, setting us in motion. After the second whistle, Mayhem and Jackson pushed off the jam line, closing in on us.

Spotting left, then right, then back to the left again, I kept my eye on her, closing gaps, opening others, hoping to get my man Jackson through while shutting down every one of Mayhem's attempts. Mason, Garrett, and Talon kept pace with me, shifting as I did while staying on Mayhem's teammates.

The pack made it halfway through the corner when Mayhem upped the pressure. Her height gave her an edge to get low and stay there. When there wasn't a gap to be had, she was impressively adept at creating one.

Wedging herself sideways in between Mason and Garrett, she gave them only illegal zones to hit, her back and front, making it impossible for them to do anything but try to squeeze her back out.

Pitching forward, she shimmied and broke through, her skate catching on Mason's briefly while they tried to put the final squeeze on her. On takeoff, Mason and Garrett collided with one another, leaving them tangled in each other's skates before crashing to the floor.

"Get up! Get up! Get up!" I yelled as they tried to scramble to their feet.

"What the hell do you think I'm doing?" Garrett shot back.

"Making out with my track. Jesus, Garrett, you're going have to get on your feet a hell of a lot faster than that."

Jackson broke through the pack then, but even with longer legs, she'd gained precious seconds and he'd never catch her.

"Get ready; she's closing in," I warned them as she made her way around, her eyes already searching for a way through us again.

We tightened up enough to make ourselves a wall on the track while stopping her blockers from opening up pockets for her to score, giving Jackson a few extra seconds to get around too and pressure her to call off the jam before he could score right alongside her.

"Don't let her through. Don't let her through…"

Mayhem went low, Tilly right there fighting to clear the way for her.

No fear between them on the track anymore, just pure concentration.

Turns out an ass beating had been the answer all along.

Despite using the coping, no matter how Mayhem maneuvered, she couldn't get past the chaos there, her every attempt resulting in a good amount of shoving, bumping, and a symphony of grunts.

Her gaze shot to the top of the track, the gap here, and she smirked. Toes digging in, she ran up the bank at an angle.

Mason spotted her, caught up, and kept pace, shoulder to shoulder until she slid back, waited for him to react. The minute he did, she shot out at a run to burst through the gap before he could even reverse his direction and blew through the whole pack for four points.

Lana blew the whistle, ending the jam and I swatted Mayhem on the ass as she skated past. "You're fast! Keep up that energy."

She smiled over her shoulder, her face hopeful and freer than I've ever seen my chest squeezed so hard it stole my breath. Blinking away an emotion I refused to name, I set up behind the jam line again.

I skated into position and shot a look at Mason and Garrett. "Could you guys stop trying to dance with each other out there. You're killing me."

"I thought you want your girlfriend to win?" Garrett said.

"I do, but I don't want you to *let* her win."

"You want her all sore and shit so you can rub her down later. I see what you're aiming for," Talon said, nodding at the ladies.

"He's got like ten years on her. He's the one who's going to need the rubdown. I've got a tube of Icy Hot with your name on it," Mason said.

I smacked his helmet. "Yeah, why do you have a tube of muscle rub huh?"

"Stole it from Garrett. Was going to put it in his underwear."

"Don't drag me into your shit," Garrett said. "Nothing wrong with my muscles. I'm a well-oiled machine."

"Hey, you ladies done chatting over there?" Lana yelled, wheeling up next to us. "Get your shit together and share your makeup tips on your own time."

Full of piss and vinegar, Lana gave us hell and I couldn't even be mad about it. I should have had her out here a long time ago. She still had a place in this sport; I just didn't see it. All this time and I didn't see it.

Well, I was paying attention now.

"She's mean," Talon said.

"Don't say that too loud; she might pull a cane on you," Garrett said with a snort.

"You guys need some new material," Talon said as he crouched in position.

With everyone in place, she blew the whistle again, sending us into another jam.

And another ass kicking.

Followed by another after that.

And another.

We finally found our footing on the fifth jam. Jackson managed to pull off two points and call off the jam before Mayhem could score her first point.

Now, we might just have a competition ahead of us—if we upped it to best out of fifteen.

No doubt Mayhem would call that cheating too.

At the whistle we took off clean, Mayhem and Jackson dead even as they closed in on us, but Mayhem didn't look for a gap this time, she kept her momentum and worked at those barriers until she and Mason went shoulder to shoulder again, running to the top of the track at an angle, but my man miscalculated, assuming she'd slide back.

She didn't.

Because she was relatively new to the bank and hadn't gotten comfortable with go-to moves yet. It would work to their advantage in Philly.

Instead, she psyched him out, dropped back a few inches, just enough to kill his forward momentum and get him going in the opposite direction. She tore ass back to the top and passed while his mouth hung open and he slid back down the hill.

Without paying attention.

You know, to the rest of us.

His teammates.

His friends.

The shit.

He dropped straight into the pack. Skates tangled, arms flew, legs kicked out to the side before flipping over into the air.

One of the fuckers caught my edge, knocking me over onto the heap where I took an elbow to my solar plexus, knocking the fucking breath right out of me.

Through the haze of sweat running into my eyes, I spotted Mayhem skating away with her team in tow, their eyes on us, their laughs echoing through the barn.

"My balls," Garrett groaned, from somewhere under the pile. "Why do I feel air on my balls?"

They all started squirming under me then, the word balls like finding out someone just took a piss in the hot tub.

"Why is there air on my balls?" His frantic shouts more erratic, his eyes wide—well, the one I could see from where it peeked through the crease of a knee and calf folded over his face.

I rolled off the pile and pushed up to my feet. "Fuck you and the air on your balls, Garrett. I told you to wear a cup, dumbass."

"Garrett," Talon piped up from the other side of the pile. "Why in the absolute fuck do I feel your balls on my hand?"

They scrambled to stand but failed miserably as they drove knees into guts and elbows into necks while they scrambled for a grip with their skates, their hysteria rising every time someone said "balls."

"Get your fucking balls off my hand, Garrett!" Talon's voice raised about two octaves. "Holy shit, man, I just felt them twitch. Get the fuck off me."

"And now Talon has a whole new nightmare," I joked with Mason as I gave him a hand up. "So much for the Icy Hot prank. Kind of hard to put muscle rub in his underwear when the dude's freeballing it."

"You probably shouldn't talk, Coach. You've been a little free with the meat yourself," Rory said, skating past before rolling into the infield.

Mason pinched the bridge of his nose. "Free with the meat? Jesus, fuck, I did not need those words in my head. If you don't mind, Lily's mouth looks like it could use my tongue," Mason said before skating away.

I caught a glimpse of Mayhem handing a helmet to Lana as Garrett and Lily tossed insults back and forth, my scrimmage quickly turning to absolute shit.

Rory rolled up to Lana next, handing her a pair of wristguards and elbow pads, followed by Sean with knee pads.

What the hell?

In under a minute, they had Lana geared up with

Mayhem on one side and Marty on the other as they rolled her to the track and stopped with her just behind the jam line.

The rest of the team piled on, all taking blocking positions.

Lana gave Zach a thumbs-up and he blew the whistle.

Mayhem and Marty pushed off, their legs flexing as they thrusted Lana forward right along with them. The blockers shifted, gaps opened and closed, as they propelled around the track, giving Lana the closest thing they could to a banked track derby jam for a woman who could no longer use her legs.

My lungs grew tight, watching Mayhem laugh, not caring how much exertion she had to put in. Not to just roll Lana around the track, but in sending her up the bank and controlling her coming back down again.

The pack shifted again, and Mayhem and Marty guided Lana through, breaking away, taking her low into the corner, and high along the straightaway, propelling her around the back, the sound of their laughter drifting away with their retreating backs and growing louder again when they turned the last corner and rolled toward us.

Yeah, I was definitely in love.

So damn in love with her the air sucked straight out of my lungs when she winked at me.

The truth of that, of the consequences—the decisions that came with the realization—would all have to wait.

And still, she'd never said my name. My real name. Hell, I'd never said hers.

Like we kept a white knuckled that one piece of our armor thinking it would protect our hearts.

Only I'd already fallen. Lilith was right that day in the barn, I had already started the devastating slide.

I needed to be more to her than the disgraced coach

stepping up to help the underdogs. I needed her to choose me and I needed to choose her. The girl she'd been before derby.

The girl who couldn't bear to give up the frayed lace of her mother's skates.

Maisy

The crowd at Banked Track spread wall to wall. Our entire team, Priest's friends, Lana and Zach, they all followed us into town for dinner and drinks. Instead of giving us menus, Patti had the kitchen keep our table full of wings, sliders, fried haddock, and baskets upon baskets of fries and onion rings with pitchers of beer to wash it all down.

Our players let loose in a way we hadn't been able to— well, ever actually.

For the first time we were all together. Everyone made the time, got babysitters, took vacation days, traded shifts, anything they had to do to be here. Marty and Rory made sure to pin Tilly in the center of the booth in case she got any ideas, but so far, she laughed along with them, the smile finally chasing away that wariness in her eyes.

Patti hopped behind the bar, keeping Milton and Gerald in beers and laughs; I guess kind of the way I did with them in the morning with decaf and tough love.

I'd always wanted to be Patti when I grew up.

Halfway there.

Now to work on more of those laughs.

Priest's cop friends drew in a bunch of other officers from Galloway Bay, and even Sheriff Chase brought in his nephew, Maverick. They stood in a cluster by the bar, giving me a few minutes to watch Priest.

Animated in a way I'd never seen him, the bonds he still had here, the ones he didn't speak about, they shimmered in the grins, laughs, the flow of conversation, and the body language as the guys circled in, a tight unit; the kind of bond that you would walk away from for a month, a year, or even a decade and slide right back into the minute you came back.

But also, the kind of bond that could stand with you through anything… as long as you let them.

That's all I wanted… for him to let them.

Even if it meant for whatever reason, he didn't choose me to stay for.

"Did you talk him into staying yet?" Lana asked, nudging me as she popped a French fry in her mouth.

Elbows on the table, I turned and propped my hand on my fist. "Does anyone have the power to do that?"

She pointed a fry at me. "If anyone can, it's you. He loves you, you know."

"Yeah? How do you know?"

She pointed at her beer, then at the *Game of Thrones* T-shirt stretched across her boobs with the words, "I drink and I know things."

I chuckled. "You're going to have to do better than that, but hey, impressive rack."

"I know, right? They look pretty great in this T-shirt."

"They look even better out of it," Zack said quietly beside her before taking a sip of beer.

"You keep saying sweet nothings like that and I might just say yes next time," Lana said as she leaned into him and nuzzled his neck.

"Say yes? Wait—did you propose?"

He stroked his fingers over Lana's hair and leaned in. "Three times."

This time I was the one nudging with elbows. "What are you waiting for?"

Lana sighed, her smile slipping. "To deserve it."

"Oh, Lana. You and Priest are just hell-bent on self-torture. Don't waste time… sometimes the supply runs short."

And the end came with no warning.

The loss that once sliced at me had waned over the years, becoming this dull ache filled with regret. More than anything, I wished my mom could see that I was okay.

It'd been bumpy for a while—I glanced up then to find Priest watching me, that turbulent look in his eyes, his past not quite done with him yet—was definitely going to be bumpy again soon, but I might have just found a place for myself here with these people.

My co-conspirators, teammates, and best friends. The kids we nurtured. The little old men who brought their feisty belligerence to my counter every morning, but always left me with a piece of wisdom. Patti, the way she had paved the way for me to stay here. Stepping in to encourage me but also ready to call me on my shit. Even the gossips. They were looking for something too. Running from hard truths. Lashing out in the only way they knew how.

All of us flawed just trying to make our way. Tempering our pride while we stoked our passions.

"I'm almost there," Lana said, wiping her hand on a napkin before reaching out and taking mine. "Thank you for what you did today on the track. I didn't know how much I missed it. I never really thought I could have it again, but you gave it to me."

I laid my hand over hers and squeezed. "Anytime you want to fly around that track, I'm your girl."

Her lips twitched and she shot a glance over at Priest. "Well, then we better do something about keeping our boy in town, don't you think? After all, it's his track."

"If he loves me like you say he does, maybe he'll stay." I'd told myself not to hope, not to set myself up for disappointment, but hope or not, there was no denying that his leaving would leave a lasting mark on my heart.

"Oh, honey… that's not the way he works. Because he loves you, he won't. He put himself under the microscope again—for you. This town isn't always loud, but the subtle judgments, the whispers—they scream louder than my mother in that ER."

I knew those stares and whispers well, but for me, they were pitying glances. First for having a mother who didn't give me what they considered stability, and then because I had no mother at all. "I don't know… she was pretty loud. Not as loud as that finger of hers, but—"

"And you threatened to fuck her up, which was rather magnificent."

I twirled my glass in my hands and winced. "I'm not proud of that."

"No, I don't suppose you would be, but you don't know what you did for me when you did it." She tipped back her glass of beer, more than half full, and didn't stop gulping until the glass ran dry. "It's the final push I needed."

"What does that mean?" I said, a tingle rolling over my skin at the determination in her eyes.

Lana glanced down at her phone, the color slowly eking from her pink cheeks. "Actually, I might need one more small push. Zach, would you get me something with an octane rating?"

"You sure?"

"Yeah."

"You got it," he said, already halfway to his feet.

The skin stood up on my arms. "I feel like I missed something. What are you up to?"

Lana rubbed her hands together. "You'll see."

Maisy

That warm fuzzy feeling I had before slipped away. I glanced around at my team as they compared injuries, both past and present, their laughter on my one side while life flipped on its damn head on my other.

Caught between the clashing of moods, and definite impending doom, I looked for Priest. As my eyes settled on him, he turned as though he could feel my stare.

His smile shifted from good-natured to shared secrets, and my stomach fluttered at the compelling transition from polite to potent. Energy crackled between us across the divide, sending a shiver right up my spine.

The same kind he delivered with the touch of his hands. The connection between us only getting stronger.

"Your drink," Zach said, setting the glass in front of Lana. He brushed his lips over hers and the girl practically swayed out of her chair. "You sure you want to do this?" he whispered.

"Yup."

"Do what, Lana?" I asked, following her eyes as they shot to the door, right as it shut behind a couple who'd just walked in.

Lana's parents.

"You know what, I need to be standing for this," she said, gulping back a good bit of the liquor in her glass.

I glanced at Zach. "Ummm—"

"Relax," Lana said, waving a hand between us. "I know I can't stand. Just get me up on the bar," Lana demanded, drawing looks from the team and a few of the patrons scattered around the room.

"What did she just say?" Sean asked.

Lana laughed as Zach swept her up in his arms. "It's story time."

"Is she okay?" Zara asked.

"Maybe she shouldn't be drinking that," Rory said.

Lana smacked her thighs. "My legs don't work, but the liver is tip-top. Now get me on that bar."

"Lana, honey, what in the hell do you think you're doing?" Patti asked, tossing her bar towel over her shoulder as Zach scooted her onto the gleaming wood.

"I hope you don't mind," Lana said despite Patti's warning look. "I just need to borrow this section right here for a minute, maybe two."

"I do mind, dammit."

"Yeah, but you love me. This will just take a sec," Lana promised as she nudged Milton's glass. "You don't mind moving down a scooch, do ya?"

"Sure, it's the least I can do if you're going to provide some entertainment," Milton said, raising his glass.

"What do you think you're doing?" Lana's mother squeaked, her widened eyes slowly narrowing to angry slits. "Get down off there."

Lana raised her glass, and her voice, ignoring her mother's demands. "I'm not even going to waste my time introducing everybody. My mom has probably been in all y'alls business here more than once. And if she hasn't, stick around, she'll eventually probe your orifices too."

Her mother's face turned red with anger. She sucked in a breath, puffing out her generous chest. "Young lady—"

"My dad will let her, of course, because he doesn't say shit. Just lets my mother railroad over everybody. Me, him, Priest."

The energy in the room shifted and popped. Priest straightened, his mouth a thin, hard line.

"You sure you're okay?" Gerald asked as he leaned across Milton, earning a swat from his longtime rival.

"I'm great!" Lana said as she took another sip of her drink and slammed the glass down, liquor sloshing over the side.

Priest approached her and took her hand. "You don't have to do this," he said quietly.

"Oh, but I do. I have a life waiting for me and I want it. And you have something waiting for you too, if you'd just get out of your own way. Maybe after this you will."

"Lana—"

"No," she said with a shake of her head. "I love you, but no."

"If you don't get off that bar—" her mother began, but she cut her off and pretended she never even spoke.

"So… a little story…" Lana started, plunging the bar into absolute silence other than the Stevie Nicks song playing in the background.

"There was this young girl, smart, funny, a bit of a wiseass, and she had a favorite movie—*Whip It*. God, it sounds so cliché now," Lana said, picking up her glass to take another sip. "Something even the best whiskey clearly can't shake."

"You get down from there right now; you're embarrassing yourself." Fists clenched, Lana's mother stomped her foot.

I almost felt sorry for the woman. To be reduced to

foot stomping when your kid decided to finally give you as good as she got had to be a solid eight on the humiliation scale.

Lana's gaze snapped to her mother's, a flash of temper breaking free. "Ahhh, let's unpack what you just said. First, can't really get down… my legs don't work," Lana said, staring down at them and I'd swear she was trying to make them move, the subtle hurt on her face stabbing straight into my heart.

"Second, young lady implies that I'm still a child. I'm not. I may be your child, but I'm fully grown and make my own decisions. Like Zach… he's a decision I made. Zach, this is my mother, Marsha and my father, David. Marsha and David." She hiccuped and giggled. "This is my boyfriend Zach."

"We raised you better than—"

"No, you didn't," Lana snapped. "Now as for that embarrassment you're so worried about. You're only worried I'm going to embarrass you. And you're right. I am."

Patti let out a low whistle, but the look of pride on her face was unmistakable.

"Anyhoo… *Whip It*. Trite. I know. Not much of an accurate depiction of roller derby, but it's the spirit of the game that I fell in love with and my parents hated the idea of it. Especially my mother." Lana leaned against Zach. "She wanted me to play tennis. I mean, really? But hey, I was already a difficult sell for them. I hated dresses, and didn't like hanging out with girls. Dolls—forget about it. I liked jokes, pranks, and sometimes, I liked to see just how much I could get away with."

When Lana's mother went to speak, Patti shut her down with a hard glare. "You just hush."

"Actually, Zach, you should know, I still do like to see

how much I can get away with, which might be why I haven't taken that ring yet."

My breath caught at the resolute look on his face sliding into a confident grin. "I'm not going anywhere."

"God, I know—you really should, you know."

He stepped up between her legs then, wrapped his arms around her, and tipped his head back. "Nope."

Lana glared even as she cupped his cheeks. "I can't walk down the aisle."

"Don't care," he said with a firm shake of his head.

"You'll have to deal with low counters forever," she pointed out.

He shrugged. "Still not convincing me."

"You'd be stuck taking care of me for the rest of your life," she said, her voice breaking on the words as she blinked back tears.

He curled his hand around her neck, pulled her in, and gave her a soft, sound kiss, so full of confident love and passion, I couldn't turn away.

"You act like that's a hardship," he said, his eyes on hers when he pulled back.

"But I don't want that for you." Her words pushed at him even as her fingers twisted into his shirt and held him there with her.

Oh, Lana… he's giving you everything. Take it.

"You don't want me to have everything I want?" Zach said, catching her in a trap of her own making.

"I might have had too much to drink for this conversation," Lana said as she straightened.

"Cop out," he said, moving to her side, his hand staying on her thigh. "Now finish your story so we can have this battle in private where it's so much easier to make up."

"Where was I?" she asked.

"Seeing what you could get away with," he tossed out, looking her parents in the eye. The way he looked at them, his shoulders straight and confident, his gaze unwavering, spoke volumes as to the lengths he would go to for Lana.

The girl better take that damn ring.

"Ah, yes, that. Turns out derby is expensive, but there were teams. As long as I could buy the equipment… as long as I was eighteen. That was a hard and fast rule. No parents signing waivers on that one. And I'd heard the coach was a real stickler for rules."

Rules Lana broke.

"And I'm no good at waiting. I had just enough in savings for the laminator and offering my services for a brief time replenished my savings, leaving me with money for equipment and a sparkling fake ID that would fool even the most seasoned cop," Lana said, meeting Priest's eyes. "Or not, but why would a coach suspect a fake anyway? It's all just paperwork."

"Lana Ann!"

"I paid for it. Dearly." Lana ignored her mother's blustering and plowed on. "And so did Priest. You made him pay the worst," Lana said, finally turning to her mother. Her voice morphed from heartbroken to angry in a split second.

"You gossiped about him, turned people against him, took every shot you could, even to this day. And you, Dad. You stayed silent while she did, knowing the whole time the money for my medical bills, my rehab, my house, and college—all of it came from him. Piece by piece you stood by and let him sell off chunks of property at Bishop Farm —while you stayed silent and let Mom vilify him. When no one else believed in me, he did, and you crucified him for it."

The farm. He'd been carving it away, chunk by chunk,

whatever he needed to do to make sure Lana had everything she needed. Anything in his power to give.

All because of the one thing he couldn't give her, her legs.

Heart twisting in my chest, I stole a glance at Priest in time to see his chest swell. Every word tortured him, trapping him under yet another microscope, but this time, a necessary one.

Tears slid down Lana's cheeks, the last of her childhood dying as she fully came came clean and took back the power she'd given to years worth of lies.

There was a kind of grieving in that. In letting go, even of the things that hurt you, because it also meant letting go of the familiar and jumping into the unknown. Forging a new path.

But Zach had her.

A splash of color rose on Priest's cheeks. His jaw locked tight. He pushed away from the high top, the picture of determination in the stubborn set of his jaw.

"That's enough," he said quietly, reaching up and sliding Lana off the bar. "It's done."

She curled into his arms and he kissed her forehead. Bending down to her ear, his jaw worked with hushed words for just the two of them before passing her to Zach.

Without another word, he snatched my hand and dragged me out into the frigid night.

Maisy

"Where are we going?" I asked as he tugged me along the sidewalk.

Priest glanced back at me, a bit of a crazed look in his eye. "To the farm."

"My place is right here. We can go upstairs and talk, if you want."

He glanced up as though considering it before shoving a hand through his hair, the chaos turning to more uncertainty now. "You know what—I, it's too close. I need to get out of here."

He was already slipping away, with our last practice done and Jackson going with us to Philly, this tiny fissure of truth Lana broke open had begun working its way between us.

Only when this ended badly, there'd be no new town, no grieving the friends I'd never see again. I'd be here with the pain. I'd see his sister, eventually meet her husband and baby, and I'd wonder.

When is he coming to town?

Would Lilith tell me?

Would I run into him?

Would I break?

Would people in town wonder what happened between

us? If I caused it. If I hurt one of their own. Because while memories were long in a small town, they could be incredibly short too.

Tales were embellished, the villain becoming the saint and the saint becoming the villain.

And maybe the transplant becoming the outcast again.

"Okay," I said, a jagged ball of doubt lodging in my gut.

"Don't do that," he snapped.

I tugged at my hand, but he only held on tighter. "What?"

"Say okay like that." He yanked open the door of his truck and spun on me. "You never just say okay, Mayhem."

"I'm not going to force you to be with me. You either want to or you don't."

Wow, so every niggling doubt I could possibly scrape from my insecurities bank was going to come out tonight apparently.

All of the things we hadn't been saying up to that point, tired of being kept hidden in the dark.

Lana told a story and left us all spinning. Now Priest and I were tumbling through uncertainty and tiptoeing around each other in spectacular fashion, parading our insecurities like prized pigs in a 4H competition.

"This has nothing to do with wanting to be with you," he growled, backing me up to the door, pinning me there with his fist curling in my hair and a hard, demanding kiss of his lips. "It's—I need to get away from people. There's too many eyes on me, Mayhem." He rolled his forehead against mine, his ragged breath fanning my cheek. "Come to the farm with me."

I need to get out of town.

So did my mother.

It should have made me feel better that he took my

hand when the urge to take off struck, but all I could think about was how easy it was for him to walk out of Banked Track and search for safety.

All because one piece of his life slid out of his tight rein of control and the man didn't know what the hell to do with himself when it did.

What the hell would he do if everything actually went his way?

"Okay," I said again, my every thought and feeling unpredictable as he spiraled in front of me.

"Mayhem," he warned.

I huffed out a breath. It was either that or the pressure building from the tips of my toes to the roots of my hair were going to launch straight out of the top of my head and singe a hole in my lucky bandana. "What do you expect me to say?"

"Shit," he bit out. "I don't know."

"So, I'm giving you a few minutes to freak out. You're welcome."

He scrubbed his hand down his face and sighed. "See, that already sounds more like you. Now get your ass in my truck."

"And that already sounds more like you. By the way, you're getting way too comfortable ordering me around," I said, even as I climbed into the cab and gave him one more piece of proof that his authoritarian voice earned compliance.

The cop in him must love that shit.

He didn't say another word as he fired up the engine, cranked the heat, and pulled out of the parking lot. As the lights from town faded away, darkness concealed him in deep shadows. Under the obscurity, he finally spoke.

"Just say it," he said, hitting the gas the minute the

speed limit sign came into view. His shoulders rigid, he kept flicking glances in the rearview.

"What do you want me to say?"

"Whatever you're thinking."

"I'm not sure now's the time to waste my colorful personality. Not when you seem like you're ready to burst into a million pieces over there, all growly and shit. Kind of takes the fun out of it."

"I don't like being put on the spot."

But he needed to be on trial. And now he wouldn't be.

At least not from anyone but himself.

That's what this was. Him poking me until maybe I stumbled upon what he couldn't bring himself to say. "Apparently, but I don't think that's all this is."

"Okay, so give it to me. What is it?"

"You covered for her for a long time." A decade giving up everything he loved. How many times had he come back here and run into her parents? Heard the whispers? Pretended he didn't see the glares?

Because he definitely came back. A man didn't take care of Lana the way he had without coming back and making sure she was okay.

"Yes," he admitted.

"All this time, you ate the shit people in this town dished out to keep her secret."

"Yes."

"I don't think you know what to do with yourself if you're not protecting somebody—if you're not protecting her."

His jaw ticked; tortured sorrow etched in the skin bracketing his mouth because although controversy surrounding Lana and her injury were a huge factor, I'd bet there was something else lurking behind it. The protection that scrutiny gave him hid whatever was eating away at him underneath.

I wanted to touch him. To smooth my fingers over the tension there until he finally relaxed. But first, I had to know… "Were you in love with her?"

"Jesus, no—" He turned to me, piercing me with a hard stare. "*No.*"

"Then why?"

"She's never going to walk again. She was suffering enough."

"And the rest? The money, the house, college…"

"I should have caught it," he said, his voice low and full of frustration.

The man wanted to rewrite history.

Didn't we all?

But if he did—if I did—would we ever have gotten to this place? Would we ever have found each other?

I didn't want to go back and rewrite one damn ache from my past if I missed this.

Missed him.

"What should you have caught?"

"Her fake. I should have caught it and I didn't. That was my mistake."

"The only crime here was hers."

"So what?" he snapped at me. "I should have turned her in then?"

Ah, and there it is. "I didn't say that, but the fact that you did says plenty."

He squeezed the steering wheel, his knuckles turning white with the force as he pulled into the driveway, rolled to a stop, and turned off the engine.

He wouldn't reach for me. Not right now, not like this. But I would reach for him.

I flipped the middle console up and slid across the bench seat until my body pressed to his.

He didn't let go. His hands flexed. His arms locked and rigid as he stared off at something I couldn't see. Something from another time. Another place.

Cupping his chin, I turned him to me.

"Tell me," I said quietly.

"What?" he said, his eyes unfocused as the past held him in its merciless grip.

"The part you don't want to say."

He made a sound in the back of his throat. The echo of tightly restrained pain… and maybe the beginning of his surrender to it. "I don't want it to touch you."

"You don't need to protect me," I said as I stroked my fingers through the hair at his temple. Over and over, my nails scraping against his scalp until he leaned into me and his eyelids slid closed.

"The last person I loved and turned in, ended up dead," he said, his deep voice gritty with pain.

I brushed my thumb along that deep dimple and over his cheek, constantly soothing—him and me. "You reported your father."

"And brother," he whispered.

"This is not your fault."

"It feels like it," he grated out. "Every single day, every single minute it feels like it was all my fault." His eyes slid closed, and he sighed before opening them again. Just a tiny release of the pressure swelling in him. "You know, our names were always this running joke," he said with a humorless laugh. "Cain and Abel. A good brother and evil brother, but my mother didn't care; she just liked the names."

"And you think you're the evil brother?"

"Are you saying he was?" he said, his tone cutting, the last of his defenses lashing out.

It's the only part of him I can keep safe now.

That's what he'd said.

Protecting his twin was not a quality just born of guilt. This was biology. Connection. Being bound to your other half even when they no longer walked among the living.

"No, that's not what I'm saying," I said, keeping my voice soft, knowing he wasn't attacking me; he was still protecting his brother—his brother's memory. "He was a child, and his father didn't protect him."

"I didn't protect him."

"No." I took his face in my hands and turned him to me. "You were a child too. And your father was supposed to protect you all. Your brother paid a horrible price for your father's mistakes, and the price you paid—the price you continue to pay—is just as high."

"You don't understand—"

"I don't understand? My mother had no ties. She moved me from town to town on a whim while I hid the tears from the heartache of leaving one more town, one more friend, a school I loved. My mother was kind, loving, and she adored me—but she was a fuckup."

"Mayhem—"

"It's okay. It's true. Every day watching you put up with the judgment here to do what's best for the people you love tore away the romanticism of what she did. She didn't end up in jail; she didn't put me in harm's way with drug dealers and criminals, but the wounds cut deep just the same." I pressed a kiss to the corner of his mouth and breathed him in as my heart ached for both of us. "When it got hard, she ran. You're weird," I said brushing my thumb over his warm bottom lip. "You run when you think they've made it easier on you, but maybe you run because when it's easy, you have no choice but to stare down the demons you've been ignoring for so long."

"What are your demons?" he asked quietly.

"I've been afraid to speak up, to rock the boat, because I'm so damn scared I would lose what little hold I had on this town because I've never had a home," I said, surprised how easily they rolled off my tongue now when I'd never dared to voice them before.

He did that.

He gave me strength and confidence to finally admit them without fear.

The same strength and confidence he gave me on the track.

But my insecurities, between never having roots and losing Tilly for so long, were a bit more distinct than his making them easier to tackle.

His twisted around one another. Loss, betrayal, guilt, and anger, he'd sought refuge from on the track and in this sport. The tug of home offering comfort, but also stark truth.

His other half—that boy was never coming back.

And all of it twisted into guilt over Lana's accident and his habit of protecting her above all.

With Lana finally coming clean, it only left lasting fragments of his past to focus on. The parts of him still left broken.

He looked into my eyes, a hint of a smile there, his face softening just a bit. "You don't have to keep fighting to hold on, because they're holding on to you."

He may be right, but I still couldn't see it. Couldn't trust the bond completely. Not quite yet.

But I could see the bond he had with them. Even at the height of scrutiny, Patti, the sheriff, his friends on the police force, his family—even when circumstances cast him in a questioning light, they never wavered on his integrity. Not once.

I brushed another kiss over his lips. "You've spent so much time protecting people all because of the one person you can't protect. What happens when the day comes that everyone is okay at the same time and there's no one else who needs you to protect them? Will you finally let yourself live life then?"

CAIN

Maisy seduced me with her soft touch and her remarkable calm, coaxing me into confessing. Drawing pain into the light before working to shape it with logic and truth.

Logic and truth I wasn't ready to accept.

I didn't know what the right thing was anymore; I just knew I was tired of watching the people I cared about pay for my mistakes.

My skin prickled and I shook my head trying to clear the thoughts—my past a cluster of aggressive vines tangling through my present.

My twin called me a traitor, the last words he ever spoke to me, my own exact replica looking back at me with such venom and betrayal. It didn't matter what anyone said; I still felt his words, and I didn't know how to stop.

But when I had a purpose, when people needed me, I could forget how much he hated me in our last moments together.

I stared at the dark house until it blurred and came into focus again. "Something's not right."

"What?" Mayhem asked, glancing over her shoulder at the house.

"The house is dark."

"Lilith probably just went to bed. She *is* actively making a whole human, you know."

"But she didn't leave our grandfather's lamp on. She always leaves it on."

"Maybe she's in the barn," she said, pointing past me. "The light's on up there."

"I told her not to worry about cleaning up. Shit." I hopped out of the truck and headed up the hill, Mayhem right behind me. Yes, I knew what I was doing. I was diving right back into someone or something that needed me. "You should be wearing your jacket."

"Some moody asshole dragged me out of the bar without it."

"You should be wearing mine then. Why didn't you grab it?"

"Because I'm sticking with you while you're in this mood. Someone has to remind you to be nice."

"I'm always nice."

She snorted next to me, her bare arms swinging in the bitter cold. "Bullshit."

She bolted ahead of me and crossed into the barn first and stopped dead in her tracks.

"So, I came up to turn off the light and surprise," Lilith said, panting out the words from where she sat on a metal folding chair, clutching her stomach, beads of sweat gathered across her pale forehead. Just a few feet away, wet concrete.

I wasn't here. This was my one job, and I wasn't here.

"Okay, let's get you to the hospital," I said, reaching her elbow.

"Nope," she said, stiffening up.

"Lilith—"

"Cain, he's coming," she said, her eyes turning frantic as they met mine. "Not only am I not going to make it to the hospital," she said, gasping as she sucked in a harsh breath. "I'm not going to make it to the house."

"Are you sure?" I asked, crouching in front of her.

"Do you think I want to have my son here?" she said, her teeth chattering.

"Okay," I nodded, glancing over at Mayhem. "I need towels, blankets, and my bag from the back seat. Can you grab them? There's a sled on the porch I use to haul gear, you can pile them on that."

"Got it."

"And on your way down, call 9-1-1."

"I'm on it," she said before turning back toward the house and heading down the hill, her phone pressed to her ear along the way.

"I'm going to turn on the heaters. Sit tight. Where's your phone?"

"I left it in the house," she said, putting her hand up the minute I opened my mouth to speak. "No lectures."

"I swear, I should have put a Life Alert necklace on you."

"Just think, after tonight you won't have to worry about me anymore," she tossed out with just enough sass to assure me we at least had a couple minutes.

"I'll always worry about you."

All four kerosene heaters fired right up. Luckily our practice ran short, so we hadn't used up the bulk of the fuel yet. In about fifteen minutes, it'd be toasty warm in here.

"I can't believe you're going to have to do this," she said, her voice breaking on a whimper.

"It's okay; I'm trained."

"There's no training to prepare a brother to see their sister like this."

"I'll tell you what, if it makes you feel better, you don't have to look me in the eye for six months."

"Deal," she said with a bit of a squeak before biting her lip.

Mayhem hauled the sled clean into the barn piled with three blankets, six towels, and my bag. "Here. Now what can I do?" she said, breathing heavy.

"Coach my sister." I grabbed the bag first, grabbing everything I needed to sanitize my hands before sliding on gloves.

"On it."

"I need to push," she groaned, her hips sliding to the edge of the chair.

I put a hand on her thigh to stop her as Mayhem wrapped an arm around her shoulder and brushed her hair back from her face.

"Not yet," I said, doing everything I could to keep my voice calm.

"Cain…"

"Lilith, blow through it. Deep breath in and big exhale. Remember what they taught you."

She breathed in, blew it out, Mayhem speaking quietly to her, repeating my words, while watching me pull out the umbilical cord clamp and bulb syringe.

"This is so not fair. Jordan's not here. I'm not ready. I didn't get to experience the first stages of labor, and now my son is going to be born a old damn dairy barn."

"But just think," I said, smiling at her, "It's going to make one hell of a story. Grandma and Grandpa would love this."

I laid out the quilt next, still folded in quarters to give her extra cushion. "Okay, we're going to ease you down right in the center. You ready?"

She hesitated. "It's Grandma's quilt."

"Doesn't matter."

"She made it with her own two hands."

"Even better."

"It'll get ruined."

She was right, but that didn't matter right now. "Lilith, get on the blanket."

She glared, but did as I told her, something I'd pay dearly for later, but as long as we got through this, she could yell at me all she wanted. "Mayhem, I'm going to need you to scoot in behind her and help support her back and shoulders."

"Okay," she said as she moved in and bracketed Lilith with her knees.

I popped off her shoes, removed her damp leggings, and draped a towel over her to keep her warm. "I'm just going to check you to see where we're at."

"I can't hate this more," Lilith said on a pain-laced groan.

"It's okay, just open for me. A little bit more. Okay, that's good."

She bowed up a second later, her jaw tight as she sucked in a breath and held it.

I leaned over her and cupped her chin. "No. Don't hold your breath, Lil. When you hold your breath your body naturally pushes and we're not ready just yet, okay?" Frantic eyes locked on mine. I forced back any niggling of panic. "Just breathe it out."

"I'll breathe with you, okay?" Mayhem said doing just that and giving my sister a reassuring smile. "You're doing great," Mayhem said, taking her hand, my sister latching on and squeezing until Mayhem's turned red with the force.

I lifted the towel and spotted my nephew's dark hair,

telling me we were a whole lot farther along than I thought. "How long were you out here, Lil?"

"Twenty minutes maybe," she said on a gasp. "Why?"

"Just checking. He's anxious to get here. I can see his head. I'm ready, so when you feel the urge to push, I want you to take in a deep breath and bear down as hard as you can for the count of ten, okay?"

She glanced up at Mayhem and back at me. "This is not how I saw this going."

"Same, Lil. Same. But we've got this. You and me, right?" She was becoming a mother right before my eyes, but when I looked at her, I still saw that young, resilient girl. And that headstrong pain in my ass. I needed her to channel that stubborn energy now. "Always. Now come on. You're strong, you've got this."

Mayhem murmured to her, a smile on her lips despite the worry in her eyes. She asked Lilith about names, if they were going to baptize him, which parent they hoped he looked like—all the happy things, naturally steering Lilith away from all the ways this could go wrong.

When Lilith bowed up again, Mayhem immediately spoke into Lilith's ear, a thread of calm in her voice, reminding her what she needed to do.

She took to every situation and stepped in doing what needed to be done with grace and dedication. No whining. No bitching. No hysterics.

Present, calming, and solid. Ready to dig in and work.

Just like my grandma.

My grandmother would have adored her.

"That's good. His head is almost out. One more big breath and push."

She followed Mayhem's every quiet direction, the two of them in sync, pushing through the fear and pain.

"That's it, his head is out." I suctioned out his nose and

mouth and dropped the bulb syringe on the pad in the sled before cupping his head gently. "Okay, listen to your body, it knows what to do. When you're ready, give me another push."

Sirens wailed in the distance.

Thank God.

Lilith bared down, his one shoulder sliding out.

"Good, now one more."

Lights flashed through the trees.

Bearing down again, Lilith let out a sharp cry as he slid out with her final push, his slippery little body sliding right into my hands.

Lilith's heavy breathing echoed in the barn, slowly, ever so slowly her breaths stretching out.

Silence.

I rubbed over him with a towel.

He didn't cry.

Mayhem glanced up at me, a stricken look on her face as her eyes turned glassy with unshed tears.

My heart pounded in my ears as I turned him over on my arm and vigorously rubbed up and down his spine. "Come on, buddy."

"He's not crying," Lilith said with a sob. "Why isn't he crying?"

This would not happen to him.

This fucking life snatched so many pieces from us. It didn't get to take him too.

No. No. No. Dammit, no!

"Come on, little guy," I whispered.

The seconds ticked off in my head as I started focusing on the narrow window we had to get oxygen in him.

Thump, thump, thump… my heartbeat pounding edge of panic in my head.

Give me this one dammit. You've taken everything else, do not take this one too.

This farm was our peace and if he slipped away from us here of all places, we'd be lost.

He stiffened in my arms, his little chest expanding before he let out a furious, shaking wail.

Relief seared through me as I kept my eyes on his angry little face all scrunched and turning more and more red with every scream.

"That's it," I murmured as I clamped his umbilical cord and bundled him in a towel. I wiped him a few more times with the edge of the terrycloth as he screamed, the best damn sound I'd ever heard.

The ambulance rolled into the driveway right as I laid him in Lilith's arms. "You did it, Mama."

"Oh, he's beautiful," she whispered with tears streaming down her cheeks. She ran her fingertip along the inside of his palm, and he responded right away by curling his wrinkled fist around her, holding on tight. "*We* did it." She shuddered, her gaze meeting mine, and smiled. Thank you."

The EMTs rolled in with a gurney and in just a few minutes had Lilith and my nephew on their way down the hill.

"You should go with her," Mayhem said, watching them take Lilith to the ambulance.

"Are you sure?" The tears had dried and the paleness in her cheeks had been chased away by splotches of pink.

"She's had a hard night. She needs you."

"Thank you." There was so much I wanted to say, but no time, so I kissed her. Took one more taste of her to take with me and handed her my keys. "So you're not stuck."

She slipped them from my fingers and gave me a small shove. "Now, go."

Maisy

Lights cut across the windows just after midnight. I peeked out from behind the curtain and spotted Priest looking at his truck before glancing at the house and looking at his truck again.

I probably should have left.

I planned to. I mean, he gave me the keys to a vehicle with real heat, but then I'd gone up to the barn and gotten everything cleaned up, turned off the heaters, and talked to his grandmother.

It sounded crazy, and obviously she didn't talk back, but for a few minutes, energy simmered in that barn. Maybe because the banked track had been reborn; maybe because Lilith brought her son into the world there; I didn't know, but I couldn't walk away.

These people made him… the man I love, and I'd swear they wanted him home just as much as I did.

Just as much as he wanted to, but didn't think he deserved to.

When I finally shut off the lights and headed for the house, I worked on salvaging the beautiful mosaic quilt first. While the laundry ran, I explored the downstairs, his grandparents' pictures on the wall—their age told in the yellowing at the corners—puzzle boxes worn from repeated use, and the thick magnifying glass lying on top of a stack of crossword puzzle books.

Touches of familiar comfort neither Priest or Lilith seemed too eager to pack away.

The house wrapped around me like a hug and I gave in to the comfort of something lasting. I turned on the lamp so important to Priest and snuggled into the easy chair for a while with a curled paperback of *Lonesome Dove* I slipped from the bookshelf.

I pretended the house was mine.

This family was mine.

My heart aching with the realization that Priest had a few battles to face before he found his way back for good—to this farm and me.

Mama, give me patience for this one. He's worth it.

He stepped through the door, that quiet intensity so much a part of him back in his eyes. "You stayed."

"I did for a bit. When do you have to go back?"

"I don't. Jordan's home. He called me to give me a heads-up that he planned to surprise Lilith and she surprised him instead."

"How's the baby?"

A proud smile curled his lips, and my heart rolled over in my chest.

"He's perfect."

The weight lifted when Lana revealed her secret and threw him into chaos, only to be settled when we found his sister in trouble and needing him. Stabilizing him even in the storm because in that moment he had a purpose.

A protector. A caretaker. A coach.

Always giving.

How would he handle receiving?

"Does this mean you'll go to Philly now?" My heart kicked in my chest while I waited for his answer.

For a yes.

His eyes narrowed and he nodded. "I'll go to Philly now."

Relief slid through me and I took a deep breath, not realizing I'd been holding in my last. But with Jordan home, his nephew delivered, and Jackson coaching us at the exhibition, he had nothing keeping him here.

He'd be back to spiraling.

Back to running.

And this time, him knowing what this town meant to me, there'd be no taking my hand before he ran.

I just hoped when he finally let go and walked away, he'd found enough here that he had no choice but to lay old ghosts to rest and come back.

"I—I cleaned up the barn and the good news is, the quilt survived. It's hanging up in the laundry room. I didn't dare put it in the dryer."

"You cleaned up?" he said, his voice low as he took a step toward me.

"Well, yes. I didn't want you to come home and have to worry about it after all you went through tonight so I— what are you doing?" I asked as he took another slow step toward me.

Stalking me.

With an unreadable look on his face.

"You stayed here and took care of everything while I was gone so I didn't have to come home and do it?"

"Yes. It's not that big of a deal."

"To you," he said quietly.

He took another step.

Energy snapped in the air between us.

"It's just laundry," I said before rolling my lips between my teeth.

He stopped within inches of me, his gaze flicking to my

mouth before meeting my eyes again. "You didn't just do the dishes. Cleaning up from childbirth is a lot more than just laundry."

"I—why are you being weird?"

He took another step, backing me up until I bumped against the counter. "No one takes care of me."

I tipped my head back and cupped his cheek, finally noticing the stubble on his ordinarily clean-shaven face. "Have you ever let them?"

His eyes closed and he tilted his face into my hand. "I don't know how," he rasped.

"Cain…" I whispered, trying out his name, his real name for the first time.

He shuddered at the sound, another barrier collapsing between us.

The air snapped and crackled with the energy of it. Of this wall we'd been keeping there to protect ourselves from pain crumbling down around us.

"Maisy," he said, his lips just inches from mine.

"What do you need?" I whispered as I ran my thumb over his bottom lip.

"Stay." He traced my lips with his tongue until I shivered and gasped—then slanted his mouth over mine, his kiss slow and deep.

Tongue gliding against mine, his hands curling around the back of my neck pulling me under him, his ragged intake of breath, and the desperation in the sound detonating in my blood.

My skin turned to fire, my breasts grew hypersensitive to the slightest pressure, and with every lap of his tongue against mine, I throbbed, wet and wanting. When our mouths broke apart, I swayed with the force of letting go, our lungs heaving, our connection beating with a life of its own in the intimate space between us.

With my eyes locked on his, I peeled my tank top over my head, offering what we both needed for what may be our last time.

He only had one commitment left now... the exhibition.

After that, he'd have to deal with his demons—and despite all the ways I could help him—his grief and finding a way to forgive himself was one reality he'd have to face alone.

He dipped his fingers in between my breasts and tugged me to him, his warm brown eyes roaming over my skin, flaring with heat and need.

Reaching behind me, the movement pushing my breasts against his chest and making his nostrils flare, I flicked the clasp of my bra and dragged the straps down my arms.

With a growl from low in his throat, he only let me make it halfway before he plundered, his hot mouth sucking my tight nipple between his lips.

Wrapping his arms around me, he yanked me against him, his hands cupping my ass as he lifted me up until my legs wrapped around his waist—his mouth on me the entire time.

Heavy footsteps echoed in the quiet house as he carried me through the living room, never once faltering as he feasted on my skin.

His foot made contact with the bottom stair, and his gaze flicked to the wall, to the picture there of two young boys, smiling, together—safe.

"Can you guess which one I am?" he asked, his voice thick.

"I don't need to guess," I murmured, pressing my cheek to his and wrapping my arms around his neck to keep him as close as we both looked at the image. "I'd know that boy on the right anywhere."

He went still and turned to me. "No one could ever tell us apart."

I slid my hand into his hair and met his eyes, the confusion there in the taut lines of his pale, haunted face.

His vulnerability stripped bare… something he'd rail against for sure the minute he realized he exposed it to me.

"I see you, Cain," I whispered the words over his lips as I dotted his chin, the corner of his mouth, and that dimple in his cheek with soothing kisses. "And when you finally see yourself… I'll be here. Waiting for you to let me love you."

His eyes flashed and swirled—almost crazed with hunger—a starving man afraid to reach for the offering.

I gave him permission to go and my heart broke with it, the ache in my chest sweeping my breath away. I gave him everything he needed to walk away without guilt, without fear of who he'd hurt when he finally did.

I offered him every last bit of security he and I both longed for—the security we never dared ask for from the people we trusted to take care of us—from the parents who betrayed us.

My mother in hundreds of little ways.

His father in a devastating blow when Cain was at his most defenseless.

Those were our false starts.

But there'd be no penalty for the wounds inflicted by the people we trusted.

And I would be strong enough for the both of us until he caught up. I'd honor everything he did for me, for the chances he took by laying everything I had on that track in two days.

And then—well, we'd see.

"Don't think—just feel," I said, settling my arms

around his neck once again. "You can doubt this all in the morning, but right now—let me love you."

Arms tightening around me, he nodded. His body trembled under my hands, his body curled into mine, and he continued up the stairs.

With our clothes in rumpled piles on the floor, with Cain lying flat on his back staring up at me, his gaze blazing a trail his fingertips followed seconds later, I rose over him.

The minute I started to take him in, inch by steely inch, he shot up, his arms banding around me, his hands in my hair, his hot gaze never leaving mine.

Holding on to me in every possible way, even as he was letting me go.

No matter where we ended up in this life, there'd never be a moment I wouldn't feel him like this. Buried deep. Stretching me to the brink. Marking me as his.

Cain wasn't a man you got over. He's a man who branded you with his reluctant, vulnerable heart.

Our bodies moved together, our hands roaming over one another, our sighs turning to moans, our fingers tightening as each roll of our hips increased our urgency— propelling us toward goodbye.

The moment he let go, his body tight, his release a low, guttural groan vibrating from deep in his chest, the broken boy he'd been showed himself in the one hot tear that slid from the corner of his eye right before he buried his face in my neck and retreated into the shadows again.

Maisy

"Well, I don't know about you guys, but I'm nervous enough to poop. You think that would be a penalty?" Rory asked as we watched the teams prep for the first round of elimination bouts.

"I don't recall seeing poop in the rule book," Marty said.

"I'm going to ask you to refrain from shitting on the track. Losing is one thing, going out like that… mmm, gonna have to give that a hard no," Eve said.

Lights danced over the track in the center of the brand-new Ascend Sports Complex. Music rumbled in the background as ad images flashed on the screens, one facing in every direction for the audience stuck in the nosebleeds.

Not that we expected to pack the place today. This wasn't about that. It was about charity… and it didn't hurt Ascend to have the bit of good press that went along with it.

Priest waved his hand at us, calling us over to a quiet spot in the corner. "Okay, a quick rundown. These teams all know each other. You're going to use that to your advantage," he said, kneeling down while we all leaned in over him. "You're not seasoned on the bank in the same way. You don't have default moves. They've never seen you play. I know it sounds like those are all negatives. But they're not. They're all going to be your advantage out there."

His gaze swept through all of us, his sole focus on the events today and getting us to tomorrow where we'd wake up and do it all again one last time.

I took my cues from him. Too much hung in the balance to do anything else but trust him and follow his lead.

Our other baggage, we'd left it in Galloway Bay. It wasn't going anywhere.

"They haven't been training the way you guys have. Their season ended just over a month ago and with the confidence they have in their experience, they would have done a few practices, but nothing even close to what you guys put in day in and day out. Use that."

Jackson passed out water—yeah, he ended up coming with us because there was no way he was going to let Priest uninvite him; something about all that powerful, feminine energy being his kryptonite or something like that.

"They're already talking about you guys because you're the only team new to bank. The conversation is dying almost as soon as it starts because they're dismissing you as a non-threat which couldn't be further from the truth. The first round they're going to think you got lucky. But by the end of the second round, they're going to realize they were wrong and should have been paying attention."

"Oh, so that's when they're going to try to kick our ass in earnest then. Cool. Got it," Tilly said, sounding just like one of us, making me smile.

I had to be honest, it was probably a dick move, but I had serious thoughts of pilfering her from her own derby team. She'd be perfect with us.

And she already worked with the kids at Crossroads like we did. It was a win-win.

"They're going to hit that point where not only are you a threat, but you're an interloper. So, they're going to be looking to put you in your place. Don't let them. They get no real estate in your head. Got it?" Priest said, piercing us with a glance one at a time.

"No room at the inn," Dixie Dom said, slapping on her helmet and letting the straps dangle. "Got it."

"You've built up stamina when they haven't. But they're going to hit you harder and tap into your energy in a new way. Don't let it psych you out. You have the endurance."

"But really, if we poop out there…" Rory said, making us all laugh, breaking the thread of tension thrumming through us as a team.

"No shitting on the track. Hide your shame like the rest of us," he said with a laugh. "Now, play hard, play clean, and remember why you're here."

Five rounds. Two quarters each.

We were the third bout of the morning. I didn't know if I was happy about having the advantage of studying some of the teams now or if I just wanted to get in there and get this done. Every minute that stretched into the next, jam after jam, bodies colliding, the shouts, the grunts, jammers breaking away, came with a growing awareness that we were just like them.

Our story beginnings may have been radically different, the time invested unmatched, but nothing on that bank was a smoking gun giving one team an edge over another.

It would all come down to communication, perseverance, and laying everything we had on the track.

"What's going on in that head of yours, Mayhem?"

Priest asked, his arm resting against my shoulder—he did that, even though we agreed we needed to focus; he kept that physical connection in the smallest of ways.

Maybe for him. Maybe for me. Either way, it was exactly what I needed to put what came after out of my head and focus on now.

"I expected to feel like an underdog, but I don't. Does that make me a conceited bitch?" I asked with a smirk.

"Not at all. You're an athlete through and through. Your level of understanding when it comes to your competitors—it's unmatched."

"I—really?"

"Really. You're one hell of a package," he said with a smile. "And you guys are about to be up," he said, jutting his chin at the bank right as the whistle peeled through the air.

"This is it," I said quietly, pressing a hand to my stomach.

"This is it," he said, pressing a kiss to my forehead. "Now go kick their ass out there."

We went up against Death Knell first. A banked track team out of California. Players who'd been practically born on the track according to their bio.

But Priest was right.

They dismissed us, and the minute we got an edge in points, they started to fracture. Glares, harsh words, ignored direction—their communication tanked entirely, giving us pocket after pocket. We broke away, finally taking the bout with a lead of fourteen points.

"Yes! That's what I'm talking about. You have an hour before you're up again. They're going to dismiss this as beginner's luck. You're going to go in and show them that it's not. You got me?"

"This is fucking great. Guys, I'm totally getting lady

bone for the idea of a banked track at Sid's. We really need to figure out how to make that shit happen," Marty said as we skated to our seats.

"Money. We need money," Sean said.

I laughed, slid my helmet off my head, and brushed my fingers through my hair. "One thing at a time, guys… Crossroads first. World Domination after that."

I glanced over at Priest, looking for a sign that he overheard Marty's comment, but he had his attention on plays, his head together with Jackson's as they looked out at the track and the team that had just started.

When he came home, I wanted there to be no flicker of doubt as to what he came home for.

Round two unfolded almost exactly like the first, until the last half of the final quarter. Shrewd stares replaced eye rolls; the communication tightened up as did their plays on the track.

We took the win, but the points margin narrowed to nine. I did everything I could to put the numbers out of my head, knowing it wasn't logical to assume the point gap would continue to close by five points each time.

"You better not be thinking about those numbers, Mayhem," he said quietly, stepping up behind me.

"Get out of my head, Priest."

"Never," he said, resting his hands on my shoulders, his fingers curling into the muscles there, making me groan.

"How's the hand?"

"A dull throb. Jackson jumped up my ass about icing it before. I should probably thank him for that," I said, letting my weight fall against his chest for just a second.

Warm and strong, he dug at the knots as we watched a penalty play out for Black Heart Barbies, giving Maximum Penalty the chance to take the lead.

"You're up against Smoke Screen next. Number 268 gets overzealous. There'll be more illegal hits."

"Shouldn't you be telling everybody."

"I will, but she goes for jammers. She likes to be in the heart of the action. She's going to come for you. Just remember why you're here and don't let her bait you, and you're going to be fine."

He was spot on. Number 268's eyes tracked me every time I set up on the jam line with the tenacity of a bloodhound. The minute the second whistle blew, I caught up to the pack, her moves so much like Tilly's had been but without the personal vendetta, making it a whole lot easier for me to resist the trap.

They were all just pieces fueled by their pursuit of a win, their chance of success shaped by how tight they tried to hold on to the control. How adept they were at shifting and changing.

By the time the final whistle blew, we'd taken them by twelve points.

Priest looked at the score and shot me that "told you so" grin.

Flaming asshole.

But my flaming asshole.

He looked good here: coaching, encouraging—completely at ease despite the stakes.

Because he belonged.

With derby and with us.

Late afternoon only solidified the fact when we pulled out two more wins under his lead.

Sending us into the finals on day two.

Several of us dripping with sweat, out of breath, every muscle screaming, fresh bruises flaring to life, we wrapped our arms around one another and leaned in a circle.

"Did we really just pull that off?" Rory asked.

"Fuck yeah, we did. And you didn't shit on the track. A raving success," Sean said with a pant, still trying to catch her breath as the final four teams for the first round on day two flashed on the screen. Beautifully Brutal going head-to-head with the Fighting Furies at nine in the morning.

"I need a masseuse. Someone suave, with an accent. Big hands," Marty said.

"Order two, please," Zara said, waving a finger as she also struggled to move air since pulling off the final three points that took the last bout.

"And a bat in his pants. That would be good too," Marty added.

"Ah, the slide from recovery to porno," Tilly said with a breathless laugh. "Always a crowd pleaser."

"Come on, ladies. You kicked ass out there. Let's grab some food, take care of the injuries, and get ready to do it all again in the morning," Priest said as he stepped up to us.

"There's the bat in the pants you ordered," Rory muttered, making us all burst out laughing.

Because we were totally immature.

And we'd just kicked ass.

We crashed by eight that night and woke up at six the next morning, stiff and hunched—nothing a swim in the heated pool downstairs couldn't fix, followed by fifteen minutes in the hot tub to get our muscles loose and ready to go.

The mood shifted at the arena on day two. More spectators, the teams in their separate corners, constant glances at the banked track.

The announcements grew more animated and frequent, thanking sponsors and players. The kind of thing you usually tuned out at sporting events, except here, when the charity feature flashed on the big screen, it grabbed me right by the throat.

Each of the four charities vying for the first-place prize got their time in the spotlight on the big screens, with smooth narration from an announcer over the sound system.

And when they got to Crossroads my heart hammered in my ears, the breath stuttering in my lungs at the picture that flashed up there. Me, with Rylee, Addison, Ellie, Noah, and Leo all piled into my arms on Priest's track, a dopey smile on my face and tears in my eyes.

"Where did they get that?" I asked when he stepped up next to me.

"Wes snapped a picture and gave it to the paper—and me."

Two emotions swept through me, going head-to-head like the final teams today—sweet relief at seeing their faces, the reminder of what I was here fighting for… and bone-chilling terror we wouldn't pull it off.

"Cain," I whispered.

His head snapped up at the sound of his real name on my lips. "What's wrong?"

"I'm wobbling."

"Nope!" He took my arms and turned me to face him as he bent down so we were eye level. "You're the heart of this team. They take their cues from you and you're not going to fall apart. Do you hear me?"

I shook my head and gulped back the threat of tears. "Yeah."

He took my face in his hands and kissed me. The kind of kiss we'd been avoiding here. Keeping our relationship and this exhibition separate.

"No wobbling," he whispered as he let my mouth go,

but pulling me right against his chest, his warm arms infusing every last bit of confidence and energy he had into me. "I'm right here every step of the way with you, Maisy. I'm right here."

Until he left.

I glanced up at the screen right before the image shifted, catching the trusting look in Rylee's eyes.

They were my future.

We just needed to do what we came here to do and not settle for anything less.

Maisy

Facing off against The Fighting Furies, the hits came harder, the knowledge that this was it for one of us keeping the pressure on the pulse point, pushing us to the brink, making tempers snap, and communication breakdown on the track on both sides.

They took the lead right away and held it through the third quarter, their defense constantly sending us to the inside and out of bounds, attacking every bit of momentum we brought.

Priest started switching us out more often, switching up our sets, keeping our jammers as energized as possible. By the time we had just a minute and ten seconds left in the bout, we only led by a point, a lead we clawed our way to and fought to hold.

"Mayhem!" Priest barked out.

"Yeah," I said, not taking it personally; he'd been barking at us all morning. Every point on the board keeping him on the edge.

"They keep giving you gaps on the high side. They aren't huge, but I've seen you blast through them before. They let up when you're at the bottom of the track, but you're fast. Pay attention to that so if they give you the shot, you can run it. Give them your back on the high side and skate through. When you come around, stay high; they'll think you're going for it again. If you need to, drop low and take the inside edge."

"Got it."

"Don't worry about anything else. Just this. Show me what you've got," he said with a flash of a smile.

I set up behind the jam line and waited for the second whistle, the jammer for the other team out of breath next to me.

Any other time I would have sympathized, but right now, I wanted to win and every struggle for air on their part was an edge for me.

The second whistle sounded, and I took off, outrunning her to the pack. All moving pieces. Action and reaction. Tilly and Eve working together to block their jammer but making a gap for me in the middle.

Closing before I could get there, I shot low and watched their players shift with me, leaving the pocket on the high side just like he said.

My breath echoed in my ears as I remember what he told me. Digging in my toes, I ran the line. Eve and Tilly moved in to block their players from getting to me at the same time. Their pivot broke away and tried to catch me as I raced up the track. I turned sideways, facing the rail, giving her my back, just daring her to take the hit as I went into the turn, veering around the corner as I snuck past, my feet burning as I held my edges before I spun forward and cleared the pack.

Their jammer broke out just seconds after me, her pace the same as mine, keeping her a few seconds back, leaving me a narrow window to score points and call off the jam before she could get points of her own and have a chance to take the win.

Tilly glanced back and I saw it coming. She went into full protection mode. Not against me, but for me.

And she knew I liked the inside.

It narrowed down to seconds. Me watching Tilly. Tilly keeping her eye on me while using her body to drive the pack up the back just enough to give me a shot.

I came in fast, got low, braced my hips, and started to slide by as one of their blockers stepped out, planting their skate in front of me.

At the last second, I pushed off the toe, jumping her attempt at sending me to the infield, cleared the pack, and called off the jam by tapping my hands on my hips.

"Yes!" Priest shouted, pumping his fist in the air as my team erupted in cheers as the scoreboard rolled over, and we took the win by two points.

By late morning, Maven Voyage had taken the win in their bout, and the final bout was set. At two in the afternoon, we'd face off one more time.

And no matter what happened, we'd already won fifty thousand dollars.

One year for Crossroads.

We'd bought time.

But we needed so much more.

The exertion began taking its toll, on our team's stamina, and on theirs. When we began again, the exhaustion and strain in our eyes mirrored theirs. Our movements were clunky at times and sometimes downright erratic.

Tempers flared. The desire to win making each side a bit more desperate.

On the line for one final jam, I took off at the whistle and caught the pack one more time. The hits came harder, some illegal as both sides gave everything they got. Skates tangled. Skaters went down but hopped right back up again.

Maven Voyage's jammer passed the star to their pivot, turning her into their lead jammer. I was just about to push through and chase her down, driving my one skate in as a wedge between two blockers, when the blocker next to me took an illegal hit to the chest, her arms flying out with the force and her elbow catching me in the eye. I crashed against the track, my skin burning as it dragged over the masonite, and Maven Voyage's jammer sailed through scoring three points.

The final jam.

Maven Voyage won.

The whistle blew and I lay there trying to catch my breath as I stared up at the iron framing in the roof of the complex, the lights shooting in all directions, catching me in the eye.

Nothing was keeping him here anymore.

We'd just lost but managed to come in second place when we shouldn't have placed at all, and all I could think is that he would spiral now.

He could check us off his list of people who needed him and I knew just what would happen when he did.

He'd run.

The blocker who took me out skated over and offered me a hand. "Are you okay?"

"Yeah, nothing some ice and a cocktail can't fix."

Except neither were going to keep me from the broken heart coming.

"I hear that," she said with a laugh. "You guys gave us one hell of a fight out there. No one will doubt you guys next time."

Next time.

Would there be a next time? Would Priest be there with us?

"They better not."

She skated away and joined her cheering team.

My crew skated up on the track and joined me, Priest cutting through all of them, wrapping his arms around me, lifting me clean off the floor.

His arms swallowed me whole as his body curled around mine. I burrowed into his heat and closed my eyes while I memorized the sound of his racing heart by my ear.

"I'm proud of you," he murmured.

I squeezed, afraid to let him go. "We didn't win."

"Second place is something to celebrate," he said, his lips next to my ear as I burrowed into him even more, grasping on to his every word. "You never forgot what you were fighting for out there."

"I'll never forget anyone I fight for," I whispered.

He stilled with my quiet words, his arms loosening on me as I slid to my feet, before letting me go entirely. My team overtook me then, and he faded into the recesses, standing next to Jackson, but with each minute further and further away.

Maven Voyage skated over, and everyone began to introduce themselves, congratulating one another, and talking about the plays, full of laughter now, the intensity of the bout slowly sliding behind us.

No animosity. No tempers.

We shared something here—misfits and mothers, artists and businesswomen, every walk of life met here on this track, what united us so much stronger than what divided us.

These were the kind of women who didn't judge how new you were in town, what kind of job you worked, or who you loved. You'd be welcome in their home and at their table. You could pull up your differences and celebrate them together, not let them divide you.

This was exactly what I'd been searching for.

With these derby sisters, the ones on my team and the ones I competed against who understood the passion and sacrifice, I was found.

After the last of us showered, all of us clean and comfortable, we poured the drinks.

"First thing next week, planning session to fund Crossroads on the long term," Marty said, handing out glasses as she filled them.

"Where's coach bat-in-his-pants and his sidekick? They should be here celebrating with us," Rory said.

Eve took a sip of her drink, winced, and dumped more liquor in. "Call them up and get their asses in here."

"What room is Jackson in?" Sean asked as she plopped on the couch in the open living room section of the suite and grabbed the phone.

"Room 308," Rory said over their heads as Dixie and Carmen got chatty and loud.

"And Priest?" Sean called out.

"Room 324," I said as I grabbed a fresh bag of ice from the minuscule freezer.

"Got it. Get ready for some testosterone, ladies, because I'm not taking no for an answer," Sean said. "I hope they like margaritas… and if they don't, well, they better just pretend they do."

"How's the eye?" Eve asked as she looked me over from multiple angles.

"Could be worse, I didn't need stitches," I said, giving Tilly the eye which only made her ass sidle on up and clink her glass to mine.

"The stitches were totally worth the outcome," she said as she wrapped her arm around me.

"Jackson's on his way. Priest didn't answer," Sean said. "Maisy, you wanna go grab your boy?"

"On it." I handed my glass to Tilly. "Don't drink that. I'm coming back for it."

"Don't come back too soon," she said with a wink as she lifted my glass to her lips.

"Hey, I mean it. That one's mine." I aimed my finger at her. "I'll be right back for it."

I padded down the hall, passing Jackson on the way, giving him a smile and a nod.

"How's that eye?" he said as he passed me.

"Great. I should look human again in a few days." I said, turning around, walking backward as I called out my answer to him.

"Try a few weeks," he said with a laugh.

"Awesome."

I glanced at the sign at the end of the hall, again, because direction has never been my strong suit, and adjusted my ice pack, my steps slowing as my skin prickled.

The empty sensation of being completely alone filled me.

"You're being stupid," I muttered, but when I got to his door, I hesitated and flattened my palm to the cool metal instead.

We had a flight in the morning. What destination had he chosen?

I knocked and waited, but there was no movement on the other side.

Sliding my cell from my pocket, I tried to call him, but it went straight to voicemail.

A lump of panic lodged in my throat, my stomach dropping to my toes as I leaned against the wall across from his room and I brought up the number for the hotel and asked for Room 324.

"I'm sorry, but the guest in Room 324 checked out."

My phone slipped from my hand.

My back slid down the wall until my butt hit the floor.

Tears burned hot trails down my cheeks, my heart squeezing painfully in my chest as I struggled to breathe past the ache.

He was gone.

Maisy

We'd been home for a week. We'd done interviews with local TV and the newspapers and a goofy ceremony turning over a big-ass check.

Yes, the numbers were big, but it was the actual check ironically that was big. Obnoxiously so.

Three feet wide to be exact.

We gave them all the tap dancing they wanted after getting their personal guarantee the program would live on for an additional year, and we'd have a grace period every year to come up with more funding.

Gee, look at us twisting their arms, when really they had us by the tits. They got money *and* us doing the work for them. But I didn't give a shit. I wanted my kids, and being able to look into Rylee's eyes and tell her with absolute certainty we weren't going anywhere was worth being small-town show ponies for a while.

A win.

And it gave me a focus.

With her worries gone, it took those kids less than sixty seconds to change the topic to Rockabilly's and the banked track, asking when they were going to see Priest again, if he would skate with them, if maybe he'd teach them how to do roller derby.

Just like that they'd latched on to him even as he let go.

I was trying not to be a bit butt hurt that they didn't ask us to teach them.

Really, guys?

I'd gone through all the motions in the past one hundred and sixty-eight hours since the last day of the exhibition. Smiled when I was supposed to, put the kids off about Priest by changing the subject, telling them he had to go on a trip—basically lying to them—and when the performance ended, I went to my apartment and cried.

And cried some more.

When I told him he could go and I would wait, I didn't know I was committing myself to the pain of being sliced in half, all the essentials still connected to support life, while I went back and forth between total and utter agony with brief periods of numb shock before drowning in the pain all over again.

Flaming asshole.

My teammates called. Eve even stopped by, threatening me with an intervention, but I didn't need an intervention.

I needed a hug.

And not by them.

By him.

I wondered if he knew he was a good hugger.

The best hugger.

And he probably needed one too. That was the worst part. Remembering that look in his eye.

Knowing his tendency to punish himself with no one there to remind him just how worthy he was of love and having someone who cared for him the way he cared for others.

"Maybe decaf ain't so bad after all," Milton said, taking a sip of his second cup that morning.

"What decaf?" I asked as I shot Gerald a look over my shoulder, catching him in the act of slipping his hand toward Milton's bacon. "Yours is coming. Be good."

"I'm a little disappointed in you, young lady. You're slipping. I've already taken one piece," Gerald grumbled.

"Don't be thinking I don't know what you've been doing back there, Maisy Jane," Milton said raising his mug. "I let you get away with it because you put up with an old curmudgeon like me," Milton said.

I rounded the counter and put my arms around both of them. "I love old curmudgeons like you."

Milton patted my hand and tipped his head against mine. "I hate seeing you sad like this, sweetheart. He's going to come back, you know."

But it wasn't just that; it was also the way he left. My last moments with him in an arena six hundred miles from home.

There were things I would have said. Feelings I would have reassured him of.

I would have told him I love him.

No hints, no alluding to it. Just three simple words.

And I would have had some sort of goodbye, that last hug to sustain me while he figured his shit out.

"You know what you need? You need to go get a sniff of Lilith and Jordan's new baby. He'll cheer you up," Milton said.

I raised my head and stared down at him. "You've seen him?"

"Sure have," he said, gesturing with his cup. "Lilith was bragging on you and how you helped her through having him. I'm kind of surprised you haven't seen him yet since you were there when he came into this crazy world."

I did do that. So, I had rights, right?

At least some sort of honorary thing. What did you call someone who did that anyway? Honorary aunt?

I could bring him a baby present, but none of that practical stuff. I could bring him something frivolous—a puppy!

Actually, a puppy probably wasn't what they needed right now, but it was a farm, and it was sorely lacking a dog.

Okay, so better than a rattle and not as awesome as a dog… kitten… but again, something that needed to be kept alive.

I closed my eyes and time sucked me back to when Cain delivered that little boy and the stricken anguish on his face in the quiet stillness after. Brief, but breathtaking, the look slid into gritty determination as he worked, and a flood of relief when he heard that first wail.

I blinked open my eyes, tears burning again, but I knew just the thing.

I slid my phone out of my pocket, made sure Scooter wasn't watching because he'd been ornery lately and no one needed more of that shit, and dialed Rockabilly's.

"Yo," Jackson answered.

"That's how you answer the phone?"

"It's early. You should be more surprised I'm awake to answer the phone."

"Have you heard from him?" I asked, trying not to hold my breath while I waited for the likely answer.

"No," he said quietly. "I wish I had a better answer for you, Maze."

Knowing what he'd say didn't make his answer hurt any less. "Any chance you can do me a favor?"

"Anything," he said, his voice remarkably swift for such a laid-back guy.

"You can make skates, right?"

"Yeaaaahhhhh," he said, drawing out the word.

"Can you make skates for say… a two-year-old?"

"Sure."

"With flames on the side?"

"I see where you're going with this," he said, his voice perking right up at the idea. "You know what, I can. I'll get started now and call you when they're done."

This was gonna be great! I just wished I asked him the timeline because I'd be watching the clock all day now.

If this was, say… a week-long job, I was in some serious trouble. I was not going to wait a week to see that baby.

I finished out my shift, ready to go home, but my phone rang instead, and thank fuck this time I knew the number.

Jackson.

"They're ready."

"Really?"

"Really. I had everything here I needed to build them. It was just a matter of looking up average sizes for that age and boom. I even have them all packaged up for you in their own box and ready to go."

A half hour later, he handed me a bag with a custom-built pair of black skates just like Priest's, with little red leather flames affixed to each side.

"If he doesn't come back here and scoop you right up," he said, holding my car door for me, "I'm going to go down to Boston and kick him in the balls for you."

"I'm going to hold you to that," I said, kissing him on the cheek before firing up my car and heading out to the farm.

I thought I'd be sad on the drive, every mile a reminder of my time out here, but the excitement of seeing the baby and the present riding shotgun next to me, the perfect present, wiped away the lingering sorrow.

Parking next to Lilith's SUV, I grabbed the bag, and headed for the door, but hesitated when I got there. I'd always knocked when we used the bathroom during practice because this was another woman's house, and it felt disrespectful not to.

But I'd helped Lilith through childbirth here.

I'd done laundry.

I saved a quilt.

Read from a well-loved book in the easy chair by their grandfather's lamp.

I'd started to let Cain go here even as I held on to him while we made love all night in his bed.

Fresh tears burned in the back of my eyes and I froze, unable to knock, unable to walk away, so damn heartbroken it choked me as I stood staring at the supply sled propped against the wall on the porch.

So much for having buried it for the time it took for a brief visit.

The door crept open, Lilith gave me a sad smile and opened her arms… where I fell apart again.

"Aww, honey, you haven't heard from him?"

"No," I mumbled against the burp rag over her shoulder. "Have you?"

"Just once," she said quietly.

"Did he ask about me?" I said, pulling back and wiping my eyes.

She didn't have to answer; the look on her face said it all with the way her mouth flattened, and the frustration flashed in her brown eyes so very much like his. "No."

"Okay." There was that word he hated, but fuck him. If he wanted to take issue with it, he could just get his ass up here and do so.

Lilith tipped her head and smiled. "Do you want to hold a freshly bathed squishy bundle of baby?" She took a step back and held the door.

"Yeah, I think I do," I said, stepping inside. "I even brought him something."

She led me into the living room where a large man with short-cropped, military-issued sandy hair I could only assume was Jordan sat with a sleepy satisfied smile on his, their son tucked in his arms.

"Jordan, this is Maisy. Maisy, my husband Jordan."

"Nice to finally meet you," I murmured, handing the bag to Lilith as I snuck a closer glance at their sleeping son and smiled at his scrunched up expression. The same one I'd spotted on his uncle's face a time or two.

"I don't even know his name. What are we calling this little cutie?"

When they didn't answer, I glanced up and found them looking at one another.

"What? It can't be top secret. Is it one of those weird Hollywood names?"

"Cain," Lilith said quietly. "We named him Cain."

"Oh—well—that's… shit." I ground my fingers into my temples. "I'm swearing in front of him already. I'm so sorry."

"I'm pretty sure he won't pick it up just yet. You're good," Jordan said with a laugh. "He learned all kinds of salty language when I checked to see if he needed changing and landed my fingers in a loaded diaper."

"He loves it, and he knows it," Lilith said next to me with a laugh in her voice.

Jordan stood and nodded to the chair. "Settle in, and I'll pass him over."

I took the offered seat and curled my legs up under me.

Jordan leaned down and laid Cain right in my arms

where he cracked an eye open, decided I was good people, shuddered out a breath, and drifted off again.

My mind went back to that moment in the barn and the way Cain muttered under his breath, like he could will his nephew to breathe with chanting words, prayers, whatever he had to say in those moments that I couldn't make out.

The relief on his face the minute the baby finally let out his first scream.

If he were here holding his nephew, I had no doubt what he would do.

And since he wasn't, I'd do it for him until he could be.

I leaned down and pressed a gentle kiss to Cain's soft forehead where it met his head full of dark hair and breathed him in.

CAIN

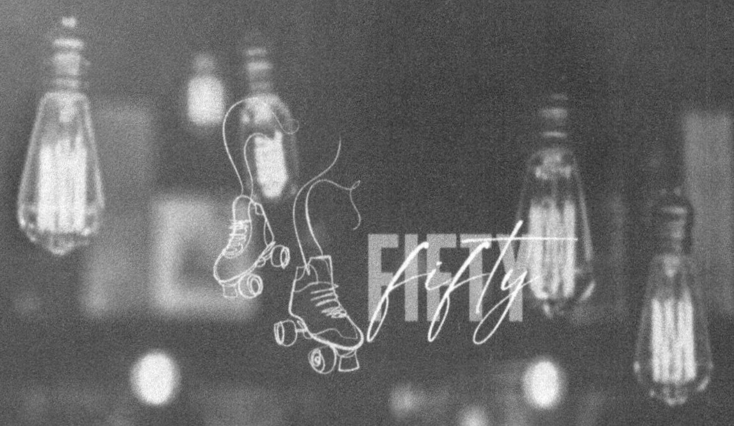

I walked through my apartment door for the first time during the daylight hours after spending more than a week working double shifts, avoiding drinks and basketball games with my friends at the precinct, waiting for something to feel normal. For anything to feel normal again.

I couldn't even find some sort of familiarity in the obscurity I once loved about the coffee shop around the corner where I counted on no one knowing my name or caring to talk. And why? Because the woman behind the counter that I was used to seeing day in and day out quit while I was gone and now, the only familiar thing I had left was the forgettable flavor of scorched coffee on my tongue that I could get from any gas station or truck stop.

On the third day, I'd taken out a pizza box to the dumpster—because that's what I did now—field trips to the dumpster, and when I'd gotten back to my door, the neighbor introduced himself, thinking I was new to the place.

I'd been here for five years.

Turns out he'd been here for four.

Neither of us could back out of that conversation fast enough.

Alone in a city of millions.

And now the stark light of day was a ruthless bitch ready to deliver a one-two punch by making sure I saw every single impersonal corner of my life in desolate detail.

The problem with the impersonal—it showcased the intimately personal.

One thing stood out. The one thing always stood out here.

Abel's ashes.

And the harsh truth that I'd been keeping him here. All this time, I'd been keeping myself in my own prison, unable to let him go.

To what end?

I'd never be able to change the last time we spoke. I'd never be able to change what I'd done when I reported them. And I had to be honest, what really bothered me is that I'd do the same thing again if I had to do it all over again today.

Because I was trying to save his life.

Being with Maisy lit me up from the inside out with so much color, so much attitude, so much heart, and no amount of being here would ever feel normal again.

I live for the both of us now.

She was right. The minute I didn't have someone who needed me, someone to save, I didn't know what to do with myself. Being here wasn't living. And how did I figure out how to live for both Abel and me when I hadn't even figured out how to do it for myself?

The sinking feeling in my gut hadn't eased since I left that hotel, no doubt making another monumental mistake with Maisy, but they had a win to celebrate and the minute the exhibition was over, the storm took hold in me one more time, and I wouldn't do that to her in her moment.

She'd say okay again and I just—I didn't want us to

turn into that. Me coming apart and her becoming the person who had to tether me to the ground again.

She wanted to take care of me, and I didn't want to be the person in her life who constantly needed to be taken care of. Who stole the joy from her wins because he still stewed in an emotional wasteland because he used people needing him as a way to avoid his emotional shit.

She called my phone just once that last night in Philly and when I didn't answer, she let me go.

And I took advantage of the fact that I knew she would.

I had to get my shit together and I wouldn't face her again until I could be the man she deserved. The one who could give and take instead of being sucked into constant doubt and memories I couldn't shake, so consumed by my past that all I did was take and take from her, leaving her with little happiness—her free spirit obliterated until okay became the standard between us instead of the glaring warning sign it was now.

I had to finally let my brother go.

I didn't know how. He was half of me and letting him go felt like I was letting myself go too. Who did I become when I was alone again?

I'd never figured out the answer... and maybe that was the answer—there wasn't one. Like words in English that couldn't be translated into other languages because the concept just didn't exist.

My phone buzzed and I glanced down and spotted Lana's number.

I debated ignoring it, but this was Lana—she didn't let anyone ignore her for long.

"Hey, is everything okay?"

"You know, Coach... I'm a pretty happy woman. I made peace with the fact that these legs are never going to work again. And until recently, I could even say I didn't miss them for anything, but you know what I miss them for now?"

I leaned against the wall and stared out at the gray city, nothing special standing out, just a spattering of nondescript buildings with no connections—no memories. A stark contrast to the lively personality on the other end of the line. "Nope, but I'm pretty sure you're going to tell me. Just do me a favor and skip any sex parts."

"No sex parts unless you count me shoving my foot up your ass as kinky."

I closed my eyes and turned away only to have my eyes go right to Abel's urn. "How is she?" I asked, my voice thick as I swallowed hard.

"You're an idiot."

I squeezed my eyes shut and pinched the bridge of my nose. "No doubt."

"She's—well, how the hell do you think she is, huh? The damn powers that be over at Crossroads paraded them around like hometown heroes; that was cute. A bit nauseating. But I get how these things go. Look, she's doing all the right things. She's slapping on a smile. She's showing up at work; she even managed to get up there to see your nephew, but she's dying inside, man."

"I'm working it out—I just, wait, what?" My skin tingled as restless energy surged through me, making me pace. "She saw him?"

"So that perked your little ears up, did it? Good. Yeah, she saw him. She brought him a present and everything. She's up here living life… a life you could be living with her if you'd stop getting in your own damn way. You're two left skates, coach, and it's embarrassing."

"Is she angry?" God, those words made me sound like a fucking coward. Like I didn't dare face her down if she was when really, it was one of my favorite ways to face her.

And I kind of hoped she was, because if she wasn't—

"No, you bonehead. She's hurt. I would kill for angry right now. Look, Zach's here and I have to go, but I'm going to give you a little tip you gave me once out on that track. Never forget what you're fighting for."

She hung up before I had the chance to say goodbye, my words coming back to bite me in the ass.

Was I going to keep fighting my past or fight *for* my present?

My phone chimed again. A fucking Facebook notification of all things, something I'd become helpless to ignore since my nephew was born, especially now that this was the only way I could get a glimpse of him.

I swiped the screen and dropped onto my couch, only to have a frozen image of Mayhem, trademark red bandana in her hair, her eyes glassy like she'd been crying, smiling down at my nephew.

My chest constricted, my head swimming with light-headedness.

I wasn't ready to see her like this.

Holding a baby. Holding him.

When I couldn't.

Or wouldn't… because it was time to be honest.

The play icon in the middle of the frame mocked me. Dared me to tap it.

The urge to save myself came, filling me with shame. To turn off my phone and not look—not see life happening without me—happy memories I could be making with her if I could just reach for it. Saving myself meant continuing to hurt her, and I couldn't do it anymore.

I wouldn't do it anymore.

I turned up the volume, not wanting to miss a single second even knowing I could play it over again.

Her soft voice slammed me right in the chest as her gentle fingertips brushed over my nephew's cheeks. My heart ached in a whole new way as I watched her living in my life—what could be our life, if only I'd step in and join her there.

For the first time a new ache overshadowed the old. The thought of living without her cutting me so deep the pain took my breath away as it roared through my blood.

Her lesson finally hit home.

I live for both of us now.

Abel's urn sat there mocking me. My exact match so full of life himself that his every feeling came out, good or bad, calling me a traitor—a scathing word that killed me for so long—but words of a teenage boy diverging from his other half as he tried to be worthy to his only living parent. A man who didn't deserve his loyalty.

But also the only parent he had left.

Why wouldn't he see me as a traitor in that moment?

And being my vocally passionate half, what would he call me now if he were standing right here to catch me hiding out?

She was doing it. Every day she was living for us and I was hiding.

She loved me so damn much she'd give me whatever space I needed to do it.

I blinked, my eyes hazed over with unshed tears, but not enough to miss the flash of something familiar in the background. I backed up the video and caught sight of it again, hitting pause, the image frozen before me.

Right there.

Hope punched a hole right through my chest. A knot lodged in my throat.

Skates.

Tiny black skates with red flames on the side almost exactly like mine.

I didn't have to wonder who got them for him. They had Mayhem written all over them.

Home.

I want to go home.

Maisy

P atti pulled me in for a hug the minute I stepped into Banked Track late afternoon to avoid the evening rush. "Have you heard from him?"

A couple of guys sat at a table in the back, but other than that, the bar was empty. I usually loved these moments where it was pretty much just us and daydreaming as I stared at her derby days hanging on the brick behind her.

But today—today was one of those days like when you got home from school and basked in the relief from the gnawing feeling in the pit of your belly after you overheard the popular girls talking about you right before lunch, so you sat away from everyone and the rest of the day you counted the minutes until you could escape and pretend it wouldn't all happen again tomorrow.

"No," I said as I hopped up on a stool—the flaming asshole's stool—and watched her work behind the bar.

"He is getting entirely too old for this nonsense," Patti said as she poured cranberry juice over ice and kicked in a splash of pineapple juice on top just like she used to when I was too young to drink, but old enough to know I wanted to sit in this bar and soak up her wisdom.

"He is kinda old," I said.

Patti gave me a warning look as she slid the glass to me complete with a quarter slice of pineapple on top with a sword toothpick sticking out of it. "Easy girl, if he's old, what am I?"

"Stop that, you're going to live forever."

"I don't know if I want that, but he better if he's gonna keep on wasting time like this. That boy is in for some lessons in etiquette the minute he steps foot in this town again. No more Brussels sprouts paninis for him either… not until he earns them," Patti said as she rubbed the flat of her palm into her chest.

I froze with the pineapple halfway to my mouth. "Hey, are you okay?"

"I'm fine," she said, waving me off. "Just indigestion. Getting old is not sexy. I do not recommend it at all."

"I went to see Lilith and the baby the other day." She'd named him after Cain, and I still couldn't bring myself to say the poor kid's name out loud. I gave him his first pair of skates, I held him, he puked on me, and I still couldn't say his name. "She said he called once to check on him, but other than that he's been silent."

And he didn't ask about me when he called.

That hurt.

Really hurt.

If he showed back up in town now, I didn't know if I'd kiss him or kick him in the balls.

Maybe have Lana run over him with the very motorized chair he bought.

Flaming asshole.

"Honey, I normally wouldn't say this because we should not have to do the chasing. We have the babies, we have the periods, we have the careers that earn seventy whatever cents on the dollar compared to a man so again, we shouldn't have to be doing the chasing," she said, slashing a hand through the air. "But go get that boy and bring him home. He's your family, right? Well, he's gone astray and maybe he just needs someone to show him the way home." She pointed a finger at me, the towel swinging from her fingers as she did. "But for the third and final time, we shouldn't have to do the chasing."

I propped my chin on my hands. "If he's having such a damn hard time finding home, he can damn well get a map."

Patti threw her head back and laughed, her palm grinding against her chest again.

Her skin took on a gray pallor right before my eyes as her laugh came to an abrupt halt, her usually pink cheeks with barely a faint splash of color.

"Patti?" I slid off my stool. "Patti, are you okay?"

She clutched the counter, her knees buckling, the towel sliding from her fingers as she hunched over. "You know what, honey, I'm not," she said, trying to catch her breath. "Hurts."

I slid around the counter and managed to get behind her as her legs gave out and she crumpled to the floor in my arms. "Call 9-1-1!"

Please not now. No dammit. No!

"Patti, can you hear me? Stay with me. Help is coming." I squeezed her hand and checked her pulse, afraid to take my fingers away once I found it. "Don't you die on me, dammit. You're my family too; you are not allowed to tell me to chase him down and check out on me a few minutes later. Do you hear me? Do you?" I demanded with a quick shake.

I couldn't tear my eyes from the rise and fall of her chest as I continued to count and talk to her. Promising her I would do the chasing, but just this once if she'd just hold on.

And if he came back for me, I wouldn't have Lana run him over; I wouldn't kick him in the balls, or let Jackson do it like he threatened.

I'd hug him. I'd curl right into him where I belonged and tell him I love him.

And then I'd make it damn clear he would never walk out on me again, so I hope he'd pulled his head out of his ass while he was gone.

She never made another sound, just lay in my arms with her eyes closed until the ambulance pulled up and the EMTs took over.

In a matter of minutes they had her strapped to the gurney with an oxygen mask settled over her face as they wheeled her out the door and loaded her in the back of the ambulance.

And all I could wonder is if I'd just seen her for the last time.

I never got my last time with my mother, but if this is what it was, maybe that was a good thing.

Because this felt like an ax right in my already shredded heart and forcing myself through every motion filled me with frozen despair.

A crowd had gathered outside and watched her go. No doubt in a matter of hours everyone in Galloway Bay would be flooding Banked Track with calls.

I grabbed my phone and dialed Rory's number, but when she answered, all I could manage was, "Patti collapsed," my voice breaking on even those two words.

"Wait, what?" Rory said, her voice breathless and thin.

"She collapsed here at the bar," I said again, choking back tears. "Can you come down and take over?"

"I'm just down the street. Five minutes. I'll be there in five minutes," Rory said before hanging up.

Maisy

Was it really only a month ago when I walked into this waiting room and wrapped my arms around Priest while he waited for word about his sister?

Before I could even get used to one change, another would hit me, and the last two, they were biggens.

The biggest.

And all I wanted as I stared out into the darkness was for Priest to show up and return the favor.

Was that really too much to ask?

I missed him so freaking much that even now, after two weeks, my heart ached with my every breath. His scent haunted me and a new stream of tears spilled down my cheeks.

Was this how Abel haunted him? Or was that even worse?

Familiar arms slid around me and a sob tore from my thick, aching throat. When his scent and heat enveloped me, every rigid muscle melted with relief. I couldn't turn to face him, not yet, but oh, how I wanted to. My heart hammered in my chest as pain, fear, and relief collided inside me.

"Are you only here because you think I need somebody?"

His chest swelled as he buried his face in my neck. His warm lips brushed over my skin as he breathed me in, his hand flexing where it rested on my belly. "I'm here because I need us."

Hope bloomed and my heart swelled with it. Eyes burning, my shoulders sagged in relief from the coiled tension locked there for hours. Maybe weeks.

"She told me I should go get you… before she collapsed," I said, choking on the clog of tears. "She told me I needed to bring you home where you belonged."

He cleared his throat and a shudder trembled through him. "I'm glad you didn't," he said, his voice thick, his breath warm over my skin.

I turned in his arms and searched his face. The exhaustion around his eyes matching mine. The lines etched into his skin around his mouth telling the story of the torment he'd been facing while he'd been gone. "Why?"

"Because you'd always wonder if I was only here because you did," he said, his thumb grazing over my damp cheek. "I don't want you to have a single doubt about why I came back—why I came to stay."

"The farm is your home—"

"No," he said quietly. "It's not." His lips settled against my forehead setting off a shuddering breath inside me. "You, Maisy. You're my home. Wherever that is, even if it's in a tiny apartment over Banked Track."

His arms swallowed me whole, and I burrowed in, my eyes drifting shut, the first real full breath filling my heavy lungs.

"I hurt you again," he whispered.

"You did." I curled my fingers in his sweater and filled my lungs with a mix of spicy, heat, and him. Just him. "But we both knew it was coming. From the beginning. It had to. There was no other way to get here."

He turned his face into mine and nestled in close. "God, you slid right through every defense I had. I never had a chance against you, Mayhem. Not from the first time I saw you on that track." Cupping my neck, he held me close, locking us in this intimate bubble for just the two of us and all the things we'd been longing to say.

"I love you so damn much," he whispered, that rumble of his voice vibrating clear through me and cradling my heart the same way he cradled his nephew.

Reaching between us, he cupped my chin, his thumb grazing over my bottom lip. Slow and smooth, he replaced his thumb with his mouth. His taste slid through me, his kiss promising me everything I'd ever longed for.

"You don't have to fight to hold on anymore, Mayhem," he said, his voice soothing every ragged edge from my past and present with resolute words. "Because I'm holding on to you."

***

Sheriff Chase had to turn on some serious charm to get the hospital to bend the rules and let us see Patti, but finally, by seven that night they led us back to her room, all of us, despite the visitor limit.

Me, Cain, Eve, Rory, Sean, Marty, and Zara, the core gang, the tried and true who never missed a night at Banked Track.

"You guys have ten minutes," the nurse said before quietly closing the door behind her.

Cain leaned in and kissed Patti's cheek and her eyes popped open, making him jump back. "What are you trying to do, give a woman a heart attack?"

"Word is you just had one," he said, taking her hand and settling in next to her.

"Look at the two of you," she said with a brief smile, until she shifted, felt the oxygen tubes in her nose, and yanked them free.

"Patti, you need—" Rory began.

"Do you think I'm going to wither away if I don't have spikes jammed up my nostrils for a couple minutes?"

"Well, no, but—"

"No buts. I only have a few minutes before miss *I want to be nurse of the year* is back in here poking at me, and I have some stuff I need to say."

"The bar is fine. People were too worried about you to drink, so we sent them all home and shut it down for the night. Told them they better handle their feelings tonight because tomorrow they needed to drink twice as much to make up for it."

"Ah, smart girl," she said, taking Rory's hand.

"And you don't have to worry about the ordering. I helped Vince and it's all set."

"You're all smart girls." She turned to Cain then, her smile turning into a scowl. "Jury's still out on you, but coming home was a damn good start. I better start hearing you make it up to her from that apartment over the bar. If I can't hear it, you're not sorry enough."

"Jesus, Patti," Marty muttered, rubbing her temples.

"What? If I were twenty years younger, I'd—"

"I think we know what you'd do," Cain said with a laugh.

"Good," Patti said with a nod. "Now listen up. I've had a few hours to think and that never happens. Anyway, the doctor's suggesting a few changes and that got me to thinking. How would you girls feel about becoming the next generation of Banked Track?"

I glanced around at my team and back down at Patti. "What exactly do you mean?"

"Take over the bar. Ownership and all. I'll stick around and show you the ropes, but you girls are the future of the sport here in Galloway Bay. Flat track or banked track. WRDF or on your own, I can't see handing a piece of history as important as Banked Track to anyone else. Can you?"

Maisy

"Toast, toast, toast," my team chanted, their glasses raised in the air as we celebrated Patti's release from the hospital… and secretly celebrated our plans to take Patti up on her offer.

"To banked tracks, exceeding expectations, second place, and that straight piece in Priest's pants," I said, shooting a smile over my shoulder at the man himself.

"Immortalized in a toast, I don't know if I should be honored or horrified," he said as he started to stroll by, cupped the back of my neck, and pulled me in for a hot kiss before letting me go and continuing on over to where Jordan and Sheriff Chase watched the latest football game on the TV screen mounted in the corner.

"Be honored and reward me hard later," I called out to his retreating back. "Oh… and with skates on."

"Anything you want, Mayhem," he said with a wink as he sat back and tipped his beer to his lips, his hot gaze running over every inch of me.

"You guys suck, man," Sean said.

"Right," Rory added. "It's bad enough we're not getting any at the moment, but to have these two sex fiends fucking each other with their eyes and making us watch? Total and utter betrayal."

"You guys are happy for me and you know it," I said, tipping my glass back, that root beer flavor hitting the back of my tongue followed by that sharp bite.

"Holy shit, look at that guy," Marty said, her drink clunking against the table, making liquor spill down her hand.

Not that she cared. Her mouth had fallen open and she'd gone nips up for whatever fine piece walked through the door.

"My God, he's just—well, damn. Damn," Rory said as she pulled out her cell.

"Way to be stealth," I said, knowing damn well she was going to snap his picture.

"Aren't you going to look at him?" Eve asked. "I mean, shit, even I'm looking at him."

"Patti's feeling okay, right? I don't want her to see him and have another heart attack," Zara said.

"She's feeling great—doh, here she comes," Rory said, craning her neck.

"And she's sending him over here."

Tall, dark, and absolutely every woman's type, the mystery man stepped up and smiled. "Sorry to interrupt, ladies. Maisy Flynn?" he said, glancing down at me.

I turned in my chair and glanced up at him and they weren't fucking kidding. He towered over our table with wide shoulders, dark and thick wavy hair brushed back, and black intense eyes all wrapped up in a power suit.

And he did absolutely nothing for me.

No buzz, no zing, nada.

His scent was positively edible, but turns out, I wasn't hungry.

But then, the only man I'd ever want sat just ten feet away, watching me with amusement in his eyes as my entire table went through some sort of mass ovary explosion.

Well, my ovaries had a very specific trigger these days, and that was Priest telling derby stories to his nephew, Cain. "I'm Maisy. What can I do for you?"

"You're a hard woman to get ahold of," he said, his full mouth curving in a smile.

"I don't go far," I said with a shrug. "Who are you?"

His eyebrow lifted and a smile twitched at the corner of his mouth. "Micah Alessi... your brother."

My drink caught in my throat, where it lodged, then came spewing back out across the table, spraying Rory and Sean in the process. Priest brought over a stack of napkins and started helping us get cleaned up.

I scrubbed at my leg and glared up at the nut. "What the hell are you talking about?"

He reached over to the empty table next to us and pulled up a chair.

Nice of the psycho to think he was invited.

"I've been trying to call you," he said as he reached into his jacket.

"I don't answer numbers I don't recognize."

He snorted, and even that sounded elegant. Must have been the tie.

"More proof we're related."

"What makes you think I'm your sister? We look absolutely nothing alike."

"Because I look like my father," he said, sliding a picture from the inside pocket of his suit jacket. "And you look just like your mother," he said as he flipped the picture around toward me.

I stared down at the image, my mother's smiling face, her arms around me, holding me on her hip, standing intimately close to a man with dark skin, thick dark hair, and the same full mouth as the man sitting with me now—with a young boy sitting on his shoulders.

"I'm sure you don't remember me, but I remember you."

I held the picture between my fingers, every nerve ending humming. "How, I mean, what—how is this possible?"

He interlocked his fingers and propped his elbows on the table. "Well, when a man and a woman are attracted to one another…"

"Ha! He's a smart-ass just like you, Maisy. Another identifier," Rory said.

"Do you have any other proof beyond the picture?" Priest asked, his fingers kneading the back of my neck and shoulders.

"We'd need to get tested to know for sure, but I remember her and after our father died, he left behind a mountain of confessions. Seventeen kids in all. I've had investigators digging up what they can and there's more, of course. Sightings, people who met Daisy and my dad together. And, of course, the two of us playing."

Every word from his mouth short-circuited my brain. I had nothing. Not. One. Damn. Thing.

"Then there was the exhibition," Micah said quietly. "Imagine my surprise when my own sister who doesn't answer her cell phone ends up in my arena and on my bank."

"Whoa," Eve said in a whoosh of breath next to me.

"Yeah," Marty said quietly.

"The exhibition in Philly was you?"

"Ascend is one of several of my projects. It's a long story that we can get into another time, but my executive assistant came up with the idea, a way to spark interest in women's sports and working with charities. Imagine my surprise when I found out you were there… and you guys were the underdog team. Another thing we have in common."

"You don't look much like an underdog," Marty said.

"Not anymore, no. Underground fighting kept me alive. I took every last dime I made from it and with some help, grew it into what you see today. It's still just money. And all of it, built on the foundation of an underdog."

"Look at her. She's stunned. Like zapped-with-a-taser stunned," Marty said as she poked me in the arm.

"Stop poking me, dammit. I just—I have a brother. I— we need to do a DNA test, right?"

"As soon as you're ready. I'm going to be in the area for another week," he said as he took out a business card embossed in gold with his personal cell number on the back. "Call me and we'll make the arrangements. Once it's confirmed, we'll talk. Sound good?" He stood and slid the chair back to the table next to us and began his retreat, but after a couple steps, he stopped. "Maisy?"

"Yeah," I said, glancing up at him.

"I haven't had a family in a long time. I'm hoping when we find out what I'm pretty sure we both know is true, maybe we can change that."

I had no concrete evidence. He was a total stranger, but that look in his eyes, that loneliness lurking there, I recognized that to my very core. He had money and power and despite it, he was here at Banked Track looking for his missing pieces.

Scraping back my chair, I walked over, catching the way his eyes widened right before I wrapped my arms around him and closed my eyes. "I hope you mean that," I said with a squeeze, "Because I hold on to my people, and once I do, I don't let go."

for all things echo...

For new books, old books, tastes-great-less-filling books,
signings, playlists, story boards, and so much more,
go to my website.

www.EchoGrayce.com

And for the latest news, and let's face it, all the
announcements I will absolutely forget to put on social
media, sign up for my newsletter while you're there!

about echo grayce

Echo wields words as a heart-piercing sword cutting through characters' souls, leaving them vulnerable yet resilient in the face of love's trials and tribulations. If you want passion-packed small towns and fierce hearts so steamy they'll grab you by the throat like the ultimate alpha-hole with skillful hands and forearm porn for days, Echo is your girl. Every book promises beautifully brutal romances with a dose of angst, a double shot of romance, followed by a scorchin' hot sexy times chaser that will leave you panting for more.

Born and raised in New England, she's got Ben & Jerry's in her heart, and real Vermont maple syrup dripping through her veins. She's an unapologetic Swiftie embracing her Fuck-With-Me-and-Find-Out era, and a certified Fall Out Boy groupie who's low-key addicted to ink and metal–hello tattoos and piercings!

When she's not plotting world domination, she's busy either crafting stories that'll make your heart race faster than a caffeine-induced heart palpitation or designing some of romancelandia's most coveted covers for fellow authors.

To all you lovely readers out there, Echo has one thing to say: she adores every one of you who read her books, turning her dreams into reality. As for talking about herself in the third person? Well, let's just say she's over it.

Echo out, but her fierce heroines and steamy stories are here to stay!